PASSENGERS

Diane Keziah Robertson

CACTUS RAIN PUBLISHING

Arizona USA

PASSENGERS

Published by Cactus Rain Publishing, LLC
San Tan Valley, Arizona, USA
www.CactusRainPublishing.com

ISBN 978-0-9829181-3-5

Front Cover Design by Junior's Digital Design
Published December 1, 2013
Printed in the United States of America.

Also by Diane Keziah Robertson

The Lacemaker's Daughter

For
Pamela

Acknowledgments

As always, I have firstly to thank Nadine Laman and Cactus Rain Publishing for their confidence in me. PASSENGERS is the story of several interwoven characters and time lines, which has made the telling of it interesting for us all.

I also thank Anita Beery and Joyce Himes for all the help and guidance they gave me. It has, as usual, been invaluable.

My friend, Carol Butcher, is also owed a thank you for reading a very rough manuscript and sticking with it.

I thank my husband, Cam, for his continued support and encouragement.

And lastly, you are thanked for taking the time to read PASSENGERS. I hope you enjoy it.

Diane Keziah Robertson ❧

PASSENGERS

Diane Keziah Robertson

Chapter 1 ❧
London – 1780

The contents of the pisspot hit the ground some five yards in front of her as she weaved through the piles of refuse between the houses and shops. Thrown from an upstairs window, the stinking nightsoil splashed against the wall of the house, just missed her skirts as she ran. She kept to the edge of the alleyway, to avoid the worst of the mess that piled up along the centre. It had rained during the night, the streets were muddy, and she prayed she wouldn't slip.

It was still early, for the bells from St. Margaret's hadn't yet rung for communion. She had to be home before anyone missed her. Through the side gate of the house, past the herb garden; she slid her hands over the wet lavender plants as she went. Round the back of the outside privy, along the turf path, she ducked low as she ran beneath the window of her father's study, lest he was inside.

At the door she stopped, breathing hard. She put her hand to her nose, smelled the remnants of the lavender, and smiled. Quickly she removed her wooden patens and held one in each hand. The soles were filthy, and she kept them away from her skirt.

She tipped her head to one side to better hear her mother, Sarah, admonish the poor washerwoman over the burn marks in the linen. Looking quickly left and right, and seeing no one, she ran down the hallway. Silken skirts dragging over the boards, moving the newly laid rushes before her like a small wave, she was making for the stairs. Head down, looking at the floor, praying she would meet no one. Hurrying.

'Elizabeth! Where have you been?' An angry man's voice demanded.

'Father!'

'I asked where have you been? You were confined to your room.' He glanced down. 'And I see by your shoes you've been outside. How dare you disobey me?'

'I'm sorry, Father, but Agnes is ill and I promised to visit.'

Agnes was the daughter of the town's mayor, a man of influence. Elizabeth reasoned that he was a man to be appeased, especially with Father in trade.

'I don't care a fig about Agnes, ill or not. You were told to stay in your room until I thought of a suitable punishment for you. That punishment, and now one for this, will be discussed at breakfast.'

Quickly turning on his heels, hands clenched at his sides, Father walked towards his study, furious at being disobeyed.

He was a tall, somewhat portly man with heavy, unkempt brows on a face that always seemed to be downcast. He viewed the world as either black or white, grey not even thought of. But then again, he hadn't achieved the success he had in trade by wavering in such a hard, cutthroat world as this.

Elizabeth slowly walked up the two flights of stairs to her room in the eaves, knowing that this time the punishment would be heavy.

But Agnes had needed me, and once you've promised a friend, you must keep your promise. That's what Father always says. He can't suit himself when he says that. Either you keep your promise or you don't. 'Trade ran on promises,' he said time and time again. A handshake was a gentleman's word. Why should my promise to Agnes be any different to his? The promise had been made before he confined me to my room, and why such a big fuss over such a small thing?

Upstairs in her room, sitting on her narrow trestle bed by the small window, she placed her muddy patens beneath, pulling on her woollen indoor slippers.

The church bells pealed, marking eight o'clock. It was time for breakfast in this, the Sharpe household. Dreading sitting at the table with her parents and three brothers, Elizabeth longed for the day when she was mistress of her own home, able to give orders and answerable to no one, except perhaps a husband.

'Elizabeth! Come down now, you are keeping us waiting,' her mother shouted. Reluctantly heaving herself up, she smoothed her hair with her hands, and taking a deep breath, opened the door to face the music.

'Thank you Lord for the food we eat,' intoned her father as they sat around the board. Starting with his wife, he looked at them each in turn, his eyes coming to rest, at last, on Elizabeth.

'Before we eat I will tell you what your punishment is, Elizabeth. I have given a lot of thought to this, and after discussion with your mother, I believe the only choice left me is that you should go to your aunt's in Honiton.'

Elizabeth stood up, angrily flinging her napkin down before he'd finished speaking.

'That's not fair, Father, it's only because I'm a girl. You'd never give such a punishment to the boys.'

'Sit down, Elizabeth, and don't raise your voice to me. I have made my decision and won't change it. Your mother shall write to her sister today to ask if she will take you.'

Elizabeth sank back onto her chair, looking at her mother, pleading in her eyes. But her mother's eyes were on her husband as she nodded in agreement at all that he had said.

Dishes, heavy with food, were passed along the table, her brothers taking huge helpings to prepare them for their day's work, eager to fill their ever-empty bellies. None of them looked at her, each concentrating on their food, not wanting to risk their father's ire.

Elizabeth refused to eat, sitting on her chair, arms crossed, lips tightly pursed, steaming mad. The boys disobey all the time; no punishment is given to them. They stay out to all hours, drinking and carousing, and well Father knows it. It's not fair that I've to go to Honiton, that godforsaken place!

'Elizabeth, you've no one to blame but yourself; perhaps some time away from London will make you realise that there are

3

rules, and that they must be obeyed.' Her mother made a visible effort to change her tone from instructive to soothing. 'It won't be so bad, you'll see. Jane is a kindly woman, and your time there will give you an opportunity to get to know your cousins properly.' She looked at Elizabeth pleadingly, silently asking her not to make more trouble.

Elizabeth refused to look at her or to answer.

Honiton, with those brat cousins, both as bad as can be. What fun was to be had there! Theirs is a pious household. And how long is a few months? Two? Three? More? I will go mad and end up in the bedlam, and then they'll all be sorry.

Elizabeth's brothers finished eating, and still without looking at her, one by one left the table, eager to leave a room where the tension was palpable. The first-born, William, was eighteen, two years older than Elizabeth, and he had formed a pleasant personality of his own right from the start. He was amenable to everyone, constantly trying to keep the peace between his brothers and younger sister. He had excelled in all subjects at school, but his favourite by far was figures. Effortlessly he could add three columns at the same time, the answer always correct. This meant Daniel, their father, at one time had high hopes of William taking over his business.

He had inherited his mother's curly brown hair, his looks already pointing to him being a handsome man when fully grown. Elizabeth loved him the most of her brothers, and was grateful his character didn't follow their younger brother, Simon, and his wicked, tortuous ways.

Next was Timothy, who at seventeen was taller than his father. He inherited his mother's curly brown hair which he wore down to his shoulders. He was the dreamer of the family, though despite that, a good leader. Forever in trouble at school for playing jests on both the masters and other pupils, he had the knack of easily making others follow him. All knew he meant no harm, which enabled him to get away with his pranks. That had proven to be good and bad.

The third son, Simon, at fifteen was a year younger than Elizabeth. A mean-spirited youth, he enjoyed tormenting his sister, indeed anyone, at every opportunity. His mouth was invariably twisted into a sneer, and his grey eyes held bitterness and cruelty.

She remembered with a shiver finding the black cat hanging from in tree at the bottom of the garden, and knew instinctively who was responsible, for Simon liked inflicting pain on any living thing, and the more they screamed, the more he took pleasure from it. It was best to steer clear of Simon.

Now, alone with her father and mother, Elizabeth tried once more for mercy.

'Father, I beg you to reconsider. I promise not to disobey you again.' She waited for an answer but none came, the decision reached, judgment given.

'Mother, please, I beg you.'

'You have had more than enough chances, Elizabeth. Your father is quite right, there is no other choice but to send you to my sister and see if she can beat some sense into you, for it's sure I cannot. I don't know what devil possesses you to be so contrary, but I only hope that Jane and her husband can help. Otherwise, I don't know what's to become of you. It's sure no man will take you for a wife if you persist in being so awkward. Hopefully living in the same house as a rector will make you see the error of your ways.'

Sarah motioned to the maid to clear the table. 'I'll write to my sister today to ask her if she will take you, though it will be a hardship for her with two children of her own. But Jane is a good Christian woman, and I don't anticipate a denial.'

She turned to Daniel. 'Husband, we will have to pay for Elizabeth's keep, and I will tell her the amount in the letter to help along our cause. Is a guinea a month acceptable to you?'

Daniel sniffed loudly, while he begrudgingly nodded his agreement. He glared at Elizabeth.

'See what your behaviour is costing me? A guinea a month! I just hope Jane is able to beat sense into you.'

He pushed back from the table, rising. 'I'm away, Sarah, for I've a busy day ahead of me. I expect Elizabeth to be on her way within the week. In the meantime, she isn't to leave the house under any circumstances.'

'Father, please!'

He ignored her as if she hadn't spoken, only tutting loudly at the maid as she got underfoot when he tried to pass through the doorway, pushing her roughly out of his way.

Alone with her mother, Elizabeth was furious.

'This is unfair; you would never punish the boys like this! It's just because I'm a girl! And that's not right!'

'Right or not, it's the way it is. Elizabeth, you manage to make it sound as if it's our fault. You are so wearisome. You have to learn obedience in everything, or you'll grow into an old maid. And who'll look after you then, I have to wonder, for it won't be your father and me, of that you can be sure. Now, go to your room and remain there for the rest of the day.'

'You can spend the time alone reflecting on how to improve.' Her mother left the room, muttering to herself at all that had to be done that day, and now on top of all that there was a letter to be written.

Elizabeth remained in the dining room for a few moments. The maid was still removing dishes from the board, rubbing her shoulder where she had been pushed against the door in Daniel's haste to leave.

'This isn't fair,' Elizabeth said aloud, thumping the board with her fists, but the maid, intent on her task, didn't answer, too afraid of the master to even think of making comment.

With no alternative, Elizabeth climbed the stairs, her feet thumping down on each step in protest of her treatment. How am I going to get word to Agnes? I promised to visit again tomorrow. Now she'll think I've deserted her, and she has few enough friends as it is. I have to find a way to send a message.

Elizabeth sat on her bed, heels kicking the floor in frustration. I'll send Agnes a note.

Needing parchment and ink, she went downstairs, even though she had been told to remain in her room. She stood in the hallway listening for her mother, whose voice this time could be heard coming from the garden to the rear of the house.

On tiptoe, she crept to the door of her father's office, safe in the knowledge he had left for the warehouse.

Entrance was strictly forbidden to all the family, including her mother, the door always kept locked. With the upset, he forgot to lock it before he left. When she pressed her thumb on the latch, the door opened. The creaking sounded loud enough to wake the dead in the cemetery four streets away. She held her breath, waiting to hear her mother's footsteps, but by the sounds of it she was still outside. Quickly closing the door, she walked quietly across the room to the desk, placed at right angles to the window that overlooked the side garden.

The desk, passed down through the generations, was a massive piece of furniture, black with age and layers of polish. The top was covered in sheets of parchment showing invoices and notes, some bound with ribbon of different colours. There was also an inkwell and three quills, along with pumice for cleaning the parchment so it could be re-used. There was a pot of fine sand for drying the ink, a large candlestick with three branches and a small silver bell, but no clean parchment.

Walking to the working side of the desk, the chair pushed tidily into the knee hole, she opened drawers. Still she found nothing she could use. Riffling through the drawer on the bottom right-hand side, there was a large oblong tin box, a dirty grey colour, with a handle at each end.

Forgetting about the quest for parchment, Elizabeth took the box out of the drawer, laying it quietly on the desktop. At the front was a small keyhole, but in her rummaging through the drawers she hadn't noticed a loose key, and presumed that her father had it on his person. Carefully putting the box back, she opened the drawer on the opposite side of the knee hole, and there found a small stack of sheets of blank parchment. Elizabeth took one sheet, for she daren't take more; her father might know how many were there. If just one was missing, he might think he had miscounted. She quickly rolled it up, stuffing it down the front of her dress and paused to catch her breath.

Closing the drawer, she moved silently to the door and listened for voices or footsteps. Hearing only distant sounds, she opened the door and slipped out. Silently closing it behind her, she raced for the stairs and the safety of her room.

Taking the parchment from her bodice, she unrolled it. Falling on her bed with relief, she tried to slow her breathing, which was fast and loud. *I wish I could have taken a quill, but there* were only three, and Father would surely know if one were missing. There's only one thing for it, I will have to use blood.

Taking the enamelled jewellery box from the shelf above the bed, Elizabeth looked inside for a small pin, and having found it, grimaced as she dug hard at her finger. She waited for the small jewel-coloured drops to fall onto the lid of the box, and used the pin as a makeshift quill.

Agnes, I'm to be sent to Honiton for how long I do not know. Write to me at The Rectory, Honiton.

She signed it, with a flourish, 'Elizabeth.' It wasn't perfect, but it was the best she could do.

While she waited for the letter to dry, she wrapped her handkerchief round her finger to soak up the oozing blood. She rolled the parchment, hiding it beneath her pillow until dinner.

At noon, still trying for mercy, she was the first one at the board and sat waiting impatiently for the rest of the family. When Alice, the young maid, brought in the meat on a platter, Elizabeth in a whisper said, 'I want you to deliver a message for me to Agnes with no one knowing.'

Alice looked in terror at her. 'But what will I say to the master?'

'Nothing, that's why I said you're to tell no one.' She sighed heavily at the girl's stupidity. 'Deliver it only to her, no one else.' She looked at the tiny face, white and fearful. 'Come on, Alice, it's only a message, there's no harm in it. I'm telling her I'm being sent away. You'll not get in trouble.' Reaching down her bodice, she pulled out the parchment, passing it quickly to the girl, who stared at it as if it held the plague.

'Quick now, before anyone comes; hide it, for heaven's sake.' With a shaking hand, Alice took it, hiding it behind the bib of her apron. And only just in time, for no sooner was it hidden than Simon came in, rubbing his hands in anticipation of his food.

Alice had been the object of his cruelty and unwanted attention on more than one occasion, and she quickly turned, edging along the wall while trying to get out of his way and almost running into William as he came in.

8

'Careful now,' William said, holding the door for her, and she gave him a grateful look as she made her escape from Simon's roving hands.

'You look pleased with yourself for someone going to Honiton,' remarked Simon, the usual derisive sneer on his face.

'I'm looking forward to it,' she said brightly, for she was determined not to let her brothers know how upset she was. 'It will be nice to see our aunt and cousins again. I will be sure to pass on your best wishes to them. Besides, London is becoming tiresome; it will be good to breathe fresh country air for a change.'

They all looked at her, uncertain if she were serious, though she certainly sounded as if she were.

Chapter 2 ❧
London

The next few days were spent in a flurry of activity. The seamstress was called to ensure that all Elizabeth's clothes were clean and in good order. She was still growing, and some of her dresses needed letting down, others letting out. As Sarah would also be travelling to Honiton to make sure Elizabeth arrived safely and to visit her sister, the poor seamstress was kept busy.

A letter had been sent to Honiton begging for lodging for Elizabeth, and even allowing for three days there and three days back, it wouldn't now be long before the reply was received. Anticipating a positive answer, Sarah fully intended to be on the first available stagecoach with her daughter.

Elizabeth spent the time lying on her bed cursing her misfortune, and with the young maid steadfastly refusing to take another message to Agnes, she was left friendless and alone. As too, she knew, was Agnes.

She had tried again on several occasions to plead her case to both her parents, individually and together, but they, in Elizabeth's opinion, had hearts of stone and refused to budge.

The more she thought of living in Honiton, the more she hated the idea. Everyone knew the county was filled with nothing but hills and smelly sheep. How did they think she was going to fill her time? Doing embroidery? Reading the Bible? Visiting the sick with the rector? Elizabeth thought not.

Jane had two daughters of her own, one older and one younger than Elizabeth. She recalled their visit to London two years earlier when Elizabeth thought she would die of utter boredom.

At that time, the elder, Anne, was a tall, painfully thin girl of ten, with front teeth that stuck out, making her look more like a rabbit than a girl. She had the added encumbrance of large ears that protruded at right angles from her head, which she constantly tried to hide beneath her hair and cap.

Elizabeth thought she was most unfortunate looking. On top of everything else Elizabeth thought wrong with her, she remembered Anne peering myopically at a book, holding it just in front of her nose. Elizabeth was surprised she could read.

The younger, eight-year-old Mary, was a constant whiner, hanging on to her mother's skirts like a baby. Elizabeth also remembered with distaste the girl's constantly dripping nose, which she wiped on her sleeves, leaving silvery trails on all her dresses. Elizabeth doubted either girl had improved.

Simon wouldn't stop his baiting, telling her time and again how she would hate her exile there, stuck amongst the sheep dung, reminding her that she would miss London and Agnes.

Elizabeth glared at him and longed to hit him, but was too scared to do so. Simon could turn vicious in a heartbeat, and she was determined never to suffer another beating at his hand. The last had been three months ago when she told Father of the hanged cat, and he assured her he would not tell his source. But as usual, she was discounted as worthy of consideration, and he broke his promise and named her.

Simon came looking for her, riding whip in hand. He found her when their parents were away from the house. He beat her unmercifully, taking care to only hit where the marks wouldn't show, and Elizabeth was left crying in pain and anger.

William and Timothy had been aware of the event, and had come to her afterwards.

'There's no point in crying,' said Timothy. 'You know what he's like, and you shouldn't have told Father. You've nobody to blame, but yourself.'

William was compassionate, asking if there was anything he could do to take the pain away. He ended up dancing round the room in a silly fashion until, eventually, he made her laugh.

11

'Take care, Bess,' William told her, 'for you know how cruel our brother can be. And there's no point in telling Father of this. Moreover, if I'm not mistaken, he is scared of Simon's temper.'

When the reply arrived from Jane, though expected, it still came as a bitter blow. Elizabeth had prayed the letter would go astray, gaining her more time, but it appeared the offer of a guinea a month for her keep had made the decision all too easy for the impoverished rector's wife, and she had accepted it with alacrity.

At dinner, Sarah broke the news. 'Elizabeth, I've heard from my sister and she has agreed to take you. I'll send William to book passage for us on tomorrow's coach, so you can prepare your belongings this afternoon.' Without waiting for a reply, she turned to her three sons.

'And while I am gone, you make sure you behave. I am fully aware of how much trouble you can get into without a firm hand.' She looked pointedly at Daniel. 'Husband, you'll need to keep the three of them busy in my absence, and I would suggest they all accompany you to work.'

He looked aghast. 'But that's not possible. I don't have time to mollycoddle them. I've a business to run; and besides, it's time they learned adult responsibilities. I'll take Timothy, but the other two, I shall set them tasks here to be completed each day.' He in his turn looked pointedly at his wife. 'Don't worry about us, Sarah, all will be well.' But the look he received in return showed how much she doubted that.

Daniel was a wine importer, one of the largest in the city. With great barrels coming from France and Germany by ship on a regular basis, they were stored and sold from a large, purpose-built warehouse at the docks by the side of the Thames River. A well-run and prosperous business, he had hopes of one of his sons taking over from him, but none, as yet, displayed any real inclination. He still held out hopes for Timothy, his main concern being, though smart enough, did the boy have what it took to build on his legacy? A leader of men he may be, but would he lead them in the right direction?

Elizabeth spent the last night in her bed, for heavens knew how long, in tears, dreading the coming of the dawn. Tossing and turning, she hardly slept, too soon seeing the first light come through the cracks in the shutters, dreading the day. She had now accepted it was useless to complain further, and with a heavy heart reluctantly joined the rest of the family for breakfast.

Her father was in a happy mood, smiling and laughing. Her mother was dressed for the journey, but for her bonnet and cape. With her possessions packed and waiting by the door, Elizabeth felt only regret at not being able to visit Agnes before the coach left.

'Eat well, Elizabeth, for it will be a long journey before we stop for the night,' advised her mother. She turned to Daniel. 'I'll require the funds for my sister, husband. Let's say enough for three months, so three guineas in all.'

'Three months!' cried Elizabeth, and instantly burst into tears. 'This is unfair when I've repeatedly said I'm sorry. Why am I to be stuck in Honiton away from my friends and my home for three months?'

Neither parent made comment, all having been said as far as they were concerned. They left her to cry into her handkerchief while her brothers sat silently devouring their food, all except Simon, who smiled maliciously at her.

'You must learn obedience, dear Bess,' he said. 'All women should learn obedience. When I am married, it will be beaten into the girl, if necessary.' He looked around as if for agreement, but neither of his brothers met his eyes, both silently pitying the future unfortunate bride.

From somewhere Elizabeth found courage, knowing that shortly she would be beyond his reach. Drying her eyes, she said, 'Father, why do you allow Simon to be so cruel with no punishment?'

She looked at Simon, daring him to gainsay her.

'He's not cruel, Elizabeth, why do you persist in this vein? He's just a boy feeling his way, there's nothing wrong with Simon that a few years won't cure.' He smiled indulgently at his youngest son.

It was at that moment Elizabeth was certain Timothy had been correct in his comment. Father was scared of Simon, and with just cause, for the years won't mellow him; if anything, he will become even more cruel.

The time for leaving came all too soon. Her father, with a final warning to heed her aunt and learn obedience if she wished to return home soon, had briefly embraced a wooden Elizabeth. She had tried hard to avoid Simon, now fearful she had spoken up as she had.

He kissed her cheek while holding her tightly by the arms, fingers biting in hard enough to leave painful bruises come the morning. 'Don't think I will forget your words, Bess, for I shan't,' he whispered. 'You won't be in that godforsaken place forever. You will have your homecoming to look forward to, for I'll be waiting for you, never fear,' As he withdrew, he smiled at her, aware their father was watching. 'Godspeed, Bess, and hurry home to us, for we'll all be waiting,' he spoke aloud and then turned away, confident she had understood his meaning.

William and Timothy were to accompany the travellers to the coach. Elizabeth and her mother led the way, holding their capes and dresses above their ankles to avoid the worst of the mud and refuse littering the streets. Elizabeth was trying hard not to cry. The boys followed with the barrow containing the travel bags, along with a small sack of food for the journey.

By the time they arrived at the coach stop, it was to find passengers already inside, claiming their seats by the windows early where they could avoid the worst of the smells.

Timothy and William handed up the bags to stow on the roof. With a threat of rain in the air, the baggage was to be covered by a large waterproof covering, lashed down to the sides of the coach with ropes.

With a final goodbye from Elizabeth to the boys, and a whispered, 'Don't despair, Bess, it won't be forever. You might even enjoy your time there,' from William, Sarah and Elizabeth clambered aboard, sitting opposite each other in the middle seats.

Chapter 3 ❧
The Journey

Sarah stuffed the bag containing their food in the space below her seat, pulling her cloak tightly around her against the morning chill. She introduced both herself and her daughter, listening to the names of their fellow travellers in return.

A large, middle-aged gentleman to her left introduced himself as Master Jeffrey Browning. He stated he would only be travelling as far as Exeter, for he was to stay indefinitely with his sister. Blustery, with a bulbous red-veined nose, he possessed a huge belly but tiny, almost childlike hands and feet. He leered at Elizabeth, giving her a sly wink that her mother didn't notice.

Opposite him sat Master Nathaniel Simmons. Dressed shabbily, he was a frail-looking light-haired man who looked to be in his late twenties. His head kept twitching in jerky movements. Elizabeth, not blessed with an abundance of patience, especially today, quickly found this extremely irritating and resolved not to look at him again.

On Elizabeth's left sat a young man of eighteen or so en route to his father's house in Honiton. He introduced himself as James Morbeck. While he had been attending school in London, his father had been taken ill. He had received word the day before from the physician that he should return home in all haste. His face was pale, brows drawn together with worry and fear.

'I'm sure all will be well when you arrive,' said Sarah, doing her limited best to comfort him. 'Very often these physicians don't know what they are talking about and create worry for nothing.' She smiled as she spoke, but he remained quiet and withdrawn, crossing his arms and staring out of the window.

On Sarah's right sat a man of some twenty years, fashionably if somewhat foppishly dressed. His shoes had large buckles made of silver, his clothes were of good quality, and he was obviously of good family.

He introduced himself as Master Philip Goldworthy, and he proclaimed to be travelling to Honiton to stay with his godmother, the Lady FitzGerald of Watermead. He looked around haughtily as if expecting his fellow passengers to be impressed with this news. But none had heard of Lady FitzGerald, much less of Watermead. They all smiled politely, not inviting further confidences. He, like Master Browning, leered openly at Elizabeth, pursing his red slobbery lips as if in a kiss, making her look away in confusion.

Unfortunately, Sarah had also become aware of his lascivious behaviour when she saw Elizabeth blush and turn her head away. She hissed her displeasure in most unladylike terms, heard easily throughout the carriage.

'What's the delay?' called Jeffrey Browning fretfully out of the window, addressing the coachman standing below.

'Just checking one of the horses, sir, it looks as though it might have trouble with a leg.'

Master Browning seemed an impatient man and he tutted loudly at this news. 'I do hope this won't delay us long,' he said, looking anxiously to the left and right out of the window, but he'd no sooner spoken than they felt the coach rock as the man climbed up to his bench. His companion, the man who had loaded the luggage above, blew the horn, warning everyone in town the coach was, at last, on its way.

Slowly at first due to the people milling around in the street, it soon settled into a steady pace, the horn blowing intermittently to warn all ahead of their approach.

Sarah, already having the measure of Masters Browning and Goldworthy, knew this was to be a long and trying journey which would take three days. The intervening two nights were to be spent at inns and staging posts along the way.

16

The wind blowing through the windows made the leather curtains, for now rolled up out of the way, bang irritatingly against the coachwork as they swayed and jolted along.

Elizabeth felt the first thrill of excitement for the journey ahead. Perhaps it won't be too bad, and at least I'll be away from Simon. She settled back to watch the houses and shops as they sped by at an amazing pace. Yes, everything's going to be well, this journey could even be enjoyable.

Elizabeth thought she would rather die than ride for another moment in the coach. It had been relatively smooth while still in London, most of the roads being bare earth, a few of cobbles. Once they hit the outskirts of the city, they were all to know the torture of deeply rutted roads, the large holes over which the wheels thumped and bumped. All the occupants inside the coach were tossed around like a hive of angry bees.

Those sitting next to the windows were able to hang on to the frames, but Elizabeth and Sarah were thrown this way then that, at times even leaving the seats when the coach hit an especially large rut.

Not an hour out of London, Elizabeth was cursing silently while at the same time glaring at her mother, blaming her and her father for having to endure this awful journey.

At ten o'clock, the coach stopped at an inn in a small village to allow those who needed to heed the call of nature to relieve themselves. They all pushed and shoved each other in a rush to leave the coach and stand on firm ground that didn't heave and roll. The coachman announced they would be there for half an hour while the horses were rested, and he and his horn-blowing companion disappeared in search of warm refreshments. Both were well wrapped against the cold, but their hands and faces were red from the cutting wind.

'Come, Elizabeth, we'll go inside and get comfortable,' said Sarah, wiping her forehead with her handkerchief, but when she took it away, it was grimy and damp. There was nothing to stop dust and dirt from entering the coach, the leather curtains usually only lowered during wet weather. They both realised they were covered in dust.

They stood brushing themselves down, with Nathaniel Simmons coughing loudly as he tried to clear his congested lungs. Everyone gave him space, fearful that whatever it was that was causing him trouble might be contagious. While the coach was in motion, they could do nothing to distance them from him, but all quickly left him alone now.

Inside the inn, Sarah asked a serving girl the way to the privy, and they were led down a dark hallway and through a door that led eventually into a back yard. The small, wooden walled privy stood in solitary splendour in a corner, leaning drunkenly against a stone wall.

'You go first, Elizabeth, I need to breath fresh air,' instructed Sarah, as she stood fanning herself with her hand, taking great gasps of air.

Elizabeth wondered where her mother would find that fresh air, for she couldn't smell much difference to the inside of the coach. A pigpen must be on the other side of the wall against which the privy leaned, for the loud grunting of the pigs could easily be heard.

Sarah went next, eventually coming out wiping her hands on her dusty handkerchief. 'Let's get a drink, Elizabeth. My throat is so dry I feel I could spit sawdust. We have food in the coach, so don't accept anything else they offer.' She led the way inside while Elizabeth trailed slowly behind, wishing she didn't have to get back on the coach.

With everyone rested, they stood outside waiting to set off once more. Everyone, that is, but Philip Goldworthy.

Even though the coachman went back inside calling for him, he seemed to have gone missing. They waited for another few minutes, and it wasn't until all had climbed aboard and the coachman was just about to whip the horses that Philip appeared. He came running out of the inn, shouting at them to wait.

Elizabeth looked out the window to see him trying to shrug himself into his coat, while he tried to hold his breeches up with one hand, the buttons obviously undone.

'Well really!' said Sarah, shocked. 'Elizabeth, close your eyes this instant!' and she hid her own face behind her gloved hand.

Philip Goldworthy flung open the door and climbed up as the coach started to move, laughing gaily and winking lewdly at Jeffrey Browning and Nathaniel Simmons, both of whom looked acutely embarrassed.

'My apologies for my tardiness,' he laughed, settling down on the seat. Without any sign of embarrassment he made a show of buttoning his breeches, and before long was snoring loudly. Even his head banging against the window frame didn't wake him.

❧❧❧

The night stop was a blessed relief, even though Sarah and Elizabeth had to share the same chamber. The door didn't lock firmly, if at all, and Sarah insisted they not disrobe, fearing who knew what. They lay on their shared bed fully clothed but for their capes, boots, and bonnets. Another two days and a night like this, however will I bear it?

They ate the last of the food they brought with them, and would from here on have to purchase what they wanted until they reached Honiton.

In the early morning, Elizabeth woke before her mother, and lay listening with growing annoyance to the loud snoring beside her.

During the night, Sarah had managed to commandeer most of the bed, with Elizabeth forced closer and closer to the edge until she was barely lying down. She had contemplated taking her cape and lying on the floor, then remembered noticing mouse droppings on the floor when they entered the room. She decided to stay where she was, it seemingly the lesser of the two evils.

The coach was due to leave on the next leg of its journey at seven o'clock, which meant being up early to have breakfast.

They ate at a communal table, the landlord and his wife serving them with cold meats and freshly baked breads. A large round cheese was set in the middle of the table for everyone to cut off huge slabs and wash it all down with small ale.

Sarah had, predictably, woken in a foul mood, blaming Elizabeth for making it necessary for her to endure this awful journey. When she remembered she would have to return by the

19

same method, she cuffed her daughter round the ear to drive home her displeasure.

The day passed slowly, the numerous bruises and sore spots from yesterday added to during the journey. When they eventually stopped for the second night, Sarah and Elizabeth asked to be taken directly to the chamber allocated to them. Sarah asked for food to be sent up immediately.

'I need to get out of these clothes, Elizabeth, before I scream,' she said, her face a picture of pure agony.

They rinsed the dirt from their hands and faces in the bowl of hot water brought to them by a small child. Sarah gratefully sank with a loud groan onto the bed, dressed only in her chemise, her nightcap holding her dusty hair off the pillow.

Elizabeth sat by the fire, wishing she was anywhere but here. She was beginning to think she would have to learn to curb her tongue, for it seemed to bring nothing but trouble when it chattered uncontrollably.

At a knock on the door, Elizabeth asked who it was, and on being told it was the maid with food, she unlocked it. A young girl of about seven years entered, obviously the daughter of the landlord, as they both had fiery red hair. She was followed by another, even younger child. The elder child carried a tray of roast meats and dishes of steaming vegetables, while the younger, barely five years old, staggered under the weight of a jug of ale. The older child then returned with a large round loaf and apples to complete their meal. Sarah and Elizabeth fell on it with relish.

Leaving the trays and dirty platters on the floor by the fireplace, mother and daughter used the pisspot, falling into bed exhausted and sore from the constant battering in the coach. The only thing keeping them going was the fact that tomorrow they would reach Exeter, and soon after that, Honiton.

Too tired to dream, even to think, Sarah and Elizabeth were soon asleep, the morning coming far too soon for either of their liking.

⁂

James Morbeck hadn't slept well, made anxious by his fear of what he would find when they eventually arrived. If his father died later, or worse, was already dead, it would mean he would now be the senior man of the family and his responsibility to care for his mother and younger brother. He didn't seek that burden. He had been quite happy at school with nothing to do but attend to his studies; his strongest wish was to become a physician.

His father was the main wool trader in Honiton, and he had always hoped his oldest son would follow him into the business. Unfortunately, like Elizabeth's brother William, James wasn't interested in the family business. He was interested in curing the myriad of diseases that afflicted mankind and that most succumbed to. Though that goal was a long way off; he needed to get through school first, and he had almost succeeded before the urgent message came to hurry home.

To make matters worse, his mother was a termagant, upsetting everyone around her, seemingly arguing just for the pleasure of it and to hear her own voice.

As the coach clattered along, James gazed unseeingly out of the window, not joining in the occasional talk of his fellows. Probably Father decided to become ill just to escape her, and who could blame him? Lord, please let him be recovered, for I shan't be able to bear it if I have to remain in Honiton. He closed his eyes, praying silently over and over that the Lord would grant mercy and allow him to complete his schooling.

⋆⋆⋆⋆⋆

Jeffrey Browning, who had told everyone he was visiting his sister in Exeter, had omitted to mention, for it was no one's business, that he had lost everything he possessed to the bank in London, having defaulted on a large loan.

Originally the loan of money had been for investment in the cloth trade, but he had become addicted to gambling, one night losing a vast amount. The next night he miraculously gained back the lost coin and more, never realising until it was too late that his fellow players were playing him for a fool. By the time he did, his capital had all but gone, and he was well into the loaned money. Losing more and more, he was unable to repay the bank, and was now deeply in debt to moneylenders. With no other choice, he crept out of London with his tail between his legs, just steps ahead of the debt collectors, carrying his few remaining un-pawned possessions with him.

He had lived in a squalid rented room, the last straw coming when he knew he would be unable to meet his rent obligation. However, there was no need for his fellow travellers to know of this, for he'd never see them again, and after all, he would be quite safe in Exeter. No one in London knew he had a sister there, and he would think up some story to tell her. She was ever a gullible and stupid woman.

In Exeter, with the change of horses for the final pull up the hill into Honiton, and the departure from the coach of Jeffrey Browning, it left more room for the remaining passengers, and knowing they were within a few hours of their ultimate destination, the mood visibly lightened. All became more vocal.

ᦰᦰᦰ

Philip Goldworthy tried to engage Elizabeth in conversation, but Sarah soon put a stop to that, remembering his running after the coach only partially dressed, his recent activity only too plain.

Chapter 4 ❧
Honiton

The countryside had been changing. The hills became softer, rounder, the fields that they could see above the hedges dotted with cattle and sheep. The air seemed different, too, or perhaps it was because Master Browning had left them. When they stopped for the coachman and his comrade to check on the horses, it was in the middle of a lane, the only sound a meadowlark soaring above them.

'How much farther, do you think?' asked Elizabeth of her mother fretfully.

'I've no idea, but it can't be far.'

'Only about another hour or so,' replied James Morbeck. He looked out of the window. 'The Devon countryside is beautiful, I do miss it,' he added, wistfully.

Sarah looked sadly at him. 'I do hope the news of your father is good, Master Morbeck.'

'Thank you, madam. I also hope so, for so much is riding on his good health.'

Almost at the end of the journey, he became garrulous. 'I pray he will have recovered and I can return to London immediately. I'm in my last year at school, you see, my ambition to train for a physician, and I'll need to get my name on the lists soon if I'm to gain entry to the school.' He looked at Elizabeth. 'What of you, if I might be so bold as to ask. What is the reason for your journey here?'

Sarah's eyes bored into Elizabeth's. Be guarded what you say.

'I've come to stay with my aunt and cousins for a while. It will be a change of air, and certainly the countryside looks very pleasing.' She looked at her mother, who nodded slightly in approval.

The coachman called down that they were making good time, and he anticipated they would be in Honiton within the hour, the end of the journey as far as the coachmen themselves were concerned. Here the horses would be removed from their traces, and the driver and the horn-blower would have a day and night to recover before they would make the return journey.

Sarah was determined she would be on that coach come hell or high water, for she didn't want to spend a moment longer with her sister and her bratty daughters than was necessary. The two had never got on, even as children. Sisters they may be, but they were as different as chalk from cheese.

In spite of Jane having married a rector, Sarah doubted she had been able to change her nature. As a child, she had dithered between this choice and that until the rest of the household were driven to distraction, and as for her children, Sarah considered them to be awful creatures.

She secretly considered Jane a terrible mother, and if truth were told, doubted she would be able to cure Elizabeth of her troublesome character. Nevertheless, Sarah conceded, at least it would give her own household a break from the constant arguing.

My task is to deliver Elizabeth safely, ensure Jane is prepared to beat sense into her, and then return to the comparative sanity of my own home and the hustle and bustle of London.

When at last they arrived in Honiton town and had all gratefully left the coach, Sarah and Elizabeth looked at each other in a state of confusion.

'Jane said she would send someone to help with the bags, but where are they?' Sarah looked at Elizabeth as if expecting her daughter to know the answer. They waited for their bags to be brought down from the roof while they looked around, but all they could see were people who were obviously shopping or standing around gossiping.

'Who are we supposed to be looking for?' asked Elizabeth.

'How should I know! All Jane said in her letter was that someone would be here when the coach arrived to help with the bags,' and she twirled around looking for anyone who looked as if they were watching for them. The two, however, remained ignored.

Master Goldworthy bowed to the ladies, winked at Elizabeth, and wished them a pleasant stay. Once his bag had been retrieved, he walked to the small landau and driver who stood waiting to convey him to his godmother's estate.

James Morbeck well knew his way home, which was within easy walking distance. Bowing in turn to mother and daughter, he bid them each a good day, picked up his bag and set off, terrified of the news that may await him.

Master Simmons, the last down, stood looking around, a perplexed expression on his pale face.

'Master Simmons, are you in need of assistance?' enquired Sarah.

'I'm unsure of where I'm to go. I'm retained as tutor to a family called Riverley, do you know of them?' he enquired hopefully.

'Good heavens no, for as you are aware it's my sister we are visiting, and we have never been to Honiton before. Perhaps ask in one of the shops or at the inn here?' Sarah looked towards the nearby inn, which stood with the main door open to welcome custom.

'Good idea, good idea,' he replied, still looking worried, and set off hauling two heavy-looking bags, one filled with books suitable for his new post.

The horses and coach were led away by an ostler to the stables situated nearby.

A weathered painted sign over the inn door proclaimed it to be the Cross Keys. In years past, the coach had dropped off and picked up passengers from the other end of town, at the top of the hill, but the inn there had been closed due to the landlord's death, his widow too feeble-minded to continue the business. She had moved to Exeter to live with her married daughter and three grandchildren, and the inn, since left vacant, had fallen quickly into disrepair.

The coach then stopped at the bottom of High Street, but that soon proved to be inconvenient, especially in inclement weather. The landlord of the Cross Keys, Master Beaker, a wily money manager, had taken up the coach business and shown a healthy profit from it.

'Well,' said Sarah, 'it looks as if we have to make our own way to the rectory. Pick up your bag, Elizabeth, no point in standing here; obviously there is no one to help us.'

Struggling under the weight of her own bag, Sarah led the way up the hill towards the rectory, which was next to St. Michael's church, according to Jane's letter. 'You can't miss the church,' she had written, 'it's at the top of the hill, and we are right beside it.'

Listening to the muttering beneath her breath, Elizabeth didn't need to be told that her mother was extremely annoyed. She only hoped she wouldn't upset Aunt Jane at the moment of their arrival.

The street was bustling, the town fully awake. Elizabeth noticed a group of urchin children throwing sticks at a pile of rags. As they drew closer she realised the pile of rags was a woman sitting, digging with her hands in the dirt among the horse droppings. Her hair was matted and filthy, her clothes in tatters.

Sarah shouted at the tormentors to stop, and they turned to see who was admonishing them. They laughed, but did move away, though not before throwing something again at the woman and taunting her with singing, 'Mad Meg, Mad Meg, all she can do is beg.'

Elizabeth and Sarah stopped, ready to speak to the woman and ask if she needed assistance, but instead of thanking them, she spouted obscenities at them, shaking her fist. Sarah grabbed Elizabeth's arm, pulling her away.

'Those had better not be raindrops I feel on my face,' said Sarah who had to turn to speak to Elizabeth, who was lagging behind in no rush to arrive. But unfortunately they were, and the two had to quickly take shelter in a bookshop, bursting through the door in a most unladylike way to avoid the downpour.

The proprietor came scurrying out of the back room at the

sound of the bell he'd fixed above the door, hopeful of a prospective customer within his needy grasp.

'Welcome ladies, welcome,' he said, rubbing his hands gleefully together in anticipation of a sale.

'We are not after books, sir,' said Sarah immediately, not wanting to mislead him. 'We only wish to avoid the rain for a moment, with your indulgence.' The bookseller had no alternative but to grant sanctuary, for looking outside it appeared the heavens had indeed opened, and they could see others scurrying for shelter through the bow window of the shop. Then again, these ladies could be a source of future revenue, so he smiled while offering chairs that proved to be too rickety for their comfort.

Elizabeth declined, preferring to look at the shelves of books after being cooped up in the awful coach, and she strolled up and down reading the titles and authors.

'Ah, I see you are a book lover,' remarked Master Catchpole.

'I do love books, sir, they help to take one to unknown places,' and she glanced at her mother. He saw and immediately understood the inference behind the look.

'Come to stay in Honiton are you, if I may be so bold as to ask?'

'I am, sir, with my aunt and cousins. You will know of them, Mistress Cardwell, the rector's wife?'

'Oh indeed, for I'm a good Christian and attend St. Michael's every Sunday. How long will you be staying?'

Elizabeth looked at her mother, who appeared to have dozed off in her chair. 'Three months, sir.'

'Well, plenty of time for you to visit my poor store again. May I enquire of your name?'

'Elizabeth, Elizabeth Sharpe, sir, and this,' Elizabeth looked at her gently snoring parent, 'is my mother, Sarah Sharpe.'

'I'm pleased to meet you, Mistress Sharpe. My name is Master Edward Catchpole, born and raised in this beautiful Honiton town. Is this your first visit?'

'Indeed it is, sir. Tell me, is there much to do here?'

'Oh yes, but only with your aunt's permission, of course,' covering himself from any coming blame. 'There is the market every Tuesday. It attracts folk from all over with many merchants from as far away as Exeter!'

Elizabeth sighed. A market. How thrilling, after all that was available in London. However am I to bear it?

She continued to look along the shelves, noting several books that could be of interest to her, and when she eventually made her way back to the window, saw the rain had almost stopped.

Without seeming to mean to, she nudged her mother's foot, bringing her awake with a start.

'What?' Sarah said, far louder than was acceptable from a lady.

'Mother, it's stopped raining, we had best be on our way.'

Sarah struggled upright, gathering herself and her bag together. 'Thank you for the shelter, sir, we are most grateful.' She headed somewhat unsteadily for the door.

Elizabeth turned to Master Catchpole. 'Thank you, sir, I hope to be able to return soon and spend more time.' Curtseying, she followed her mother out the door, leaving Edward Catchpole to come to the window to watch them head towards the church at the top of the hill.

'I certainly hope you do return, Elizabeth Sharpe.'

Chapter 5 ⁊

Rectory

Through the garden gate, which Elizabeth let close with a decided bang, they approached the front door. Sarah's first thought was that it was in bad need of a coat of paint.

The little that remained showed as dark blue. The brass knocker hadn't been polished for some time, presenting a dull and unwelcoming face to the world.

Even through the closed front door they could hear shouting and wailing, and Elizabeth groaned. It sounds like my dear cousins are in their usual good form. Aunt Jane too, by all accounts.

Sarah steadfastly refused to look at her daughter, afraid of seeing what she knew would be a mutinous look on her face. After the third use of the knocker, the sound, more strident with each time, was at last heard amidst the hubbub inside. It was suddenly wrenched open by a girl of about ten, whose red eyes and blubbering mouth told a sorry tale.

'Yes?' asked the blubbering mouth.

Sarah quailed. If Jane couldn't control her own daughters, what hope was there for her controlling Elizabeth?

'I'm your Aunt Sarah, and you must be Anne.'

'No, I'm Mary. You'd best come in, though you have arrived far too early and Mother isn't ready for you yet. She won't be best pleased.' Mary stood back, grudgingly allowing them entrance.

Sarah glared meaningfully at Elizabeth as if to say, 'Not a word, my girl."

They could still hear shouting from upstairs, abruptly cut off with a slammed door. They looked to the head of the stairs, where they first saw skirts, and then a whole person appear, hands pushing wayward hair under a cap. The face beneath it was flustered and red, just like Mary's.

'Sister,' called Sarah, giving warning that they had arrived.

Jane came to a sudden halt halfway down. 'Sarah, you're here already! This must be Elizabeth. Oh dear, was it today you were to arrive? I seem to be all at sixes and sevens.'

Sarah, tired and sore, now became angry. 'Indeed it was, as I made plain in my last letter. You assured me there would be someone to meet the coach and help with our luggage.'

'Did I? How very odd, for there is no one to help with the luggage. Why would I have said that? Still, you are here now and that's what matters. Except your rooms haven't been prepared yet, what with one thing and another, but it shan't take long to see to that. I expect you'd like something to eat and drink?' Without waiting for an answer, she continued. 'Yes? I thought so, come away into the kitchen and I'll see if I can prepare something.'

Leaving Mary sniffling in the hall, Sarah and Elizabeth left their bags by the front door. They followed Jane along the dark, narrow hallway into the kitchen, which was situated at the back of the house.

'The kitchen girl is sick with the toothache and has taken to her bed, so I have to make the food myself.' This was said with a heaving sigh, as if it was all too much burden for one poor woman. She gave a kick to a pile of rags, that proved to be the kitchen girl lying on a pallet beneath the long table.

Jane looked embarrassed. 'Anne will join us shortly, she is a little vexed at present as I refused to order a new dress for her, but with money short as it is...' She left the rest of the sentence unfinished.

She prattled on while filling the pan with water and setting it on the hearth to boil. 'It's not as if the one she has now is short, and with funds as mean as they are...' Again she left the sentence hanging out for them both to see, making it clear the guinea a month for Elizabeth's keep would be spent to the last farthing.

'Still, no need to burden you with my troubles. Now where is that Anne? She could at least come and greet her cousin.'

Jane disappeared in search of her youngest daughter, who remained upstairs, the thumping and crying clearly heard.

Sarah and Elizabeth were left to look at each other, both still wearing their bonnets and capes.

'Don't say a word, Elizabeth; I'm sure it won't be as bad as it seems. We have just arrived on a bad day for your aunt.'

Elizabeth didn't reply, though mutiny was written clearly on her face.

'Besides, the weather is improving and you will be able to get out and about, exploring the town and everything.'

Silence.

'Don't look at me like that, child! It's your fault you're here; if you had only obeyed your father you could have remained at home. And it's only for three months, you'll see, the time will go quickly.'

'I hate it here. I hate Aunt Jane and I hate those stupid, snivelling, whining brats.'

'Elizabeth! That's not a Christian way to talk, for doesn't the Lord say, "Love Thy Neighbour?" I am sure He meant it for family, too, so you might as well make the best of it.'

Jane appeared again, dragging Anne behind her, whose eyes, like her sister's, were rimmed with red from crying and her nose running.

Dear Lord. Three months of THIS?

'Now, be polite to your Aunt Sarah and cousin Elizabeth, Anne. Perhaps after they have had a drink and something to eat you could show Elizabeth round the church?'

'You'll like the church, dear,' she said, addressing her clearly mutinous niece. 'It's old, with interesting wall drawings inside. Did you know it has five bells? No? Well, it does. Do wipe your nose, Anne, for goodness sake.'

While she talked, she prepared tankards and a jug of ale, leaving Elizabeth to wonder why she had put water to boil.

31

Taking out some oatcakes from a pantry cupboard, Jane placed everything on a tray.

'Let's go to the front room, we can get to know one another better.' She sailed out of the kitchen followed by Sarah.

Elizabeth, as usual, trailed along. Anne lagged behind, sniffling loudly, still not having blown her nose.

'I'll get Mary to help me prepare your rooms, it shouldn't take long. I just have to make the beds up. It should have been done yesterday, but with one thing and another. Do sit down and make yourselves comfortable, I'll go find Mary, and leave Anne to entertain you.'

They both turned to face Anne, who seeing her aunt and cousin looking expectantly at her, let out a loud wail and ran from the room in pursuit of her mother's skirts.

'Oh dear,' said Sarah. 'This isn't going well, is it?'

'And I'm stuck in this godforsaken place for three months, Mother! Three months!' wailed Elizabeth, and she, too, began to cry at the sheer injustice of it all.

Chapter 6 ❧
Morbeck Home

James Morbeck unashamedly dragged his heels on the short walk home. On one hand, he was eager to find how out his father fared; on the other, he was dreading bad news. *I could not bear it if I have to leave school and return here. I have no interest in running the business, and I should be terrible at it.*

His brother David, younger by a year, had always shown genuine interest when his father was talking of the day's events, asking about suppliers and workmen. *Why not let him run it? Why drag me back?*

The family home was situated off High Street, and as he turned down the lane that led to it, he could see the familiar large pink house on the left, set at the front of an acre of land. The house, with its black timbers, was sheltered from the worst of the winds by large trees planted by his grandfather. A short earthen path led to the weathered oak door. Knowing it would be kept locked to keep out thieves, he knocked. After a few moments he heard footsteps approaching, which echoed loudly on the bare flagstones.

When the door opened, it was to find Gwyneth, his mother's maid, staring at him as she wiped her hands on a snowy white apron. He hadn't been home for almost a year, and he hadn't realised how much he had changed.

'Yes, what is it?' she demanded, preparing the close the door again.

'Gwyneth, what a way to welcome me home!'

She started, peering at him through cloudy eyes. 'Oh goodness me, if it isn't our Master James, home at last and welcome. Come in, come in,' and she opened the door properly, allowing him entry.

'Who is it, Gwyneth?' called his mother from upstairs.

'It's Master James, mistress. He's come home.'

'James? He's really here?'

Gwyneth said, 'Go on up. Your mother will be pleased to see you home, for sure.'

'Before I go, how is my father?'

'He's doing a little better, I think. The physician comes most days, and he was bled yesterday, which seems to make him a little easier. But go, don't waste time talking to me, your mother's anxious enough.'

He smiled his thanks for the news, patting her shoulder. Looking upward, the stairs stretched into darkness, no candles lit during the day.

With Gwyneth's news about his father apparently feeling better, surely that would mean he needn't stay; and he hoped he would be able to return to London within a few days, but he couldn't leave too soon or his parents would be offended. Bracing himself with hopes to the good, he went upstairs, his spirits rising with each step.

His mother had stayed in their bedchamber, and James knocked on the door. Although it stood open, he wanted to give warning he was outside.

'James, thank goodness you are home,' said his mother, hurrying to him, clasping him to her breast.

'Mother, you are well?'

'I'm well, thank you, and more importantly, your father seems to be on the mend. Come and greet him.' Leading James by the hand, they went to the large four-poster bed, the woollen curtains drawn back and tied neatly to the four corner posts.

James' father, Septimus, lay between snowy white sheets, half sitting up, supported by large bolster pillows. Still wearing his nightcap to keep any wayward draughts off his balding pate, his face lit up when he saw his oldest son.

'James, this is indeed a happy day for us, how good it is to see you at last.'

James took his father's hand, the skin so papery dry he could almost feel the veins beneath.

'Father, I hear from Gwyneth you are feeling better?'

'Indeed I am, and the more so for seeing you. I told your mother there was no need to send for you, but you know how she frets!' He turned and smiled at his wife to take away any sting from his words.

'How does your schooling go? Are you top of your class? Do you still wish to follow your chosen path?' The latter question was asked with a searching look, obviously hopeful James would have changed his mind.

'Yes, Father, on both counts. I am indeed top of my class for, thankfully, learning comes easily to me, and no, I haven't changed my mind, I still wish to train for a physician. Though let's not talk of that just as I arrive. Tell me, what does your physician say? How long before you are up and about again?'

'I should be able to sit in the garden within the week, which is still too long away, for I am vexed with looking at these four walls!' They laughed, all grateful if for different reasons, for a promise of better health to come.

'Come, James,' said his mother, 'wash the dust of your journey away. Your room is waiting for you, just as you left it. Let your father rest, you can talk again after dinner.'

Margaret Morbeck ushered him from the room, following him along the corridor to his room at the back of the house, overlooking the garden.

Gwyneth had told the young kitchen boy to bring James' bag, which he had left at the foot of the stairs, and it now stood waiting for him just inside the bedroom door.

'Take your time, son, for you must be tired after such a dreadfully long journey. We eat at twelve o'clock, remember? I'll be downstairs helping Gwyneth, so come down when you're ready.' She suddenly reached up, hugging him again, kissing his cheek. 'It's good to have you home,' she said, and left, quietly closing the door behind her.

James took off his coat and hung it on the hook behind the

door. He looked around the room, and indeed found it just as he had left it, the bed freshly made in anticipation of his arrival.

There was a small knock on the door, and opening it, found a lad, hired since he was last home.

'Mistress Gwyneth sent me with hot water for you, master.'

'Did she indeed, that's kindly of her. Bring it in for me, if you please.' He watched as the young lad struggled in with a large pitcher, his tongue sticking out of the corner of his mouth with the effort.

'What's your name, lad?'

'Edwin, master.'

'Well, Edwin Master, I thank you.' Edwin looked at him, not understanding his humour, and he decided not to pursue it, quickly nodding his head and rushing instead for the door.

James could hear his light footsteps hurrying down the stairs while he sat on the bed. He chuckled to himself.

Chapter 7 ❧
Meadowacres

Unfortunately, things weren't looking as promising for Master Simmons. He asked a gentleman on High Street if he knew of the Riverleys, and if so, where they could be found. The man looked at him as if he carried the plague, hardly stopping, never mind giving information. Then he saw a man who was obviously of a religious bent, dressed all in black from head to toe, including his hat, with something clasped in his hand. He was heading down the hill. As he drew closer, Nathaniel realised he was carrying a Bible.

'Excuse me, sir. May I ask where I would find the Riverley house?' The rector stopped with a slight smile on his rubicund face.

'Why certainly, sir, they are about a mile and a half out of town.' He looked down at the two heavy-looking bags the stranger was carrying, then up to the sky. 'Too far to walk with such a burden, I fear, especially with rain threatening. There is a smithy not far, and I'm sure the farrier would, for a small fee, be willing to hitch up his cart and take you there.'

Nathaniel was crestfallen, for even a small fee could well be his breaking point. 'Oh dear, I was given to understand the house was within the town, and I'm unsure now what to do.' He stood, dithering, his jerking head becoming even more agitated with the stress.

The rector took pity on him; after all, wasn't it his Christian duty to help those in need?

'Come, sir, let me show you the way to the smithy. I'll have a word myself and smooth your path, never fear. Allow me to carry one of your bags for you,' and he took up the one that looked the lightest.

'Have you recently arrived on the coach?'

'Yes, my name is Simmons, Nathaniel Simmons, and I'm hired as tutor to the Riverley children. And you, sir?'

'My apologies, I should have introduced myself. Rector Cardwell at your service,' he said with a small bow. 'But come, we will soon have you at your place of employ.'

Nathaniel walked beside him, down the way he had just come, turning right along a lane. He could smell the horses immediately.

The smithy was a busy place, the farrier proving to be a broad-shouldered man with long thinning dark hair tied behind his neck with a string. He had a dark beard below a thin, humourless-looking mouth, and one eyelid drooped alarmingly. A young boy, whom Nathaniel presumed to be the farrier's son, was keeping the fire hot with a large pair of leather bellows, sweating from both the effort and the unremitting heat.

'Master Farrier, meet Nathaniel Simmons who is in need of transport to the Riverleys'.'

'Oh aye.' The farrier looked at the newcomer, taking in his poor appearance and the two heavy-looking bags. 'I'll take thee for sixpence.'

'Sixpence?' squeaked Nathaniel, for he only had a shilling and a half to his name, the accommodation and food needed for the journey being more than he had anticipated.

'Oh come now, Farrier, show a little Christian charity to the poor man,' urged the rector.

The farrier glowered. 'All right, threepence then, but not a penny less!'

Rector Cardwell looked at Nathaniel, silently urging him to accept.

'Very well, threepence,' agreed Nathaniel. It was still more than he could afford, but he could feel the rain starting again, and the thought of walking a mile and a half burdened as he was left him with no choice. Besides, the holes in the soles of his shoes weren't going to get any smaller, and he was already cold and tired.

'Right, hold on while I finish up here. My son will hitch up the horse.' He yelled at the young lad, who eagerly left the bellows and scurried out, heading for the stable, welcoming any chance to escape the heat and his father.

'I thank you for your assistance, rector. I hope to see more of you during my stay,' said Nathaniel, shaking the cleric's hand.

'No doubt you will, for the Riverleys attend church on Sunday, sometimes twice. I can invariably be found at St. Michael's at the top of the hill, should I be needed. Well, I must get on, my wife will be wondering where I am.' He raised his hat in farewell, nodded to the farrier and headed out into the lane, leaving Nathaniel leaning against a wall, waiting for the boy to return with the horse and cart.

≈≈≈

'That's it, through them trees,' said the farrier, pointing over to the right.

'I can't see anything.'

'Are thee blind? There, plain as nose on thy face,' and indeed, once they had cleared a small copse of trees, Nathaniel did see his destination, though it looked more of a castle than a home.

'Good Lord,' he said, 'does the family own much land? By the looks of the house they must be exceedingly wealthy.'

'Aye, about 700 acres. Wealthy they may be, but miserable buggers they are for all their money. Thee won't have much reason to laugh once thee enter through those doors, I'll warn thee now.'

Nathaniel felt a chill go through him, and was, if at all possible, even more despondent.

Chapter 8 ❧
Rectory

'Elizabeth, there's no use crying like this, it will just make you ill.'
Sarah was sitting on the bed in Elizabeth's room, trying her best
to comfort her heartbroken daughter. 'Come now, the time will
go quickly, and I could even try to convince your father to allow
you home earlier. If he receives good reports from your Aunt
Jane, it may be possible.' She looked hesitantly at Elizabeth, for
she knew her daughter's character. 'And you don't want the
rector to see you with a bloated and red face, now do you, for
what would he think?'

It was impossible to say how much Elizabeth had heard for
she was crying so hard, and it appeared no amount of heartiness
and encouragement was going to help. Sarah stood; sympathy
for others was never one of her attributes, quickly giving way to
annoyance.

'Very well, if you wish to behave in such a manner, there's
little I can do for you. When you are done making a spectacle of
yourself, I shall be found either in my room across the hall or
downstairs helping my sister prepare supper. Elizabeth, did you
hear me?'

Elizabeth continued to lie on the bed, her head buried in a
pillow. Sarah flounced out, thoroughly irritated, slamming the
door behind her.

As soon as she was alone, Elizabeth stopped crying, sat
up and smoothed her hair. Clambering off the bed, she poured

water from the jug into the basin and rinsed her face, wiping it dry on a towel hanging from an iron rail on the wall.

She had heard every word her mother had uttered, particularly relishing the part about asking her father if she could return early. So, the tears had worked. Deciding to wait upstairs rather than face her miserable cousins, she sat back against the wooden bed head, pulling the pillows behind her to make it more comfortable.

The window to the foot of the bed had magnificent views over the countryside; even in its winter hibernation, a sight to behold. The fields in spring would be bright green, but now were a dull, muddy colour, and with the leaves off all but the evergreen trees it was possible to see for a great distance.

As she sat listening to the noises from the rooms below, she wondered how Agnes was, if her ankle was fully recovered. All this led her thoughts back to London, and the excitement of her life there. Three months, how am I to bear it?

'Elizabeth, come down now, supper is about to be served,' her mother shouted.

Reluctantly Elizabeth rose from the bed, heaving a great pitiful sigh.

Everyone was seated round the table, the rector at the head, Sarah to his right with space for Elizabeth beside her. Mary and Anne sat opposite, with Aunt Jane at the end of the table facing her husband.

With the night settling in, the lamps had been lit, casting moving shadows on the walls. The maid of whom Jane had spoken earlier had, by the looks of it, partially recovered. One side of her face showed swollen and angry looking, a rag tied from the top of her head to under her chin. Obviously still in pain, she was dribbling as she walked round the table offering a dish of meat and vegetables, and it was clear she could hardly wait to escape from the room when all were served.

'That girl looks ill,' said Sarah to Jane. 'What is she doing about her tooth?'

'I told her to go and see the farrier to have it drawn, which she promised to do tomorrow. Hopefully that will cure her depressing face!'

Mary, addressing her mother said, 'What is Lizzie to be doing while she's here?'

Lizzie?

'She's here to spend time with her family, Mary.' Jane looked around nervously. 'I'm sure there will be more than enough to keep her occupied.'

Mary looked at Elizabeth.

'She doesn't seem very happy to be here, if that's the case. I've not seen her smile since she arrived.'

Sarah sensed Elizabeth's anger rising and quickly stepped in. 'Nonsense Mary, she's just tired after the journey, isn't that right, Elizabeth?'

The question went without answer, for why tell a lie unnecessarily, best to save it for something really important. She wasn't tired. She didn't want to be here, it was as simple as that.

Quickly changing the subject, Sarah commented on the tenderness of the meat, meagre servings though they were, and the conversation gradually drifted away from the contentious.

Elizabeth sat, pushing her food around her plate while listening to the endless droning from around the table.

'After supper,' said the rector, 'we could play a game or two. That sounds like fun, doesn't it?' He looked around the table, but none of the faces registered delight. Jane looked worried. His two daughters looked bad-tempered, as usual. Sarah mirrored her sister's worried expression, glancing frequently at Elizabeth, who looked plain mutinous.

'Oh dear,' he thought, 'a household of women, all at odds with each other.' Taking advantage of the end of the meal, he stated he had a sermon to prepare for the coming Sunday. He beat a hasty retreat to his study, firmly closing the door behind him, shutting out the ill feelings. Or so he hoped as he lit his pipe.

Sarah and Jane left, taking a few dishes with them to the kitchen, Jane at last taking pity on the little maid, though only because Sarah set the example. Elizabeth was left alone with Mary and Anne.

'I would prefer not to be addressed as 'Lizzie,'' she hissed. 'My name is Elizabeth, and that is what I answer to.'

'Just listen to her,' said Anne, addressing her sister. 'Just because she comes from London she obviously thinks she's better than us.'

'Well, that's up to her, Anne. All I know is it's going to be an unpleasant time while she's here if she continues in this vein.' Mary looked down her nose at her cousin as if there were a bad smell in the room.

'But come, sister, let's away to our room and leave Lizzie alone, for there's no doubt she prefers her own company.' Mary and Anne rose from their chairs, sweeping out the room in a flurry of skirts and petticoats.

Elizabeth went straight to her room. Outside it was now fully dark, and after undressing, she lay once more on the bed, gazing out at the blackness beyond the glass. With no houses overlooking, there was no need of curtains, the dark total except for the moonlight. Sarah would leave soon to take the coach back to London, leaving Elizabeth to her fate.

Chapter 9 ❧
Watermead

For Philip Goldworthy, his time thus far at Watermead had been productive.

Upon arrival, he had gone directly to greet his godmother, Lady FitzGerald, who awaited him in the main salon. He kissed her cheek in greeting.

'Philip, I am relieved to see you arrive safely. I remember the journey from London is long and arduous. How is your dear mother?'

Philippa Goldworthy had been a lifelong friend of Lady FitzGerald from when they were each first married. When Philip had been born, Lady FitzGerald had been the obvious choice for a godmother, making their friendship even stronger.

Upon the death of her husband, Philippa had visited Watermead on several occasions, staying sometimes for up to two months; the journey for a lady of advancing years being difficult, time was needed to recover.

Philip and his hostess sat by the fire enjoying the warmth, as Philip sipped old brandy.

'The journey was passable as always; there were no other passengers of interest, I fear, but the time passed well. What of you? And Watermead?'

A pleasant hour was spent exchanging news, Philip's glass refreshed when it emptied, which it did often. Before either knew it, it was noon and time for dinner, after which Lady FitzGerald retired to her room. Philip went to the stables to see the new horses his godmother had spoken about then returned to his own room and spent the afternoon relaxing. The two met again later in the afternoon, and Philip regaled his hostess with tales of mutual acquaintances in London, some of it spitefully done. As the supper hour approached, he retired to his room to wash and change, Lady FitzGerald doing the same.

As her maid arranged her hair for the evening, Lady FitzGerald said, 'Dodds, tell me if you hear of anything untoward of Master Philip during his stay, won't you?'

The maid, Laura Dodds, looked at her mistress' face in the mirror, trying to gauge the reason for this.

'Of course, my lady.'

Lady FitzGerald was an astute judge of character, quickly able to tell the wheat from the chaff, and she had an uneasy feeling about young Philip for all his charm and nice manners, and she felt vaguely disquieted by his spiteful comments.

꙳꙳꙳

Lady FitzGerald was again seated in the salon waiting for her godson to join her. Unable to put a solid finger on her uneasiness, she was now wondering on the prudence of asking Philip to visit.

Originally the invitation had been for him and his mother, but her old friend was unable to accept on this occasion due to pain in her knees, instead asking if Philip could come unaccompanied.

At just twenty-one years old, Lady FitzGerald knew Philip had a lot of maturing to do. Her thoughts kept returning to her long departed and dearly loved husband, for at the same age, he had been mature well beyond his years. She couldn't help but compare the two.

Perhaps it was because Philip's mother had mollycoddled him as a child, refusing to allow him to go to boarding school as was customary, instead hiring a tutor. Or perhaps, as she suspected, he was just plain spoiled. Now she was in two minds whether it was good to have him with her at this time, for she had her nephew, Thomas Stanton and his wife Susannah joining them in a few days.

Thomas was the heir to Watermead, and these days Lady FitzGerald felt each of her years. With the ague in her knees and hands, the winters were torture at times, the cold and damp seeming to concentrate all their fury on her. Even with the salves the physician prescribed for her, there was little relief. She knew it wouldn't be long before Thomas was master of Watermead.

It is always good to see the newlyweds. It had been nearly a year since they had last visited. Thomas' estates spread over vast distances, requiring his full attention. As she sat alone waiting, the warmth of the fire felt comforting on her aching body. She told herself again not to fret, that the visit would go well.

⟡⟡⟡⟡

She felt rather than heard the door open, the candles on the table besides her flickering wildly in the draught, and turning, saw Philip approaching.

'Hello, godmother, my apologies if I have kept you waiting. I couldn't find my clean boots and hunted everywhere. Eventually I summoned the maid, who told me they had been taken for cleaning, and of course, by the time they were found and returned, it made me late. So, blame the bootboy, whom I clipped round the ear, not me for my tardiness.' He flopped down heavily in the chair opposite, rudely throwing a leg over the arm.

Lady FitzGerald didn't like Philip blaming her staff; after all, they were only doing their job, and she gave a small tut of annoyance.

'On the contrary, Philip, I would have thought you should have thanked him for ensuring you were well turned out rather than scolding him.'

'I don't agree. These people must be made to understand who their betters are. Perhaps you are a little too lax with them.'

Lady FitzGerald was saved from an even tarter reply when the door opened once more, and the butler announced that supper was served.

Leading the way to the dining room, she tried to calm herself, for to lose one's temper while eating was well known to cause dyspepsia.

After they had been served the soup, the footmen leaving them alone with only the butler in attendance, she said, 'Did I tell you that Thomas Stanton and Susannah will be joining us tomorrow or the next day?'

He stopped with his soupspoon halfway between the bowl and his mouth. 'No, you didn't.' He was annoyed, for he had wanted to approach Lady FitzGerald for a loan, which now would have to be done this evening, before Thomas and Susannah arrived. 'When are you expecting them? In the morning, you say?'

'Could be; they are at one of his estates in Dorset, and will probably set out early. Why do you ask?'

'No reason, just of interest.' Damn and blast! This had really upset his plans, he would have to speak to his godmother before they arrived, and he hadn't yet prepared his story.

It was also imperative that his mother not know of his request, for she had already turned him down on two occasions, with the latter discussion ending acrimoniously. In fact, he had wondered if she really was not well enough to travel this time, or if she was still angry with him, wishing to distance herself from him for a while.

But no matter, he felt sure he could convince Lady FitzGerald to accommodate him, for he didn't like to think of the alternative. And whom else did she have to spend her considerable fortune on? Thomas Stanton was, obviously, independently wealthy with no need of her money or lands. She was too old to be gadding about in town spending it on high living. No, he felt sure there wouldn't be a problem. He turned his attention to the excellent meal.

≈⋆≈⋆≈

The next morning dawned clear and dry, though still cold. Philip hadn't had an opportunity to speak to his godmother the night before, for after the meal she had announced the beginnings of a headache, leaving immediately for her bed. Left with no other choice, he would have to speak to her the next morning.

She ate breakfast in her room, and he was forced to wait for her to appear. He thought of visiting her in her bedroom, but he balked at that. He would have to hope that Thomas and Susannah didn't arrive until he had a chance to plead his case.

Deciding not to not waste the morning, he ordered one of the estate horses to be saddled, and took himself off riding across the hills. Gone for three hours, he returned in time for dinner to find his godmother had made a miraculous recovery and gone into Honiton to visit the sick, which she considered her duty. Philip was convinced the gods were conspiring against him.

Lady FitzGerald heard from her maid that Master Septimus Morbeck had been ailing, though now thankfully was on the way to recovery.

The cook made up several baskets consisting of fresh bread and preserves, each with a wheel of cheese made of milk from the estate for her to take along. Well wrapped against the cold, her feet resting on a stone bottle filled with hot water, the carriage set off, and she gave a sigh of relief she had managed to leave without encountering Philip. She had a definite suspicion he wanted a favour of her, and no matter what it was, she was determined she wouldn't grant it. It would do him good to let him stew.

৯৪৯৪৯৪

Outside the Morbeck house, the footman helped her from the coach, handing her one of the baskets.

Gwyneth answered the door, instantly recognized her ladyship, and gave a low curtsey.

'Your Ladyship, please to come in from the cold.' Showing her into the parlour, she begged indulgence while she went in search of her mistress. Margaret came rushing downstairs, removing her apron on the way, throwing it over the banister, and smoothing her hair under her cap.

'Your Ladyship,' she said, curtseying, 'this is indeed an honour.'

'Mistress Morbeck, I was distressed to hear your husband was ill. How goes he?'

'He's much improved, thank you, but please, do sit down.' Margaret indicated the best chair, waiting for Lady FitzGerald to be seated. 'May I offer some ale, or something to eat?'

'No thank you, mistress, for I have eaten. I brought along some provisions that I hope you can use. The cheese is made from our milking, and the bread is freshly made today.' She moved aside the napkin covering the contents of the basket.

'That is kindly of you, indeed it is.' Margaret hesitated. 'I'm afraid my husband cannot leave his bed to thank you, the physician said it would take at least another week.'

'Of course, I don't expect him to exert himself until he's fully recovered. Did I also hear that your son had returned from London?'

Margaret wondered how she had heard that piece of news. 'Indeed he has, your Ladyship, he came on the coach yesterday. Such a long and trying journey, especially in this weather.' She tutted, shaking her head. 'But it's good for him to see his father, and the other way round too.'

'Is he still intending to study for a physician?'

'Yes, we were hoping he would take over the wool business, but it's not to be.' She sighed. 'Still, we are lucky we have another son who is interested, so all is not lost!'

'Indeed not, you have been most fortunate. Please pass on my best wishes to your husband and wish him a speedy recovery. Thank you for your hospitality, Mistress Morbeck.'

Margaret saw Lady FitzGerald to the door, waiting until she was once again safely in the carriage and on her way before closing the door, returning to the parlour to pick up the basket and taking it to show her husband.

Of James there had been no sign, and she was angry that he hadn't shown himself to her ladyship, especially when she had been so kind to make the visit especially to see his father. Margaret went in search of him, finding him in his bedroom, his nose, as usual, in a book of medicine.

'Didn't you hear Lady FitzGerald arrive, you ungrateful boy? You should have come down and greeted her in the absence of your father. Where are your manners? Have they all disappeared since you went to London? I was never so mortified in all my life!'

But James had long since learned to be deaf when his mother began to complain so, and while he was looking at her, nodding when it seemed appropriate, his mind was thinking over the effectiveness of bleeding a patient.

Chapter 10 ❧
Meadowacres

Nathaniel Simmons, meanwhile, was preparing to join the Riverley family for dinner. The bedroom allocated to him was on the fourth floor, and as he followed a servant, who begrudgingly carried his bags, Nathaniel was huffing and puffing.

'Just one more floor,' said the servant who was used to the climb. 'You'll soon get used to it, never fear.'

Nathaniel doubted that, having to pause frequently to catch his breath, the servant having by necessity to wait also, with obvious bad grace. When they eventually reached the room allocated for his private use, it was to find a small, dark, and very cold room in the eaves.

One small candle and a copy of the Bible stood on a table beside the bed, which in turn was also small in length, and Nathaniel was of above average height. A small window no larger than a foot square on a level with the floor was the only source of light, but the fireplace opposite the end of the bed held promise. He turned to the servant.

'Is it possible to have the fire lit?' he asked. 'The room strikes cold.'

'I dunno about that, you'd have to ask the housekeeper, but you'd have to catch her when she's in a good mood, which ain't often.' The servant laughed. 'As I said as we came up, you'll soon get used to it; you just have to dress warm. The family eats at six o'clock, but meets in the library for drinks at five-thirty so make sure you're down by then. You should hear the bell, from up here as a warning to get yer'self down there. There's fresh water in the jug,' and he indicated a table to the right of the window that contained the jug and basin. 'It's four floors down to the privy for you.' Still laughing, he disappeared out the door and back down the stairs.

Nathaniel stood for a moment, looking around at his home for the next who-knew-how long? What have I come to? A poorly paid tutor, living in the eaves?

There was a battered three-drawer chest to the left of the window, obviously to hold clothes, and a frail-looking, cushion-less chair beside it. A table, obviously unwanted in the rest of the house for one leg had been broken and patched together badly, stood at the foot of the bed.

Nathaniel picked up the bag containing his books, taking them out and placing them on the table, but with its patched leg it immediately began to wobble and he quickly removed them, placing them instead on the bed. Looking in the chest, he found it at least dry and cedar lined, so he unpacked his few clothes and linens, placing his spare pair of boots beside it. He daren't sit on the chair, certain it wouldn't hold his weight, so with no other choice, sat on the bed, which proved hard and uncomfortable. The sheets felt coarse, and when he looked closer found they had been turned 'sides to middle' to extend their use. One thin blanket was folded at the base of the bed.

He looked through the small window that overlooked the stable yard, and felt very sad and alone. Reluctant to go downstairs, he remained in his room all afternoon, growing more and more hungry until his timepiece told him it was nearly time for supper.

After washing in the icy water and changing his dusty travel clothes, Nathaniel had opened the door the better to, hopefully, hear the bell commanding all to attend in the library, and luckily he did, albeit faintly.

By the time he reached the second floor he realised he didn't know where the library was, for no one had shown him around the house, and once he reached the hall he had to stop a manservant to ask for direction. Without greeting, or showing any interest in who this new face belonged to, he was told to follow the hall to the front doors and turn right, through four rooms until he came to a door painted dark red, and there he would find the library. The servant disappeared before he could give thanks, and Nathaniel set off, counting rooms as he went.

The dark red door now faced him and he knocked, in what he hoped was a respectful way.

Yet another manservant opened it, but this one had obviously been told to expect him, for he turned to the room and announced, 'Master Simmons, your lordship.'

Nathaniel entered the room to find six faces turned inquiringly at him, four of which were adult. So which of them were Lord and Lady Riverley? He decided to resolve this dilemma by bowing low and waiting to be approached.

No one moved, they either stood or sat, like a tableau with not a greeting smile between them. Now even more unsure what to do, he said in the direction of the two men, 'Lord Riverley?'

'Yes, I'm Riverley.' A tall, rather unattractive middle-aged man with a florid complexion stood by the fireplace, his arm resting proprietorialy on the mantle. Overly long greying hair was brushed back, dark brown eyes with large bags beneath standing out, a mouth pursed in annoyance.

'Good evening, Lord Riverley,' answered Nathaniel. With no reply, he was left to stand by the door like a poor relation begging alms. The rest of the company returned to their conversation, leaving the two children staring at this, their new tutor, and obviously finding him wanting.

The mood around the Riverley's dining table was anything but welcoming. Nathaniel, when under stress, found his head twitched and bobbed worse than ever, and though the children were not present, as they had left and were being fed in their nursery, the agitated motions were obviously annoying the adults.

'Tell me, sir,' said Lord Riverley, 'what makes your head move so?'

Nathaniel was mortified, for it was only good manners that one's infirmities were not mentioned unless you chose to do so yourself.

'Lord Riverley, I have been afflicted thus since birth, so I'm used to it.' He looked down at his plate, his face burning hot, and misery in his eyes.

'Well, I doubt very much if we shall get used to it. I think in future you had best eat with the servants. I can't have the ladies upset.'

Nathaniel could have shrivelled into his chair, wanting to run away and never return, but he was bound by a contract for a year. Certain Lord Riverley would pursue him with a legal case he would be unable to defend due to lack of funds, he had no choice but to acquiesce.

'Certainly, Lord Riverley, as you wish.'

The other diners totally ignored him throughout the meal, and he might as well have been invisible. Indeed he wished he were. Even as a child at school, his fellow scholars hadn't treated him so cruelly, and everyone knew how unkind children could be to one who was different. He had been raised in a loving and supportive house, his parents frequently telling him how valued he was. Only rarely had he been ridiculed, and he could almost physically feel himself disappearing into nothingness. If the parents can be so rude, heaven help me tomorrow when I have to start teaching the children.

The six-course meal at last came to an end, and with each successive remove he noticed that his plate had been filled with less than half of everyone else's.

The farrier was right; it's going to be hard to find any joy in this employment. How I wish I'd never seen the advertisement for this position in the Spectator. Starvation would almost be preferable.

Chapter 11 ❧
Meadowacres

At the same moment Thomas and Susannah walked through Watermead's imposing front doors, Nathaniel Simmons entered the kitchen at the Riverleys' residence, Meadowacres.

He had slept fitfully, the draughts blowing through the window as if there was no glass there at all, and the thin blanket provided on the bed was nowhere near warm enough to offer comfort. During the night he had risen and dressed, hoping that would help, but it hadn't. Each time he awakened from the tossing and turning, he looked outside to find it was still full dark, and he had no idea of the time. He had lain awake reading The Franklin's Tale by Geoffrey Chaucer until far too late, and the one candle provided had burned down to nothing. He had not thought to look for another in any drawer or cupboard before it gutted out, so with no choice but to wait for the dawn, he lay in shivering misery in the dark.

In the best houses, maids would come in the early morning to re-lay and light the fire, but none came near his room. The servants would consider him one of them, not someone to be catered to.

Reminding himself to seek out the housekeeper and request, no, demand, a fire, he could only dream of being warm. He must have drifted off to sleep, for the next time he looked there was a lightening of the sky through the curtains. He had to wait awhile before he could see his timepiece, which showed it was nearing seven o'clock.

When he did rise, the water in the jug had a layer of ice on the top, which he had to break with his fist. Too cold to wash properly, Nathaniel contented himself with quickly rinsing his face and hands, and left the room.

Down the three flights of stairs to the dining room he went, only to find there was no one there, the table unlaid, no food on the sideboard.

Nathaniel stood scratching his head and decided to seek the kitchen. Leading off from the hall there were several doors, and he had no idea where they led. He wasn't even sure if he should knock or enter freely.

He hadn't asked last night what time they wished the children's lessons to start, for he had been too nervous, especially when told he would have to eat with the staff and Lord Riverley's hostile manner. Lord Riverley had said he could not eat with the family, and he had no choice but to find the kitchen if he wanted to eat. He was uncertain what to do or what was expected of him.

He looked at the doors, hoping to see one that looked like it led downstairs, but none looked likely. Just as he was despairing, the butler, Hoskins, came through a door behind the stairs.

'Good morning,' said Nathaniel in greeting. The butler sniffed quietly. Nathaniel waited for a reply that obviously was not to come. 'Could you tell me where I could get some breakfast, please?'

'Lord Riverley told me that in the future you would be eating with the staff, and we ate an hour ago.' He looked at Nathaniel with distaste. 'You will have to ask cook if she can find you something, though she won't be pleased.'

Nathaniel squared his shoulders. He wouldn't be spoken to so rudely by a mere butler.

'Pleased or not, tell me where the kitchen is, man,' he demanded. Hoskins looked at him with, if possible, even more distaste, and this time the sniff was long and loud.

'Through this door, follow the noise,' and with that, Hoskins walked around Nathaniel, giving him a wide berth as if this newcomer carried the contagion.

Nathaniel opened the door, which looked exactly like all the others in the hall, went down three steps and followed the noise as instructed. Once on the other side of the door, the floor changed from white tiles to crude stone flags, and his footsteps sounded loud against them. More doors led off the long corridor, Nathaniel looking inside as he passed each one.

The hubbub was growing louder; one strident voice was heard above all others, while pots and pans were clattered around. The added incessant barking of a dog made it seem like chaos was reigning.

Faced with a door from which the noise was emanating, he pushed it open to find himself standing a good six feet above the level of the kitchen, a wooden railing in front of him, well-worn stone steps going down to both left and right.

Nathaniel could have stayed there all day without anyone taking notice of him whatsoever. It wasn't because everyone was busy; on the contrary, it seemed a young girl washing the pans was the only one working, and she was barely able to see above the sink. She wore a wraparound apron far too big for her, for it draped on the ground at her feet.

At the table, which had to be twelve feet long, sat two people. At one end was an unattractive woman, her head covered in a cap that even from a distance looked in need of a good wash. Extremely large, she occupied all and more of a chair that looked hardly suitable for a person of her girth. She appeared to be about forty years old, but her features were deceiving, she could have been older or younger. The hair that had escaped the cap was a dull, lifeless brown. Her hands, pudgy and obviously afflicted with the ague, were holding a large beaker of a hot liquid, the steam rising towards the ceiling. Nathaniel presumed this was the cook.

To her right sat another woman, completely opposite in appearance. Painfully thin, her nose stuck out like an eagle's beak, curved and pointed. The flesh on her face was sunken, sharp cheekbones obvious. Also wearing a cap, though hers had a frill of lace, she wore a grey linen dress, which was severe in appearance, and Nathaniel glimpsed a large bunch of keys attached to a belt around her waist and surmised her to be the housekeeper. Nathaniel coughed politely, hoping to gain their attention, but they continued to talk, even though the cook couldn't help but see him standing elevated at the door. He coughed again, more insistently, but the result was the same. Now angry, he walked down the steps, approaching the table with a firm tread.

'Good morning.' The cook looked at him in astonishment, as if he'd dropped down from heaven into the middle of her kitchen. 'Who you be?'

He bowed. 'I'm Nathaniel Simmons, the new tutor. I spoke to Hoskins and he told me to ask you for food.'

'Well I never!' said the cook. 'What time do you call this to be looking for food? We eat at six, there's nothing for you now,' and she turned back to her companion, ready to take up their conversation.

Nathaniel looked pointedly at the table where a plate piled high with freshly baked biscuits stood.

'And pray tell what are they?'

'They are for the staff later, in case they are hungry.'

'Well, since I am staff and I am hungry, I'll have some.' Without waiting, Nathaniel pulled out a chair and moved the plate closer to him. 'I will join everyone for breakfast tomorrow, but as no one told me the routine of the house, I would be grateful if I could also have something to drink, preferably hot.' He smiled at the cook, waiting for her to argue with him.

He had been at Meadowacres for less than a day, and none of his former colleagues would have said he was an assertive man, but he knew that if he was to survive his tenure, he would have to learn this quickly.

He and the cook stared at each other for a moment, and then with a loud laugh she banged her hands on the table, calling over her shoulder to the young girl washing the pots.

'Bring Master Simmons here a hot toddy, Bessie. Pleased to meet you Master Simmons, but those biscuits won't hold you for long,' and without warning, she bellowed, 'Frances!'

Around a door came a girl of about twelve years wiping her hands on her grubby apron.

'Find Master Simmons here some bread and cheese, and there's some of the leftover chicken from last night, no doubt he'd like that, too.'

'Indeed I would, and thank you.' He smiled again at the cook. Turning to the other lady, he said, 'Good morning, mistress. You must be the housekeeper.'

'I am,' she said, although with not nearly as much warmth as the cook, and certainly no welcoming smile.

'Then I'm pleased I met up with you, for I nearly froze to death last night, even before I met the children I'm to tutor.' He paused to smile at his humor. 'And I'll have the fire lit in my room, for it's fearful cold. More blankets for the bed, and the candle has burned down to nothing.'

'My, my, you don't want much, do you?' said the housekeeper coolly. 'We aren't put on this earth to have all our creature comforts taken care of. Some suffering is good for the soul.'

'Indeed it is, madam, but when it will interfere with the education of Lord Riverley's children due to my freezing to death, I think that suffering has gone far enough! I shall expect a fire, more blankets, and a good supply of candles for this evening.'

Nathaniel was furious, but determined to stand his ground. Without a word, the housekeeper stood, nodded farewell to the cook and swept out of the kitchen, her anger obvious in the straightness of her back.

'Don't take no notice of her,' said the cook, laughing. 'Frances! Where's that food?' she bellowed again as the poor girl came flying through the door carrying a tray laden with food.

'I'm coming, I'm coming,' she cried.

With the food before him, Nathaniel felt he had handled himself very well so far. Of course, he had yet to properly meet the children.

Chapter 12 ⟡
Rectory

In the morning, households awoke to driving rain brought by a strong wind from the northeast. Elizabeth lay listening to the rain beat on the window of the rectory.

Sarah travelled to London today, and with the coach leaving the Cross Keys at eight o'clock sharp, they were all out of bed early. The kitchen maid had once again taken to her bed with the toothache, so it was left to Elizabeth, Mary, and Anne to put food on the table and light the fire in the dining room. The wind was so strong the smoke blew back into the room, making it look as if a fog had come inside to shelter from the weather.

Each who entered waved their hand in front of their face to clear the air, but to no avail. While Sarah couldn't wait to leave, there was a small part of her that did so with trepidation. She felt worry for Elizabeth being left with the two girls and Jane, who had proven to be a most ineffectual mother. Sarah realised that there was little hope of Elizabeth being brought into line, for Jane couldn't control her own brats.

Jane, the younger of the two sisters by a year, was always treated by their parents as the favourite, a fact Sarah had never forgotten nor totally forgiven, even though the Bible urged it. However, as they say, 'needs must,' and Elizabeth had to realise her behaviour was not that of a well-brought-up young lady. Sarah decided not to tell her husband of her misgivings; what he didn't know he couldn't fret over. More importantly, her life would be easier in the bargain.

Breakfast was eaten in silence, the rector joining them once they were seated. After a brief prayer of thanks, they dove into the bread and cheeses, a large platter of cold meats left from the night before, and a bowl of hard-boiled eggs. At least Elizabeth won't want for food with such good country fare, thought Sarah as she bolted her food, eager to be gone from this miserable place.

The only person not eating was Elizabeth.

'Come, Elizabeth,' urged Sarah. 'Dinner will be a long time away, and a growing girl needs sustenance. Eat something, do.'

Nevertheless, Elizabeth continued to sit mutely.

Jane, Sarah, and the rector looked at each other with troubled faces, while Mary and Anne giggled behind their hands.

'Come, Lizzie, best eat something,' mimicked Mary.

Elizabeth didn't answer, didn't even look up. I'll get my revenge on you, Mary, you see if I don't. And it won't be long before I do.

When Sarah went upstairs to collect her bonnet and cloak, her bag already at the front door, Elizabeth stood at the bottom of the stairs waiting to bid farewell.

'Now, Elizabeth, remember to help your Aunt Jane as much as you can, and do write to us, won't you, dear?' She saw the sad face in front of her, the tears gathering in Elizabeth's eyes. In a chivvying tone, Sarah said, 'Now come, daughter, the time will go quickly and even more so if you heed your aunt. If she sends me good reports, I will speak to your father about returning for you earlier than the three months.'

At that Elizabeth looked up, hope in her watery eyes. 'Do you promise, Mother?'

'Yes, I do, but as I said, I'll need good news of you from Jane.' Sarah realised this farewell was best concluded as quickly as possible, and with a kiss for Elizabeth, and one for Jane and each of the girls, she took her bag from the rector. With a last wave, Sarah stepped out into the wind and rain, down the hill to the Cross Keys and, ultimately, to London.

Jane and the girls went back inside, the weather forcing them in, while Elizabeth remained on the step, watching until she could no longer see her mother, wishing she was going with her.

'Elizabeth, help clear the board,' Jane said once she was back indoors, the front door now firmly closed against the weather.

'But where are Mary and Anne?' Elizabeth made a good show of looking around for her cousins.

'They have gone upstairs to read for a while, but that's none of your business,' replied Jane, picking up dishes and stacking them one on top of another. 'I'm sure I don't know when that maid will be better, for if anything, her tooth seems to be worse this morning.'

All the time she was talking, she was bustling around the table, plates teetering precariously. 'Well don't just stand there, girl, there's work to be done and the dishes won't do themselves!' She glared at Elizabeth. 'Don't you think your life is going to be easy, for in this house we all have to help.'

'But Mary and Anne aren't helping.'

'I've told you, that's none of your business, and I won't have you speak ill of them, for they are good girls on the whole.'

Elizabeth longed to disagree, for she thought them ill mannered, lazy, and spoiled. How Mother thought this would be good for me, Lord only knows! At home I don't have to work, why should I here? Nevertheless, she picked up a bowl of apples, which nobody had touched, and who could blame them when they looked so mealy and wormy, along with the platter of meat, and headed reluctantly for the kitchen.

The maid, named Rose, was lying on her pallet beneath the kitchen table, her face even more swollen than yesterday, moaning piteously.

'Haven't you been to the farrier yet?' asked Elizabeth, feeling sorrow for the girl.

'No, but I must go this morning, for I can't stand the pain another minute.'

'Do you want me to come with you?'

'Would you? You'd have to ask the mistress for permission, though. I'm frightened he'll pull the tooth and I can't stand any more pain,' and she sat up, rocking back and forth in her agony.

'I'll go and ask,' said Elizabeth and left the dishes on the table, returning to the dining room.

'Aunt Jane, may I go with Rose to the farrier to get her tooth pulled? She looks poorly, and if he pulls it, she may need assistance getting home.'

Aunt Jane looked hard at Elizabeth. 'That will be the only place you'll go, you are both to come straight back here afterwards and help with the work.'

'Yes, Aunt Jane,' and before there could be a change of mind, she hurried back to the kitchen, telling Rose to be quick about putting on her wrap, for she could accompany her. The poor girl looked relieved, though she knew the tooth would have to be pulled and she was filled with terror.

⁂

The farrier's was to be found at the bottom of the hill just off High Street, and neither girl was in a rush to reach it. Rose led the way, but her steps kept faltering, which Elizabeth found understandable when she thought of what was to come.

Rose was afeared of the farrier's pincers; she had never had a tooth pulled but had heard many a tale of the agony suffered by countless others. Elizabeth didn't hurry her steps because, even with the wind and rain, it was a relief to be away from the rectory and those within.

The street was deserted due to the weather keeping most inside and dry. She stopped to look in the bookshop window, but saw no sign of Edward Catchpole. Perhaps he hadn't bothered to open today, anticipating the lack of trade.

But, they couldn't meander too long or Aunt Jane would be angry, a state she seemed never to retreat from.

'Come, Rose, we must get on,' said Elizabeth, even though it was she who was wasting time.

Rose trailed behind, holding her hand against her swollen face, terror in her eyes. She was only nine, a small slip of a thing that the wind, had it been any stronger, could easily have blown away.

She had been the maid at the rectory since being taken in as an orphan, the rector doing his Christian duty, so he said. In reality, she was merely cheap labour; she did have a roof over her head and food in her belly, but it was a hard life for one so young. If anyone would have asked, Rose would have considered herself lucky, except for that tooth.

The rain dampened down the smell of manure from the farrier's, but it was still pungent. Even with the cold, the young lad, the same one who had hitched up the horse and cart for Nathaniel Simmons, was sweating profusely as he worked the bellows keeping the fire going for his father.

Upon seeing the two girls, he stopped, calling to his father somewhere out of sight.

'Pa, Pa, there's people here.'

The farrier came through into the yard, raising his eyebrows when he saw them.

'Yes?' he asked gruffly.

'Please, sir, I've the toothache,' said Rose, already trembling in anticipation of the pain that was to come.

'Well, let's have a look at it, then.' Walking over, he grasped Rose's small face in one large fist. Turning her face to the meagre light he said, 'Ah, I see thy problem, it's all black and swollen.' He poked roughly at the rotten tooth with his finger, making Rose howl. 'Won't take but a minute to get that out.'

Rose hid her face in her wrap.

'What are thee crying for?' he asked, impatiently. 'Do thee want it out or not? Make up thy mind, girl.'

Elizabeth spoke up. 'Yes, of course she wants it out. She's scared, that's all. Will it hurt much?'

'Nay, done in a trice,' said the farrier. He went to the makeshift table that held all manner of tools, selecting what seemed to Elizabeth to be one of the largest. She glanced at Rose, who still had her face hidden.

'Come on, Rose, it has to be done, and think how much better you will feel after.'

The farrier had neither the pity nor time to coax the girl. 'Sit down on that stool and open thy mouth.'

With shaking knees that threatened to collapse under her, Rose walked to the stool with tears streaming down her face.

The farrier took another look at the tooth to make sure he didn't pull the wrong one. Unfortunately, he had done so in the past, much to his patient's displeasure. As he had said, within a trice the tooth reappeared at the end of the pincers, leaving Rose howling with fright and pain.

'That will be a penny,' he said.

'You never said anything about payment, sir,' replied Elizabeth.

'I don't do it for nought, girl. A penny it is. Due now.'

'We didn't bring any money, I'll have to return.' She looked him straight in the eye, daring him to argue.

'Very well,' he said, but with bad grace. 'I expect it by this dinnertime, mind,' and he turned from Elizabeth. Replacing the pincers on the table now minus the tooth, which he had thrown on the midden heap, he yelled for his son to get the forge fire going again.

Handing the crying maid her own handkerchief, Elizabeth helped Rose from the stool, holding onto her arm, which was shaking violently.

'Come, Rose, let's go back to the rectory. I'm sure the pain will soon subside now.'

With Rose shuffling along beside her and leaning heavily on her arm, Elizabeth led the way back to High Street. Her heart ached for the young girl who looked so pitiful that she, too, couldn't help but cry. There they were, two young girls climbing the hill to the rectory, both feeling sorry for themselves if for different reasons.

Chapter 13 ❧
Watermead

Susannah's return to Watermead was bittersweet. How could she be so close to the cottage at Offwell and her life there with her parents and brother and not mourn for them? Tending the graves at the cottage, of course, would have to be kept for a dry day, for she would want to spend some time there, preferably alone.

They had been among the poorest of the poor, but she remembered the good times with Ma combing her hair, humming as she pulled the comb through the knots. Ma had died far too young, and her pa had died in Honiton saving others from danger.

Susannah seldom thought of her father, and on the rare occasion she did, it wasn't with happy memories. But it would be good to visit Giles Bentley at Upper Hambley once more, for he had been kind to her and Peter when they were in such dire need of help. So many memories were flying around her head it was hard to keep them all straight, but visiting Peter and his shop was uppermost in her mind.

When Susannah sold her lace as a young girl to Lady FitzGerald, she always went to the back door, but now the carriage drew up smoothly to the front of the house.

The butler, watching for them, opened the doors wide to welcome them in, a young maid standing to one side waiting to collect coats and Susannah's bonnet. With the wind and rain coming from the north, the entrance, which faced south, was sheltered from the worst of the weather. As the footman helped both her and Thomas from the carriage, Susannah stood for a moment, taking in how good it felt to return to Watermead.

Looking down the long driveway she used to walk, the years disappeared and she saw herself as that small, undernourished child responsible for keeping her and her crippled younger brother from starvation.

'Come, Susannah, my aunt awaits.'

'Yes, of course, I'm sorry, Thomas,' and she turned back to smile at her husband who stood with arm outstretched to escort her inside.

The fireplace in the entrance hall was well lit, candles glowing against the dull day, making them welcome. Susannah shrugged off her cloak and bonnet, handing them to the maid who accepted them with lowered eyes and a small curtsey.

'Thank you,' said Susannah smiling at the girl, who looked up, giving a shy smile in return.

'Her ladyship is in her bedroom, Lord Thomas,' said the butler. 'Do you wish to go there first or refresh yourselves?'

'I think we'll go to our room first. We are rather early, I doubt if my aunt has even had breakfast. We'll give her some time to prepare for us,' and he looked at Susannah for confirmation, who nodded agreement.

'Very good, sir, you are in the Green Room as usual, and your luggage will be brought up directly.' He then turned his attention to Susannah.

'Your maid will instruct the staff, my lady, as to your personal items, and I'll have some refreshment brought up to you.'

'Thank you, Hanna will be here shortly, for she wanted to stop in Honiton first. I'll care for myself until then, but the refreshment would be most welcome.'

Thomas and Susannah followed the servant up the wide curving staircase, Susannah's hand gliding smoothly over the wrought iron handrail, savouring the feel. As they ascended, she couldn't resist looking back at the black and white chequered floor originally glimpsed through the doors as a child.

Chapter 14 ❧
Watermead

Philip Goldworthy, luxuriating in his bed, stretched until his bones cracked. Daylight showed through where the curtains didn't meet in the middle, so it was after seven o'clock, but he was in no hurry, the day his own.

He had one task, though; speak to his godmother about the loan. He had lain in bed going over his speech and thought he had it just about right. Mind you, he'd tried a version of it on his mother to no avail. But, stuck in this godforsaken hole, he hoped Lady FitzGerald was unaware of his past sins and she, no doubt, would not have heard the gossip from London. He was confident all would be well. Turning over and burying his face in the pillows once more, he drifted back to sleep.

The maid whose task it was to light the fires in the bedrooms was as quiet as she knew how, but even so, Philip was awoken with the sound of logs going into the grate.

'What's this noise!' he bellowed, reaching down the side of the bed for a boot and flinging it in the direction of the poor girl. 'Get out, can't you see I'm sleeping!'

The maid abandoned the basket, and gathering her skirt ran from the room in fright.

Wondering what time Thomas and Susannah would arrive, he knew he must speak to godmother before then, but the feather bed was far too comfortable to leave just yet.

From the other side of the door he heard voices. He thought it was the maid then realised one voice was male, commanding.

Philip leapt from the bed, wrapping a sheet around his nakedness. Opening the door he peered out, but saw no sign of life. Then the voice came again, this time answered by a woman.

'It's good to be back at Watermead,' said the man.

'Yes, the air always feels fresher in Devon,' replied a woman.

Philip became aware the voices were drawing closer. He pushed the door to, peering through a thin slit. Thomas and Susannah had arrived.

Damn! Now what do I do? He closed the door noiselessly, turning back to stare sightlessly at the room. Lady FitzGerald would be occupied with her guests. He knew he had left it too late. He had to get money or the debt collectors would start knocking on his mother's door, if they hadn't already. Those damned horses!

The thought had crossed his mind to find a betting game in Honiton and try and recoup some of his losses, but sense had taken over; he was far enough in debt as it was. He couldn't afford any more; indeed, he couldn't afford what he already had.

He opened the door and bellowed for hot water, and after shaving and dressing quickly, he strode down the stairs to the dining room. Upon entering, he found Thomas and Susannah sitting at the table.

'Thomas! What a pleasant surprise! And Susannah, this is good news. It's been a long time since we saw each other.' His voice, even to him, sounded unnaturally loud, and he told himself to moderate it.

Thomas rose. 'Good morning, Philip. I heard you were visiting.' The two men shook hands, and then Philip went around the table to kiss Susannah's cheek.

Dishes were on the sideboard and kept hot with small candles beneath. Philip inspected each one in turn, deciding on two eggs and sausages, and then helping himself from a plate of bread on the table. Susannah was eating a piece of toast, a cup of tea at her elbow, while Thomas' plate was heaped with an assortment of eggs, bacon, sausages, kidneys, and mushrooms.

'How long are you staying?' Philip asked Thomas, trying to sound casual.

'We have no firm plans. I don't have to be back in Wiltshire

69

for a month or so, and Susannah is especially fond of Devon.' He smiled lovingly at his wife, who smiled back.

'I have a few ideas for while I'm here,' said Susannah, 'But really, it's lovely not to have to do anything one doesn't want to.' They all laughed, Philip's somewhat forced.

'And you?' enquired Thomas.

'Oh you know, this and that, here and there, a bit of riding, if the weather holds. As you said earlier, Susannah, it's good to smell sweet Devon air.' He looked at each of them, smiling benignly.

In spite of her easy demeanor, Susannah wasn't comfortable. She had mentioned the air to Thomas as they that had gone upstairs, which meant Philip had been listening to a private conversation.

A good judge of character, she suddenly felt unsettled. Sitting back in her chair, she left the conversation to the men, and it predictably quickly turned to hunting and shooting, neither of which interested her. She concentrated on her breakfast, her mind going over once more the conversation with Thomas when they arrived, more certain than ever they had been alone when she mentioned the air.

'If you will excuse me, gentlemen, I'll go in search of Lady FitzGerald and leave you to your blood sports.' Both men stood while she left the room, Thomas following her with his eyes.

'What are your plans for today, Thomas? The weather looks as if it will be fine for the morning at least,' said Philip.

'I have to go into Honiton, some business to be transacted with the solicitor there. And you?'

'Perhaps I'll ride with you, there's a man I want to see about a horse,' and he left it at that though he didn't miss the sharp look from Thomas. 'Leave in half an hour?'

'Certainly, I'll get two horses saddled and brought round,' said Thomas. His food finished, he left the room, the beginnings of a frown on his face.

Susannah went in search of Lady FitzGerald, who these days rarely appeared before dinner. The years had passed quickly, and she found it hard to believe that Thomas' aunt, her benefactor as a child, had grown old. Now nearing seventy years, Lady FitzGerald still carried herself with a straight back and head held high. There was, however, rarely a reason for her to rise from her bed early, and if anyone urgently needed to speak to her, they could go to her bedroom.

Susannah knocked on the door, waiting for the maid, Dodds, to answer.

'Mistress, do please come in, her ladyship said you would be here early.'

Susannah smiled her thanks.

The bedroom overlooked the back of the estate, the formal gardens laid below for the mistress of the house to enjoy from her room. The countryside beyond the hedges and walls stretched into infinity, the different hues of green and gold standing clear in the sunshine.

The room was large, indeed large enough to need the two fireplaces it contained, one set into each side wall. The huge bed was set at right angles to the fire on the right, keeping its precious occupant warm while still able to see the gardens, her pride and joy.

'Susannah, I am pleased to see you. I heard you and Thomas had arrived, and so I have been anticipating your visit with pleasure. Sit down and tell me all the news.' She patted the side of the bed, and as Susannah sat they held hands.

'Thomas and I are glad to be here, Lady FitzGerald; we have been looking forward to the visit since your invitation arrived. Indeed, if you hadn't invited us, we would have invited ourselves!'

'What's this "Lady FitzGerald" business? We are family, Susannah, and I think it only appropriate you called me Aunt Sophie.'

'Thank you, Aunt Sophie, I will.' Susannah paused, looking out at the gardens. She turned back to Lady FitzGerald and paused, stumbling over the words. 'Thank you for all you did for my brother and me. We know that you kept us from starvation by buying the lace when we were so desperate. Make no mistake,' she looked meaningfully at Lady FitzGerald, 'we were desperate. All I have now I owe to you, especially Thomas.'

Lady FitzGerald continued to hold her hand, tears showing in her faded, rheumy eyes. 'Nonsense, child, it was the right thing to do, and how could I not buy the lace, for it was so beautiful?' She smiled impishly. 'Did Thomas ever tell you what I did with it?'

Susannah shook her head. 'No, though there would have been a lot of it. But what would Thomas know of it?'

'Yes there was, you were a prolific lacemaker indeed! Thomas bought it, every piece.'

'Surely not, for he never mentioned it. I thought you sold it to ladies in London.' Susannah was shocked. 'There must be dozens of pieces, surely? Where is it now?'

'When he came to Watermead, he purchased whatever I had.' Lady FitzGerald lay back against the pillows, speaking gently. 'He loved you from the first time he met you when the lace fell in the stream, Susannah, and he waited impatiently for you to grow to the woman you are now.'

Susannah felt her face grow warm, and knew she was blushing. 'I'm sorry to say that I remembered him only as a stranger who helped me out of the stream and fed me the best breakfast I had ever eaten.'

'I trust you have eaten breakfast this morning?'

'Yes, I did, thank you.'

They sat in silence, content in each other's company, looking out at the beautiful garden and the gardeners who toiled there.

Chapter 15 &

Morbeck Home

James Morbeck, impatient to be on his way back to London, showed himself at meals, spending the odd hour with his father, but mostly his time was spent reading in his room.

When the physician attended his father, James made sure to be present, gleaning as much information as he could. Dr. Cork had, upon his own father's death, taken over the practice and been physician in Honiton for the past twenty years. Like most country doctors, he knew all the family secrets; which child had been born on the wrong side of the blanket; and which, for whatever reason, hadn't been born at all.

All of his patients liked to think he kept their secrets, but they were aware that Dr. Cork had a fondness for drink, and he was seemingly unable to hold it well. When sober, he was an upright, correct man. When drunk, which was often, he was a fountain of information about each and every one of them. He was also the only physician for thirty miles around, and so with little choice they tolerated him, doing their best to keep the worst of their sins from him.

He had been trained under his father, never actually attending medical school, so the title 'physician' was merely a complimentary one. But he was the nearest thing they had if they discounted the old woman who lived in a run-down cottage in the woods who professed to heal with herbs and flowers.

James was determined to become a proper, licensed physician, and for that he needed to go back to London. It didn't mean that he wouldn't come back to Honiton once he had passed his final exams and could at last call himself 'physician,' but it did mean that he would have a world of possibilities in front of him. While there were towns and cities springing up all over the country, there were far more places like Honiton, good places to grow up in where people worked hard. Yes, the possibility existed he would be interested in coming back, but only if Dr. Cork was no longer the town physician.

Having seen the man with his father, he felt unhappy with the service being provided. However, his father seemed to be improving day by day, and after all, what did James know that Dr. Cork didn't? If his father continued the way he was, James hoped he could be on his way back to London within two weeks.

He found life in the small market town claustrophobic, used as he was to his own routine consisting of school and his studies. His mother hadn't improved since he left and was still terrorizing the servants, and if truth were told, her husband too.

David, James' brother, kept out of the way. He spent as much time as possible at the wool business, returning each evening to report to their father.

James, lying in his narrow bed listening to the household settle for the night, thought of his life to come, master of his own fate at last.

Chapter 16 ஜ
Honiton

Susannah's brother, Peter Brigginshaw, looked around his workshop. In early morning, everything was quiet, the smell of sawdust and glue redolent in the air. He thought how this had to be his favourite time of day; he had the room to himself, his apprentices still to appear from their beds looking for food.

Mistress Chapman still cared for the house, though he could see the years were taking their toll. Her thinning hair was pure white, and her face lined. Never a tall woman, she was now stooped and frail. On several occasions he had asked if the upkeep of the house was becoming too much, but both she and Master Chapman assured him she was able to cope.

Henry Chapman was still involved with customers, though had long been unable to work the wood himself. Ague in his hands and feet had made life difficult for him, but he was so pleased to still have a part in the joinery. Each evening he gave thanks that young Peter had come into the business, for without a son to his name, it would have had to be closed, and what would he do with himself then? The days would be long and tiresome, and more importantly, money would be short. With Peter doing so well, his heart soared, knowing now that the business would continue after his death.

Not only the joinery business had grown, Honiton had grown in leaps and bounds. St. Michael's church was packed to the gills of a Sunday, and the weekly market was drawing more traders with a wider variety of goods for sale.

Unfortunately, along with the increased populace came those who wanted to separate the hard-working people from their money.

The watchman who had been responsible for mistakenly taking Susannah into custody so long ago had died two years previously, his post now taken up by two citizens to share the load. Market days were the worst, thieves and scoundrels looking for the weak and incautious, working usually in pairs; one would distract, the other snatch a purse or goods.

They also tried their luck in the shops, the keepers now wise enough to have extra help standing guard. Luckily, Peter's shop was off the beaten path, and so far he had not been bothered, but he knew that eventually the thieves would seek him out. One of the reasons he had remained untouched was that his goods were too big to spirit away unseen, though the tools could be at risk.

His furniture had gained a favourable reputation, commissions being received regularly from as far away as Plymouth, as word of his good work spread. Though still young, he possessed a forward-thinking mind, always looking for the best wood, the newest tools, and the best apprentices.

He had started with one, but with the volume of work increasing, he was soon forced to engage another. There had been several applications for the last position, due to Peter's reputation as a good master having grown. It had been a difficult decision to make, but after talking it over with Master Chapman, Peter decided on the youngest applicant, a lad by the name of Anthony whose family hailed from Exeter. Bright and eager, he absorbed information like a sponge, and Peter had high hopes for his future.

However, of Peter's own bright future there was but one thing missing; a wife. His infirmity had done nothing to thwart the attention of the town girls, and with his prosperous business, he was considered a worthy catch. While all the local girls were comely enough, none stirred his heart. For the present he was satisfied to wait, but not for too long.

The success of the business posed another problem, for they were quickly running out of space. Raw wood was stacked everywhere, even leaning against the walls in his bedchamber. Room had to be kept downstairs to receive customers. Shelves were strung along the walls to hold some of the wood, but even that hadn't helped for long. There was nothing for it; he would have to find bigger premises.

For some time he had his eye on a two-acre piece of land owned by Squire Hawkins just outside the town boundary. Nearly 100 acres in total, it had been in the family for generations, but the present, unmarried squire couldn't care less about it. He spent most of his time in London favouring the gambling dens and brothels. The family house, empty for most of the year, retained a small staff and occupied a small portion of the land about a half-mile from that in which Peter was interested.

The proposed workshop wouldn't be visible from the main house, and the small stream that ran along one edge of the property ran first past the squire's house, then past the land in question, so no fear of contamination there. The entire area had been allowed to go to weed and grass, no forestry or coppicing had taken place for years, and no animals were grazed anywhere. As far as Peter could see, it was just wasting away. For a fair price, he felt sure the squire would be pleased to sell such a small portion.

The estate manager spent most of his time in the local inn, and after a couple of drinks needed no encouragement to speak disparagingly of his frequently absent master. Peter reminded himself to speak to the solicitor regarding approaching the squire, and in his head was already drawing up plans for a new house and workshop.

The Chapmans would move with him, and Peter could see no flaw in his whole plan. The house would have to be big enough for him and his future family, the Chapmans, and the two apprentices. A separate workshop, a good-sized office, and large separate buildings for the storing of wood and finished pieces were also planned.

A garden was also needed, for a wife would surely wish to grow her own vegetables and herbs. Yes, he could see it all in his mind. He could even sell the existing building for a profit to help fund the work, but it would have to be planned carefully, for he couldn't afford any loss of work time.

Busy with his thoughts, he was unaware of a figure outside, and it was only a moment later when he heard a tapping on the window. Swiftly moving to open the door, he was amazed to see Susannah standing there wearing a grin from ear to ear.

'Susannah! Come in, come in, do.' He stepped back, holding the door wider for his sister and her voluminous skirts.

'Peter, it is good to see you.' They embraced, standing back at arm's length to look at each other. 'You look well and happy.'

'I am, Susannah, how could I not be when I'm doing what I love? How long are you in Honiton for? When did you arrive? Are you well? Is Thomas with you?'

'Questions, questions,' laughed Susannah. 'I'm well, thank you, and Thomas and I are here for about a month, so plenty of opportunity to see you.' She looked around at the crowded shop. 'And the business, it goes well?'

'Very well, as you can see,' he waved his hands around at the cramped showroom. 'In fact, I was just planning on moving the shop to bigger premises, but need to speak to the solicitor first.'

Susannah looked at him, questioning.

'I want to buy land from Squire Hawkins to build on. About five acres should do it, and he is just letting it go to waste. It has good access to the town, next to the stream, and I already have plans in my head as to the layout of the buildings.' He stopped, suddenly remembering his manners. 'But forgive me; can I get you something to drink? Or eat?'

'Heavens no, nothing. I know it's early, but I couldn't wait to see you, it seems to have been so long.'

'It has, since just after your marriage. A lot has happened to both of us in that time. I now have two apprentices because the work is so plentiful, and Master and Mistress Chapman are still with me. Let me call them, they will want to see you.' Peter went through to the back room, shouting as he went.

Susannah looked around, seeing the wood stacked everywhere, furniture crammed in every available spot. Indeed, Peter does need somewhere bigger, it's good to see he is so successful.

Peter returned, followed by the Chapmans. Mistress Chapman immediately insisted she provide food and drink, and bustled off to the kitchen. Master Chapman, however, was quite overcome at the sight of Susannah, remembering the young girl who had brought her brother for an apprentice, and now look at her. Confident and assured, she was a lady in the truest sense of the word. With tears in his eyes, he kissed her hand, begging her to take a seat. But he looked around, finding none.

'Please come through to the kitchen, if you please, my lady.'

'My name is still Susannah to you, Master Chapman. And I would be honoured to come to the kitchen.'

Master Chapman led the way, followed by Susannah and Peter.

Mistress Chapman set out beakers of ale, breads, and meats on the well-scrubbed table, and after indicating the best chair for Susannah, all waited for her to sit. It didn't take long for them to start chattering at once, Mistress Chapman wanting to know everything that had happened since the wedding, and Peter talking to Master Chapman about the proposed move. The kitchen was warm and comforting, the years slipped away, and Susannah felt herself enveloped in an overwhelming contentment.

Chapter 17 ❧
Meadowacres

Contentment was far from Nathaniel's mind. He hated the children, hated the house, hated his master, and hated his life. Every morning he lay in bed dreading the day ahead, fearing what the children would do next to make his life a misery.

The list of their misdemeanours seemed endless. They refused to read the books assigned to them, complaining to their father in tears that Nathaniel had forced, yes forced, their noses into the pages, demanding they learn the text. Lord Riverley had yet again looked down his nose at the tutor, demanding an explanation, but when Nathaniel tried to naysay the children, their father had asked why should they lie, perfect children that they were?

One evening he had left pages of written questions on the table in the schoolroom only to come in the next morning to find ink had been spilt all over them, making them unreadable. When he looked in anger at the children they had snickered, daring him to complain to their father.

The children, David, the eldest at ten, and Daniel, eight years old, were demons in human form as far as Nathaniel was concerned. He found a dead toad in his bed, all the candles removed from his bedroom on another occasion, and with no lock on the door, he was unable to prevent them entry.

They had obtained a cane, beating themselves over the knuckles enough to raise welts, and then complained to their father that he beat them when they gave the wrong answers.

Nathaniel had been called to account in Lord Riverley's chancellery, and while he tried to explain he had never seen the cane before, and certainly hadn't brought it with him, Lord Riverley all but called him a liar and a bully, demanding it not be used on the boys again.

Humiliated and furious, he had gone in search of the children, but they wisely hid, only turning up the next morning looking guiltless. Still steaming from the night before, Nathaniel confronted them, but both looked at him as if he had gone quite mad. He was even more determined to leave this dreadful employment, even if it meant starvation, and wrote letters to former colleagues begging for their help in gaining other work. His only friend was the cook, and he poured out his frustrations to her of an evening as they sat in the kitchen after supper.

'Little buggars, those boys; why, if I told you everything they've done, it would make your hair fall out,' she said. 'All the maids are afeared of them, and if they are like this at the age they are now, what will they be like as they grow older, I dread to think. I'm just glad I'll probably be in my grave by then.'

All this talk did was to make Nathaniel even more morose, more determined to flee. The next day was Sunday, and he vowed to attend church, already forming a prayer asking for deliverance.

꿍꿍

As usual, St. Michael's was packed for Sunday morning services, and Peter arrived late. He had been awake for a good part of the night planning the new buildings, sleeping in as a consequence.

Master and Mistress Chapman could no longer make the climb up the hill for the services, so they presumed he had already left when in fact he was still fast asleep, only waking to the sound of the bells as the morning service began. With his bad leg, it took awhile to walk the distance, and the third hymn was already underway when he pushed open the huge oaken door.

People were standing right in front, blocking access, so he quietly retreated, walking down the path to the east end of the church, heading for the smaller door to the left of the altar. The rector had his back to the congregation, his arms raised in

81

prayer when he saw Peter sidle in, and without a break in his speech managed to glower at him.

Peter stood to one side, jostling shoulders with the baker and his family, also late. His eyes roved over those facing him. Everyone stood, only the extremely elderly or infirm allowed a seat.

The rector's wife was singing heartily, her eyes raised to the heavens, oblivious to her daughters' giggling and pushing each other. Peter noticed the girl beside them and wondered why he hadn't seen her before, thinking surely he would remember if he had, for she was beautiful.

Unable to take his eyes off this new penitent, Peter was unaware of the rest of the service, making responses out of habit, singing the hymns by memory. What's her name? Is she family to the rector? She's so beautiful.

Without a word spoken between them, and Elizabeth oblivious of his existence, Peter fell irretrievably in love.

Chapter 18 ஃ
Morbeck Home

James Morbeck's father, Septimus, was extremely vexed with looking at the same view for so long, and felt stifled in the dark bedchamber. He demanded to be taken out to sit in the garden.

Margaret fussed and fluttered around the bed, smoothing the sheets and fluffing the bolster, suggesting they wait until the physician's next visit to obtain his opinion. Septimus was adamant, stating he wouldn't settle until he could breathe good fresh Devon air. He sat up, pushing the sheets Margaret had just straightened away from his legs. 'Get my robe, woman, and tell James to get a chair ready for me outside.'

Margaret rushed off, torn between helping her husband and instructing her son. If truth were told, Septimus, sitting on the side of the bed, his thin pale legs dangling over the side, felt dizzy, but he wouldn't tell Margaret or she would forcibly prevent him from getting outside.

Waiting for his robe, he took advantage of the time to take deep breaths and wait for his head to clear. For the last few days, and especially now that he was feeling better, he had started thinking about the business and how it had fared in his absence.

His manager was a good enough man, trustworthy too, but he didn't have the vision required to be truly successful. Septimus himself bought the wool from farmers in the area each spring, selling it at the wool market to the Flemish who came to buy good quality English wool.

He had, he hoped, come to terms with James' desire to become a physician and not be his heir, but it still rankled. It was one more thing he didn't discuss with Margaret, for she couldn't understand why James was so intent on a different path, especially when there was a ready-made one at his fingertips.

When Margaret returned with the robe, he pushed his arms into the sleeves, wrapping the heavy wool round his thin frame, and carefully stood up, afraid of the dizziness returning. Thankfully, his head remained clear and with his feet pushed into his slippers, he shuffled to the door preceded by Margaret, who continued to fuss.

The stairs were more difficult than he had imagined, but after insisting he go outside, he couldn't lose face by changing his mind; slowly but surely, and by holding tightly to the railing, he went down the stairs until both feet were firmly planted on the ground floor.

Gwyneth stood at the front door waiting for him to approach, and as he drew nearer, they smiled at each other.

James had taken a chair out to the front where the sun was strongest, and carefully stepping over the sill, Septimus held onto the doorframe, and raised his face to the warmth of the sun.

Margaret waited until he was sitting down, and then covered him with a blanket brought from upstairs, lifting his feet onto a low stool. From her pocket she produced his nightcap, insisting he wear it to prevent a chill. So there he sat, swaddled like a newborn, fussed over by the two women and his son, but happier than he would have thought possible to be away from his bedchamber.

Several neighbours passed by, all stopping to greet him and say how pleased they were to see him improved in health. Septimus returned their greetings with his thanks, unable as he was to release his hands and arms from the robe and stifling blanket. The sky was blue, the air so clear that it seemed he could see forever, and sheltered from the wind the sun was warm and comforting.

Margaret sent Gwyneth to their chamber to change the bed linen while Septimus was outside, but it was a scant ten minutes later that he declared he had had enough fresh air for one day, trying to rise from his chair to return indoors. However, he now found himself weak, his legs trembling as he hung onto Margaret, who called once more for assistance from James.

The front door closed behind them, and Septimus looked at the stairs leading upwards, silently cursing his insistence to go outside. They soared upwards, and he knew if he wanted to return to his bed he had to climb them, but it seemed far too much, and he quickly begged a chair to sit on. James brought the one from outside, placing it behind his father's knees, guiding him to sit.

'I told you it was too early to get up,' scolded Margaret, her face flushed with temper. 'And how you think we are going to get you back upstairs is quite beyond me. Why did you insist so?'

'Do stop fussing, woman, I'll get upstairs, don't you fret,' Septimus said, wiping the sweat from his forehead. Though how, he wasn't quite certain.

Margaret fussed around like an agitated hen that couldn't find her chicks, with Gwyneth repeatedly asking how he felt until Septimus felt he would scream.

James, however, had seen his father's ashen face and shaking limbs and taken control. Back outside, he had stopped the first man he saw, their neighbour Stuart Blackmore.

Master Blackmore was a tall, heavily built man with eyebrows that met together like a long black caterpillar above his nose. His hands were huge, with nails chewed down to the quick. A widower for the past five years, he was the terror of the females in Honiton, for after too much drink he would think himself irresistible to the opposite sex. The Watch had cautioned him on more than one occasion about his behaviour, and each time he had professed himself sorry, swearing it would never happen again. But, of course, it did.

Stuart followed James into the house saying loudly, 'Now, now, master Morbeck, we'll soon have you up in your bed,' and before his unwilling burden could protest, picked him up as if he weighed a feather and trumped up the stairs, Margaret preceding him, shaking her hands in agitation, leading them to the bedchamber.

Depositing the ailing man on the freshly made bed, he wiped his hands together, as if wiping off dust. 'There now, back you are in your bed,' as if he doubted Septimus could work that out for himself.

'Oh thank you, Master Blackmore,' said Margaret. 'That's right kindly of you. Do stay and take some refreshment. I'll just get my husband settled and join you downstairs,' effectively dismissing him.

'Yes, indeed, thank you, sir,' said Master Morbeck, on the one hand grateful for not having to climb the stairs, on the other humiliated at being thought of as a weak baby, especially by someone so obviously strong and healthy as Stuart Blackmore.

Chapter 19 ❧
Rectory

Elizabeth lay on her bed staring at the ceiling. Her legs and back ached from all the work she had to do. Fetching and carrying until she lost count of the number of times she went up and down the stairs, helping Rose carry wood for the fires, raking out the ashes, washing endless dishes. Have I really only been here a week? It seems like months. I'm never going to go home. I've become a maid to my aunt and her wretched children. She wondered if she wrote to father begging to be allowed home, would he be angry?

Elizabeth wrote a letter to her father begging to come home, leaving it on the hall table along with other letters to be taken to the coach. Later, she had heard Mary and Anne laughing in the garden, and when she went out to ask what they found so amusing, they turned to her, Anne waving the letter in the air.

'So, Lizzie! You want to go home already? Don't you like it here?' They leaned against each other in their laughter.

Elizabeth was furious. 'Give me that!' she said, ominously calm. 'You had no right to read it; it's addressed to my father!'

'We have every right,' replied Anne. 'It was on the table for anyone to see. We shall show it to Mama, won't we, Mary? You are here for three months at least, and if you know what's good for you, you won't write any more silly letters to your family. They don't care about you, that's why you're here, you stupid girl,' and they broke into laughter again.

Elizabeth tried to snatch the letter from Anne's hand, but it was whisked away out of reach, and the girls ran into the house calling loudly for their mother.

Running up the stairs to her room, Elizabeth slammed the door behind her, falling onto her bed, beating her hands and feet against the hard mattress in frustration and anger.

Her muffled cries covered the sound of approaching footsteps and the door opening to reveal a very angry Aunt Jane.

Elizabeth looked at her through teary eyes.

'What's this I hear, Elizabeth, writing to your father begging to go home? I've never heard of such a thing. Here you are and here you'll stay until he sends for you. The rector and I will be watching for the mail. If you want to write to your family, I will read it first,' and she left, slamming the door.

Downstairs, Jane went into the salon taking a seat and trying to calm her breathing. We can't afford for the girl to go back, we need the guinea a month. We can afford good meats now, and the girls need new shoes and dresses, and there's that lovely bonnet I saw, indeed that I deserve. We'll have to be vigilant.

꧁꧂

To Elizabeth, each day was a nightmare. While Rose prepared the meals, she had to help with the dishes, something she had never had to do at home.

She was sure that if she wrote to Agnes it would help her feel better. The rector and Aunt Jane kept an eagle eye on her, and if they saw her writing, demanded to know to whom it was addressed. She may not be able to mail the letters, but they couldn't prevent her from writing them.

The rector had parchment for his correspondence and sermons, and with plenty of ink and quills available, the material side of her problem wasn't an issue as long as she wasn't caught taking them.

Getting extra candles into her room was another. They were kept in a locked box affixed to the wall in the salon, and Aunt Jane controlled their use with an iron fist. Once burnt down, the scrags were used in the kitchen and for use in the lanterns for the outhouse at night, though more often than not the thunder pots were used if the weather was bad.

The scrags were lined up on the mantelshelf over the fire, and on her next trip to the kitchen Elizabeth made sure she noted how many were there, counting six. With the days getting longer there wasn't such a need for candles, and looking quickly around, she could hear Rose somewhere in the back, but no other sounds.

She estimated each would burn for about thirty minutes, so quickly lifting a chair to the fire, she took down two scrags, hiding them down her bodice, spacing the remainder out.

Hurrying to her bedroom, she hid the two stubby candles amongst her linen. Even if Mary and Anne, or Aunt Jane snooped – for she knew they did – they would just think she wanted to read at night in the privacy of her room. Or so she hoped. With only the parchment, ink, and quills left to procure, she felt happy. With the rector so forgetful, he'd never realise their loss.

Over the next two nights, Elizabeth wrote her letter to Agnes, detailing the awful journey by coach from London, and in far more detail the horrors of her life at the rectory. Deciding not to hold anything back, for she was only being honest, she relayed the characters of Anne and Mary, the lack of control of her daughters by Aunt Jane, the awfulness of the rectory, and church twice on Sundays, with the utter boredom of the rector's hour-long sermons.

Elizabeth's tone changed when she wrote of the Devon countryside. The robin with a nest in the lilac tree outside her bedroom window was written of in detail, her beautiful song each morning that helped to cheer the day, the two blue eggs waiting to bring their tiny inhabitants to life.

Much was written of Edward Catchpole and his kindness in allowing her to read from his books, and the hope that he would agree to place her letters on the coach.

The kitchen maid was also mentioned, for she and Elizabeth had become friends. The rector had taken in Rose on the death of her parents, each of a fever, and the poor girl had spent the intervening years slaving away for the family. Not knowing any different, Rose considered herself fortunate to have a place that was relatively warm in winter, and at least she was fairly well fed, albeit mostly from the table scraps.

Mistress Cardwell, Aunt Jane, felt saintly in giving the child, in her opinion, a loving and caring home. She never failed to mention it to her husband's flock whenever the opportunity arose, though they all knew how hard the child worked.

Rose, referred to as 'poor Rose' in town, was for the most part happy with her lot in life, but had found an ally in Elizabeth.

Anne and Mary were equally unkind to both of them, and many glances went back and forth in silent understanding and commiseration.

⁂

She continued to write, but once written where to hide the letters? She had no doubt that Anne and Mary, and probably Aunt Jane too, searched her room. She daren't hide them in her room, and there was nowhere downstairs, for the house was small and each room well used. The garden? No, there was only the outhouse, but no one liked to linger too long. For the first while she took to carrying them on her person hidden beneath her chemise and tied around her body with a long ribbon. Then they became too bulky and Elizabeth was left with a problem.

It came to Elizabeth that maybe Master Catchpole could care for her letters and put them on the coach to London. Her heart lightened as she thought of writing to Agnes of her dreary life. She could ask Agnes to write back in care of Master Catchpole, and then her aunt wouldn't know about the letters.

She clapped her hands in joy, smiling broadly, for she felt she had solved her problem.

'And what are you so happy about?' asked Mary, who as usual had entered Elizabeth's room without knocking. She stood in the doorway, her hands on her hips, and the usual scowl on her already unattractive face.

'Nothing,' replied Elizabeth, 'absolutely nothing.'

With her plan now in place and knowing it would be at least another three days before she would be allowed to visit the bookshop again, she thought those three days could be spent in composing another letter to Agnes.

It was the next Saturday when Elizabeth felt she could ask to go to the bookshop, and tentatively approached Aunt Jane at breakfast. Deciding that a roundabout way was best, she said,

'What a beautiful day,' to no one in particular, though as usual, none answered her. The rector was busy reading a letter that had arrived from the bishop the previous day; Aunt Jane sat peeling an apple, while the girls appeared, from their faces, to have nothing in their heads at all.

'It looks as if the sun will shine all day,' she said, and already being certain of the answer, addressed Anne and Mary. 'I think I'll go for a walk, would either of you like to join me?'

'Walk? Where to?' replied Anne, her nose wrinkled in distaste. 'Why?'

'Why not? Why stay closeted inside when the good Lord has given us such a day?' replied Elizabeth, sure that the rector would hear His name and think well of her.

Anne and Mary looked at each other, Mary answering for both. 'I think not, I want to mend a bonnet, and Anne shall help me.'

Elizabeth frowned, as if disappointed. 'Oh well, I'll go on my own then.'

Aunt Jane woke up enough to say, 'You let me see you before you leave, I can't have you going to town unseemly dressed.'

'Yes, Aunt Jane,' Elizabeth replied, and wiped her mouth with the napkin, hiding her smile.

Rose came in to remove the dishes, and between the two of them everything was quickly cleared away. The temptation to run upstairs was great, but Elizabeth forced herself to walk slowly, not wanting to give away her eagerness and set minds to wondering.

Wearing her bonnet and a thick wrap over her shoulders, for the morning was still chilly, she presented herself to Aunt Jane.

'You wanted to see me before I left, Aunt?'

Jane looked her over carefully, for all intents and purposes checking her dress, but really looking for forbidden letters. Reluctantly she said, 'Very well, you may go, but just to the bookshop, mind. And be back in time to help with dinner.'

'Yes, Aunt Jane.'

Elizabeth left the rectory, gently closing the front door behind her. With no one to see her face, she grinned widely, restraining herself to not whoop with the sheer joy of it.

Chapter 20 ❧
Honiton

Elizabeth went straight to the bookshop, and Master Catchpole came into the shop from the back room when he heard the doorbell.

'Mistress Sharpe, to what do I owe the pleasure?' he enquired, bowing low.

'Good morning, sir, I have a small favour to ask. Would you be able to give this to the coachman going to London next time he comes?' She produced the letter to Agnes from beneath her wrap and held it out.

Master Catchpole took it in a shaking hand, reading the name on the front. He looked at her quizzically. 'I don't understand, mistress, the coach will not be here for another two days, why not bring it back at that time?'

Elizabeth hadn't anticipated this question. Why indeed?

'I'm afraid I have another engagement that day, and I was hoping you would deliver it to the coach on my behalf?' She looked up at him from beneath her lashes, a small tremulous smile on her face.

Master Catchpole looked again at the letter, flicking it against his thumbnail.

Elizabeth continued to smile.

'Of course, mistress, I would be happy to oblige.'

Elizabeth gave a sigh of relief, for if he had refused, she would have had to take it back to the rectory, and one of the three snooping women would surely have found it.

'My thanks to you, sir.' She turned to leave the shop, but just as she reached for the door, Master Catchpole spoke up.

'However, mistress, one good turn deserves another, I believe.' He paused, waiting for Elizabeth to turn around and face him.

She did so, slowly. 'And what could I possibly do in return for you, sir?'

'I was thinking that perhaps after church next Sunday, we might go for a walk together down to the river?' His face held a decided leer. Elizabeth knew exactly what he meant. Returning to stand in front of him, she held out her hand for the letter.

Master Catchpole held on to it.

'Sir, the letter isn't that important, it can wait a few more days until I can deliver it to the coach myself.'

Edward Catchpole clutched the letter in both hands, panic on his face. 'Mistress, you misunderstand, I meant nothing by it. I just thought it would be a pleasant walk with a friend.'

'No doubt it would, sir, but as I said, the letter is not that important.' She reached out and took the letter from him. Bidding him good day, she once more turned to the door and walked into the street, turning right to go down the hill.

He must be at least thirty years old. As if I would go walking out with him! Though what do I do with the letter?

Heading straight for Cross Keys Inn, she entered and asked the girl who was sweeping the flagstone floor in the entranceway if she might speak to the innkeeper, and the girl, still carrying her broom, scurried off to find him.

Master Beaker came out from his chancel room. 'Yes, mistress, what can I do for you?'

Elizabeth curtsied. 'Please, sir, the coach to London stops here, does it not?'

'It does.'

'Can I ask if you could give this letter to the coachman, please? I have an engagement that day and won't be able to bring it myself.'

Master Beaker looked at her. Elizabeth felt his eyes boring into hers, as if he knew she was being devious. After a long pause he said, 'I don't see why not. You're Elizabeth Sharpe from London, aren't you? Staying with the rector and his family?'

'Yes, I am.' Elizabeth felt her face growing red, sure now he knew she was up to something.

He shrugged. 'Well, as I said, I don't see why not.' He reached out his hand and Elizabeth placed the letter in it.

He looked at the name on the front. 'Aye, well, I'll give it to the coachman when he next comes, but that won't be for two days yet.'

'I know, but it's not important, just a letter to my friend. She's the daughter of the mayor of London.' She realised she was talking too much, and bit her tongue to make herself to stop.

'I can see that.'

'Well, I'd best be off, I told my aunt I wouldn't be long. I had to go to the bookshop, you see.'

I'm doing it again. Stop talking.

Master Beaker stood silently, a slight, knowing smile on his face.

'Well, thank you, sir.' Elizabeth turned and rushed out of the inn, heading this time up the hill on her way to the rectory. She hadn't gone far when she saw a face she recognised coming towards her, though it wasn't a cheerful face by any means.

Nathaniel Simmons, his eyes focussing on the ground, didn't see Elizabeth until he was almost beside her.

'Master Simmons, good morning. How are you enjoying your position? It was with the Riverleys, if I remember?'

He bowed. 'Good morning, mistress. Yes, it is.' He gave a huge sigh that seemed to start at his boots. 'But truth to tell, it's not going well.' He pulled a handkerchief from his sleeve, covering his mouth to cough.

Elizabeth looked hard at the man before her. She saw a pale face with a forehead lined with worry and care, his shoulders slumped in all too obvious defeat.

'I am sorry to hear that, is there anything I can do to help?'

Nathaniel, a tremulous smile showing briefly replied, 'Unfortunately not, but I thank you for your kind offer. My employment is for a year, and I have no choice but to honour it.'

He looked away from her, his eyes sad. 'Though how I will bear t, I do not know,' he said quietly. His head jerked this side and that, a sure sign of his unhappiness.

'The time will go quickly, sir, and I am sure it will get easier for you.'

'I hope so, the boys I was hired to tutor are undisciplined, and I am not allowed to control them. They play terrible tricks on me, and when I complain to their father, he makes it appear as if I provoked them. It is an intolerable situation.'

Elizabeth thought of her brother, Simon. If they were anything like him, heaven help the poor man.

'I am sorry to hear of your troubles, Master Simmons. If you change your mind and find you need my help, I am at the rectory.'

'Thank you, Mistress. That is indeed kind of you. I have to say that just talking about it has helped me. When my time here is over, I can look for other, more pleasant employment.'

Nathaniel's demeanour had changed during the time he had been talking. Elizabeth noticed he stood taller, and his face had become less sad.

'I had best be on my way, my aunt will be wondering where I am.' Elizabeth turned to go, but Nathaniel reached out as if to take her arm.

'Mistress, please don't misunderstand me, but would it be acceptable to you if we met again? Just to talk? I feel you understand, you see.' His eyes darted this way and that, hoping she would not take offence at what could easily be construed as an inappropriate suggestion.

Elizabeth understood what he meant. 'Of course, sir. Do you come into town often?'

'I am allowed one half day a week away from my duties. Usually I like to take Saturday after dinner for myself when possible. Perhaps we could meet here, where we are now, at, say, two o'clock?'

Elizabeth thought rapidly. What excuse for leaving the rectory alone on a regular basis could she give her aunt?

'That would be convenient, sir. Though you must realise that there may be times I just can't get away.'

'I do understand. I know only too well what it is to not be your own master or mistress.' With a small bow he continued on his way. But this time, he was a happier man.

Elizabeth watched for a moment as he continued down the hill. Poor man, she thought. At least I will be going home in three months, hopefully sooner if Mother can convince Father.

Starting out once more for the rectory with slow footsteps, her mind was firmly fixed on coming up with an excuse for next Saturday. When she arrived at the rectory, it was to the expected recriminations.

'About time you came back, I told you there was work to be done. What have you been doing that took so long?' Aunt Jane stood in the hallway, hands on hips, the usual scowl on her unpleasant face.

Elizabeth was aware of her cousins sitting at the top of the stairs, sniggering at her discomfort. 'I haven't been that long, Aunt. Surely the girls could have helped, if there was work to be done?'

'The girls are tired, and besides, Elizabeth, you are not sent here for a rest. This is a big house and we have a position to keep up. People expect to come to the rectory and be welcomed. That takes work. From each of us. We need the firewood brought in, you can do that.' Feeling she had handled the situation well, Jane returned to the kitchen to find fault with the young maid, seemingly a favourite occupation of hers.

Elizabeth started up the stairs to change her clothes, while the girls continued to snigger. Pushing past them, she went to her room, closing the door hard behind her.

For a few moments she was furious, and then found herself thinking of the day. Of the pleasant time spent with Nathaniel Simmons, with hopefully more to come. There was still an excuse she had to think on, but a few days for that. The letter to Agnes had been safely delivered to Cross Keys, for onward travel in two days' time. All in all, it had not been a bad day.

Chapter 21 🕊

Watermead

Excuses were one thing Philip Goldworthy never had trouble thinking up. He had, at a young age, become an accomplished liar. Each was spoken with a look of pure innocence on his well-scrubbed face. Up until the age of five or so, his governess had thought nothing of it, feeling sure he would outgrow this childish behaviour. She had tried on occasion to discipline him, but realising that her young charge had a vicious streak, she had quickly learned to ignore his behaviour as best she could, especially as he grew bigger and stronger.

Philip spent the intervening years honing his craft, and though he still hadn't had an opportunity to approach his godmother for a loan, he wasn't too worried. He trusted implicitly in his ability to spin a yarn suitable for any occasion.

Each time he went in search of his godmother, either Lady FitzGerald's maid was hovering around or the wretched Susannah was sitting with her keeping company. When it wasn't Susannah, then the housekeeper was discussing household accounts or seemingly never-ending menus. He didn't like to admit it, but he was becoming desperate.

One letter, forwarded by his mother, had reached him. It was from his bookmaker demanding, again, payment of his debts. He knew she wouldn't have opened it, merely re-addressed it. His fear was that one of the servants would let slip to the bookmaker where he was.

He didn't have a good relationship with the household staff in London. They were never insolent, they knew their livelihood depended on their currying favour, but at times, it came close. If he had ever stopped to wonder why, the blame lay entirely at his own door. Servants, however lowly, were still human and he treated them no better than doormats. Impatient, intolerant, almost any adjective would fit to his detriment.

It hadn't taken the staff at Watermead long to arrive at the same conclusion.

The young bootboy, a mere eight years old, still had ringing in his ears where he had been punished for not cleaning a pair of Philip's boots to his satisfaction, and having returned them late.

The chambermaids quickly learned to exit a room should he enter it, and eventually took to working in pairs if there was even a chance he should appear. Complaints by them to the housekeeper, though met with sympathy, went no further.

Philip decided he had to approach Lady FitzGerald this day. No more excuses. Dinner was over, and he went in search of her before she retired to her bedroom for a rest. He found her in the salon reading. For once, she was alone.

'Godmother, how are you feeling today?' He took a seat to her left, effectively blocking her view of the garden.

'I am well, thank you, Philip. You?'

Here was the perfect opportunity, better to get it over with. 'A little worried, if I were honest.'

'I'm sorry to hear that.'

Philip was instantly on the alert. He had hoped she would ask what trouble he was in. Now he was forced to bring it up himself.

'Yes, and I can't see my way out. I find myself a little short of money at the moment, and have a debt I need to pay.'

'As I said, I'm sorry to hear that.' She looked down at her book.

Philip laughed, which even to his ears sounded too loud.

'All very awkward, of course.' He continued, 'It's not as if it's a large amount after all, but the damn fool is threatening legal action.' He waited, hoping she would offer help, but Lady FitzGerald just looked at him briefly, then returned to reading.

'I can't ask Mama, she wouldn't understand.' Again he waited.

There was nothing for it. He was forced to ask outright, before anyone interrupted them. 'So I am hoping, godmother, that you will oblige me. Just this once, you understand. As I said, it's a small amount. Nothing to you, I'm sure.' The palms of his hands were sweaty, and he couldn't stop himself wiping them on his breeches.

Lady FitzGerald put her book on the nearby side table, taking her time before answering.

'Why wouldn't your mother understand, Philip?'

'Oh, you know what mothers are like.' Once more he laughed too loudly.

'Yes, I do. The only reason I can think of is that she had to pay off debts for you before, and is now thoroughly sick of doing so.'

Philip felt sick. 'Just one or two, certainly nothing to be concerned about. You know what it's like.'

'No. I don't. Obviously they were enough to concern your mother. The letter that arrived for you, was that from a creditor?'

Philip was surprised that she knew of it, he had presumed it had been brought straight to him, and for once, he forgot to lie.

'Yes, a very unpleasant man, as you would expect such a man to be.'

'Nevertheless, a creditor to whom you owe money. How much, exactly, do you owe, Philip?'

She could almost see him deciding whether to tell the truth or lie. He decided on the truth.

'A thousand guineas.'

Lady FitzGerald sat silently, absorbing this 'small amount,' while Philip held his breath.

'No.'

'But godmother, it is only a thousand guineas.' He could hear the desperation in his own voice and knew she could too.

'I said no, Philip.' Lady FitzGerald picked up her book, taking her time finding her place once more.

Philip sat, stunned. Now what was he to do? She had been his last hope. The reality of his situation now stared him full in the face.

Without another word, he left the salon and headed to his bedroom. 'Damn, damn, damn,' he said under his breath.

Chapter 22 ❧
Morbeck Home

Two days after Elizabeth had met Nathaniel Simmons, James Morbeck stood beside his father's bed, his hastily packed bags outside the door.

'I'm glad you are better, Father. Each day will find you stronger, I'm sure.'

'I certainly feel better, but I tire easily. I'm sure that will pass.' Septimus knew his son was eager to leave the house, to leave the sickbed and return to his studies. 'Thank you for making the journey, James. Your mother is also grateful for your support. She was frightened this was to be my deathbed.'

'That won't be for many years yet, Father. And when I'm a qualified physician, I will be able to help not only you but others in Honiton, too.'

'That won't be for some time though, and in the meantime we must deal with the physician we have, qualified or not. Go with God, James, and don't forget to write, for your mother worries about you.'

'I won't forget. Thank you, Father, for understanding that I must follow my own path. You do have another son, who is far better able to carry on the business than I.'

They shook hands, staring for a moment into each other's eyes. James turned away, pausing at the door to take one more look at his father.

He laid in bed, wrapped in a thick woollen wrap against the draughts, the nightcap on his head. James thought how old his father looked, how shrunken he had become.

Kissing his mother and Gwyneth goodbye, he left with hurrying steps to wait for the coach at the Cross Keys Inn.

Chapter 23 ❧
Exeter

Master Browning spent most of his time in his bedroom at his sister's house, which didn't suit her at all. A widow for ten years, Nan had grown used to having the house to herself. Her late husband had been a wealthy merchant who died young. She soon proved to be an astute businesswoman. Where her husband had, in her opinion, merely toyed with the business, she worked hard at it.

The shop, for there had been one at the beginning, sold fabrics and notions. But realising the population was growing in leaps and bounds, she knew there was far more money to be made by being forward thinking. From one shop another had sprouted, then another.

Each afternoon she made the rounds between the three, keeping a careful eye on the ledgers and the manager she had installed in each. She and she alone counted the money, for she would only trust the managers so far.

With everything planned and ordered, the last thing she needed was her wastrel brother. He had told her, upon his sudden arrival, some cock and bull story about needing to live near the sea for his health. Even as a child she could tell when he was lying, and could tell by his furtive glances out the window there was more to it than that. There was little doubt he owed someone, or several people, money. She decided to give him a roof over his head for a couple of months, but then he had to go. She didn't care where, so long as he went. And more importantly, that he never came back.

Master Browning knew, instinctively, that his creditors were closing in. On his last visit to the inn, the man serving had told him there had been a stranger asking if any knew of him. Racing back to his room at his sister's house, he slammed the door after him. He sat on his narrow, hard cot in the eaves, hugging himself from fear. He beat his fists against his forehead in exasperation. He heard someone crying, realised it was himself and clamped his hand in front of his mouth as if that would stop it. But it didn't.

Nan, changing her dress in her bedroom below her brother's, heard the sobs, but there was no pity. Two months, then he must leave.

ﮰﮰﮰﮰ

Philip Goldworthy needed to get away from Watermead to think, and not being in a position to return to London, decided to go to Exeter for a few days.

Good manners demanded that he let his godmother know of his change in plans, and so it was that he visited her in her bedroom just as her food arrived. With the usual enquiries of her health and comments on the weather behind him, he plunged right in. He never gave thought to telling the truth when a lie would do.

'Godmother, I have received word this morning that a friend of mine is staying in Exeter, and he is asking if I could spend some time with him. I can see no reason why not, so shall be leaving shortly. I have no idea how long I will be gone.'

'That's very pleasant for you, Philip. Have your known this friend long?'

'Um, a few years, you know.'

'And where did you meet him?'

'Oh you know, around,' he replied evasively. 'Anyway, I'm sure you won't mind.'

'Not at all. Tell me, how did you get word he was nearby?'

'A note was delivered this morning. He must have heard from mutual friends I was here. You know how it is.'

'Indeed I do.'

He was eager to be away from the rather unpleasant atmosphere that had developed since his request for a loan. His bag was packed, and he had given instructions for a horse to be ready. Kissing his godmother farewell, he fairly sprinted out of the door.

The horse stood patiently waiting for its rider, a young stable lad holding the reins. Flinging the bag up and tying it securely, he mounted the horse. Without a thank you to the boy, he kicked it into an instant gallop, racing down the gravel driveway.

Lady FitzGerald, still in bed, summoned her maid to her side. 'Dodds, did a note come for Master Philip this morning?'

'No, my lady, nothing was delivered.'

'Thank you, Dodds.' She sat, tapping her fingers on the edge of the tray, mulling over the conversation with her godson.

What trouble is he going to get into in Exeter, I wonder? Perhaps I should write to his mother, though I fear she is already aware of his character. No, perhaps not, I'll wait and see what happens in Exeter. Instead I'll write to the rector there, Richard Troak. He will be able to tell me all I need to know.

Master Browning, at last venturing from his self-imposed prison, made his way to the inn, where he proceeded to drown his sorrows in copious amounts of ale, eventually falling asleep at the table. Oblivious to other patrons coming and going, it was nearly dark when his foot was kicked hard. He woke to look blearily around him.

Another sat at the table, his hands cradling a large pot of ale, a look of deep worry on his face.

'Whas' a matter?' slurred Master Browning.

'Mind your own bloody business,' replied Philip Goldworthy. He didn't even look at the man to whom he addressed. If he had, he would have seen a face as downcast as his own. The two sat, each absorbed in their own worries and fears. Soon, however, they would begin to talk.

Chapter 24 ❧
Rectory

Elizabeth sat; for once her thoughts were happy. All her attention was given to finding an excuse why she needed to go to town alone the following Saturday.

One she thought would do, was discarded as too flimsy. Another she thought as opening up the possibility that Mary and Anne would accompany her, and that would never do. She had to be alone. A knock on the door brought her back to the present.

'Miss Elizabeth, are you in there?'

'Come in, Rose, come in.'

The young maid opened the door and brought in clean linen, laying it on the bed. 'Are you all right, Mistress?'

'I am well, thank you, Rose. Why do you ask?'

'No reason, just you look preoccupied today.'

Elizabeth, knowing that Rose was grateful for the help she gave her, suddenly had a wonderful thought.

'Rose, remember when you had your tooth pulled?'

The girl blanched. 'Indeed I do. Right painful it was, too.' Her hand went to her face, remembering the pain.

'It must have been. I feel a toothache coming on, too.'

'Oh no. That's awful. You'll have to go to the farrier and have it pulled, like I did.'

'Yes, I will, won't I? What's today, Rose?'

'It's Thursday, Mistress.'

'Is it? Well, I think, that by Saturday, it will be just about ready to pull.'

'Really? How can you tell that?' Rose looked searchingly at Elizabeth's face. 'It's not swollen or nothing.'

'No, not yet it isn't, but it will be by tomorrow.' Elizabeth jumped from the bed. 'Thank you, Rose, you have been most helpful.'

Rose looked perplexed. 'I'm right pleased about that.' She made for the door, stopping to look back. 'If you go to the farrier, I could come with you, return the favour like.'

'No, I will be well, but thank you, Rose. I shall be fine.'

After Rose left, Elizabeth continued to make her plan. That will take care of this Saturday. I'll let the next one take care of itself nearer the time.

At supper that evening, Elizabeth played with her food, pushing it round the plate, taking small morsels then holding the side of her face. Anne and Mary ignored her as usual, but in the end Aunt Jane couldn't keep quiet any longer.

'Elizabeth, what's the matter with you? Why aren't you eating?'

'I've a toothache, Aunt.'

'I'll get Rose to find you some clove oil to rub on it. That will soon sort that out.'

The seed sown, Elizabeth sat back in her chair looking sad. Truth to tell, she was hungry, and it was all part of the pretence, but she could get food from Rose later.

She asked Rose for the clove oil, and took it away with her to her room, though she never applied it.

Early the next morning, before anyone was awake; she stole down to the kitchen and rummaged in the larder for food. Rose, hearing the noise, crept out from her pallet under the table. Elizabeth held her finger to her lips in a shushing gesture, and Rose gratefully returned to her bed and much-needed sleep. Taking cheese and bread back to her room, Elizabeth sat, munching happily.

Before breakfast, she tore a corner from her handkerchief, stuffing half into her mouth to make it look swollen, returning the other half to her pocket. Without a mirror to look in, she could only feel the small bulge with her fingers, and feeling that it was just about right, practiced speaking. The most difficult part was not opening her mouth too wide so the linen fell out, but she soon got the way of it, and went downstairs to join the family for breakfast.

They were all sitting at the table when she entered, dragging her feet and looking very sorry for herself.

'Elizabeth, what is this? What's the matter with you? You haven't got a fever, have you?' All members of the family shrank away from her.

'No, Aunt, I've the toothache something awful,' she mumbled.

'Is that all? Well, you'll have to have it pulled. I heard the farrier isn't in town today; he had to go to Watermead to see to all their horses. You shall have to wait until tomorrow.'

'Oh no, however shall I bear it?' cried Elizabeth, holding her cheek and rocking backwards and forwards in her chair.

Anne and Mary couldn't resist making fun. Both held their own cheeks, both rocked back and forth. 'Oh no, however shall I bear it?' they cried in unison, and then fell to laughing at Elizabeth's pain.

'Stop it, girls. A toothache is no laughing matter. You'd best go back to bed, Elizabeth. I'll get Rose to bring you food there.'

'Thank you, Aunt.' Slowly leaving the room, she climbed the stairs back to her room. But she still heard Aunt Jane's comment.

'She must be ill, for I've never her known her so biddable before.'

Closing the door, she lay on the bed. Elizabeth, reviewing her plan, was pleased with herself. She had thought of everything that could go wrong, and discounted them. Tomorrow she would meet Nathaniel Simmons. She wasn't interested in him as a suitor, how could she be with that twitching head? But the knowledge that she had pulled the wool over her aunt's eyes, well, any risk was worth that.

Early the next morning, Rose brought a tray of food to Elizabeth. Remembering to stuff her cheek with the handkerchief, Elizabeth answered the door, taking the tray from the maid.

'Are you still feeling poorly?' enquired Rose, concern plain on her face.

'Yes, but once I get to the farrier I know I'll feel better. Thank you for the food, Rose, but I don't feel much like eating. Perhaps I'll save it for later.'

'I understand, I didn't eat when I had the toothache. I'll tell the mistress you've kept the tray.'

'Thank you, Rose.' Elizabeth closed the door, placing the tray on the table by the window. She was terribly hungry, but only had a few more hours to keep up the pretence.

When the church bells struck one-thirty, she put on her bonnet and wrap, and made her way downstairs. Finding Aunt Jane in the kitchen, Elizabeth told her she was leaving.

'Ttake care. Do you want one of the girls to accompany you?'

'No, I'll manage.' Elizabeth left the rectory through the kitchen door, making her way round the house and through the gate that separated the rectory from the church proper.

High Street was a hive of activity, and Elizabeth felt no one would take notice of her, intent as they were on their own errands and activities. Walking quickly past the bookstore, and being careful not to look in the window in case she caught Master Catchpole's eye, she slowed her steps as she approached the spot where she was to meet Nathaniel.

The arrangement had been they were to meet on Saturday at two o'clock, just up from Cross Keys Inn. The church bells struck two. Elizabeth made a show of looking in various windows and looking occupied. The bells struck the half hour, and she realised she had been waiting for thirty minutes with still no sign of Nathaniel.

The first stirrings of concern made their way into Elizabeth's mind, but she quickly convinced herself that she had the time wrong, and they arranged to meet at half past the hour. Not wanting to stand too long in the one spot, she walked down the hill, past the inn, turning left down a lane. She came to stand before the windows of a workshop; she looked up at the sign above the door, where she read 'Peter Brigginshaw, Joiner.'

The name meant nothing to her, and she turned and walked back to High Street, turning once more past the inn. There was still no sign of Nathaniel, and now the bells were ringing the hour.

She paused, looking in the window of a candlemaker. The reflection showed a girl with a swollen face, and it was only then that Elizabeth remembered she still had the handkerchief stuffed in her mouth. Quickly she spat the slimy wad into her hand, throwing it to the ground in disgust.

When the bells rang the quarter hour again, there was no other choice but to accept that Nathaniel wasn't coming, and all her planning had been for nought. She stamped her foot in temper, and turning, bumped into another, who was just leaving the candlemaker's.

'I am sorry, mistress. Are you hurt?' enquired the young man standing before her. The first thing Elizabeth noticed was that he had two sticks to aid him walk.

'No, I'm not hurt.' She smiled at him, noticing his clear blue eyes beneath well-formed brows. His nose was slim and well shaped, and his pleasing mouth mirrored her smile.

'I have seen you in church, I believe. Allow me to introduce myself, I'm Peter Brigginshaw.'

'I know of you, you have the joiners down the lane, do you not?'

'I do. May I ask how you know of it?'

'Oh, I was walking by and happened to see it.'

'Next time you are "walking by," please come in. I would be happy to show you around, for I'm proud of my shop.'

'I may. I don't often walk that way. I shall see.'

Peter looked with amusement at this young girl, whose chin was raised as if she thought herself far above a mere joiner.

'Well, I will look forward to seeing you in church next Sunday, though I'm afraid you have the advantage of me, for I do not know your name.' Peter knew full well who she was, including her name, but she didn't need to know that.

'Elizabeth Sharpe, sir. I am staying with my aunt and her husband, he's the rector.'

Without waiting for a reply, only a quick curtsey, Elizabeth headed up the hill to the rectory, her face flushed and her breathing fast with a feeling she couldn't name.

The rector had been absent for most of the morning. Two of his parishioners were living out their last days, and he liked to visit them as much as possible. One, a wealthy widow, had promised to mention the church, and the rector in particular, in her will. He believed in keeping his face in front of her, just to aid in her remembering. She lived alone but for two elderly servants, in a large rambling house just off High Street.

The other was also a widow, though a pauper, who lived with her son and his family in a hovel on the outskirts of town. With nothing to leave the church, she still deserved the ministrations of the religious, and he didn't begrudge the half-hour walk there and back.

After comforting the poor woman, he cut back to town by walking over the bridge that spanned a small stream, entering the town from the bottom of the hill.

The first person he met was the farrier. They greeted each other as old friends.

'How is Elizabeth, Seth?' the rector asked.

'I've no idea,' was the perplexed reply.

'But didn't she come to you today to have a tooth pulled? She's been complaining of the toothache for two days now, and set off this afternoon for your smithy.'

'I've not seen the girl. I had to return early to Watermead, one of their horses had trouble with a hoof and needed a special shoe, which I made last night.'

They stared at each other. The rector knew the farrier had no cause to lie, while the farrier thought the rector didn't know what was going on in his own home. Deciding it best to drop the subject, the rector asked after the farrier's family, and by the time they parted, the rector had forgotten about Elizabeth. Almost.

Walking in the front door of the rectory, Elizabeth remembered at the last moment to hold her handkerchief to her mouth.

Anne met her in the hallway, and immediately mimicked her. Elizabeth pushed past her, heading for the stairs, though not in time to avoid Aunt Jane.

'How did you do, Elizabeth?'

Mumbling incoherently, Elizabeth rushed up the stairs to the comparative safety of her room. The tray of food from the morning was still there, and she fell on it ravenously. It was only when she had finished every morsel did she remember Nathaniel, and wonder why he hadn't met her as arranged. Though perhaps it was just as well, she thought, for if he had she doubted she would have met Peter Brigginshaw.

When the family met for supper at six o'clock, Elizabeth joined them. Yet again, having recently eaten, she wasn't hungry.

After the rector said prayers for the food, he addressed her.

'How is the tooth, Elizabeth?'

'Better, thank you, Uncle.'

'I'm glad to hear it. Did the farrier remove it?' He continued to carve the meat, doling out meagre slices on each upheld plate.

'Yes, he did. But it didn't hurt too badly.'

'So you should be able to eat your food well?'

'Oh yes, I will have no difficulty.'

'I'm glad to hear of that, too.'

The rector turned to Jane. 'Wife, I met the farrier today.' He paused, giving Elizabeth time to absorb this. Jane, and Elizabeth, who held her breath, waited for him to continue.

'Oddly enough, he wasn't at the smithy, having to return to Watermead to tend to a horse with a difficult hoof.' He looked meaningfully at Elizabeth, whose heart sank to the floor. Jane knew what this meant immediately, while Anne and Mary, too busy piling food onto their plates, didn't.

'Go to your room, Elizabeth. I will to speak to you later.'

Only too glad to escape the accusatory look from the rector and Aunt Jane's furious face, Elizabeth fled.

As usual, Elizabeth hadn't thought the plan through. When Aunt Jane at last appeared, she was prepared for the worst.

She was told a letter would be sent to her mother telling of this, but it would also be recommended that Elizabeth stay for at least two more months. This would, said Aunt Jane, give her a chance to knock some sense into the girl.

More importantly, it would also mean two more guineas for the rector and his family.

Chapter 25 ❧
London

At Elizabeth's home in London, her mother and father sat by the fire after Sunday dinner.

'Have we heard from your sister regarding Elizabeth? Is she behaving?' asked Daniel, lighting his pipe and making himself comfortable on the settle. Sarah had been prepared for this and had her reply ready.

'Yes, I received a note from Jane this morning. Elizabeth is enjoying her time there, settling in well. But Jane feels another two months will be necessary to make sure she has control of the girl.'

'Another two guineas?'

'Yes, but worth it, don't you feel?'

Daniel drew on his pipe, looking at the smoke curling above his head. 'Yes, I think I do. Send the two guineas, Sarah.'

'Yes, Daniel, thank you. I will do it tomorrow.' She heaved a silent, heavy sigh. Two more months of peace and quiet. The one giving trouble now was Simon. There had been yet another complaint from a well-respected merchant about their youngest son. The man had accused Simon of harrying his daughter. Even though he had been warned off, Simon persisted, and it now appeared that the girl was frightened of leaving the house in case she should be accosted.

What with that worry, and rumours of typhoid to the south, Sarah felt as if the weight of the world were on her. Her parents had both died of the fever, and Sarah herself had been ill, taking months to come back to health. At least Elizabeth is out of it, she'll be safe in Honiton with Jane. No need to worry about her. But what's to be done about Simon? Would it be possible to send him to Jane, too?

≈≈≈≈≈

While Elizabeth was furious that she was to spend an extra two months in Honiton, when she thought it through, perhaps it wasn't so bad after all. Hopefully by the time I do return to London, Simon will have found someone else on whom to vent his anger, she reasoned.

The reply from London, when it came, agreed with this pronouncement. With the remainder of this sentence left, another two now added, it was a bitter blow. But a blow that even Elizabeth couldn't deny was laid squarely at her door.

Chapter 26 ❧
Meadowacres

Nathaniel Simmons, laid up in his attic bedroom with a bad attack of ague, cursed his life, his frail constitution, and his employment, in no particular order. He had been anticipating with pleasure his meeting with Elizabeth Sharpe, now he could only hope he would meet her again in town next week. Confined to his room in the eaves of Meadowacres, Nathaniel felt forgotten. The cook would send up food for him, but the servant instructed to bring it only did so when his other duties were completed. Breakfast appeared nearer dinnertime, supper sometimes arriving close to nine o'clock in the evening. With only two meals a day, Nathaniel was growing thinner and weaker.

Lord Riverley had sent a message within two days of the onset of Nathaniel's illness asking him how much longer he would be indisposed. The servant who relayed it then added his own comment when he brought the dinner tray.

'You can't stay in bed much longer, we all think you are shirking because of the boys, so you'd best get yourself back to the schoolroom. His lordship isn't the kind to take fools gladly.' He smirked as he said it.

Nathaniel hadn't even bothered to reply, just turned his head to the wall. He knew he should see a physician, but didn't want to ask for him to be sent for, certain this request would get back to his employer. He told himself every evening that tomorrow he would feel better. But he didn't. Each morning he felt worse. The breakfast was collected, untouched, when the dinner tray was delivered.

In the end the decision was taken away from him. On the sixth day, the cook, worrying about him and the untouched food, made the long breathless trek up the three flights of stairs to Nathaniel's bedroom. One look at him, lying supine in his bed, his face red, the sweat pouring down on to the already soaked pillow, and she fled downstairs. When the butler came to the kitchen for his morning snack, she told him of the tutor. He immediately sent the bootboy into town on the nag for the physician, telling the other servants not to enter Nathaniel's room for fear of contagion.

When the bootboy arrived at the physician's humble dwelling down by the river, it was to find him absent, and not having been told to leave a message should the doctor not be in, he decided to take advantage of his freedom. Kicking the old nag into a trot, he carried on up the hill into High Street. Tying his mount to a convenient post, he walked off to explore.

When the church bells struck eleven, he suddenly realised that he should be on his way, and quickly collecting the nag, he urged it back to Meadowacres, rehearsing his excuse to the butler.

He met the cook first. 'Is he on his way?' she enquired, wiping her hands on her floury apron.

'He wasn't there.'

'But you told the housekeeper he should come as soon as could be, didn't you?'

'No, I wasn't told to.'

The cook flung her hands in the air. 'You idiot boy! You shouldn't have to be told to use common sense. Now someone else has to waste more time to go back there.' The boy ran from the kitchen, while she looked around her, but there were only the kitchen girls, and they couldn't go. She headed outside.

The first person she saw was the young stable boy, John. 'Take one of the horses and get to the physician's in Honiton, tell him we need him here. If he isn't there, leave a message with his housekeeper. Tell them it's urgent, that the tutor is very ill with a fever.'

116

Back in the warmth of the kitchen, she sat in the rocking chair by the great fire, hoping he would be in time.

The physician arrived just as cook was finishing off the dinner, the maids waiting to carry the platters to the table. Sharply telling him to take a seat, and making sure he had a glass of ale at his elbow, she finished the preparations for the meal. Only when all was done did she join him by the fire.

Without preamble, she told of her visit to Nathaniel's room that morning and of her concern for him. Taking his time to finish his twice-replenished ale, he collected his bag and made his way up the stairs to the eaves, carrying a candle to light his way.

As soon as he opened the door, he knew he was too late. The air was cold, almost hostile, and there was a smell of death in the room. He gave an involuntary shiver. The candle by the bed had gutted, and he was glad he had brought his own.

He approached the bed where Nathaniel lay, but when the physician touched the forehead of the still figure, he was unsurprised to find it quite cold. He stood, head bowed, for a few moments then quietly left the room, closing the door behind him.

The cook was still sitting by the fire, awaiting his return.

'How is the lad?' she asked, concern on her kindly face.

'I am called too late. He has long been dead.'

Her hands went to her face in horror. 'Oh the poor lad; dying alone. He should have said he was so poorly, we could have called you sooner.' She began to sob, the kitchen girls stopping their work to stare in bemusement.

'Now, now, now. Nothing could be done.' The physician was worried. If he had died of a fever, where had he caught that fever?

'Do you know ought about him? Where he came from? How long has he been here?' he asked.

'He came from London, but that's all I know. He came, what, awhile ago?' She looked around for confirmation, and the girls nodded in agreement, time meaningless for all.

'Well, he couldn't have brought the fever from London then, that's a good thing.' But it didn't answer how he had become ill.

The physician, thinking over the symptoms the cook had described before he had gone to Nathaniel's room, was at a loss. The rage of Lord Riverley at the man dying in his house didn't bear thinking about. He intended to be away before the news was taken to the head of the household.

'I'll arrange for his body to be collected, but who'll pay for the burial?' enquired the physician, edging to the door.

The cook, wiping her eyes on her apron, had no reply. The staff of Meadowacres hadn't liked the poor man enough to offer to help, and it was certain Lord Riverley wouldn't.

'I'll speak to the rector, perhaps there's money in the paupers' fund we could use.' With the cook still not replying, he escaped into the courtyard to collect his horse.

Riding to town, the physician thought how unfair life was. A young man, who should be in the prime of his life, dying alone in a house that didn't care whether he lived or not, except for the cook, the only one he had seen who had shed tears. He just hoped that when his turn came, there would be someone to cry for his passing.

Chapter 27 ❧
Rectory

The physician knocked on the door of the rectory, which was opened by Elizabeth.

'Is the rector at home?' he asked.

'Yes, sir, please come in.' Closing the door behind him, Elizabeth led him to the rector's study, knocking on the door.

'Uncle, there is a man to see you.'

The door opened, the rector and physician greeting each other as old friends.

'Elizabeth, perhaps you would be good enough to bring two tankards of ale?' asked the rector. The physician entered the study, placing his hat on a side table, and taking a seat facing the desk.

Returning with the ale, Elizabeth caught the end of the conversation.

'Poor man, he hadn't been tutor there long, and we all know Riverley won't pay for the funeral, so no use looking to him. I was wondering if you had money in the paupers' fund?'

'Tutor? At the Riverleys'? What of him?' asked Elizabeth, the tankards of ale spilling as the result of her shaking hands.

The physician turned to her. 'You know of him?'

'If the tutor's name was Nathaniel Simmons, then yes, I know of him.'

The rector looked suspiciously at Elizabeth. 'How would you know of a tutor?' he asked.

'He was a passenger on the same coach as Mother and I.' She placed the tankards on the desk top, mindless of the papers on which she placed them and the resultant soggy rings.

'What has become of him?'

'He died earlier today of the fever.' The physician spoke matter of fact, death not unknown to him, and after all, he hadn't know the man personally.

Elizabeth felt cold, her fingers tingling with the shock. Poor Nathaniel. She remembered him as she had last seen him on High Street when they arranged to meet. How grave his face was, how pleased he looked as they made their plan. He was too young to die, how could he have caught a fever? She ran from the room, taking the stairs two at a time, her skirts bunched in her hands. Flinging herself on the bed, she buried her head in her arms and sobbed.

Anne and Mary, hearing her, walked in to her room without a by-your-leave.

'What are you crying for, Lizzie?' asked Anne. They sat on her bed, crowding her. Elizabeth lifted her head, glaring at her two hated cousins.

'Go away, you awful brats! Leave me alone.'

They left, both running to be the first to tell their mother that 'Lizzie called us brats.'

When Aunt Jane came into Elizabeth's room ready to reprimand, it was to find a distraught girl indeed. For once, Jane did the right thing. 'Come, Elizabeth, what can be so bad you have to sob so?' Aunt Jane's voice was gentle. She, like her daughters, sat on the bed. She stroked Elizabeth's hair, smoothing it behind her ears.

'Oh, Aunt Jane, Nathaniel Simmons is dead,' she wailed.

'I know, and I'm sorry to hear of it. Not that I ever met the man, but your uncle tells me he came on the coach with you and your mother?'

Elizabeth wiped her nose on the back of her hand.

'Yes, he was a poorly man. His head twitched, and I was irritated by him, but he was a harmless soul.' She couldn't say that they had planned to meet last Saturday, so had to swallow her grief for her one friend in Honiton. If she didn't count the newly met Peter Brigginshaw, that is.

'Well,' said Aunt Jane, 'the church is going to pay for his burial, but it will have to be in a pauper's grave, sad to say.'

Elizabeth sat up, taking a handkerchief from her sleeve, and giving her nose a mighty blow while Aunt Jane nattered on, talking more to herself than her niece.

'I wonder who will lay him out. Hopefully someone at Meadowacres will take pity on him, for no one should go to their grave unclean.' This only brought Elizabeth to sobs once more. Poor, poor Nathaniel.

With no family nearby, or so the rector presumed, there was no need to wait for their arrival. The decision was made to bury Nathaniel in two days' time.

Predictably, the cook was the one to take pity on him. Two of the men servants, none too carefully, brought his body wrapped in a sheet down the three flights of stairs.

Cook had scrubbed the long kitchen table to within an inch of its life, and then placed clean sheets on top of that. Nathaniel's body was placed upon it.

Shooing all the young girls from the kitchen, she undressed him and, using a clean rag and soap, washed his body. All the while she talked to him.

When her husband died, the rector had told her that her husband could still hear her if she wished to talk to him. Presuming the same would apply to a tutor, she uttered soothing words as she washed the grime from his face and hands, drying them on another towel. Progressing to his body, she tried not to look at his private parts, giving them only a cursory wiping.

Leaving his body alone for a moment, she called to one of the girls to go to his room and pick some clean linen to dress him in. Meeting the young maid at the door, she received the clean linen, a pair of much mended breeches, a linen shirt in the same repair, along with a jacket, shiny with age and wear. Lastly came Nathaniel's spare pair of boots.

Once he was dressed, with some difficulty, Nathaniel's body was placed in the pure woollen shroud purchased from Master Morbeck's warehouse earlier in the day.

Unable to keep him in the kitchen for the heat, the body was taken out to the yard, a place found for it in one of the little-used sheds until the time came for burial. The kitchen table was again scrubbed down with boiling water and soap, after which cook sat there alone, her elbows on the damp surface, wiping the tears from her face.

ᶘᵃᶻᵃᶻᵃ

The rector, Elizabeth, and the cook were the only ones who attended the funeral, not counting the two gravediggers. The Prayer for the Dead was said, but since nothing was known of him, there was little time spent before the earth was filled in, covering up poor Nathaniel's head, now still.

Once the others left, Elizabeth stayed on. 'I am sorry we never got to meet again, Nathaniel. I'm sorry if I was irritated with you because of your twitching head, I know you couldn't help it. I promise I'll try and be more patient with people, and when I start to get annoyed, I'll think of you.'

The large oak trees that surrounded the paupers' part of the cemetery were being blown around in a strong wind that had sprung up, and their boles creaked as if they, too, were crying. She held onto her bonnet with one hand, wiping her eyes with the other.

She had brought a small posy of meadow flowers with her, which she had placed at her feet during the brief service. Though looking at them now, she thought how mean-spirited they looked. But she had nothing else to give, so bent down and laid it gently on the freshly returned earth.

'Goodbye, Nathaniel. I shan't forget you,' she sobbed. Then she turned and walked away, not looking back.

After dinner, Aunt Jane, seeing how upset Elizabeth was, excused her from the table.

'Why don't you go and lie down for a while? Anne and Mary can help with the clearing up today.'

This brought howls of protest from the two girls, which Elizabeth ignored.

'Thank you, Aunt Jane.' Excusing herself, Elizabeth left, climbing the stairs to her room, though once there, she felt a strong need to be out in the air.

Slipping her wrap round her shoulders she returned downstairs, leaving the rectory by the front door. Heading for the small orchard at the bottom of the garden, she felt more tears gathering in her eyes. She allowed them to spill and run unchecked down her cheeks.

That night, lying in her bed, her thoughts kept returning to Nathaniel. He had been kind to her while she had silently mocked him, but now he was gone, she found herself both ashamed and bereft.

Chapter 28

Exeter

Lady FitzGerald, comfortably tucked up in her large bed with its feather mattress and linen sheets, lay wide awake. Watermead may slumber, but its mistress was far from rest.

Philip had been gone for several days with no word from him. She decided if he hadn't returned by dinnertime tomorrow, she would have to write to his mother, and that was not a task she looked forward to. Where on earth could he be, and more importantly, what trouble was he in?

Philip had found a fellow sufferer of life's woes in Master Jeffrey Browning at the inn in Exeter. Once sober, recognising each other from the coach ride, they drowned their respective sorrows in copious amounts of ale at the inn where Philip was lodged. Jeffrey was only too glad of a sympathetic ear, and the seemingly endless pocket of his acquaintance.

Philip in his turn played the role of a sympathetic ear to exquisite perfection. There was no need for this bumbling fool to know that the ale was being purchased on the tab.

On his arrival in Exeter, and in need of shelter, Philip had made his way to the nearest inn, taking a room for a week. The innkeeper, seeing before him a gentleman dressed in fine clothes with silver buckles on his shoes, made the mistake of presuming he had funds to pay. Little did he know Philip was already planning his departure, and this drunken fool looked as likely a means as any other. The horse Philip had ridden, belonging to Watermead, was stabled two lanes over. The ostler, not as trusting as the innkeeper, had demanded a week's board in advance, effectively depleting Philip's meagre resources.

Jeffrey Browning let slip that his sister was a wealthy merchant, and went on to describe in detail all the plate she owned. When he stated he was a resident in her home, the answer to Philip's problem showed itself to him. Jeffrey Browning, now well in his cups, couldn't return to his sister's house unaided, and Philip was only too happy to assume the role of the Good Samaritan.

The innkeeper gave directions to Nan's house, and with Philip supporting the now very drunk Jeffrey, they prepared to leave the inn. The innkeeper reminded Philip that the front door may well be locked on his return, it now being after midnight, but that the kitchen door would be left unlatched.

Philip, taking his wobbly burden outside, lowered him to the ground around the corner of the inn, quietly returning through the front door and slipping unseen to his room. Quickly throwing his few belongings into his bag, he just as quietly returned to his fellow sufferer. Dragging him to his feet, Philip hauled Jeffrey unceremoniously along, following the directions of the innkeeper.

When Nan's house was reached, Philip's hopes rose even more. Standing alone behind a low stone wall, the house was impressive.

'If the contents are anything as good as the outside, my troubles will be over,' he whispered to himself.

Leaving his small bag outside the unlocked front door, getting Jeffrey up the stairs to his chamber was far from easy. Twice he asked directions to his chamber, and each time a different answer was given.

Nan, woken by the commotion outside her bedroom door, pulled the bedclothes tight up to her chin, her heart thumping wildly in her chest. Not wanting to light a candle and show she was awake in case she was asked to help, she was grateful to the kind soul who was looking after her fool of a brother.

When eventually she heard one set of footsteps descend the bare wooden stairs, she waited until she heard the comforting sound of the door closing. Vowing to wait a few moments before going down to lock and bolt it, she slipped unknowingly back into sleep.

Philip, crouched behind the sheltering wall, also decided to wait a few more minutes before re-entering the house, then carefully lifted the latch and slipped inside.

It was difficult to see as there were no windows close by, but he remembered seeing a closed door to the right of the stairs when he brought Jeffrey home. This was, he presumed, the parlour, and he headed there first.

The door opened without a sound. The wooden shutters had not been closed over the windows, allowing the moonlight to enter.

On a side wall opposite the window stood a large wooden dresser, exactly as had been described by Jeffrey. At the top, three shelves stretched the length of it, cupboards below. Each shelf was laden with silver cups and plate, worth a king's ransom. He gasped, not believing his luck, but how was he to carry it all? He only had the small bag he had brought with him from Watermead, and it couldn't possibly hold all of this, far more than he had anticipated. He looked around at dark shapes showing various chairs and tables.

To his left was a fireplace, ashes still glowing behind the screen, a yawning cavern in the night. To the right of that stood a large wooden chair, and beside it on the floor was a large bag. Tiptoeing over, he carefully felt inside. It contained material and thread, obviously a sewing bag. Taking care to not make a noise, he quickly emptied everything out onto the floor.

The noise as one piece of plate touched another seemed so loud to him as he laid it in the bag, but being as careful as possible, he continued, though fear made his hands tremble.

Once the larger items were inside, he started on the smaller. When both bags were full, he carefully wrapped the top closed and snuck, like the thief that he was, out of the house.

But Philip hadn't thought through the plan for leaving town. His horse was in the stables, and a young lad slept among the horses. If he tried to bring the horse out, the lad would awaken and alert the innkeeper. So what to do? There was nothing for it, he had to return to his room and wait until first light, then make his getaway. With Nan's sewing bag now over one shoulder, his own bag in his hand, he returned to the inn.

Nan, cosy in her bed, awoke later than her usual six o'clock, the room already light. Disturbed by her brother's late return she felt groggy and out of sorts. Pulling a wrap over her nightclothes, she went to enquire of the kitchen servant regarding breakfast. As she came down the stairs she noticed the parlour door ajar, though felt sure she had closed it the night before. The servant wouldn't have entered during the night; she was far too worn out by her daily labours. Pushing the door farther open, she looked around, still too groggy to take in the missing silver or her sewing, now in a pile on the floor.

After asking the servant to fetch small ale, Nan returned to the parlour, intending to spend a little while on her sewing before starting her day. Seated in her chair, she laid her head back, thinking of all she had to do.

She still did not realised her loss. It was the servant, stumbling in with the ale that raised the alarm. 'Mistress, where is the plate?'

Nan stared at the dresser, then at the floor to the discarded sewing, realisation at last dawning. With that came her voice. A loud and prolonged scream rend the air. The servant scurried from the room with her hands covering her ears against the racket.

'My plate! My plate!' Nan yelled, running to the front door and flinging it open. Down the short path, she stood, her hands tightly gripping the top of the entrance gate. 'Watch! Somebody call the Watch, I've been robbed.'

The Watch, when he at last arrived, was met with a hostile glare.

'It took you long enough to get here,' remarked Nan. A good hour had gone by since the alarm was raised, and she was finding it almost impossible to keep her temper. 'He's miles away by now, and my plate along with him.'

'I am sorry for the delay, mistress, but I haven't been to bed all night. I've been lying in wait at the silversmith's, there's rumour he is to be the victim of a thief, it took them awhile to find me.'

'I care nothing for the silversmith. My plate has gone and I want to know what you intend to do about it.' Hands clasped under her bosom, she was still dressed in her nightclothes. Her mouth was pursed in annoyance, aimed between the Watch and the maid who had been the first to see the loss, as if it were their fault.

Jeffrey Browning, woken from his drunken state by the screaming and commotion, had decided it would be better to remain in his bed. He pulled the cover about him against the morning chill, and clasping his hands behind his head, lay warm and content.

He remembered going to the inn and meeting up with Philip Goldworthy. He could remember some of their conversation, their mutual need of funds caused by a shared gambling problem, but as to how he had made it back to Nan's and ended up in bed was totally lost to him.

He got up and used the pisspot, taking pleasure in his emptying bladder. Tucking the pot safely under the bed, he returned to his musing.

He had been in Exeter a short while, and was enjoying having the maid look after his chamber and the kitchen maid cook his meals.

Perhaps I could persuade Nan to let me stay. After all, I am her bother. If I tell her I will look for employment, pay something towards my keep, why should she deny me? After all, this is a big house for one person.' He settled himself more comfortably. But it was difficult to think with all the noise, and he decided to go downstairs.

Dressed, though not yet washed, he entered the front room to find Nan talking to a man. When Nan addressed him as the "Watch," Jeffrey recoiled sharply. He held on to either side of the doorframe, convinced the Watch had come for him; that word had arrived from London of his default on the loans. A sweat broke out on his forehead, and he felt sick. Nan turned to him.

'About time you got up,' she spat. She turned back to the Watch and said by way of introduction, 'This is my brother, Master Browning. He's lodging here temporarily.'

The Watch gave a nod, which Jeffrey returned.

'I've been robbed,' said Nan, indicating the empty dresser. 'All my plate has gone.'

Relieved beyond measure, Jeffrey cleared his throat. 'I'm sorry to hear that, Nan. When did it happen?'

'Last night. It was still on the shelves when I damped down the fire before going to bed. What time did you arrive home?' she enquired of Jeffrey.

'I've no idea. I'm afraid I drank too much at the inn and really have no recollection.'

The Watch spoke, 'If you were the worse for drink, how did you get back?'

'Someone I met at the inn must have brought me home, or perhaps I made my own way. But as I say, I really have no idea.' As he spoke, he became aware of a terrible feeling of doom. It started in his boots and was slowly creeping up his legs. Oh God. What was his name, something Goldworthy? Jeffrey stood looking out of the window, fearful of letting Nan see the terror in his eyes. It had to be him. He must have brought me home. I spoke of my need of funds, but he did also. Oh God. He's stolen Nan's plate. If she finds out I brought him here, she'll never let me stay. He turned back to look at the Watch.

The man was looking intently at him, his eyes boring into Jeffrey's as if he could read his mind.

'What are you standing here for?' demanded Nan of the Watch. 'You'll never catch him standing in my parlour.' Her hands were on her hips, her chin thrust forward as if her determination alone could get the man moving.

'I understand that, mistress, but until I know who I'm looking for, I would just be going round in circles.' He turned once more to Jeffrey, who was slowly backing out of the door.

'Did anyone follow you home?'

He spread his hands, shrugged his shoulders. 'As I said, I was the worse for drink. I wish I could remember, but I cannot.'

Now out of the room, he ran back up the stairs to his room, slamming the door behind him. Falling onto the bed, he sat hugging himself, rocking back and forth. Oh God, oh God. That fellow has stolen Nan's plate.

Philip Goldworthy had returned to the inn and made it to his room without meeting anyone. His breath came in great gasps, and he closed the door behind him, carefully dropping his small travel bag along with the sewing bag filled with the plate at his feet. Leaning against the door, he wiped the sweat from his face and walked with trembling legs to his bed.

As soon as it's daylight I'll get the horse. Hopefully they won't realise the plate has gone until I'm out of town. Nobody saw me at the house, but the innkeeper saw me leave the inn with the fool. If anyone asks him, he's bound to remember.

He retched. This was the first time he had stolen. Or to be exact, the first time he had stolen anything of real value. The punishment if he was caught didn't bear thinking about, so he didn't. He thought instead of where he would sell the haul, and what he would do with the proceeds.

He knew it couldn't be anywhere near Exeter, for the Watch, when alerted, would be on the lookout for it. Honiton was far enough that perhaps he could sell some of it there.

I will have the funds to repay some of my debts, there is no reason why I couldn't return to London and rid myself of this godforsaken county. Of course, it depends how much money is raised, but I would pay off part of the bill to my tailor and boot maker, just sufficient to keep them off my back. There were also some members of my club I would need to satisfy. Perhaps I should do that before I pay off the creditors. It has been getting awkward, fellows starting to avoid me. But surely once he showed he could repay his debts or at least some of them, he felt certain all that unpleasantness would be forgotten.

His trembling slowed, and then stopped. Thinking back, he felt quite satisfied with his night's work.

His plan of escape had worked, and now at the doors to Watermead, Philip left the horse outside the main door and called to the boy to come and take it back to the stable. With a bag in each hand, he walked up the steps that led into the house, where the butler held the doors open for him.

'Welcome back, Master Philip. Did you have a pleasant time?'

He looked at the servant with distain, a cordial answer beyond him, and walked over the black and white tiled floor and up the curved staircase to his room.

The butler watched him, his face, as always, impassive.

The likelihood of being caught was very small, Philip convinced himself. Who would dare accuse the godson of Lady FitzGerald of Watermead in the county of Devon? He laughed out loud. No, no need to worry. He had every reason to think he was safe here.

Chapter 29 ❧
Rectory

Elizabeth wrote to her parents, begging to be allowed to return home. Giving the letter to the innkeeper at the Cross Keys, for transfer to the coach, she waited impatiently for the answer, which she knew would take about a week.

She had decided the only way to deal with her wretched cousins was to ignore them as much as possible. It was only when her aunt and uncle were present that she minded her manners.

When alone with the girls, she had decided to fight fire with fire. After long and hard thought, she had looked for their weak spots. Mary was worried silly about her looks even though, as a rector's daughter, she knew full well the pitfalls of vanity. Anne was afraid of spiders. Not just afraid, but petrified.

Elizabeth decided to concentrate on Mary first. At every opportunity she niggled away at her appearance, her hair, anything she could think of. If Aunt Jane made comment about how nice Mary looked, Elizabeth waited until they were alone then made a point of making a negative comment to her cousin. Slowly but surely, she watched Mary's confidence sag.

In between times, hours were spent collecting spiders, the larger the better. In the old rectory they were in abundance, an accepted part of living there. It was almost as if they knew they were to be trapped, for finding them was the easy part, trapping them was not.

The finding of a large nest one morning was a particular treasure, carefully drawn into a tin box for safekeeping, then opened and secreted in Anne's linen drawer when the girls were out.

Anne subsequently found spiders in her bed and her shoes. Each time she screamed for her mother to come immediately and kill them. But when her linen drawer was opened to find it teeming with baby spiders, it was more than she could bear and she ran from the room screaming, her face white with fear. Elizabeth joined the family in trying to calm down the hysterical girl, but as soon as she could escape to her room, she rolled around on the bed, her hands over her mouth to quiet the laughter.

Elizabeth felt sure her parents were now missing her and would welcome her home early. But the long-awaited letter, when it did arrived, was a bitter blow.

The summer heat, it said, had brought disease to London, and Sarah was ill. Not only Sarah, but also William and Simon were confined to their beds. There was no way she could return until the danger had passed.

The letter, penned obviously in a rush by her father, warned her not to ask to come home until he wrote and gave permission. 'My patience with you is wearing thin, Elizabeth,' he wrote.

Not even the fun of terrifying Anne, nor making Mary think she was even plainer than she was, could bring a smile. All Elizabeth wanted was to go home.

❧❧❧

Peter Brigginshaw, rushed off his feet with an influx of new furniture orders, was in the middle of finalizing plans for his new workshop and home. As he had correctly anticipated, the owner of the land was only too willing to strike a deal, and couldn't believe his good fortune with the price offered. Immediately contacting the family solicitor, he made it clear that nothing could be allowed to prevent the sale. Peter had offered twenty guineas for each of the five acres he needed, an amount that wasn't quibbled about by the gleeful seller.

The first spade full of earth had recently been turned, and the footings of the buildings were well on their way. Peter spent the early part of the mornings working with his apprentices on the various orders, and then left just before lunch to visit the new worksite.

Each Sunday Peter attended the church service, making sure he placed himself where he could look at Elizabeth over the congregation. He would spend the time during the service mindlessly singing the hymns, thoughtlessly answering the responses. All he cared about was looking at Elizabeth. The beautiful hair that showed beneath her bonnet, her almond-shaped blue eyes framed with long, dark lashes. She filled his dreams each night and his spare thoughts during the day. Peter whispered her name, lingering over each syllable.

Chapter 30 ❦
London

Sarah Sharpe lay in her bed, wracked with fever. William was slowly recovering, though Simon also was abed, covered in sweat and muttering incoherently.

Daniel was beside himself with worry. The maid had fled as soon as the mistress fell sick, seeing immediately the problems that were falling upon the Sharpe house. That left Daniel to care for his sick wife and sons, and every day he cursed his decision to send Elizabeth to Honiton. On the one hand, the girl was safely out of danger, but it left him at his wits' end.

The sweat-soaked bedclothes had at first piled up with no one to launder them, then he resorted to reusing them, which only resulted in the contagion being passed backwards and forwards.

Still with the wine business to run, Daniel's days were racked with worry for his loved ones and worry for his livelihood. Timothy was doing his best, but with some of his workers also afflicted, each day was proving to be more and more difficult.

The citizens of London were frightened to venture out for fear of catching the typhoid. The streets and alleyways were sparsely inhabited. With the disease spreading its deadly wings to the west and north, people were fleeing to the south and east.

People in Kent were forming groups to keep those from London out, hoping to prevent the contagion. When it quickly became obvious that nothing they could do would stem the flow, they were forced to retreat and accept the inevitable. Word of the disease in the country's capital had spread to Honiton, and Elizabeth was worried about her family.

The last letter had been from her father telling her she could only return when he gave permission, and she found that day-by-day she was becoming more and more despondent.

On Saturday afternoon, she told Aunt Jane she would be going into town. When asked if she would like Mary or Anne to accompany her, she declined, somewhat forcefully. Desperately needing to get away from the cloying atmosphere in the rectory, she didn't care if her aunt thought her uncivil.

Once outside, the air was fresh and slightly chilly. She pulled her cloak closely around her, she went through the gate and onward down the hill. Several people passed her, and since everyone in Honiton attended the church, they all knew her as the rector's niece. All nodded their greeting, which Elizabeth returned. Her steps had a mind of their own, leading her here and there, first looking in this shop window, now moving on, all the time going down the hill.

Looking along a side lane, Elizabeth saw the joiner's shop, and found herself drawn to it. Shielding her eyes from the sun, she looked through the window to the gloom within.

Wood was stacked everywhere, leaning against the walls, lying on the floor, and just as she was thinking that it must be hard to walk between it all, the door opened, the doorbell jangling noisily.

'Good morning, mistress, how nice to see you again,' said Peter. He stood on the step, smiling at Elizabeth, his shoulders hunched against the chill.

'Good morning. I'm sorry if I seemed inquisitive, I just wondered what was inside,' remarked Elizabeth.

'No need to wonder, come along in and see firsthand.' He held the door open, a smile on his face that lit up his eyes.

Elizabeth stepped inside and stood for a moment, absorbing the smell of the wood shavings and glue. One of the apprentices, a small lad of about thirteen with bright red hair, poked his head round the doorway at the back of the shop, then just as quickly disappeared, to be replaced by Mistress Chapman, Peter's housekeeper.

Wiping her hands, she said, 'Good morning, mistress. Are you here to order a piece of furniture or come to visit Master Peter?' She looked between Peter and Elizabeth, a small smile playing on her lips.

'Oh no, mistress, I was passing and wondered what was inside. I've not come for furniture.'

Peter introduced the two women, taking pleasure in saying her name. Elizabeth Sharpe.

'Well, no matter. I was sitting down to some refreshment and fresh bread. Will you join me?'

Elizabeth looked at Peter, who stood silently. He was biting his lower lip, and she could just see a small piece of white front tooth, which she found surprisingly attractive. She forced herself to answer.

'Thank you, I would like that.' She followed Mistress Chapman through the back door, turning to the right, and down two small stone steps into the kitchen. The housekeeper indicated she should take the chair by the fire, which burned welcomingly in the blackened grate. There was a redolent air of freshly baked goods, which caused Elizabeth's mouth to water. Sitting where indicated, she removed her bonnet, laying it on the stone floor beside the chair.

Peter had followed her and stood leaning against the doorjamb, unable to take his eyes off her, a most welcome visitor.

'Don't stand there gawping, Peter, get Mistress Sharpe a drink while I put out the bread.'

He coloured and instantly pushed himself straight, hurrying to the dresser to pick up a tin jug and going outside to the shed where they kept the barrels of ale.

Elizabeth sat back in the large, comfortable chair and looked around the welcoming room. Mistress Chapman nattered on about the weather and the coming market to be held in town the following week, and Elizabeth found herself smiling with the joy of it all. For the first time since she had come to Honiton, she found herself happy.

After a short while, Peter excused himself to continue his work, leaving Elizabeth alone with Mistress Chapman. They continued their talk as if they were old friends instead of just met; the age difference of no matter. When the time came to leave, Elizabeth hoped she would see Peter again, but he was obviously busy, and she could think of no reason she could ask for him.

Promising to visit the kindly housekeeper again, she left to make her way back to the rectory, deciding to go by the Cross Keys Inn to see if a letter had come for her on the last coach. She went in search of the innkeeper, Master Beaker. Not finding him in his chancel office, she looked in the main eating room, which was almost empty.

A man sat with his back to her, and upon hearing footsteps, turned to see who came behind him.

'Well, well, well, if it isn't my little stagecoach companion. I haven't seen you since then. Come here and sit with me.'

Elizabeth sensed immediately that the man was drunk, and recognizing him as Philip Goldworthy, wanted to be as far away as possible. While hesitant to be outright rude, she said, 'Thank you, no, sir. I must get back to the rectory. I have already been gone too long.'

He had risen from the bench while she spoke and was headed towards her, weaving between the tables. Before she could turn he grabbed hold of her wrist, twisting it painfully.

'Please, let me go,' she cried as she tried to release herself, but his grip was too strong, and very painful.

'What's going on here?' asked a man's voice, and her attacker turned, wrenching her wrist even more.

Philip was angry. 'Mind you own business, man,' he slurred, all the while holding hard at Elizabeth. He had hardly finished speaking when a huge fist swept past Elizabeth's face and connected with Philip's jaw with a loud crack. He released her wrist and dropped senseless to the flagstones, hitting his head on a bench on the way down.

'Are you hurt, Mistress Sharpe?' asked Master Beaker. He held her elbow, lowering her gently to a chair, for her face was ashen and tears were rapidly gathering.

'I am not hurt, thank you, sir. You have my word; I did nothing to provoke him. I only came to see if there was a letter for me,' she sobbed, hiding her face in her hands.

'I know Master Goldworthy requires no encouragement to make a nuisance of himself. If it wasn't for the fact that he is Lady FitzGerald's godson, he would be barred entry here.' He looked worriedly at Elizabeth, for she was shaking. 'Can I get you some small ale? Perhaps that will help settle you.'

'Thank you, yes, please,' replied Elizabeth gratefully.

'But first, let me get rid of him.' Master Beaker jerked his head towards the recumbent Philip. With awesome ease, he lifted him over his shoulder, taking him out the front door, which he closed firmly behind him. He returned quickly with Elizabeth's ale.

'You will have to excuse me, mistress; I have someone here to see me to discuss some new chairs and tables. You may sit here for a while until you feel ready to return home.' He left Elizabeth sitting alone, cradling the tankard and wiping her face with her sleeve.

Peter Brigginshaw was waiting for him outside his chancel office, a parchment roll of new drawings showing samples of chairs and tables under his arm.

'I'm sorry to have kept you waiting, Master Brigginshaw. I have Elizabeth Sharpe here. She stopped by to see if there was a letter on the coach for her, and that fool Philip Goldworthy got hold of her. Right shaken up she is. I've left her to come and speak to you, but I don't like to leave her too long.'

Peter made no reply but hurried to the eating room where he went straight to Elizabeth.

'Mistress, I'm sorry you have been upset. Please allow me to escort you home.' He knelt before her, concern deep on his face.

'I am sure I will be fine on my own, there's no need to take you away from your business, but thank you.'

'I insist. Master Beaker and I can always meet later, tables and chairs are of no importance compared to your safety.' He stood, holding out his hand.

Elizabeth took it gratefully, and together they left Cross Keys, turning left to walk up the hill to the rectory.

Chapter 31 🍃
Honiton and Exeter

Master Beaker returned outside and stood looking down at Philip Goldworthy, shaking his head. What he had told Elizabeth was true. If it weren't for the fact that the fool was Lady FitzGerald's godson, he would not be allowed entry to the inn.

From his rare visits to Honiton, Philip was well known by the townsfolk as a 'nasty piece of work.' They, like the innkeeper, had no wish to bring sorrow to a most-favoured lady, and all kept quiet. Their silence had only resulted in Philip thinking he could get away with anything.

Emptying a jug of cold water on Philip's head, Master Beaker took two paces back and waited for the man to come round.

Philip sat up, shaking the water from his eyes and looking around him with bemusement. His jaw hurt where he had been hit, and one of his bottom teeth was loose when he explored it with his tongue. Always belligerent, he looked up at the innkeeper. 'What do you mean by attacking me? You'll regret this.' He staggered to his feet, all sign of drink now gone, replaced by pure raw anger.

'Get away from my inn, and don't come back. If you do, I'll set the dogs on you. I don't care who you are, you attacked a young maid on my premises. You walk back through my door and I'll go straight to her ladyship and tell her what a right bastard you are.'

The two stood, and at equal height and weight, they were nose to nose.

'Get away,' Master Beaker repeated, louder this time.

The kitchen girls were peering round the door, thrilled and frightened at the same time at seeing their kindly master red faced and furious.

Philip whipped up his hat that Master Beaker had thrown at his feet and turned, ready to make his way back to Watermead.

The innkeeper followed him with his eyes.

Standing on the road, Philip looked back. 'You'll regret this,' he said, his voice full of venom, and marched off to collect his horse.

⁂

Back in Exeter, Jeffrey Browning had kept to his room for two days after the theft of Nan's plate, hoping that those who had seen him in the inn with Philip would forget the brief acquaintance. Besides, he didn't want to be anywhere near Nan while she was still so furious about her loss. Now, hoping that the fuss would have died down, and in need of good ale, he crept from his room in the mid-morning and made his way back to the inn. His decision that day was to have consequences for not only himself, but another.

Upon entering, he stood for a moment, giving his eyes time to become accustomed to the dim light. Though a meagre fire burned, and a few lanterns stood on the rough wooden tables, it was cold inside. A few single customers sat cradling their ale. A man and woman shared a table in a corner, whispering behind their hands while looking furtively around them.

Jeffrey took a seat at an empty table, and without asking, a pot of ale appeared before him, put there by a young girl. Thin, with knotted and dirty hair, she couldn't be more than eight years old. He felt a momentary rush of sympathy for her, which quickly left when he thought of his own troubles.

He hadn't finished his first pot when the landlord came over to him. 'I'm surprised to see you here again,' he said. 'I would have thought your sister would have thrown you out by now.' He stood, looking down at Jeffrey, a hard expression on his face.

'Why would she throw me out?' he asked, trying to sound confident though even to himself his voice sounded weak and uncertain.

'After the theft of her plate? Be serious, man. Your drinking companion came straight back to his room after taking you home, and me giving him directions too, for which I'll never forgive myself. It doesn't take great thought to put two and two together and make five. Besides, he arrived with one small bag and left with a second one, a much larger one as well.' He edged closer, crowding his pitiful customer. 'Now what do you suppose was in that other bag?'

'I don't know. How would I know? He just guided me home. I have nothing to do with the theft.' Master Browning stuttered and made as if to rise. The landlord's large fist pushed him back on to the bench.

'Well, the thief probably thinks he's not known here, but he is. One of my customers that night recognized him and rumour has it that he owes a great deal of money up in London. Besides that, the stable boy saw the Watermead mark on the horse left in his charge. Now what do you think Lady FitzGerald would say to that?'

'Lady FitzGerald? What has she to do with this? Why would she care about the theft?'

'Oh, I don't know. Probably she wouldn't if she didn't know the thief.' The innkeeper stood back, enjoying the look of horror of Jeffrey Browning's face.

'She knows of him? How?'

'Why he's her godson, that's how. Now, I wonder how much she would pay me to keep quiet.' He looked into the fire, calculating once again how much he could wring from the richest person in the county.

'Blackmail? You wouldn't. You couldn't.' Jeffrey was appalled, all remaining colour draining from his face.

'Couldn't I? How much would you pay me not to tell your sister you introduced the thief into her home?'

'But I have no money!'

'No, but your sister does. Let's start with ten guineas, shall we? Tomorrow at this time?'

As it dawned on Jeffrey what terrible trouble he was in, the landlord walked away, leaving him shaking and terrified.

Chapter 32 ❧
London

Daniel Sharpe sat at the kitchen table with a plate of stale bread and mouldy cheese in front of him.

Sarah was not getting better, if anything she was worse. Simon couldn't be roused from what seemed to be a deep sleep. He lay unmoving in his bed with its soiled and stinking sheets. He no longer sweated, and his breath came in shallow gasps that terrified his father when he dared venture into the room.

William, on the other hand, had recovered, and though still weak was able to leave his bed and make his way to the kitchen, not that there was much to eat there.

Many of the merchants had fled, their only concern to keep their families safe. Boarding up their shops if they had them or filling their wagons with wares and families, they had left for the country. Those who had made the decision to stay, while still frightened, were reaping the extra custom.

Daniel was doing his best, but he was becoming increasingly aware his best just wasn't good enough. Timothy was just hanging on down at the warehouse on the dock. The wine was still coming into port, and instead of ordering the men to cope with the heavy barrels, he found he had to help the three or four men still turning up for work on a daily basis.

Daniel had previously arranged with Timothy that he would try to leave a note on the door of the warehouse advising of conditions at the house when he could leave his wife and son.

However, reality meant that several days went by between messages.

Each note that was left for Timothy spoke of both the sick, and the worsening conditions inside the house. Timothy was stricken, feeling the full responsibility of keeping the family business going and fear for his family.

Sleeping each night at the warehouse, the workers kindly sharing their scant provisions with him, he had no other choice but to take one day at a time and pray.

꒰ꕤ꒱ꕤ

James Morbeck, however, confined to his school premises, found the contagion of great interest. More than ever he wanted to study medicine, and his tutors had assured him he would have no difficulty getting into the school, but now with the typhus here, he was worried.

Many of his fellow pupils had left London to return to their homes in the country. All professed they too would rather stay, but James could see in their eyes they thought him a fool for continuing his studies while the devil himself swirled about the city.

He had received word from his mother that his father continued to progress well, and most importantly, that the disease hadn't found its way to Honiton. With that knowledge, he felt able to concentrate on his own affairs and spent hours, usually well into the night, over his books. The few other pupils who did remain spent the nights carousing and drinking, the noise making sleep all but impossible.

Food was becoming scarce as the merchants fled, but somehow the cooks in school managed to serve up something of substance at least once a day. Even so, he felt his clothes becoming looser, the veins in his hands standing out prominently purple against the white skin.

Exams had been postponed, which irritated him greatly. He had studied long and hard, and couldn't accept the fact that more time was to his benefit. Twice he had asked his tutor if he could still sit for them, and twice been declined. These would be his final exams at this school, and once passed, a fact of which he had no doubt, he could apply to medical school. Now with the contagion, and no one able to tell how long it would last or how far it would spread, he felt a prisoner of fate.

Keeping to his room as much as possible except for lessons and meals, James found himself turning more to his faith for support. Taking time each morning and evening for prayers, he found a sense of peace, and knew that whatever the outcome of his staying, it was the right choice for him. If he had returned to Honiton, as others had fled to their homes, he could have taken the disease with him. He could never have forgiven himself for that.

ᘓᐤᘓᐤᘓᐤ

On the other side of London, huddled in a rough blanket against the cold, Daniel wept in despair. With no food in the house, and afraid to go outside when the morning came, he could bear it no longer.

Sarah had died the day before, and numb to the grief of it, he had carried her emaciated body down to the yard. Wrapping her in cloth he found in the lean-to, he left his beloved wife of twenty years by the wall in front of the house. Horse-drawn carts came by regularly to collect the dead, loading them higgledy-piggledy on top of one another, no thought or time given to preserving their dignity.

Simon still lay upstairs, and with Daniel too frightened now to go into his room, he knew not if his youngest son was dead or alive. He could only give thanks William was now safe.

Timothy, frightened by the lack of information from his father, had come twice to the house, but he had now stopped. He, too, was afraid of catching the fever. He struggled on at the warehouse with the few men who still came and the now-dwindling wine barrels as word spread abroad of the horrors taking place in London.

Sitting alone in the cold, dark warehouse, he thought of his family when they had last been together. He thought of Elizabeth, crying and vowing to be more obedient and Simon, smirking as usual. His parents, determined to send Elizabeth away. As it now turned out, this decision had been for the best. At least she was safe and happy.

Chapter 33 ૨✦
Honiton

Elizabeth may have been safe, but she was rarely happy. The only time she smiled was when she thought of or met Peter Brigginshaw, and he was far too busy to see much of her.

When he had escorted her safely home from the Cross Keys after the terrifying incident with Philip Goldworthy, she had lain awake that night thinking of all he had said. Her first thought was that he was a gentle, fair-natured man, and she had barely noticed his disability. Though he struggled as they neared the top of the hill with the effort of walking, he never showed any self-pity, nor did he seem to expect pity from her. He accepted what God had given him and was making the best of it.

Peter had spoken of the new building and his plans for the future, but had also listened to Elizabeth. And not just listened, but truly heard her. She had told him why she had been sent to Honiton, and he had laughed aloud, and for the first time she found herself seeing the funny side of the whole thing, and joined in his laughter.

When he asked how much longer she was to remain at the rectory, and on being told it would be for some time, he smiled at her and she felt her face grow hot.

'Well, mistress, we shall have to make the most of that time, won't we?'

A week had gone by since then, and Elizabeth found herself thinking of a way to meet him again.

She knew he came to church of a Sunday, and had noticed that he was invariably late and had to push his way in amongst the crowd. Elizabeth, being considered part of the rector's family, had little choice but to sit in the front pew with her aunt and bratty cousins, so there was no way for them to meet there.

Though perhaps there was a way after the service was over. Perhaps she could dally and happen to be nearby when he emerged from the church. With his disability she had noticed he tended to avoid being caught in a crush of people. It stood to reason he would hold back and wait for the congregation to leave first.

Her plan for once worked beautifully. The following Sunday, as the others left the church, she deliberately wandered among the crowd of those waiting to speak to the rector, and timing it perfectly, met Peter.

'Master Brigginshaw, how do you fare?'

'I'm well, mistress, and even better for the chance to speak to you. I am hoping you are able to join me after dinner. I'm visiting the new building and wondered if you would like to accompany me?'

Elizabeth's heart skipped a beat. 'I would, but I need permission from my aunt.' She looked around, searching amongst the departing congregation for the unattractive bonnet her aunt was wearing today. 'She's over there, will you wait while I ask?'

Peter nodded.

Elizabeth pushed her way through the throng and stood waiting for Aunt Jane to finish speaking.

'Aunt, may I go into town after dinner? Master Brigginshaw has asked me to visit his new building, and I should dearly love to see it.'

Jane looked over Elizabeth's shoulder, seeing Peter standing alone, a hopeful expression upon his face.

In truth, Jane was growing bone weary of the constant battles with her strong-willed niece. It was bad enough dealing with Mary and Anne on a daily basis, but to have bear. The thought of another argument with the girl was too much.

Elizabeth too, well, there was only so much one poor soul could

Then she thought of the guinea a month being paid, and what she was able to do with it. Still, she considered herself hard done

147

by. Here was a way to get Elizabeth out of the house, and one of the girls at the same time.

'You may, but only if Mary or Anne go with you.'

'Why? Why do they have to come with me? We are only going to the new building.'

Aunt Jane sighed heavily. 'Because it's not right you should go off on your own, unmarried as you are.'

'I'll never get married if I don't!'

'Don't talk nonsense, Elizabeth. Either you take one of the girls with you, or you don't go.'

Elizabeth had no choice. 'This is silly, Aunt Jane.'

'Silly or not, that's the way it is. I don't want people in the town saying that I'm not caring properly for you, nor word of it reaching your mother.'

Elizabeth, for once biting her tongue, returned to Peter. He knew from her face that she was upset.

'I'm allowed to go, but only if Anne or Mary accompany us.'

'It's only what I expected, no need to look so downcast. The main thing is you will get to see it.'

'Yes, it is.' Elizabeth looked at his kind face, and knew she didn't care if Mary, Anne, Aunt Jane, the rector and the rest of Honiton came, so long as she saw Peter again.

Chapter 34 ⋈
Exeter

Jeffrey Browning had been given a scant two days by his sister, Nan, to make other arrangements.

Still furious at the loss of her plate, Nan had heard mutterings about town with regard to her brother's role in the theft. Word was freely circulating in Exeter that he and Philip Goldworthy had been responsible. Her friends, such kindly souls, had made sure she had heard them.

On her way to one of her shops early the next morning, she bumped into the Watch, who had been avoiding her at every opportunity. Caught off guard, he had no choice but to greet her.

'What about the theft of my plate?' she demanded, not even greeting him.

'Mistress, I've asked around, but no one has reported being offered any of it for sale, it just seems to have disappeared into thin air as it were.'

'Then why is the town talking of my brother and this godson of Lady FitzGerald's? If others know of it, why don't you? Why aren't you on your way to Honiton to ask questions of this Philip Goldworthy or whatever his name is? Just because he is her ladyship's godson doesn't mean he's above the law.'

The Watch drew himself up. 'I am well aware of that, mistress, but I can't simply accuse him. I have to have proof.'

'What more proof do you want? It's the talk of the whole town, and worst of all, my brother is said to be involved. I have told him to be out of my house within two days, but I shall still look like a fool. So tell me, when do you go to Honiton?'

'I'll have to think more on that; I can't just accuse a man of theft. He could be innocent after all.'

'Well, you'll never know unless you go and find out, will you?' Nan was furious at the apparent reluctance of the man to confront someone of status. 'I'll give you the same two days as I've given my brother, and if you haven't been to talk to him, I'll want to know the reason why.'

The Watch walked away with as much dignity as he could muster after such a tongue-lashing. What made it worse was that he knew the woman was right. With none of the plate surfacing in Exeter, he was running out of ideas as to where it could be. Even he had heard the rumours of Nan's brother and Philip Goldworthy, and he was fast approaching the time when he would be forced to confront them. Though just not yet.

⋅⋅⋅⋅⋅

Jeffrey Browning waited, determined to beg if necessary, to be allowed to remain. He sat in his room under the eaves rehearsing what he would say.

He could remind her of when they were children and what good times they had growing up together; he could remind her of their mother's deathbed wish that they should always remain close and look out for each other. How could she refuse such a request? He settled instead on buttering her up.

When he heard the front door slam and his sister's voice giving a command to the maid, he plucked up his almost non-existent courage and descended the stairs.

Finding Nan in the front room, he couldn't stop his head turning to look at the empty shelves of the dresser, and almost immediately felt the sweat bead on his forehead as he thought of his part in the whole affair.

'What do you want?' demanded Nan. 'Remember, you only have two days to get out.'

'Yes, Nan, how could I forget, for you keep reminding me?' He felt his knees tremble, and leant against the table for support. 'And that's what I wanted to talk to you about. I assure you, Sister. I had nothing to do with the theft, for you have been nothing but kindness itself in giving me shelter this short while. As you know, I've nowhere else to go, and I don't believe such a kind and thoughtful sister would demand that I should leave her house based on such flimsy evidence.'

Nan snorted loudly. 'You've made the mistake of taking me for a fool, Jeffrey. The whole town knows you and that man stole my plate, and I won't be satisfied until I get it back, every piece of it. I met the Watch this morning; he's been avoiding me like the plague. I gave him an ultimatum that he was to go to Honiton and confront the scoundrel. I care not a whit that he is the godson of a wealthy lady.'

'I want you out of here in two days, and there's no more discussing the matter. I worked hard to get where I am, and nobody, and that includes you, brother, is going to take it away from me and make me a fool in the bargain.'

Jeffrey stood, his mouth open, his knees trembling worse than ever. He pulled out a chair and plopped down into it under the seemingly endless onslaught of bad feeling.

'Is there nothing I can say that will change your mind, Nan?'

'Yes, there is. Tell me where my plate is and when I'll get it back.'

She swirled round, heading out the door and up the stairs.

≈ Watermead ≈

Lady FitzGerald sat in the salon talking to Susannah who sat by the window working on a delicate piece of lace with the benefit of the morning light.

'Have you seen Philip this morning?' Lady FitzGerald asked.

'Briefly, at breakfast. He seemed out of temper, has something happened to upset him?'

'I was hoping you could tell me that. Ever since he came back from Exeter it's as if there is a black cloud hanging over him. I'm told he won't let the maid clean his room, not even to light the fire. And in this weather the room must be chilly.' She looked down at her hands, at the rings that adorned each finger.

151

'I don't feel good about him, Susannah. I thought of writing to his mother, but on reflection decided it wouldn't be right to worry her. After all, he is a grown man.'

'I agree.' Susannah looked with worry at Lady FitzGerald. 'Would you like me to speak to Thomas, find out if he knows anything?'

'Would you?'

'Of course I would. If there's anything to know, Thomas will have knowledge of it.'

Susannah returned to her lace, Lady FitzGerald to her musing. *Something is wrong, and I just hope it doesn't affect Susannah and Thomas. I can't settle to anything until I know what it is.*

❧ Exeter ❧

Jeffrey Browning, packed of his few belongings, gave one last look around his room at Nan's. His stomach was clenching, for he had no idea where he would spend this night. He didn't possess a horse, and with no money to buy or even hire one, he had no choice but to walk.

Nan had left the house that morning without as much as a farewell, even though Jeffrey stood at the head of the stair in full view. He had raised his hand, which she had seen, but turned and left.

Utterly despondent, he stood outside the front gate, looking to left and right. To the left lay the various inns of Exeter, to the right, Honiton and Philip Goldworthy.

Tossing and turning through the all-too-short night, he had eventually come to realise that if he were to get back into Nan's good books, then her comment, 'Tell me where my plate is and when I'll get it back,' was the only way that would happen. He turned to the right.

The lane was busy, carts laden with produce coming into town from outlying farms, and Jeffrey kept his head down, avoiding eye contact with all who passed.

The weather was bitterly cold, and his coat nowhere near up to the task of keeping him warm. Without gloves or hat, he was utterly miserable. His shoes had been made for city cobbles not country walking, and he tried not to think of how far he had to travel.

Drinking at the inn the previous night, the keeper had asked about the ten guineas to buy his silence, and Jeffrey assured him he would receive it soon, no need to fret, he would be getting it in the next few days. He had then enquired for directions to Honiton, and been advised to follow the coach route, that being the most direct. When he then enquired as to the distance, he was told it was seventeen miles, give or take a mile.

He had not thought, however, of asking if there were suitable places for lodging along the way. He had left Nan's just before dinner, and estimated he could walk about ten miles before darkness fell.

After a short while he left the last few cottages behind, and watching the road for ruts and holes, he walked on.

❧ Watermead ❧

Thomas had returned cold and hungry. Wherever he travelled, there always seemed to be estate business to be conducted, and he had spent the morning at the solicitor's in Honiton.

Known by all but the newest inhabitants, he found it took a great deal of time to do the simplest thing. All stopped to speak to him, usually asking for advice in one form or another. He couldn't refuse any, and invariably ended up sitting in the Cross Keys over a jug or two of ale.

Master Beaker passed the time of day at some length imparting this piece of news or that. The main news today swirled around Philip.

'He's a bad lot, your lordship. None of us like to speak ill of him to her ladyship, but I'll tell you what I told him. If he comes near my inn again, I'll set the dogs on him.'

Thomas sat back and took his pipe from his pocket. Next came his tobacco pouch, and he tamped a wad into the bowl. He had no need to comment, for he sensed the innkeeper was only too ready to unburden himself. After the pipe was drawing well, he looked at the innkeeper, waiting for him continue.

'He attacked a young girl here, in my inn if you can believe it! She's the rector's niece, and had come to enquire of some mail when he got hold of her.'

Thomas sat up. This was more, and worse, than he had expected.

'What happened?'

'I hit him. I had no choice, you understand. He was yanking her around, and she was crying in pain. I had no choice, believe me. I had to stop him and save the girl; it was the only way.'

'Oh, I believe you, Master Beaker. Was she harmed?'

'Frightened more than harmed. Peter Brigginshaw saw her safely home. I told Master Goldworthy outright I would set the dogs on him if he returned, and threatened him with telling Lady FitzGerald, though I would never do such a thing as it would be too hurtful to her. But like I said, he's a bad lot. You mark my words; he'll come to a bad end.'

Thomas drew on his pipe, blowing the smoke towards the low, discoloured ceiling.

'Anything else?'

'Well, I hardly like to mention it. I mean, attacking a young maid, that's one thing, but – '

'Go on, man.'

'Well, it's nothing I can prove, you understand, so I would be obliged if you didn't mention where it came from?'

Thomas gave a short nod, then realised his teeth hurt from clenching the pipe stem too hard. He relaxed his jaw.

'I've had some travellers here from Exeter. Word is going round there that he is responsible for the theft of plate from one of the town's biggest merchants. And that she won't rest until she gets it back.'

Thomas looked through narrowed eyes at his informant. Master Beaker had now gone too far to withdraw, and like Jeffrey Browning, had no choice but to go on.

'He wasn't the only one involved, seems there was the merchant's brother also part of it, not that that knowledge makes it any better for Master Goldworthy.'

'No, you're right. It doesn't. Did the travellers mention when this happened?'

'Just a couple of nights ago, to all accounts.'

Thomas leant his head back against the wall. That fits in with Philip returning to Watermead. Since then, he has hardly been out of his room. What has that fool got himself involved in?

'Leave it with me, Master Beaker.'

'Willingly, but like I say, if he comes here I shan't be held responsible, you see if I won't.'

'I think we can both rest assured he won't be coming to Honiton again, or attacking young maids.'

Thomas rose, knocked out his pipe into the fireplace, and stowed it in his pocket. He shook the innkeeper's hand and went outside to mount his horse that was tethered to the post at the door, and turned it towards Watermead.

Master Beaker watched from the window. That should fix the bastard.

Chapter 35 ❧
Rectory

Elizabeth lay on her bed reminiscing about her afternoon with Peter. Even the presence of Mary couldn't cast a gloom over the day. Sited some way out of town, Elizabeth wouldn't have cared if the new building had been ten miles away, for it meant she had more time with Peter. Mary had the whit to walk behind, though her frequent complaints about the walk both she and Peter chose to ignore.

The weather was cold, and all were well wrapped against the wind that blew over the hills. Being the Sabbath, there was no work in progress, but it was easy to see where the various buildings would be. Set well back from the road, the foundation stones of the main house stood removed from the workaday buildings. Peter was rightly proud of it all, and spent some time explaining what it would all look like when finished, which he said would be in about five months' time. Master and Mistress Chapman would be moving with him into the new premises, and their living quarters would be to the rear of the house, easily accessible to both.

The apprentices would be housed above the large workroom, which was comprised of two floors. Their quarters would be on the upper, and Peter had planned that each would have a room of his own.

There would be a separate building for the storage of raw wood. Next to that would be another, also separate, for the storage and display of finished items awaiting delivery. The front of this building would be a shop similar to the present one in the town, but with room for seating and discussion of special commissions.

The land, when purchased, was fronted by a stone wall, accessed by a single iron gate, and the entrance had immediately been widened to allow access to the various carts and wagons filled with building supplies.

Mary sat on a pile of stone, impatient from the first to return to the rectory. She repeatedly called to Elizabeth to ask if she was ready to leave, and for the first time Elizabeth had replied. She then decided that Mary wasn't worth the bother and ignored her. Nothing was to spoil her time with Peter.

When it was, at last, time to return to the rectory, Peter had escorted them. Mary ran on ahead once they reached High Street, giving Elizabeth the much longed for time alone.

Now she lay remembering everything that Peter had said, how he had looked as he said it. She lay on her back, hands clasped behind her head. A sigh escaped her. Not daring to speak aloud, as Mary slept in the next room, she repeated his name. 'Peter.'

Chapter 36 ❧
Watermead

Thomas Stanton, on his return to Watermead, had called for food and drink to be brought to his room as hurried up the stairs to speak to Susannah. Not finding her in their suite of rooms, he found her with his aunt in the salon. Both looked up as the door opened, and he came forward to kiss Susannah's cheek. 'Hello, Aunt, you look pensive.'

The two women looked at each other, Lady FitzGerald's eyebrows raised in question.

'Thomas,' said Susannah, 'have you any knowledge of Philip? Aunt Sophie is worried he is in trouble.'

Thomas looked at his aunt. 'Now why would you think that?' he enquired.

'You know me, Thomas; I am sensitive to atmosphere. Philip has disappeared into his room and won't have anyone enter, not even to tend the fire.' She looked searchingly at his face. 'Have you any knowledge, Thomas? I have written to the rector in Exeter to ask if he knows anything, but have yet to receive a reply.'

Just as he was about to speak, there was a knock on the door and a footman entered followed by a maid carrying a tray laden with food and drink. Thomas indicated to put it on a nearby table, after which they both quickly left the room. 'I was in Honiton this morning, as you know, and stopped at Cross Keys. The innkeeper there could hardly wait to tell me of Philip.' He hated telling either woman of Philip's conduct, but on the ride to Watermead had been unable to think of a way to avoid doing so.

'He has been banned from the inn and threatened with having the keeper's dogs set on him.' He paused. 'And that's not all; there is talk he has stolen.'

Lady FitzGerald clasped her hands to her breast with horror clear on her face.

'Surely not, Thomas. Philip?' Susannah, not related to Philip, didn't have the same sense of shame, but keenly felt Lady FitzGerald's distress.

'I'm afraid so. Plate is missing from a merchant in Exeter. I have a feeling that is the reason he won't let anyone into his room, because the plate is there.' He rose, and fetched the bread and cheese from the nearby table, returning to his seat and the worried faces of these two, much loved, women.

'What are we to do?' whispered Lady FitzGerald.

'I can think of only one way to confirm or dismiss the talk, and that is to search his room. The mere request to do so is tantamount to an accusation of guilt, of course. The whole thing is extremely awkward.'

'What if you find it there?' asked Susannah, glancing at Lady FitzGerald with concern.

'Then we have to inform the Watch, and Philip must take his punishment like any other thief.'

'But what of his mother, what will I say to her?'

'I have the feeling that it won't come as too much of a shock to the poor woman, Aunt. That's not to say I don't feel for her, but I'm sure she knows her son. And what he is capable of.' He finished the bread, placing the plate on the tray.

'When will you do it? Search his room?' enquired Lady FitzGerald. She sat, her back straight, head held high. Never one to shirk the unpleasant, if something was to be faced, then face it she would.

Thomas stood as he brushed his hands together, smoothing down his coat. 'Now is as good a time as any. Has anyone seen him this morning?'

'No,' answered Susannah. 'The maids said his breakfast tray had been left outside his door as he requested, and he has taken it inside. It hasn't been put outside again, so he must be there.'

'Well, in that case, I'll go now. I'll take a couple of footmen with me to stand at the door if that is all right with you?' Lady FitzGerald nodded, not trusting herself to speak.

'Right. I will return as soon as I can. Hopefully, with news that we are all wrong in our thoughts.' Thomas left, quietly closing the door behind him, leaving Lady FitzGerald and Susannah looking at each other in mutual dread.

Knocking on the door of Philip's room, he called out, demanding entrance.

'Why, what do you want? I am unwell and am abed,' came the reply.

'Open the door, Philip, or I will break it down.' The footmen looked at each other, hardly believing what they had heard.

Thomas waited a minute, and then as he was to tell the men to put their shoulders to the door, it was pulled open by a couple of inches with Philip's face peering through the gap.

'What do you want, Thomas? I told you I was unwell.'

'Unwell or not, I am coming in,' and he pushed the door back gaining entrance. Motioning to the men to remain where they were, he closed the door behind him, and taking Philip's arm, pulled him roughly over towards the window.

Keeping his voice low, he said 'What the devil have you been up to, you fool? Are you aware there is talk in Exeter you are responsible for the theft of a quantity of plate?'

'What?' squeaked Philip. 'Me?'

'Yes, you must have been recognized, and hiding in your room refusing entry to the maid is just hammering your guilt home.' He shivered, and looked over at the fireplace, cold and empty. 'It's freezing in here. I'll get the fire lit.' He made to return to the door, but was stopped by Philip, who held his arm.

'No, I don't want anyone in here.'

'Why not? You are responsible for the theft, aren't you?'

Philip walked to the bed, slumping down, resting his head in his hands.

'Yes, I stole it.' He looked up, pleadingly, at Thomas. 'I was desperate. I asked my godmother for funds, but she refused me.

I can't return to London, for I owe too many people money. I was desperate, can't you understand?'

'No, I can't. You have brought disgrace and shame on your family and friends, and even worse, on my aunt.' He looked with contempt at the pathetic figure before him.

'Where is it? Where's the plate?'

'What will you do with it?' asked Philip, now snivelling. He wiped his snotty nose on the back of his hand.

'What do you think? It must be returned, you fool. Where is it?'

Philip stood and walked to the press and opened the doors. Hidden beneath his linen was a large fabric bag from which, when he pulled it out, loud clunking noises emanated.

Thomas took it from him, and to the bed. After untying the drawstring and looking inside, he saw what he had hoped not to see. 'You idiot. You know this is a transportation offence, don't you?'

Philip stood, looking down at the floor, utterly broken. There was no need for him to answer, for he did know. Despite his behaviour, he wasn't a totally stupid man.

Thomas called in the two footmen, telling one of them to take the bag down to the salon. He and the second footman remained with Philip.

'I have to restrain you, Philip. Don't insult us both by asking me why.' He turned to the footman. 'Take this man to the cellars and lock him in. When you've done that, bring me the key, I'll be in the salon with her ladyship.'

'Yes, my lord.' The man held onto Philip's arm, leading him to the door. Philip went quietly, all dignity gone from him.

Thomas waited a few moments before returning to the women. Damn the fool.

≈ Honiton ≈

Jeffrey Browning, his feet blistered and bleeding into his shoes, couldn't take another step.

After a miserable, endless night spent under a hedge with his head resting on his bag, he had met the dawn frozen and stiff as a board. He hadn't thought to bring food from Nan's house, and now loudly cursed his misfortune, albeit of his own making.

He had no idea where he was, no idea how much further it was to Honiton or when he would get there, and the thought of another night spent in the open was terrible to think of.

He had passed only one cart headed in the opposite direction. Headed towards Exeter, the man walking beside the horse just pointed without speaking when asked how much further it was. Jeffrey was left looking after the disappearing figure with despair. With no other choice, he continued on the coach road.

Unaware of the typhus in London, and as a result the coach not running to avoid spreading the disease, there was no hope of a ride. Painfully he put one foot in front of another, and blew frequently on his frozen fingers. His ears were blue with cold, his nose running without end. He was miserable beyond bearing. *I'll kill that Philip Goldworthy when I see him. I wouldn't be in this mess if it weren't for him. Damn the man.*

⁊ Watermead ⁊

Philip was led still without protest by the footman down the back stairs. The man left him by the kitchen door to request the key to the cellar from the butler, but when he returned, it was to find Philip gone. Frantically he called for help, and quickly explaining what had occurred upstairs to all within hearing, they split up to search for the thief.

However, for all intents and purposes, in the short time he had been left alone, Philip had disappeared off the face off the earth.

The butler, as head of the servants' household, knocked on the salon door, which was on the second floor of Watermead, and asked to speak to Thomas alone. It was in great trepidation that he had come.

Following the butler out into the hallway, he waited for the man to speak.

'I've bad news, my lord. Master Goldworthy has made a run for it.' He continued quickly before Thomas could voice his all-too-apparent anger.

'It wasn't the footman's fault, my lord; he had to get the key from me and left the man by the door. He didn't bring him into the kitchen as he wanted to avoid any more disgrace being brought onto him. He did what he thought was right.'

He waited, giving Thomas time to understand the fact that his sympathies were with the servant. Thomas nodded his understanding, and waited for the man to continue.

'The footman wasn't gone but a moment, but master Goldworthy had disappeared. I have the men out in the grounds looking for him, and the gardeners have joined the search. The maids are searching the house, and if he's still here, we'll find him. I thought you should be told as quickly as possible, my lord.'

'Have the stables been checked? He'll be looking for a horse,' said Thomas.

'I will go there directly.' The butler turned, preparing to run.

'No, I'll go. Stay near her ladyship and my wife in case he comes back,' and Thomas made for the stairs, taking them two at a time.

The object of the search, cold and terrified, was well hidden in the bushes about two hundred yards from the house, but he knew the chase would be on. Hearing shouts, he watched four men come running from the library door. They split into two groups, the men heading to the left shouting out to a couple of gardeners wheeling barrows across the lawn. The gardeners stopped, one removing his hat while they waited for the footmen to reach them.

Philip didn't wait around to see more, and keeping low, he headed deeper into the woods, with no idea which way he was heading. He had only the clothes he stood up in, and no money. And if truth be told, little hope.

Thomas found all the horses accounted for in the stables. The lads were surprised by Lord Thomas' sudden appearance, but assured him all was well, and that nothing untoward had occurred. From there, he ran to the back of the house, where he met the butler who was standing talking to some of the footmen. The butler had stayed with his mistress and Susannah as Thomas had instructed, but after just a few minutes, Lady

FitzGerald had released him, saying he would be more use searching for Philip.

'I've left a footman with them both,' he said, aware Thomas had told him to stay with the women. 'He can't have gone far; the men were searching in good time. What of the stables, is a horse missing?'

'No, all are accounted for, which means he must be out here on foot, or still in the house. Get the rest of the gardeners looking outside and send some of the footmen back to the house. If he is inside and one of the maids come across him, it could turn unpleasant.'

'Yes, my lord.' The butler turned again to the footmen to relay the new orders, and Thomas returned inside.

The two women sat, hardly able to sit still but frightened to move. Lady FitzGerald's hands were clenched tightly in her lap, her knuckles showing white.

Susannah had picked up her embroidery but couldn't concentrate, and when she looked closely, realised she had made such a mess she would have to unpick one of the flowers. She placed the sewing on the chair beside her, reluctant to make any more mistakes.

'Try not to worry, Aunt Sophie. Thomas will find him.'

'I know he will, my dear. I just keep wondering what I will say to his mother. Philippa has been such a dear friend to me for so many years, how do I tell her that her son is an admitted thief? What if she thinks I am at fault? After all, this happened while he was with me.'

'Aunt Sophie, you admit she has been a good friend, and as Thomas said, I doubt it will come as too much of a shock. You will find the words, and she won't blame you for her son's behaviour.' Susannah moved over to sit next to Lady FitzGerald, putting her arm around shoulders that shook beneath her embrace. Susannah rose, fetching a woollen wrap that lay on a chair back. She wrapped it around Lady FitzGerald, who gave a small smile of thanks.

They sat in silence, waiting for Thomas to return with news.

⁓ Devon Countryside ⁓

Philip was exhausted. Hot from running, he could see his breath clouding in front of him whenever he paused to breathe. He gave no thought to how cold he would be when he stopped, for he couldn't imagine stopping. He had to keep running as far and as fast as possible.

He leant against a tree, his breath coming in great ragged gulps, the sweat running down his face and into his eyes, making them sting. He had fallen several times, and the knees of his britches were wet and caked with mud, while his hands were scratched and bleeding from pushing through holly and bramble bushes.

In the distance he could hear the dogs and his bowels clenched. Five more minutes of running brought him against the estate stonewall, which stood seven feet high. He stood for a moment, trying to bring his breathing under control. He backed up, then raced forward to jump up and grasp the top of the wall with his painful hands, his feet scrabbling frantically for a toe-hold. Pulling himself up, his arms screaming with pain, he lifted one leg over, to lie, prone, on the top of the wall. The dogs sounded closer, and he could hear men shouting to each other. He let himself drop down on the other side, landing in a painful heap at the base of the wall, but with no time to rest, he forced himself to get up and set off again. His legs could hardly move, but he had to go on, or face the consequences.

Chapter 37 🕮
London to Honiton

Daniel Sharpe, too frightened to enter Simon's room, pressed his ear to the door, listening for any sign of life. Hearing nothing, he knocked, saying tremulously, 'Simon? Can you hear me? Simon? It's me, your father.' There was no reply, and Daniel felt for the latch. Taking a deep breath, he opened the door.

'Simon?'

The stench was unbelievable. Holding his hand against his mouth, Daniel moved further into the room. The sun was shining through the window, the light falling onto the bed set against the wall. A pile of covers lay in a heap on the floor, the figure lying on the mattress uncovered except for a nightshirt that had ridden up to the waist.

Simon lay on his back, his long legs showing white against the filthy bed sheet. His hands were clenched and tucked beneath his chin as if in supplication. He had vomited copiously, his face and pillow smeared with the aftermath. His lips were drawn back to show his blackened teeth and gums.

Daniel whimpered, screwing his eyes up in the hope that when he opened them, Simon would be alive. But nothing had changed when he dared look again, and he turned and fled from the room, keening loudly.

A few days before, William Sharpe, recovered from his bout of illness had, on his father's instruction, reluctantly left the house in London. His brother, Timothy, had advised him not to join him at the warehouse, and William had taken a day to decide where to go. He hadn't wanted to leave his father and mother, but felt better knowing that Simon would be there once he recovered to support them in his absence. After much thought, and with no need to remain in London, he decided to journey to Honiton to visit his sister, Elizabeth.

Unknown to him, and during his own illness, the twice-weekly coach trip to Honiton and back had stopped to avoid spreading the disease, which William found out when he made enquiries.

Fortunate to have no time commitments, and no shortage of money thanks to his father, the next day he bought a horse from a nearby stable and all the provisions necessary for his journey. Eager to be on his way, he climbed up onto his new, roan-coloured companion. With his bag tied to the pommel in front of him, he set off.

⁂

News of the typhus had reached Honiton only when what turned out to be the last coach arrived, though rumours had been swirling for some time. The driver told Master Beaker to let anyone enquiring know that he couldn't say when the coach would run again, but he hoped it would be soon.

With a wife and six children at home, he badly needed the money. He also had a mistress at one of the staging posts on the route, and had learned that she was to have a child. Cursing his bad luck even though he was solely responsible for his worries, he at times gave serious consideration to walking away from the lot of them.

Without the coach, William took a few days to reach Honiton, stopping when and for how long he liked. Nights were spent at inns along the way, wholesome, filling meals eaten at communal tables with fellow travellers or local people. He listened with delight to the various stories of local life, the hardships and highlights that shaped each character. During the day he followed roads and tracks at whim, wending his way through the countryside in the general direction of Honiton.

As he left each inn in the morning he asked the landlord for directions to his next place of lodging. With the last night on the road now behind him, he took the track described to him, easy to follow until he drew his horse, whom he had named Endeavour, to a halt.

The path meandered zigzagging down the side of the hill. A large wood lie ahead, the taller trees full of rooks' nests, the irritating cawing easily heard even from a distance. Endeavour shook his head as if advising William not to proceed, but William stroked his neck, calming him. Moving into a walk they started down the hill.

Now within a few hours reach of Honiton, William let his mind wander. How surprised Elizabeth will be to see me, and there's so much to tell her.

The closer they came to the woods, Endeavour became more and more jittery. Talking quietly, William reassured him that all was well, it was just a wood, and the noise was just the rooks – nothing to fear.

Into the wood, the trees stood tall, crowding out the light so it became darker the farther he progressed. William found his horse's nervousness was beginning to infect him too, and he looked around with concern as he felt the hair on the back of his neck lift. Unable to calm his own fear, he kicked Endeavour into a trot, which the horse took up willingly, as if he too would be glad to be out into the open again.

The trail was still easily discernible, beaten down by countless feet and carts. William kept telling himself that they would soon be out of the wood, and how glad he was to be alone so no one else could see his fear. Looking ahead, he thought he saw the gloom lightening and felt himself begin to relax. Now feeling safe, he slowed his horse and laughed out loud that he had overreacted.

The path had narrowed, just wide enough for a small cart and horse to pass. Ahead he could see the end of the wood and the countryside beyond, the light now able to penetrate fully. At the base of the trees the bushes were thick and heavy, some nearly six feet high, making it difficult to see far to the side. Trails of ivy snaked across the path, ready to trap an unwary foot or hoof.

Endeavour reared, and William found it difficult to keep his seat. His bag loosed from the pommel. Falling with a thud to the ground, some of the contents emptied into the dirt. It took a few moments to gain control of the horse, but slowly Endeavour calmed and William was able to dismount to retrieve his bag.

Re-packing the bag and tying it again to the saddle, making sure it was held with a strong knot, he sensed someone behind him. Turning, he saw a man, but before he could react, something hard hit his jaw and everything went black.

ᦧᦲᦧᦲ

The drizzle woke him, falling on his face and hands in a cold mist. Shivering, he lay on the ground amongst the leaves looking up at the canopy of trees. Unable to comprehend why he was here, he felt his aching jaw with probing fingers. Pushing himself up, he looked around. It was still light, so he hadn't been unconscious for long, he reasoned. He called Endeavour, but the only sound was the wind and the crows. The horse had gone, taken by whoever had attacked him. Rising carefully to his feet for his head spun, he walked unsteadily down the track and, thankfully, out of the wood.

Endeavour and his bag were gone with no sign anywhere. He gave thanks that he had kept his funds in his boot; at least the thief hadn't left him penniless as well.

ᦧᦲᦧᦲ

Jeffrey saw, with great relief, the beginnings of the town. Small hovels were now scattered along the side of the road. Children and chickens grovelled together in the dirt, both running in and out of the open front doors, despite the chill and damp. Wood smoke curled from chimneys, and he could smell cooking as the women prepared a meal for their families. Jeffrey found his mouth watering, but he dared not stop and ask for food. He didn't know how much farther he had to travel, and didn't want to spend another night in the open, especially in such chilly weather.

Faces appeared to look anxiously at this strange man who walked by, but he ignored them, keeping his eyes on the ground. When he reached the town proper, he saw the sign of Cross Keys, and thinking that here, at last, was somewhere he could comfortably lay his head, he walked in.

Taking a seat quickly by the large fire that sputtered and smoked with wet wood, he placed his bag at his feet. He ordered a tankard of ale and food from a young girl who came through from the kitchen. Master Beaker, on hearing an unfamiliar voice, came from his office.

'Good day,' he said in a friendly voice. 'Passing through?'

'I'll take a room for the night, if you have one,' replied Jeffrey, ignoring the question and not matching the easy tone. 'I'm on my way to Lady FitzGerald's estate. You know of it?'

The serving girl came through from the kitchen again, placing the ale in front of him then quickly scurrying back to get his food.

'I know of it, it's not far. You'll want to stable your horse for the night?'

'I have no horse.' Jeffrey drank the ale off quickly, smacking his lips as he put the tankard back on the table.

'No horse? How did you get here? The coach isn't running.'

'Walked. From Exeter.'

'I see.' The innkeeper now took more interest in the stranger. 'And you are on your way to Watermead, you say?'

Jeffrey looked at him through lowered lids. 'You said it wasn't far, how long will it take me to get there?'

'Walking? About an hour should do it, though I could rent you a horse to make it easier for you.'

'No, I will walk.' Jeffrey looked away, not wanting to answer any more questions. He certainly didn't want everyone in Honiton knowing of his troubles, and he knew full well how quickly gossip spread.

Master Beaker took the hint and returned to his office, though he sat in his chair with the thought that something was wrong, though what, he didn't know.

☙❧❦☙

Word of Philip's escape had reached the town, and a lot of the men had joined in the hunt, initially organized by the Watch. Lord Thomas had offered a reward of ten guineas for the man who could bring him in alive. He had stressed 'alive.' Ten guineas was a small fortune, and all who could, took up the challenge, telling their wives and families to expect them when they saw them. Stopping at home only to take a small sack of food with them, they gathered on High Street to decide which direction each would search, and full of hope, they started out.

They had been told Philip was on foot, and had neither warm clothing nor funds. They were each and every one of them, confident it was just a matter of time before they caught him. Some carried heavy sticks for defence. All carried large knives, and those who thought ahead carried thick rope. This would mean they could bind their prisoner when they caught him, which would make it easier to haul him back to Lord Thomas and his ultimate fate. And their reward.

But now, with night drawing in, one by one the searchers returned to their homes, despondent at not catching their prey immediately, but determined to set out again at first light.

≈≈*≈*

Jeffrey Browning, retiring early to a clean, soft comfortable feather bed, slept dreamlessly. He gave no thought as to how he would pay his bill, for why worry about things he could do nothing about? He was penniless, and he felt confident he could skulk out without paying. It just showed how frantic he was, for he had already forgotten he had told Master Beaker where he would be heading the next morning. He was ever a stupid man.

Chapter 38 ❧
Honiton

The rector had locked up for the night, his routine to go round the house checking each door and window in turn, for even the clergy weren't immune from those with criminal leanings.

Jane was already in bed, though it was just on nine o'clock, and Anne and Mary could be heard upstairs quarrelling. He shook his head. It was all they seemed to do. Nothing was ever right for them, and he suspected they would grow to be nags like their mother.

Elizabeth had disappeared upstairs even before her aunt, pleading a headache, though the rector suspected she needed to escape the perpetual arguing of her cousins. He could commiserate.

Entering his study, he closed the door on the domestic mayhem upstairs and placed the candlestick on the small table beside his chair. Taking up his book of devotions, and relishing the comparative quiet afforded by his private room, he settled in the chair by the fire and pulled a wrap round his shoulders against the night's chill.

Deep into his book he faintly heard the doorknocker, but it didn't sound loud enough to disturb his pleasure. Again it sounded, now louder, and much more insistent. Jane upstairs heard it, and thumped on the floor with the cane she kept by her bed in case of intruders. Feeling put upon, the rector sighed loudly and rose from his chair, taking the candle with him.

'Who is it? What do you want?' he called through the heavy oaken door.

'It's William, sir, your nephew. Elizabeth's brother.'

The rector released the bolts and turned the large key in the lock. Pulling the door open he peered out to find his nephew looking back at him, his face drawn.

'Come in, come in. Let me close the door against the rain.'

William gladly stepped inside, the rain puddling at his feet and onto the flagstones.

'What are you doing here, my boy?' asked the rector of a shivering William. 'Forgive me, you're cold and wet, come to the fire,' and he led the way to his study. 'Take a seat and warm yourself, I'll build up the fire.' The rector added another log, which flared quickly, then turned to William. 'You look terrible, what has brought you here in this state?'

William sat, hugging himself with cold. 'I was on my way to see Elizabeth but was attacked in a wood, and my horse stolen. It has taken me most of the day to walk here.'

'I'm sorry to hear of this. You must be exhausted, are you hurt? Are you in need of a physician? Shall I summon the Watch?' the rector asked with concern, making as if to head to the door for help. William told him he needed something to eat and to get warm, that it had just started to rain and he wasn't soaked through.

'Of course. I'll get you a plate and then tell Elizabeth you're here.' Leaving William to rest and warm himself before the now-growing fire, he took another candle from a shelf, lit it from the one on the table, and made his way to the kitchen in search of sustenance.

As he came through the hall, and on hearing a noise, he looked to the head of the stairs. Four frightened face looked back down at him.

'Who is it?' asked Jane tremulously, still brandishing the stick.

He ignored her, instead addressed Elizabeth directly. 'It's your brother, William. He has been attacked in the wood and has walked a long way. Come down and greet him while I get him food and drink.'

Elizabeth ran down the stairs, not caring that she was in her nightgown. She burst into the study, and rushed headlong into Williams' arms.

'Uncle said you had been attacked. Where are you hurt?' She pulled from his embrace, holding him at arm's length while she searched his face for sign of injury.

'I wasn't injured, except for a hefty wallop to my chin that knocked me senseless.' He touched his face.

Elizabeth's eyes following him and seeing a large bruise.

'Nothing else?'

'No. Unless you count the thief who stole my new stallion.'

'Stallion? The coaches are not running? Is there still disease in London?' Elizabeth's thoughts had gone immediately to her parents and brothers left behind.

'Yes. I was ill, though thankfully I am recovered. Timothy is taking care of the warehouse for Father, Mother is unwell and the maid fled in fear.'

'Dora has gone? Who is there to care for Mother, besides Father? Simon would be useless, he's so caught up in himself.' She looked at William, who stood in silence before her.

'Simon's not sick too, surely?'

'He was sickly when I left, but I'm sure he will recover, just as I have. Don't worry about him, Elizabeth; it will take more than the typhus to bring Simon down.' They both laughed at the thought of Simon confined to his bed and no one to tend him. How angry he would be.

The rector returned carrying a plate in one hand and tankard in the other, kicking at the door with his foot for entrance. Elizabeth opened it, and William sat down, eagerly devouring the food.

Aunt Jane and the girls appeared, and leaving William to take his fill, Elizabeth told them all she could of both his journey and the family. Aunt Jane held her face to her hands when she heard of her sister, Sarah.

The rector, completely out of patience with his family, said, 'Don't fret so, Jane, I'm sure she will recover like William. In the meantime he must stay here, for he can't return to London until the typhus has passed. And neither can Elizabeth.'

He looked around at his study, as if trying to decide the sleeping arrangements now there was one extra male, and a handsome one at that, in the house.

Anne and Mary stood behind their mother. Mary batted her eyelashes at William whenever he glanced her way, which he steadfastly pretended not to notice. Jane ushered them out of the door and back to their rooms, telling them they could speak more to their cousin in the morning, disappearing with them only to return shortly after with blankets and a pillow.

'Until we can sort ourselves out, you'll have to sleep here, William.' She looked at the rector, daring him to naysay her now that he was faced with the loss of his only sanctuary.

'It will just be for the one night, husband,' she assured him.

Leaving the men to sort themselves out, she waited for Elizabeth to say goodnight to William, and preceded her up the stairs and back to bed.

The rector said goodnight shortly after, leaving William to make himself as easy as possible on the hard floor. Blowing out the candle, William lay back against the pillow, unable to get comfortable. I am never going to be able to sleep like this, he thought, turning restlessly. The dying embers of the fire gave a small amount of light, but eventually the warmth, along with the events of the day, took their toll, and William slept.

༄༅༄

A knocking on the study door woke him. William rubbed his sleep-heavy eyes, uncertain of his surroundings, and watched the rector enter.

'How did you sleep, my boy?'

William struggled up to lean on one elbow. 'Surprisingly well, thank you. What time is it?' he asked, trying to collect himself.

'Seven o'clock. We take breakfast shortly; join us in the dining room when you're ready.' With a smile, the rector disappeared, closing the door quietly behind him.

William lay back again, stretching his arms and legs until they cracked. The fire had long since died, and all that was left was a heap of grey ash, but the room was still warm.

Stiffly he hauled himself to his feet and left the study in search of the privy. Washing his face and hands at the outside

Diane Keziah Robertson

hand pump, he smoothed his hair into some semblance of order and went to join the family for breakfast.

Chapter 39 ❧
London

James Morbeck, despite feeling he should return to Honiton to make sure his parents were well, was reluctant to leave London. While exams had been postponed, with the typhus at last loosening its grip on the city, he hoped they would be held soon.

With so few students at school it had been quiet, even at night, and James took advantage. Every available moment was spent in study, for nothing was as important as entering medical school. Once, when he had taken a break from his studies, he had walked outside for the first time since the contagion started, and seen the toll that it had taken on the inhabitants of the city. Unafraid of being infected, he found the streets were virtually empty; but as he walked along, children, dirty and half-starved, appeared as if from nowhere, begging him for alms. Behind them came adults holding out their hands for anything he could provide. But he had no help to give.

His father sent funds monthly on the coach, which were kept for him at the coach stop until he could collect them. With no coach transport between Honiton and London, James had found himself unable to pay for three meals a day. Reducing it to twice, then once a day, he purchased a small dinner, hoping it would help him to sleep without his stomach cramping.

Returning with relief to his room, he slumped on the bed. With his head in his hands he wept for those he had seen but to whom he could offer no relief. Praying that now, with the disease seemingly abating, life would soon return to normal, he hardly dared think of the consequences should the typhus reach Honiton.

Chapter 40 ❧
Rectory

Elizabeth ran downstairs in the morning to greet William, and found him already in the dining room seated next to their uncle. Giving her brother a kiss, and greeting the rector with a curtsey, she sat beside William demanding to know all the news from London.

Before he could reply, Anne and Mary came into the room. Mary looking sullen when she saw there was no chair beside her cousin. Realising she would be better able to see him if she sat opposite, she walked around the table only to have to push Anne out of the way, for she had the same thought. Immediately they began arguing, pushing and shoving at each other. Elizabeth looked at William as if to say, 'See what I have had to put up with?'

The rector, still annoyed at the loss of his study, shouted at them to be silent or to return to their rooms. Both girls sat down but continued to glare at each other, and at Elizabeth, as if she were to blame.

Aunt Jane was still abed suffering from a headache brought on by worry for her sister. Elizabeth breathed a sigh of relief that William wouldn't have to listen to her irritating whining, for now at least.

'You must speak to the Watch this morning to tell him about the loss of your horse and possessions, but I don't hold out much hope they will be found,' said the rector glumly.

'I could accompany you,' said Anne, looking at William from beneath her lashes.

Her father answered immediately. 'No you couldn't. William doesn't want a silly girl trailing along behind him while he's on important business.' He turned to William. 'Would you like me to come along? I have to speak to him myself on a parish matter and planned to go this morning.'

'Thank you, yes,' replied William.

The kitchen girl came in with the leftover meats from last night, placing it on the table along with bread and cheese. Waiting while the rector said a prayer of thanks for the food, she left the family to eat, returning to the kitchen to sit next to the fire to break her own fast in blessed peace and quiet.

༄ེ༅ེ

William walked beside his uncle down the hill, breathing thankfully the clear air, looking round with interest at sights never seen before. Everyone looked prosperous, all were well dressed and none looked in need of a good meal, unlike those in London.

How had Honiton escaped the typhus? What was different between the two places? Here the streets were wide, and while there were still the central runnels for waste he was used to, the houses and shops were well away from them. In London, the buildings were cheek by jowl, the second floors overhanging the lower, blocking out the daylight. In London it was common to see rats running in the streets, foraging for food; but here, he realised, there were none, or rather any that he could see. Could this be the reason? Could the typhus be spread by rats? Or was the clean air and plentiful food the difference?

Although he had recovered from his illness, the long walk exhausted him. He must have slept well, for he couldn't remember waking up at all during the night, but he still felt weary clear through to his bones. He stopped and turned to look back up the hill. He wasn't looking forward to making his way back up.

They found the Watch standing talking outside the door of the inn, and the rector stood to one side, waiting for him to finish his business. The Watch noticed him and nodded in recognition, then looked at William. After a few moments, his conversation with the other fellow finished, he turned to them both.

'Rector, good morning.'

'Good morning to you, John. My nephew here needs to speak to you. William, this is John Hopkins, the town Watch.'

'Good morning, lad,' said the Watch. He was a tall, thin man, about thirty and five years. His eyes were alert, moving all the time, and William had the impression he was taking in all that happened around them, missing nothing.

'I arrived last night, too late to speak to you, but I was attacked on the road here. Just one man, I believe, for I saw only one. He stole my new stallion and my bag, and I particularly want to get my horse back.'

'Where did this happen?' ask John. 'I've not heard of any trouble for some time. Did you get a look at him?' As he spoke, he suddenly had a thought, but decided to hear William' first.

'I was coming through a wood, a good two hours walk away. Something caused my horse to rear and the bag fell. When I got down to retrieve it, that's when I was set upon. I've no doubt it was a man, he hit me hard enough to knock me out. When I came to, both the horse and bag were gone.'

The Watch turned to the rector. 'I bet I know who is responsible for this. You've of course heard of Lady FitzGerald's godson, Philip Goldworthy?' The rector nodded, realization dawning.

'I bet it was him,' continued the Watch. 'We know he was on foot when he fled Watermead with only the clothes and boots he escaped in. To find your horse and bag with fresh clothes would be a godsend to him.'

He turned back to William. 'You won't have heard, but we have a thief on the loose, and most of the town's men are already out hunting him down, though they believe him to be on foot. If he's got your horse, he could be miles away by now. I'll have to let the searchers know they are probably wasting their time.'

He looked at the rector, shaking his head. 'They'll be greatly disappointed. Lord Thomas had a ten guinea reward for the man who brought him in. But you'll excuse me, I need to spread the news and send a rider to Watermead to inform his lordship. But before I go, give me a description of the horse, along with your bag and what was in it, we will need that information too.'

William complied with as much detail as possible, then he and the rector bade farewell to the Watch as he strode off to give the bad news to the searchers.

The rector looked at William. 'Well, that's not good news. If it's true, he'll be desperate now, and the likelihood of you getting your horse and goods back can't be very high. I didn't get a chance to speak to the Watch of my matter, and I must go after him. You'll find your way back?'

'Yes, Uncle, I'll have no problem. I'll look for the church.' The rector laughed, quickly following the Watch who was rapidly disappearing round a corner.

William liked the look of Honiton. Most of the shops and houses were of wood, a few of stone, but all looked well cared for. Deciding not to return immediately to a house full of arguing women, not counting Elizabeth, he took advantage of his freedom and wandered down a side lane, coming upon the sign stating that the attached building was Peter Brigginshaw's joinery. As he approached the door opened, and down the steps came a young man who walked with the aid of two sticks.

'Good morning,' said the man, moving the sticks into one hand to enable him to close the door.

'Good morning,' replied William.

'I haven't seen you in Honiton before?'

'No, I only arrived last night. I'm staying with my uncle, the rector.'

Realisation dawned with Peter, noticing the Sharpe family likeness. 'Are you by chance related to Mistress Sharpe?' he asked.

'Elizabeth? Indeed I am, for she's my sister.'

Peter, now down the steps, took more notice of the tall, well-built young man before him.

'And you've come from London. I hear there is disease there, though hopefully it is now abating.'

'It is, and the reason for my coming to Honiton. I've recently recovered, thanks be to God. My father wanted me to be away from town.'

'I'm glad you're better, and that your sister is safe here. How long will you be staying?'

'I've no definite plans. I wanted to make sure Elizabeth was well.With the coaches not running we haven't had word of her. I had to let her know that our mother and brother are now ill.'

'I'm sorry to hear of it, I hope they also recover.'

They stood before the shop, both seemingly reluctant to move.

William looked at the sign over the door. 'Are you Peter Brigginshaw?'

'That I am. Forgive me, Peter Brigginshaw at your service.' He removed his hat and gave a small bow.

'William Sharpe at your service, Master Brigginshaw.' William looked at the shop. 'I saw your sign from High Street, and was interested in a look inside.'

'I would be delighted, but forgive me; I have an appointment I must keep.' Peter indicated his sticks. 'It takes awhile for me to make my way, so I must leave immediately, but please look around.'

William hesitated. He liked the look of this man and wanted to look inside, but also wanted Peter there when he did so.

He smiled. 'Thank you, but I'll wait until another time when you are available.'

'I should only be about an hour; shall we meet here at that time?'

'I'll look forward to it.' They walked together to High Street, parting ways there.

William, now with time to kill until he met Peter again, wandered down the street coming to Cross Keys. Chilled by the wind, he entered the inn in search of a warming drink. Once inside, he was met by the raised voices of angry men venting their anger. William followed the noise down the passageway, pushing his way into a large room.

One man, blocked from sight by those in front of William, stood at the back of the room. He was obviously trying to make himself heard, but the men, who all had tankards in their hands, weren't in the mood to listen. Twice the man tried to quiet the crowd, and then decided to wait them out. It didn't take long.

'I've told you,' said the man, 'it's not my fault. He stole a horse and could be anywhere by now.' The crowd muttered.

'I know his lordship offered a reward and you can still claim it, but you have to catch him first.' The crowd grew restive once more. How could they catch him if he had a horse? And where were they to start looking?

William raised his hand and the Watch caught the movement over all the heads.

'Now quiet everyone, there's someone who wants to speak,' he shouted, grateful to have the attention away from himself. The noise slowly stopped, and the men looked around them for the one who had something to say.

William forced his way through the tired, dirty and stinking men who had obviously spent time searching for the thief. He stood next to the Watch and addressed the room.

'My name is William Sharpe and it's my horse he stole.'

The men glanced at each other, unsure if they should feel sorry for the loss of the animal or angry that it was his horse that enabled a thief to escape, thus depriving them of the ten guinea reward.

William, thankfully, said the right thing. 'No one is sorrier than I that he stole my horse, especially since I heard there is a substantial reward out on him.' The men nodded agreement. 'But there's nothing to be done about that now. He gave me a hefty wallop, too. I want him caught, so I can return the favour.' He rubbed his chin.

The men laughed, some raising their tankards in agreement. The Watch noticed the atmosphere calming, the crowd no longer out for blood, and his blood at that.

A large brute of a man spoke up, though he was difficult to understand with not a tooth in his head. 'So what do we do? That reward would have meant the difference of a long winter and a comfortable winter for some of us.' All turned to look at William as if expecting him to work a miracle.

'I can show you where I was when he set upon me and perhaps you could follow his tracks. Does anyone have a better idea?' he asked, looking around at the honest, weather-beaten faces. None had.

The Watch joined the conversation. 'So, it's a place to start.' He turned to William. 'It will take awhile for the men to get their horses and carts together, as some live out of town. Can we meet back here in, say, two hours? We will still have a lot of daylight left.' All turned to William for his answer.

'Yes, two hours from now,' he repeated. The Watch stood beside William as the men quickly finishing their ale, headed out of the room.

'Thank you for that, Master Sharpe, the men were turning ugly. I had told them the thief had a horse when you came in, and I'm grateful for your help. They are right, the reward would have made a difference to their winter.'

'Well, it still might. I can show them where I was attacked and we can pick up the tracks.'

The two men parted company, William to return to Peter Brigginshaw's, the Watch to collect his horse from the stable and ready for the hunt.

⊱⊰⊱⊰

Elizabeth couldn't bear it any longer. She needed to speak to William and was determined not to wait until his return. Pulling her wrap round her shoulders, she found her aunt in the kitchen.

'Aunt, I'm going into town to find William. I don't think he told us all he knew about Mother and Simon and I'm anxious for news.'

Aunt Jane straightened up from ladling water into the pot over the fire.

'But there's work to be done, Elizabeth. You can't leave when you feel like it.'

'On the contrary, Aunt Jane, I can. I'm not a maid. Mother and Father are paying you a guinea a month for my keep, which to my mind, makes me a paying guest. So I shall leave when I feel like it.'

'But the work,' began Jane again, feeling she was losing control of the girl as well as the conversation.

'Mary and Anne can do it. It's time they did something other than argue with each other.'

Jane stood, her mouth open, speechless.

Elizabeth took advantage of the silence and almost ran to the front door, rushing through it before Jane came to her senses.

With no idea where to find her brother, Elizabeth walked up and down High Street, peering into shop windows as she passed. Almost at the bottom, she saw a welcome figure coming towards her. It was Peter.

'Mistress Sharpe, this is a pleasant meeting.'

'Indeed it is. I'm looking for my brother, but you won't know of him.'

'But I would. He and I spoke earlier, and we have arranged to meet at my shop shortly. Why not come with me and meet him there.'

Elizabeth was thrilled. Not only would she be able to spend time with Peter, but also she would find William. She happily fell into step with Peter.

As they turned into the lane, it was to see William disappearing into the shop, and each heard the jangling bell sound above the door. Elizabeth was in no hurry, and Peter couldn't walk quickly, so when they did arrive, they found William talking to one of the young apprentices.

Master Chapman, Peter's former master, rarely came into the shop. Older now, his mind was beginning to wander, mixing up customers and orders. He was also becoming deaf, so when Peter was out, one of the two apprentices came through from the workroom should a customer appear. At the sound of the bell, William turned.

'Elizabeth, what are you doing here?'

'I came to find you and met Peter on my way. He told me you had arranged to meet here, so, here I am.' She looked between the two men, smiling happily, the apprentice having disappeared when Peter came in.

William spoke to Peter. 'I can't stop long, I fear. I am to show the Hue and Cry where I was attacked in the woods. We hope to be able to follow Endeavour's tracks.'

Peter looked blank.

'Endeavour is my horse. I had only had him a short while, but he's a beautiful and very biddable. And I want him back.'

'I can understand that,' replied Peter. 'But will you be able to find the spot in the woods? It would all look the same, surely?'

'I'm certain I can, for I told the men at the inn I could and none seem the type to take fools gladly.'

'Do you have another horse?' enquired Elizabeth.

'No, but some are bringing horses and carts, I can ride with one of them.' William spoke with more confidence than he felt. He didn't want to think what would happen if, firstly, he couldn't find the spot in the woods, and secondly, if they couldn't follow the tracks.

'You have enough to do,' said Peter. 'Come back when you have more time, I will gladly show you around then.' He realised he sounded curt. 'Forgive me, William. There is so much to do and I find myself overwhelmed at present. To add to everything, I am having a new shop built, and it seems my presence is ever in demand there as well as here.' He waved his hand around, a worried look on his face.

'Can I help you?' asked William. 'I'm a good organizer and good with figures. Elizabeth can tell you.' He looked to his sister, eager for confirmation.

'Indeed you are, William; Father relies on you.'

'Let's talk more when you have been out with the Hue and Cry, William. I must admit I need the help, but if you are only here for a short while, I'm not sure what you can do.'

William interrupted him. 'As I said, I have no immediate plans to return to London.'

Elizabeth looked at her brother with a silent question in her eyes. But she was not to get an answer this day.

Chapter 41 ⚭
Honiton

Blissfully unaware of the trouble swirling round his quarry, Jeffrey Browning spent a trouble-free night, waking at seven o'clock to the sound of the church bells. Breakfasting well, he returned to his room to collect his coat and hat, only stopping by the landlord's office to tell him he would require the room for another night.

Master Beaker, still smarting from the sharp answers he had received the day before, merely nodded his agreement. He gave no thought to telling the lodger of the identity of the thief. Indeed, all talk was of the thief, but his name never said aloud, as if the mere mention of his name would bring shame on Lady FitzGerald. Later, when he found out that the visit to Watermead was to confront Philip Goldworthy, he didn't regret his omission. Master Beaker was a firm believer in the old adage that you reap what you sow.

The day was fine; the temperature moderate as if autumn was taking a break and returned to late summer. Jeffrey asked directions to Watermead and with a thankful heart that his journey was almost at an end, set out once more.

The estate proved easy to find; turning through the stone gates and up the driveway that led to the house, he found his step lightening and his thoughts becoming more optimistic.

He had no doubt Philip would have seen the error of his ways and would be only too eager to return Nan's plate to Jeffrey's safekeeping. It wouldn't be long now before he was back in Nan's good books.

The house, when it came into view behind a large stand of oak and alder, proved impressive. Far bigger than he had envisioned, Jeffrey gave a small laugh. This will be easy. The fool won't want anyone here knowing of his theft, he will be only too eager to give me the plate to ensure my silence.

At Jeffrey's knocking, the doors were opened by the butler. As he demanded to speak to Philip Goldworthy, he watched the butler's face change from a normal, healthy colour to ashen grey.

'Your name, sir?' he asked.

'Master Jeffrey Browning. I know he's here, and I'm prepared to wait for as long as it takes.' He stood, legs spread as if determined to take root if necessary. The butler didn't ask him to enter, telling him to wait on the step. The doors were closed.

After what seemed an age, he heard footsteps approaching, accompanied by male voices. The doors opened once more, revealing the butler and another man.

Without preamble, the other man spoke. 'You wish to speak to Master Goldworthy, I understand.'

Jeffrey, faintly aware that things were not going as planned, spoke up. 'I do. And I'm not leaving until I do.' He thrust his chin out belligerently, daring the other to argue.

'Well, you've a long wait, for he's not here.'

Before Jeffrey could protest, the man spoke again in a cold, cutting tone. 'Might I ask, sir, how you know of Master Goldworthy?'

Jeffrey hesitated. He hadn't anticipated this. He thought Philip would be produced upon demand. 'Well,' he stuttered, 'I met him recently in Exeter, and we have some business together.' Then after a short pause, he added, 'Unfinished business.'

'As I said, he's not here. I don't anticipate him coming back, so your business will have to remain unfinished.'

Jeffrey was furious. 'What is this? I know he's here. I was told he was Lady FitzGerald's godson and this is her estate. I demand to see him, sir.' He made as if to push his way in, but the butler quickly moved in front of the other man and from nowhere two footmen appeared, looming large and threatening in the background.

'I have told you, he's not here, nor likely to be. I suggest you look elsewhere,' repeated the man.

'And who are you to tell me what to expect or not?' asked Jeffrey, his face growing red with pent-up frustration and anger.

'I, sir, am Lord Thomas Stanton. Lady FitzGerald is my aunt. I have every right to tell you what to expect where Philip is concerned.' Thomas turned away, then stopped, turning back to face Jeffrey. 'And if by chance you do find Master Goldworthy, tell him that if he darkens these doors again, he will be fortunate if all I do is set the dogs on him.'

The butler closed the door with a firm hand and Jeffrey heard the bolts being shot. He stood, facing the wood, no further forward than when he left Exeter what seemed like a lifetime ago. Damn the man. Now what do I do?

He couldn't return to Exeter without the plate, and even then he doubted if Nan would allow him back into the house if he were honest with himself. He couldn't return to London in case his debts there caught up with him, and having left without paying his rent, had nowhere to live even if he did. What do I do? Where can I go?

The long walk back to Honiton now faced him. He had no choice but to return there to collect his bag. He had no money to pay the landlord for the night's lodging, and he cursed telling the landlord he would require the room for another night.

Chapter 42 ✒
London

The typhus left London almost as quickly as it arrived. Timothy, who was still struggling to keep the warehouse going and keep in touch with his father, was at his wits end. He had sent message after message to the house, but none had been answered. One boy who had been paid to deliver the note had the sense to come back to tell him there was no answer to his knocking. He had slipped the note under the door, but that's all he could do. Timothy knew this to be true, and thanked the boy for at least letting him know, giving him an extra farthing for his trouble.

That night when the workmen had gone home, he sat on a box, the candle in its holder guttering beside him. If there was no answer, that could only mean one thing, all were dead; Mother, Father, Simon and William. Unaware that William had been sent out of town, he thought his entire family, but for Elizabeth, was gone.

All through the contagion he had been strong, keeping the business running, dealing with the moneylenders, paying the men, dealing with the customers that remained. But the thought that all were dead was too much. Alone, cold and hungry, Timothy, his arms on his knees, his head in his hands, sobbed. Long into the night, the candle dead, he listened to the skittering of the rats as they looked in vain for food.

Timothy lay on the pile of rags and blankets he had fashioned into a bed and cried as if he would never stop.

The next morning, waking up with a terrible headache, he left a note on the door for the workmen that he would return shortly and set off for home.

Using his key to enter, he found the note the boy had said was slipped under the door. The air was stale and cold. When he had last been here there were voices, the noises of everyday life. Now, only silence greeted him. He made his way to his father's study, pushing open the door and peering inside. The shutters were over the window, and he opened them, letting in the weak sunshine. Displayed prominently on the desk, propped against the inkstand, was a piece of paper, and written in his father's scrawled writing on the front the words 'To whoever finds this.'

Taking it to the window, Timothy sat on the window seat and read the contents.

We are all dead or dying. Sarah, Simon, both have been taken for burial, though I didn't enquire where, and I have little time left. I sent William away. He left for Honiton to tell Elizabeth we are ill. I knew we were dying. I hope Timothy has survived, for he can carry on in the business. When the typhus is passed, custom will improve again. Whoever finds this, tell Timothy, William and Elizabeth that I love them.

All I leave must be shared equally between those who survive. I hope they use it wisely.

Timothy let the letter fall to the floor as he sat in the window in the sad, empty house.

Later, but no idea how much later, he picked up the letter again. If Mother and Simon were taken away, where was Father? Not still in the house, surely?

There was no alternative. His breathing quickened as he moved from room to room, though each proved empty. He had deliberately left his parents' room until last, reasoning that his father had died in his bed and not wanting to find him there. When he did summon the courage to open the door, it was to find the bedroom as empty of life as the others.

Timothy walked to the window, looking down at the small garden to the rear. There was his father's body, lying in the mud, sprawled on its back wearing a nightshirt. His long hair had fallen over the ravaged face, making the remains seem even more grotesque. Without warning, Timothy vomited onto the floor, though with an empty stomach it was clear bile.

Wiping his mouth and chin on his sleeve, he went down the stairs and out the front door. Standing by the front gate he called desperately for help. Any help. 'Someone, please help me!'

James Morbeck, returning to school from attending church, heard cries of grief and altered his course to see if he could help. The cries grew louder, more frantic, begging. As he turned the corner, it was to see a crowd gathering outside a large house, more people pushing past him to find out what was amiss.

Rain had started to fall; James pulled his coat collar up as he joined an elderly man standing off to the side of the crowd.

'What's wrong?' James asked.

The man, huddled inside an old worn coat, turned to him. 'Seems this young lad has just found someone dead in the house; must have died from the typhus.' He crossed himself as he spoke, and James found himself doing the same, though he wasn't Catholic.

'I'm sorry to hear of it. Does he have family who can help?'

The man snorted at James' ignorance. 'Obviously not, or he would not call for help, would he?' He spat; the disgusting glob just missing James' foot.

'No, perhaps not,' agreed James. Leaving the old man, he pushed himself to the front of the crowd, only then seeing a young lad about the same age as himself, who leaned with both hands on the gate as he gasped for breath. None around him appeared to be of help, for all stood there watching his misery through dull eyes.

So many had died in London from the plague that James could fully understand, if not condone, their indifference. With death such an everyday occurrence even without the typhus, all who were left were only concerned on their own survival, Timothy's pain only of interest as a change from their own.

'What help can I give?' he asked, touching Timothy on the shoulder to get his attention.

'My father, he's, he's–,' but Timothy couldn't finish the sentence, looking at James for help.

'Your father is what? Is he dead?'

Timothy nodded mutely as the tears poured down his face.

'Show me,' said James firmly as he opened the gate and guided Timothy back inside the house. As he turned to close the door behind them both, he saw the crowd was already starting to move off, the spectacle over.

He introduced himself. 'I am James Morbeck, sir. Where is your father?'

'He's at the back of the house, in the garden.' Timothy, now that someone was helping, had stopped weeping and stood straighter. 'My name is Timothy Sharpe, and I thank you for your help.'

He led the way through the passageway and down the three steps into the small kitchen. James put his hand to his nose to mask the smell of rotting food as they passed through; taking a deep breath of air once they were outside.

He didn't need Timothy to show him where his father lay. The nightshirt stood out starkly against the muddy earth, the thin pale legs sticking out from beneath it, toes with long yellow nails pointing skywards.

'Stay here, Timothy.' James approached the corpse, though not getting too close. It was obvious he had died of the contagion and all to be done was to call the death cart.

'I'm sorry, but he is dead.'

'I know. They are all dead.'

'Your family?'

'Mother, Simon, now Father. All dead. I thought William was too, but he's gone to tell Elizabeth. Father left a note that I found in the study.' Suddenly he began to shake violently, and James rushed to his side, fearful he would collapse.

'Come back inside, Timothy. Sit down, I'll find you a drink.' But once inside, there was no drink, only rotting food.

'You can't stay here. Come with me, we will lock the house and I will call the death cart. You can stay the night with me. .

Your father must be buried as quickly as possible.' He wondered how to say the next part, but truth had to be told, no disguising the ugly part of it.

'You won't have a choice, I'm afraid, where he will be taken. With so many dead already–.' He had no need to finish

Timothy nodded, now in control. 'I understand. Thank you.' He stopped by the study to retrieve the note, effectively a Last Will and Testament, for he would need it for the solicitors. Without glancing back, he followed James out of the front door, locking it behind them. Grateful beyond words that someone had taken control, he walked beside James, not noticing where he was going.

He gave not a thought to the warehouse and the men who would be waiting for him there.

Chapter 43 ❧
Honiton

Elizabeth, now that she didn't fear telling her aunt she would come and go as she chose, made a point of walking into town every morning. Hurrying past the bookshop, lest she catch Edward Catchpole's eye, she wasn't concentrating on her surroundings. Only at the last moment did she hear the sound of the horn, stepping back barely in time to avoid being run over by the coach as it sped past to pull up before Cross Keys.

Master Beaker immediately came out the door to greet the passengers, and Elizabeth found herself walking nearer to see who had arrived.

'Welcome,' said the landlord, addressing the coachman. 'How was the journey, John?'

'Good. It's a relief to be back on the road again,' came the reply as John climbed down from his seat. The lads from the stables were already unhitching the horses, to be led away to well-earned oats and rest.

Elizabeth ran forward. 'Are you come from London?' she asked excitedly.

'That we are, and glad to be in work once more,' laughed the driver as he helped the first of the passengers down the narrow coach steps.

Elizabeth clapped her hands with joy, for now her letters could continue to Agnes, and she could write to her parents to ask if she may return.

'So the typhus, it's finished?' she asked excitedly.

'More or less for now,' replied the horn-blower cynically as he stood on the roof of the coach, ready to throw down the bags to the waiting passengers.

Elizabeth ran back to the rectory, eager to tell William of the news. Now they could both return, and they would be a family once more. Then she remembered Simon's warning that he would be waiting for her, and despite the warm sunshine, she shivered.

A few days later, William and Elizabeth went into town. William wished to speak to Peter Brigginshaw with respect to his suggestion that William join his company. Overnight, while tossing and turning, he had thought long and hard of the prospect of remaining in Honiton.

Timothy was caring for the winery until his father could take control again. Besides, William had no wish to toil amongst wine barrels. Even as a child he had hated the London docks, whereas Timothy had found it fascinating and invigorating. Simon had felt the same way as William, avoiding visiting the warehouse at all costs. Simon's idea of enjoyment was spending time in the local alehouses with his friends and chasing the serving girls into almost-willing submission.

The more thought he gave, the more he became enamoured with the idea of working for Peter. He wasn't particular of the terms of his employment, so long as it entailed staying in the town. He had only been in the county for a short time, but already had found it a pleasant, gentle landscape. All those he had met had been friendly, and had obviously taken well to Elizabeth.

Leaving the rectory they had arrived at the shop to find it still closed, the door locked and darkness within.

'Let's just walk for a bit,' suggested Elizabeth. 'It is so nice to get away from Aunt Jane and the wretched girls that I don't want to waste a moment.'

William laughed as they headed back to High Street. 'Yes, they are annoying. I feel sorry for our uncle living with so many women.'

Elizabeth playfully smacked his arm. 'Hey,' she said, joining in his laughter.

'I'm not including you in my criticism, Elizabeth, though how our uncle puts up with them all is beyond me.'

They had reached the end of the lane-way where Peter's shop lay. Looking down the hill, they saw horses being led out of the stables, harnessed and ready for the coach, which must be due shortly.

'Let's wait for a few minutes,' said William. 'It looks as if the London coach is due, and perhaps there's a letter from Father.' Brother and sister slowly walked in the direction of Cross Keys, enjoying watching the stable lads control the large, powerful horses with ease.

While waiting, Elizabeth was aware of mutterings coming from behind a clutch of young saplings that grew beside the inn. Leaving William, she wandered towards the sound. There, on the ground, sat the old woman Elizabeth had seen on her arrival. Dirty and dishevelled from head to toe, she was digging in the dirt with her bare hands, but the ground was so hard she was hardly making any progress. While watching, Elizabeth wondered what the woman was digging for and why in that spot? Surely even the roots of young trees would be impossible to dig through with bare hands. The woman raised her head and saw she was being watched.

'What yer looking at?' she shouted. 'Get away, this is mine, all mine.'

Elizabeth didn't answer, just gave a small smile in return, but the woman raised a dirty fist and shook it at her, shouting obscenities. Returning to stand with William, she told him what she had seen.

'Digging? For what?' he asked.

'I don't know, and it seems such a peculiar place to dig.'

It wasn't long before they heard the horn, and stood still as they watched the coach come around the corner, drawing to a halt before the inn door. Master Beaker appeared and looked around. On spying Elizabeth, he raised his hand in greeting, and then turned his attention to the arriving passengers, hoping for custom.

William and Elizabeth waited until the passengers had emerged, found their bags, and left for their various destinations either alone or with friends who had met the coach. None stopped at the inn for breakfast, preferring to be on their way.

William approached the driver. 'Do you have any letters from London?' he asked politely.

'That I do, I have three.' He rummaged in various coat pockets, eventually pulling the crumbled missives into the open.

'Anything for Elizabeth or William Sharpe?' asked William hopefully.

The driver made a great show of peering at each piece of paper while they waited impatiently. 'Yes, there's one.' He handed over a folded sheet with a red seal, and three words written on the front of it.

'Elizabeth Sharpe. Honiton'

Taking the letter eagerly, Elizabeth tore it open, William standing behind her, reading over her shoulder. It was from Timothy.

It told of the death of their parents and of Simon. It spoke of Timothy's pain and of James Morbeck's assistance at such a dire time, and that Timothy was keeping the wine business going, if barely.

It spoke of brother and sister not returning until all trace of the typhus had gone from London, and of their father's deathbed note instructing all his possessions to be shared amongst his surviving children.

Elizabeth and William read all this in horror, hardly able to comprehend its import and the change in their lives the typhus had brought. William looked at Elizabeth's ashen face, and fearing she was about to faint, held her elbow tightly, ushering her into the inn and leading her to a chair. Calling for ale, he sat his sister down at the nearest table, taking a seat next to her.

Both stared numbly at the table top, noticing as if it were of great importance the scarred and shiny surface of the wood, keeping at bay for a short while longer their worst nightmare.

Master Beaker, alerted by the serving girl of the two customers who looked devastated, came into the eating room. He knew Elizabeth and introduced himself to William. He noticed immediately their dull and shocked eyes, the pallor of their faces and the automatic replies to his greeting.

199

Without asking, he sat across from William. 'What is it, lad?' he asked gently.

William numbly handed over the slip of paper that had changed their lives forever. As he read, Master Beaker looked up, searching their faces once more, seeing abject grief.

'There's nought I can say, except I am truly sorry to read of this.' He paused, looking at William with a worried expression. 'Does the rector know?'

'We have only just received the letter from the coach driver,' replied William, turning to look at the departing horses. 'No one else knows.' He looked then with concern at Elizabeth, who if possible, seemed even paler.

'We had best get back to the rectory, Elizabeth. Aunt Jane will need to be told.' Elizabeth didn't answer, seemingly not hearing.

'I don't think Elizabeth should walk up the hill after receiving this news,' said the kindly landlord. 'I'll get the cart and take you myself.' With only a grateful nod from William, Master Beaker went to hitch up the horse to the inn cart.

William took Elizabeth's hand, which felt clammy and cold, then drew her into his arms. 'Come now, we will manage, Elizabeth.'

She looked up at him, tears brimming. 'But how? Timothy says not to go home yet, and we can't stay with Aunt Jane forever.' She looked over William's shoulder with dull, pain-filled eyes. 'What's to become of us, William?' she asked in a whisper.

But he couldn't answer, for he didn't know.

Master Beaker dropped brother and sister off outside the rectory, telling them that if he could be of any more assistance, they should send word. He watched them enter through the door, and then turned the horse and cart away.

In Honiton, death was a common occurrence, and he thought that by now he should be hardened to its visitation, but he found himself this time sad at the lives the two would now have before them. Like everyone, Master Beaker had had his share of loss. His own parents, his younger sister, were all taken before their time. His late wife, too, had died along with their babe, in torturous childbirth. So why had this news unsettled him so? He hadn't was different. She was certainly different from the rector's known the dead, he should have been able to give his sympathies and carry on untouched. But he couldn't.

He thought it was because he had grown to like Elizabeth, though he had only seen her when she came to deliver or collect mail from the coach. There was something about her that two spoiled brats. Although new to the town, all he spoke to had only good things to say of her, so he knew he wasn't in the minority.

'There is something different about Elizabeth Sharpe.'

'What did you say?' asked a voice beside him.

With a start, Master Beaker realised he had spoken aloud and that Ben Weaver was standing with a smiling face at the side of the cart. He was carrying a bag with him.

'Were you talking to me?'

'Yes, Master Beaker, I was. But by the looks of it you were far away.'

'You're right there. It's a chilly morning, Ben.' Both looked up at the heavy, overcast sky.

'Looks like rain, too.' Ben shook himself as if it had been he who had been dreaming. 'Well, best get on. I hear the coach is running again from London.'

'Yes, so more custom for the inn, thank goodness. Times are hard enough as it is without the lack of custom.'

Both men nodded farewell, Master Beaker clicking at the horse to get it moving and Ben continuing on his way to his mother-in-law's house to deliver food his wife had prepared.

Elizabeth and William entered the rectory to the usual hubbub of noise. Aunt Jane was obviously in the kitchen giving instructions to the kitchen girl, while Anne and Mary were upstairs arguing. Of the rector there was no sign.

Elizabeth removed her bonnet and wrap, laying them on the bottom stair. She looked at William with a silent, 'Shall I tell them or will you?'

With a short nod, William led the way to the kitchen. Upon opening the door, they saw before them the kitchen girl sitting at the long wooden table, her apron held to her face while she sobbed as if her heart would break. Over her stood Aunt Jane, pieces of a broken platter in her hands.

'And how do you intend to pay for this, you stupid girl?' she shouted. 'This was my best platter that was left me by my mother. What do you intend to do about it?'

The girl sobbed even more loudly, not taking her face from her apron as if not seeing the broken pieces would make them go away.

'I'm sorry, mistress, it was an accident. It slipped through my fingers,' she cried.

'You stupid girl,' replied Aunt Jane, and gave the girl a hefty clip round her head, which only drew louder cries.

Into the noise, William spoke.

'Aunt Jane, Elizabeth and I need to speak to you, please.'

Jane looked at them, and they saw her face was a vivid hue, her eyes angry, mouth pursed. 'Can't it wait; can't you see I'm busy?'

'No, it can't wait. We will await you in the parlour,' replied William. He took hold of Elizabeth's elbow, gently easing her out the door and along the passageway to the front of the house.

Elizabeth sat on a chair by the window. William stood to the side of the fireplace which, at this time of day, nearly noon, was laid but unlit. Neither spoke.

Some five minutes later Aunt Jane entered. Her face was still flushed, anger clear on her face. She didn't take a seat, stood facing William with an impatient air. 'What is so important that it that couldn't wait, William?' she demanded.

'The coach is running again from London.' He looked at Elizabeth, at her pale, pinched face. 'We have received a letter from our brother, Timothy. I'm sorry to tell you, Aunt Jane, but Mother has died of the typhus.' He stopped, suddenly finding his throat constricting, unable to continue.

Jane looked from one to the other. 'What is this you're telling me? My sister is dead? It cannot be, for she was just here bringing Elizabeth.'

'I'm sorry, but it is true. Timothy wouldn't lie, nor has he reason to. Not only Mother, but Father and Simon also have died.'

'No, there must be some mistake.' She turned to Elizabeth. 'This is your doing. You put William up to this so you could return to London. Haven't I done all I could for you? Haven't I cared for you these past months? Haven't you been pampered and spoiled enough?'

Elizabeth looked at her aunt as if she had gone mad. 'Spoiled? Pampered? On the contrary, I have worked hard since I have been here. The only two who have been spoiled are Anne and Mary.'

Aunt Jane flopped down in a chair, a hand to her mouth, tears spilling from her eyes. 'And after all I've done for you; you have the temerity to criticize your cousins. How could you!'

Elizabeth rose and went to her aunt. Kneeling before her, she put her hand on Aunt Jane's, which was clenched in her lap.

'I'm sorry, Aunt. Let's not argue at such a time. Our mother,' she nodded at William, 'your sister, is dead. Can't we come together in our grief?'

Aunt Jane reached out for her, holding Elizabeth tightly, while both cried heartily. William, decided it was best to leave the two women and went in search of the rector. He found him in the church.

Upon hearing the news, the rector fell to his knees in front of the altar, William joining him.

Later, the rector said, 'I had best return to Jane and Elizabeth, they will need comfort.'

As William walked the short distance between the church and the rectory, he thought of what was to come for him and Elizabeth.

Timothy had told them not to return to London yet; he would send word when it was safe to do so. He couldn't continue to stay at the rectory. Nor could he continue to sleep in the rector's study. His thoughts turned to Cross Keys Inn.

The rectory was now in mourning. Jane had hurriedly changed into deepest black, though Anne and Mary adamantly refused to do so. Elizabeth, though she knew she should wear mourning, had none to wear and didn't want to spend the funds to purchase it. Aunt Jane was appalled, repeatedly asking Elizabeth what she was supposed to tell the congregation when they asked why, with half her family dead, Elizabeth was still wearing her everyday clothes.

Elizabeth had replied that as far as she was concerned, Aunt Jane could tell them whatever she liked. She couldn't bring herself to believe that wearing black would help her family, and she knew it certainly wouldn't help her.

Chapter 44 🙦
Devon Countryside

Philip Goldworthy, cold and extremely hungry, had never felt more alone. Fed up to the teeth with sleeping in the open air, he longed for a warm bed, preferably with the companionship of a lusty young and willing maid.

When he had attacked William in the woods, he hadn't meant to harm him. He merely needed the horse, had hit him without thought.

On reflection, he regretted his action, but salved his conscience by telling himself that he hadn't meant to hurt the lad, and he should only have a small bruise to show for it. So any injury suffered was the lad's fault, not his, he thought unreasonably.

Once out of the woods and leaving William lying on the path, he hadn't ridden more than three miles by his estimation, when he came upon a stream. Urging his mount forward brought little reward, for the horse seemed to dig its hooves solidly into the ground. Utterly frustrated, Philip dismounted, taking the reins into his left hand and leading the horse forward. But it refused to budge, rearing up and thrashing around with its front legs. Without benefit of a whip, Philip flailed at it with his free hand, but with a final loud neigh the beast broke free from his grasp.

Without hesitation, it ran through the stream that moments before it had refused to enter and took off at a fast gallop through the thicket that stretched before it. Philip ran after it, through the water, yelling and shaking his fist, but it was all to no avail. The horse grew smaller as it rushed away while he could only stare in panic at his mode of escape as it forced its way through a hedge.

None of this came close to the sense of utter panic that overtook him as he woke the next morning beneath a large holly bush. He had chosen it as his shelter the night before in the belief that the sharp leaves would help to keep night creatures away. He had not given a thought to the ground-living crawlies that usually he wouldn't have cared a fig about. Safe in a comfortable warm bed the presence of spiders, worms and other creatures were unknown. But in the open air they were in their natural habitat, and all came to see who this strange thing was that had forced its way into their domain.

Without benefit of a timepiece, Philip was unable to tell the hour. His possessions had been left in his room at Watermead, and he bitterly regretted not having returned in the night to collect them. Dressed only in indoor clothes, he was freezing; his boots still sodden where he had walked backwards into the stream with that wretched horse. All he could do was wait until it grew light, however long that took. And to think.

Should he make for the coast and take ship to the continent? How could be pay for his passage? He didn't even have benefit of the plate he had stolen, and surely by now the Hue and Cry would be out for him.

Worse still, word would be on its way to his mother of his crime, and at the thought, he hid his face in his hands as if others were berating him. He tried not to think of what she would say or of her shame and humiliation when her friends found out, for find out they surely would. All he must think of was how to get out of this mess he had created, but each time he set his mind to a solution, his mother's mournful face appeared before him, and he found himself again hiding his face in dishonour. If he had known that the men from Honiton charged with the task of capturing him had all but given up when told he was now in possession of a horse, he would have felt much more cheerful.

Surely, he thought, he couldn't be too far from the coast, and he could offer his services as crew in return for his passage. His clothes, so obviously those of a well-born man might be a problem, but that could be rectified. There must surely be cottages and hovels along the way where he could trade or steal more common clothing, and it was with these happier thoughts that he set off.

Any fool knew in which direction the sun rose and keeping in mind Honiton, which he thought to be behind him, he only had to head due east and he would soon smell the salty air of the sea.

As he walked, he whistled to keep himself company and to scare away any animals that may be around. Tired from his sleepless night, hungry from missed meals, he plodded on. Through hedges, gates, and fields, through streams he went. Confident he would soon be away from England.

Chapter 45 ❧
Honiton

William had moved to Cross Keys the day after the news from London arrived. Elizabeth found herself craving solitude more and more. Aunt Jane seemed to have at last recognized, if not accepted, that Elizabeth had a mind of her own and had more or less given up trying to get her to do work within the house.

Anne and Mary were left to do the work that had been Elizabeth's task before, and their venom towards their cousin knew no bounds.

Whenever William visited, which was usually every other afternoon, their bad temper disappeared on the instant. They offered food and drink, both vying for his attention, seemingly oblivious of the fact that their whispered arguments and name-calling could easily be heard as they rushed to prepare whatever he requested.

Elizabeth also made sure he knew of their feelings towards her, so their mercurial shift of character was totally wasted. Mean-spirited girls held no appeal for eighteen-year-old William.

When brother and sister were alone, which usually meant leaving the rectory, they talked over what would they do while waiting for Timothy's letter advising them it was safe to return to London.

With William lodging at Cross Keys, he had plenty of opportunity to speak with Peter. Word of William and Elizabeth's loss had quickly spread throughout Honiton, and Peter had been one of the first to give his condolences. Peter had again broached the possibility of William working for him.

'My business is expanding faster than I can cope, and I admit that I find myself in need of help. Have you given any more thought to my offer?' he asked William at one of their chance meetings. They had met on High Street, though Peter had suggested they retire to Cross Keys for ale, and this is where they were now talking.

'I have. But you don't know anything about me, and I've none around, beside the rector, who can speak to my good character,' William had replied. 'Elizabeth and I are still awaiting word from our brother as to when we can return to London, for I've no doubt there's a lot to be done there. Timothy is running the wine business, and he will need help with the house and its contents.' William suddenly found himself unburdening his heart of all its worries, seemingly unable to keep them inside any longer.

'And there's Elizabeth to think of,' William continued. 'I don't care for her returning to London until I have a chance to clear out the house of our mother's things, her clothes and such. Oh, I know it should be Elizabeth's duty, but she's still so young, and the deaths have affected her badly. Timothy wrote that he had found a note in the house from our father stating that all the estate was to be split between Elizabeth, Timothy and I, which was generous of him.' He stopped, looking down into his tankard as if all the answers were to be found floating on top of the ale. 'But in answer to your offer, when I get back and if you have satisfactory report on me from our uncle, then yes, I think working for you would suit me well.'

Peter held out his hand, which William took. The two men looked directly at each other, both liking what they saw.

That evening, when William had climbed gratefully into his bed, he lay listening to the noise from the inn below. As the patrons finished their drinking and slowly drifted away to their own beds, the inn settled into slumber. Master Beaker told the serving girls to stop work for the night, and he walked around locking various doors and windows.

Warm and comfortable, William said his prayers, asking for mercy for his family, dead and alive. He gave thanks for being given the opportunity to come to Honiton where, it appeared, his life would continue, away from London. Who, he thought, ever knew where life would take them. You were born in one place, but there were no guarantee one would live there forever, though that was usually the case. Surely you should follow the opportunities that presented themselves and hope that they were right for you. He had a strong feeling Honiton would be right for him.

Chapter 46 ❧
Watermead

Jeffrey Browning was convinced Honiton was at the root of all his problems, not only Honiton, but also Exeter. He cursed the day he had decided to leave London for Exeter and his sister, Nan. He should, he thought, have remained in London. Perhaps he could have changed his name, and then his creditors would never have found him. Even as he thought it, he knew that wouldn't have been the case. He owed so much money they would have found him even if he had moved to the Low Countries.

After being summarily turned away from the doors of Watermead, he had stood looking up at the house, thinking of the money needed to not only purchase it but to maintain it. They have so much, he thought, while I am asking for so little. I only want Nan's plate. Nothing more. He felt himself not only hard done by, but also treated shamefully. He was convinced that rogue Philip Goldworthy was inside, and that, what was his name? Oh yes, Lord Thomas Stanton, was bound to be lying, covering up for his family. But Jeffrey had no intention of being taken for a fool. He decided to lie in wait at the end of the driveway, convinced that Philip Goldworthy would journey down it at some point.

He hid among the bushes where the driveway met the lane. To the left was Upper Hambley, to the right, Honiton. Jeffrey settled himself down on a thick piece of sward, his back resting against a small birch. Wait till I catch the bastard, he thought. He'll rue the day he ever met me.

Philip was closer than Jeffrey could have hoped. Having lost the horse he had stolen from William, his courage had failed him when it came to making for the coast and catching passage to the continent. He had come upon a hamlet with no more than three or four small hovels huddled together in a clearing in the woods. One of the women had washed her man's coat and left it hanging from a limb of a tree at the back of the cottage, thankfully not overlooked by a window.

Unused to skulking about amongst the undergrowth, for the longest time he was frightened to come into the open, but as day turned slowly to early evening and the temperature dropped, he knew he had no choice. To his ears he was making an awful racket, try as he may to keep quiet. He was certain all must hear him, and it took nearly an hour for him to summon the courage to dart out and grab the coat and as quickly run back into the shelter of the trees and bushes.

With the light fading fast, he ran as far into the woods as he dared, the overhanging canopy almost completely stopping what little light was left. Twice he stumbled over roots. Only when he felt he had totally escaped from the soon-to-be irate goodwife and her husband, did he feel it safe to rest.

He had been making his way back to Watermead. He had thought long and hard of a plan to escape the trouble he was in, and had, he thought, come up with the answer.

He would, under cover of the next night's darkness, cajole one of the kitchen maids to give him entrance. He could use the back stairs to give him access to his room. There he would find his clothes and the little money he had. The coat he had stolen was only required to keep him warm for the night and next day. Threadbare, patched and mended numerous times, it proved too small for him. When he put it on he realised he was unable to button it, the sleeves tight and uncomfortable.

He sat on a fallen log, leaf mould thick beneath his feet. Removing the coat, he turned it so his chest was covered, and tucked his arms beneath it to keep warm. Extremely hungry, thirsty and cold, Philip felt utterly beaten. He couldn't be seen at Watermead, extreme care would have to be taken there. He couldn't return to his mother's house in London, for word would have reached her by now. No doubt all of Honiton knew of his crime.

He wished he could explain it had been a momentary weakness on his part; surely, he thought, he should be forgiven. It was merely a boyish foolishness. If given his chance, he tried to convince himself, he could explain away his mistake and forgiveness would be given.

Darkness now total, he did his best to wrap the coat around him and lay on the earth among the mould and worms. Utterly exhausted and his stomach cramping with hunger and despair, he fell into a deep sleep.

※※※

The next morning he was woken by something on his face. Brushing it away with his hand, he kept his eyes closed, determined to return to sleep and blessed oblivion. Whatever it was returned, now tickling his ear. Again he made an attempt to brush it away. Again it returned.

With an annoyed 'tut,' he opened his eyes only to find three men standing above him, each with a triumphant grin on his face, one of them using a frond of fern to tickle him awake.

'Reckon we got 'im,' said one to the other two.

'Reckon we have at that. Ten guineas split three ways, seems to me this be our lucky day.' All three burst into laughter, and then reached down, hauling a shaken Philip to his feet. Taking a length of rope from a pocket, one of the men pulled Philip's hands behind his back, where they were tied tightly.

The stolen coat had fallen to the ground on the rough handling, and was now picked up by the man who had spoken initially. 'This be Tom's coat, too, the one his goodwife said was stolen, so we can add the theft of it to the stealing of the plate in Exeter and young William Sharpe's horse.'

Philip was roughly pushed forward, with no choice but to follow where he was led by another rope which now had been tied, though not too tightly, round his neck. The men spent the walk back to Honiton discussing how they would spend their share of Lord Thomas' reward money.

Oh God, what will mother say, and Lady FitzGerald?

213

Jeffrey Browning had decided he could wait no longer for Philip to appear. As the hours crawled by, he vacillated between the sure knowledge that Philip would appear momentarily, and the increasingly sure knowledge he would not. If he did not, what was he to do then? He had to return to the inn to collect his belongings, but he couldn't afford to be seen by the landlord or any of the servants. Indecision ran rampant, one minute he would rise stiffly and make as if to set off to Honiton, the next he would sit down again.

What if he returned to Honiton and he couldn't enter his room? What if the landlord had already guessed he couldn't pay his bill and had taken possession of his goods? But what if he didn't return to Honiton, but to Exeter instead? What if Nan saw him, and without the plate? Jeffrey found himself shivering, and not only from the chill evening air.

Perhaps he should return to London and take his chances with his creditors. Surely, he thought, they would have given up looking for him, and if he took lodgings in a different part of town, kept a low key, they would never know he was there. Perhaps he could even take employment somewhere. That thought was instantly dismissed, for he didn't know what he could turn his hand to.

Before he had fallen so much into debt, he had worked as a clerk for a solicitor in the Middle Temple. The hours had been long, sometimes as much as fifteen hours a day when a case was being heard, and he wondered now how he had ever coped. His release and relaxation had been in the gambling. It hadn't really mattered if it had been horses or cards, so long as he could gamble.

That thought led him in a different direction. If he could gamble in London, why not in Honiton? Usually inns were the place for game; though he had a feeling the landlord of Cross Keys wasn't the type to allow it in his establishment. But someone would know where he could find like-minded men.

Once more on the positive side of life, Jeffrey set out in the gathering dusk and with a firm step to Honiton.

Chapter 47 🍂
London

Timothy, after the initial shock of finding his father's body, was regretting sending such a terse letter to Elizabeth and William. Perhaps, he thought, he should have couched his words with more compassion instead of baldly stating their deaths. But those had been the facts, and he knew he had been badly shaken when he wrote it.

In the days since then, he had come to know James Morbeck, and liked what he saw. Both of approximately the same age, Timothy felt he could unburden his heart to his newfound friend, and James willingly listened.

With Father's body now removed, the house didn't feel so terrifying, and Timothy found he was able to enter each room without seeing ghosts of family passed. Decisions had to be made, but he didn't feel he needed to make them immediately. Besides, Elizabeth and William should be party to those decisions, for their father had wanted it so. Even if Father hadn't so stated it, Timothy himself would have wanted it that way.

The men at the warehouse had been saddened to hear of the deaths, but also not surprisingly concerned about their continuing employment. Timothy had conveyed to them he would now be running the business, and that with the typhus almost over, demand for wine would soon increase. They had no cause to worry.

He would write to Elizabeth and William letting them know it was safe to return, but return to what? The house was large, and

Timothy doubted the feasibility of keeping it. Elizabeth had been in Honiton for a while now, and for all he knew, with the death of their parents and brother, she may not wish to return, preferring instead the open, disease-free air.

William had always made it plain he had no wish to run the winery business, while Timothy was suited to it, and already well experienced. Dealing with the men and the ships' captains was like meat and drink to Timothy. He had long thought the business could be expanded, perhaps now was his chance to bring his dream to the light.

James returned to the house each night after his schooling. Coming straight from his lessons, he stopped at a pie shop and bought two each for himself and Timothy. Funds were still in short supply, and frugality had become commonplace since the time when the coach between Honiton and London had stopped.

He found the quiet of Timothy's house conducive to study, and both men enjoyed having company that respected the quiet. It took only a few days for Timothy to make his offer.

'How are your chambers?' he asked James one evening when they had finished eating.

'I have a room to myself, mother insisted on it when I told her I wished to study in London.' He chuckled. 'She thought I would be murdered in my bed if I shared a room. Why?'

'I am rattling round in this house, which seems quiet and empty to me. I was wondering if you would find it better for your studies if you lodged here instead of your room at school. It would suit both our purposes. I have to write to Elizabeth and William to let them know it is safe to return should they wish to, but once they are here, there is plenty of room for us all.'

'Write to them? Where are they?' enquired James.

'My sister went to Honiton some months ago and remains there. I wrote to tell her and William of Mother, Father, and Simon's deaths. I told them I would let them know when to come home. I think it is safe for them to come back, don't you?' He looked at James as if he would know the answer.

Realisation dawned with James. 'But I was on the coach with your sister and your mother! My father had been taken ill, though not the typhus, a heart ailment. I remember them both well.'

'You know of Elizabeth?' replied Timothy excitedly. They were sitting opposite each other, both resting their arms on the kitchen table. The rotting food had long been tossed out, and Timothy had scrubbed down all the floors and surfaces in the house with lye. The linens had been boiled by the washerwoman who Timothy had hired.

'I only saw her those few days, but she appeared unhappy for the whole journey.' He sat back, a large grin on his face. 'I'll take you up on your offer and willingly. I will be able to study far more easily here than at school. Most of the other pupils are only there for the carousing and drinking and keep me awake until the early hours. It will be good to be able to study in peace.' He paused. There was bound to be a catch, for this suddenly seemed too good to be true.

'I will need to pay my way, though. Perhaps you should tell me what you will require before I accept.'

'Let's just say it will be good to have the company. Once Elizabeth is home she can do the cooking, or we can get another maid to do it. Until then, if you pick up the dinner on your way from school, we'll say that's your payment. Does that appeal to you?'

'Indeed it does, Timothy. Indeed it does.' The two shook hands, sealing their arrangement, both convinced they had the best of the deal.

James would have to inform the school of his departure and advise them of his new lodgings. Also, he would have to tell his parents of his decision to lodge with Timothy, though he wouldn't tell them he barely had enough to feed himself after his room was paid for. Once he had moved, he would only be responsible for bringing their supper home, and he hoped he would have enough funds to buy a small dinner also. Things, he felt, were definitely looking up.

Chapter 48 ❧
Honiton

Philip knew things were as bleak as could be. Held in the town gaol, a round, stone-built structure with a sturdy oaken door and small, barred window, he was given food twice a day by the watch's goodwife. At least the food was edible, and usually hot.

The gaol itself was cold and damp, and contained a small cot with one thin blanket for sleeping. A basic three-legged stool and a pot for nature's call comprised the rest of its contents.

He had been told he would remain within until the magistrate arrived from Exeter, and God knew when that would be. He had mistakenly thought that Thomas Stanton was the magistrate for the area, which were it true, he had hoped would mean an early release into the custody of his mother in London. He was horrified to find out he was totally wrong.

Now a total stranger would decide his fate, though he presumed his aunt, Lady FitzGerald, would know of him. Perhaps he even dined at Watermead upon his visits to Honiton. If he could only speak to his aunt, or failing her, Thomas, he could convince them he meant no real harm, it had been only a boyish prank, and they could then speak on his behalf to the magistrate.

Through the long day and interminable night, all manner of thoughts went through Philip's head, but he couldn't escape the fact that, if he were honest, his future looked less than promising.

❧❧❧

Thomas sat in the parlour with Susannah and his aunt, Lady FitzGerald. Evening, too soon for supper, they sat companionably in front of the roaring fire which cast shadows into the corners of the room. Candlesticks were placed on all the tables, and with the fire, the room felt oppressive despite the cold outside the windows.

'Where is he, Thomas?'

'Philip? He's in gaol in Honiton, Aunt. He will remain there until the magistrate comes.'

Susannah was looking pensive, and Thomas knew she was worried about his aunt. Never having encountered anything like this before, Lady FitzGerald was unsure how to behave. She was only too glad that Thomas and Susannah had been visiting, and that Thomas had taken control of the situation and all its repercussions.

She had that morning written to Philip's mother at her London house. If Philippa were staying elsewhere, it would be sent on. But all of that would take precious time, during which Philip would remain locked up where he could do no more harm. Lady FitzGerald had tried to be as gentle as could be in the telling, but Philippa would read between the lines and know that the situation was far worse for her son than was being conveyed.

Lady FitzGerald spoke to Susannah and Thomas. 'He was always a wayward child, forever getting into trouble. When his father was alive he was kept in hand, but since his death, well, Philippa did her best, I've no doubt.' She turned to each of her companions, as if seeking solace.

'Perhaps I should have been more involved in the boy's upbringing, but it never occurred to me, I'm afraid.'

'You can't possibly feel you are to blame, surely, Aunt,' said Thomas. 'He wasn't your responsibility while his mother was alive. If anyone should have interceded, it should have been me.'

Susannah now spoke. 'Stop it, both of you. Neither of you are to blame. Philip is responsible for his own behaviour and actions, not you. From the little I have seen of him, he is self-centred and lazy, easily led into wrongdoing.'

Lady FitzGerald leaned forward to interrupt. 'No, Aunt Sophie,' continued Susannah, 'I won't have you blaming yourself, nor you, Thomas. Philip has brought this upon himself. He had the choice whether to steal the plate in Exeter, and to steal the horse and assault its rider. The fact that he made the wrong choice is his responsibility, and his alone.'

'I know you are right, Susannah,' replied Lady FitzGerald, 'But I feel so for my poor friend, who now has to face the world and its scorn.'

'I am sorry also, but facts have to be faced. Philippa will survive the shame with the help of her friends, and she will find out now who they are.'

With nothing left for any of them to say on the matter, Thomas turned the conversation to estate matters, the spring plantings, the horses and cattle. No work would be possible without the tenant farmers who tended the fields and animals, coppiced the woods, or those who worked in the great house of Watermead itself. Each depended on their neighbour so all could eat through even the harshest winter.

The three men who had captured Philip had been paid the ten guinea reward that same day, all thrilled to have this extra coin in their possession. Thanking Thomas profusely, they returned to their cottages and wives to sit around their own, humbler fires and to tell of the villain's capture and their respective bravery, such as it was. None thought it necessary to mention Philip had been sleeping when they came upon him, the easy taking of him more through luck than effort.

ॐॐॐ

Jeffrey Browning heard the news of Philip's capture as he sat in Cross Keys downing ale. He noticed that the innkeeper, Master Beaker, was ever hovering nearby, as if he knew Jeffrey was intent on scuttling away once night came, leaving his tariff unpaid.

He had been lodged at the inn waiting his chance to confront Philip, but now it seemed that he wouldn't get the chance. Bitterly resentful, he had spent the afternoon and early part of the evening eating and drinking. He sat alone, muttering to himself occasionally to give the impression to others that he was well on his way to being sotten.

His plan, if it could be described as such, was to shortly stagger up to his room, and lay on his bed to snore loudly. Should anyone listen from outside, it would appear he was totally drunk and in no state to abscond. Once the inn settled and all took to their beds, he would creep down the stairs and make his escape.

He felt sure once he spoke to Nan and explained he had spent the last days while trying to retrieve her plate, her harshness towards him would soften and she would allow him back into the house. Now that Philip was arrested, he reasoned the plate would be returned to Nan and all would be forgiven.

He could see nothing wrong with his reasoning, and saw no need to change his plan in any aspect. It was foolproof. All that remained was for night to come.

Chapter 49 ⁊
London

Timothy Sharpe and James Morbeck were sitting down to their evening meal, which, as agreed between them, was purchased by James on the way home from school. Today it was eel pie, full of gravy and vegetables. Both savoured the moist pieces of eel, neither speaking until their plates were scraped clean, and on James' part, licked clean.

'Have you written again to Elizabeth and William?' asked James.

'No, I have been busy at the warehouse, but I know I must do it tonight. With the typhus over, there's no reason why they shouldn't come home if they wish.' He stopped and looked around the familiar kitchen, once so full of life, now just the two of them.

'But what will they come back to, James? With Mother, Father, and Simon dead what is there here for them?' He looked at James as if he held the answer, but James merely nodded, kindly eyes commiserating silently with his newfound friend and landlord.

'I am running the winery, and not doing a bad job in my opinion. Trade is coming back, indeed if it continues in this vein I shall have to hire more men to replace the three who died with the typhus. What would Elizabeth do? Would she be content to keep house for us? Well, you've met her, James, what do you think?'

James laughed. 'I only knew her for a few days, but I can't see your sister being happy doing anything other than what she wants to do. I think you are right, though, Elizabeth isn't the type to look after a house full of men, for that's what it would be if William did return too. Why not write to them tonight, explain all we have spoken of the last while, and let them make their own decisions?'

'I will. If you'll excuse me, I'll use Father's study.' He rose from the table. 'Can I leave you to clean up?' he asked.

'Of course, it's the least I can do,' replied James, also rising and collecting the two plates. It would take but a moment to wash them, and then he meant to study in the peace and quiet.

Taking a candle from the table, Timothy walked along the hall, entering his father's study. Closing the door behind him both for privacy and to keep out the ever-present draught, he hesitated before taking a seat behind the large desk, for it didn't seem right. He had never sat there while his father was alive, and he had to force himself to pull out the ladder-back chair and sit down. Placing his hands upon the desk top, the flickering candle cast shadows on the bookshelves containing the company records not held at the warehouse.

Forcing himself, he took parchment and quill from the desk that would now be his, and began to write. Stopping often to make sure he had included all his thoughts, the candle was almost a scrag before he was satisfied.

He asked Elizabeth and William if they were in agreement with his taking over the business; that if they wished, he would sell the house and move to smaller accommodation. If they agreed with him remaining, he told them, then James Morbeck would be company for him, as the house at the moment was filled with unsettling memories.

Father's bank account had been extremely healthy, and he suggested that the funds be split between them, giving all ready money for whatever they wished in life. They should have no worries in that department for many years, or indeed ever, if they used it wisely.

The house, he continued, would be sold only if all agreed and the proceeds from that and the furniture would be split equally between them.

If they were in agreement, would they advise him forthwith, or if they had other ideas would they convey them as soon as possible? He would, if they preferred, consult a solicitor to have the agreement then formalized.

He told Elizabeth he had disposed of their mother's clothes, except for her linen and a fur wrap, which he kept for her.

He read the letter through once, then again, making only small adjustments, then re-wrote the whole thing on fresh parchment, signing it with a flourish.

Hearing the church clock strike ten, he put down the quill and sanded the ink. He left the letter on the desk and determined he would look at it once more when he rose from his bed to ensure he had included everything necessary. If he were still satisfied, he would take it to the coach stop after breakfast for onward transportation to Honiton.

The candle now out, he made his way by moonlight to the door and wearily climbed the stairs to his room. He lay in his narrow cot and looked out of the window at the waning moon, one moment hidden the next clear of clouds. Certain in his mind he had done all he could, and glad he had at last written what had been such a difficult missive, he turned over and was instantly asleep.

Chapter 50 ❧
Honiton

William, as was his usual routine, waited at Cross Keys every morning the London coach was due, each time hoping for word from Timothy. When the letter at last arrived, he didn't open it but hurried to the rectory to share the news, whether good or bad, with Elizabeth.

Finding her in the kitchen talking to Aunt Jane, and hearing that the rector was out on calls to the sick and elderly, he asked if they could use the rector's study. Upon being given permission, they went straight there, closing the door on nosy eyes and ears.

Elizabeth sat on the chair before the large desk while William leaned against it. Elizabeth waited while he read through it first, though the suspense was more than she could bear. Utterly relieved when he had obviously come to the end, she looked expectantly at him while waiting for him to speak.

William did so, reading aloud slowly and carefully to ensure they both understood what their brother was telling them. At the end, William didn't speak, merely looking at Elizabeth to indicate she should go first.

'That seems clear enough, doesn't it, William?' she asked tremulously.

'I think so. Timothy raises a good point. Does either of us want to return to London? What is there for us? I'm not in the least interested in the winery. If you return, what will you be, Timothy's housekeeper? You're too good for that, Elizabeth. I could understand it if it were your own house, your own husband, but looking after Timothy and this James Morbeck? Is that something you want to do?'

'No. I know I came here under protest, but I've grown to love Honiton and the people in it. London is far too big, I hardly knew any of our neighbours there, and Agnes was my only friend. Here I know so many more. I'm not saying I want to continue living with Aunt Jane and the dreaded cousins, but if you are staying, surely with Father's money, we could join it together and buy a small house of our own?' William didn't speak immediately; too pleased to hear which way her heart was leaning.

'Have you thought any more of Peter Brigginshaw's offer of employment, William?'

'I've thought of nothing else. So are we of a mind? We shall remain here and look for lodging of our own? It would have to be furnished, for I don't want to have to purchase new; besides, it will give us a chance to see if we can make a go of it.'

'Yes. Let's make a life for ourselves here. We are still young, many years before us, God willing. Shall you tell Aunt Jane, or shall I? Or shall we do it together?'

William pushed himself up from the desk. 'We'll do it together. She won't be best pleased at the loss of a guinea a month, but don't let her dissuade you, for she will try, Elizabeth.'

'I know she will, and I can't blame her, but I won't.'

With a hug, as if sealing their agreement, they left the study to give Aunt Jane the news that as soon as they had found their own lodging, Elizabeth would be leaving. She couldn't wait.

The rector joined them, Jane telling him that Elizabeth would be leaving and he didn't need telling that the loss of the guineas would hit hard.

When needing solace, he turned to his study. With Elizabeth leaving life would become difficult, Jane even more shrewish at the loss of the extra coin, which she had come to rely on. But try as he might, he couldn't think on this too long, for that afternoon he had lost one of his flock; the wealthy widow he visited on a regular basis had died.

Summoned to the house by one of the servants, he attended the corpse. He knew she had no relatives near, for her only son had left for the Americas to try for his fortune. She had been a well-known figure in the town, so he didn't fear there would be no mourning for her. He did, however, feel sorry for her elderly servants who were now facing the loss of their employment.

A letter from the solicitor would have to be dispatched to the son advising of his mother's passing. He supposed that until a reply was received, the servants would remain in the house, which would no doubt have to be sold.

He was used to death; it held no fear for him. He felt more for those left behind, bereft and more often than not, alone. Seated at the desk in his study, and with a heavy heart, he began to write a sermon for the funeral.

❧❧❧❧

Philip, still in the town gaol, was becoming increasingly despondent. The only complaint he didn't have was the quality of the food. Supplied by the Watch's goodwife, it was wholesome and plentiful. It wasn't the same as he had enjoyed at Watermead or at his mother's home, but all things considered in that regard, he couldn't complain.

When it came to everything else, however, he had grumbles aplenty. The gaol was alternately cold and damp. The pisspot was not emptied often enough. He demanded a change of clothing, which was granted and brought from Watermead the next day. The Watch stood outside guarding the door and window to prevent anyone peering in while he changed.

At other times, faces would appear from nowhere to stare at him through the bars of the door or the small window. Children would bring boxes or chairs on which to stand, and throw scraps of rotten food at him. He had never known such misery. Each day he would ask the Watch when the magistrate would come, each day he was told it would be soon. Each day was a living nightmare.

Thomas Stanton had come twice, once accompanied by a local solicitor who barely spoke to Philip. Thomas told the prisoner he would pay the fee for the legal representation, making a point to tell Philip it wasn't on his account that a solicitor was hired, but for Philip's mother, so she would know all had been done that could possibly be done. Thomas also advised him not to lean on false hope. His punishment would be severe.

227

Upon asking what had become of the stolen plate, Philip was told it was being held in Watermead to be returned to its rightful owner when the magistrate had pronounced Philip's sentence.

He enquired of Thomas if word had been received from his mother, but the answer was no, nothing had been heard. Alone, his thoughts rushed here and there, coming to no resolution. Has she washed her hands of me? Is this the final humiliation and she can take no more? What can I tell the magistrate? Whatever shall I do? Oh God. Please help me.

The magistrate arrived almost two weeks to the day since Philip had been captured. The site of the courtroom was the large storage barn at the back of the Cross Keys Inn. Two tables, each with a chair, were set up at the back of the building for the magistrate and his clerk. Facing these was a table for Philip and his solicitor. Benches and odd chairs were placed in higgledy-piggledy rows before them for the witnesses and spectators. Philip would have shackles placed upon him while inside the gaol, and then the Watch would lead him to the temporary courtroom.

The Watch, accompanied by another man, came for him. Neither met his eyes, and remained silent to all Philip's questions and pleas. The other man, tall and heavyset, stood on the inside of the gaol door while the shackles were placed roughly on the prisoner. He carried a heavy stick, which he banged repeatedly against the wooden door to remind Philip he would use it on him if necessary. He looked as if he would relish the chance.

It seemed as if all of Honiton and the surrounding area were crammed into the barn. All the benches and chairs had been taken early, now it was standing room only.

Pushing their way through the heaving mass of bodies, Philip, with the Watch and his assistant, found themselves before the magistrate. The chains were placed round the shackles, then round the posts. The noise died down, all present excited that the long-awaited proceedings were about to start.

Thomas Stanton and the solicitor sat at their table. There was no chair for Philip.

The magistrate, dyspeptic and clearly annoyed at having to journey here while feeling unwell, glared at all before him. Philip felt the last of his hope drain from him, and his legs grew weak.

The solicitor rose to speak, placing Philip's defence, such as it was, before the court, though Philip had barely even spoken to the solicitor, how could he know of the chain of events that led to the theft or the assault on William Sharpe? He had made sure that William had not seen his face; how, therefore, could he be accused, he reasoned. It was a measure of his fear that Philip hadn't realised that being caught with the clothes which William recognized and confirmed to the Watch was proof enough. And the plate was found in his room made it certain of his guilt.

The magistrate himself didn't seem to pay attention, closing his eyes and leaning his head back as if wishing he were anywhere else.

Thomas spoke briefly, telling of Philip's lack of fatherly direction and of his mother's concern, though stopping well short of pleading for mercy.

The proceedings went forward as fast as lightning, leaving Philip's head in a whirl. He wanted to speak in his own defence, trying to catch the solicitor's attention, but the solicitor told the magistrate that Philip regretted his actions, which had been brought on by too much drink, all the while making shushing movements with his hands to keep Philip quiet.

Nan's plate stood piled on a long table set beside the magistrate's chair. There was a prodigious amount of it, and the crowd looked at it with envy; a king's ransom to all those in attendance. Not fifteen minutes after the court had been called to order, sentence was pronounced: Transportation.

The judge told the Watch to return the plate to its rightful owner, picked up his papers and stopped to shake Thomas' hand, then the solicitor's, and pushed his way through the crowd eager to start the journey to home and his bed.

Stunned and unbelieving, Philip looked around for help, but none could give it. In his panic he looked for someone, anyone, who would intervene on his behalf. He recognized only one person. Two rows back was a small, pinched face that looked back at him. The one face in the courtroom that showed pity: the girl from the coach. He tried to concentrate on remembering her name, anything to forget what was happening to him. But his mind was empty.

Thomas approached him. 'You idiot. You'll never see England or your mother again. And for what? Some plate and a horse.' He spun on his heel and followed the solicitor out the barn door, leaving Philip chained to the post in shock of all that had occurred.

Later, he couldn't remember the walk through those who remained to jeer at him, or the walk back to the gaol.

Philip was wrong in his thinking that he recognized only one person. There was one other, but his face didn't bear Elizabeth's look of pity and concern. Jeffrey Browning, late arriving and forced to stand at the back of the crowd, could hear well the solicitor's pleading, the sentence handed down. He couldn't disguise his pleasure that Philip would be sent away, for he was the one person who could speak of his own hand in the theft.

Then he heard the magistrate tell the Watch to return the plate. Jeffrey, however, had other plans for it. He wanted to be the one to take the plate to Nan, for then, he had convinced himself, she would be grateful and would willingly allow him to lodge with her. So how was he to get it?

If he told the Watch he was Nan's brother, what if the Watch had heard of the suspicion that Jeffrey was involved in the theft in the first place? Would he also be arrested? Would he be transported like Philip? Wouldn't that be an irony, to be on the same ship as Phillip?

No, he reasoned, there's no way for it, I'll have to waylay the Watch on the road to Exeter. As always, Jeffrey hadn't thought through his plan. If he attacked the Watch then presented the plate to Nan, wouldn't the Watch know it had been Jeffrey who had attacked him? Jeffrey was ever a stupid man.

The barn emptied quickly, all returning to their daily chores. Philip was led back to gaol to await his fate and a final visit from the rector.

Elizabeth and William went directly to Cross Keys in the hope of another letter from Timothy. Master Beaker heard William's voice and came from his chancel office, the much-anticipated letter in his hand.

He had been too busy to attend the trial, but news had already reached the inn. He couldn't pretend to be upset by it. He had avoided having to tell Lady FitzGerald of her godson's behaviour, but he knew she would be devastated by the news. His heart went out to her. Handing over the letter to William, he left the two alone.

By silent consent, they left the inn, making their way out of town and along to the river. The day had turned warm, the sky a cloudless blue. Once sure they were alone, Timothy read the letter out loud.

Absorbing the information it contained, Elizabeth and William looked at each other, neither willing to be the first to speak, as it contained much the same as the previous letter. They continued to walk by the river, both mulling over Timothy's words. William voiced his thoughts first.

'Are you distressed, Elizabeth, that Timothy has removed Mother's clothes?'

'No, I'm not. I wouldn't have relished the task and I'm grateful he took it upon himself. Timothy is right; they would have been a terrible reminder of our family as we once were. What are your thoughts?'

'He is doing well with the business, and if there is more money than we thought, it will take a burden from us all. It also means I don't have to return to London, as he has all in hand. I'm pleased he has taken in a lodger, for the house must seem empty. You know of this James Morbeck, Elizabeth?'

'I do. He was returning to Honiton, for his father was ailing. He told us he was at school, only interested in becoming a physician. He seemed a pleasant young man, one who definitely knew his own mind. I am glad Timothy has taken him in.'

'As to selling the house,' Elizabeth continued, 'I see no reason to. If we decide to go back for a visit, there will be somewhere for us to stay, and as Timothy said, we don't need the money from its sale.'

'I agree. Timothy can be trusted to be fair with us.'

They came to a bend in the river, large reeds growing against the banks. Paddling between the reeds was a mother duck with seven young ones following. Elizabeth watched them as they madly clambered up the opposite bank to keep up with their mother with their short, webbed feet.

'Which brings us back to us,' said William. 'We are both in agreement we should have lodging away from the rectory, and Timothy's letter means we can now pursue that. I'll speak to Master Beaker at the inn this evening to see if he knows of anywhere, but as I said, it will have to be furnished.'

'I'll also speak to our uncle at dinner, he may be aware of a suitable place,' offered Elizabeth.

For the first time since coming to Honiton, Elizabeth felt a deep sense of peace. William was with her, she was making friends, and truth be told, she was happy here. Or rather, happy for the time she was away from Aunt Jane and the brats.

⋆⋆⋆⋆

William sat in the eating room at Cross Keys. Surrounded by townsfolk taking refreshment after their daily work, he was also vaguely aware they were discussing Philip Goldworthy's trial. His mind was focussed on finding somewhere for him and Elizabeth to live. He had spoken to Master Beaker earlier, but the landlord had no immediate thought of a vacant furnished property.

⋆⋆⋆⋆

Dinner at the rectory was a sombre affair. Jane was grieving her lost sister, and the rector was at a loss as how to give her comfort. His usual ministrations for those in mourning had fallen on deaf ears. Jane had turned on him as if it were his fault. Lying on their bed, her face and eyes red with weeping, she had refused to join them for dinner.

The rector looked round at his table with sad eyes. Mary and Anne were bickering as usual. Elizabeth hardly spoke, except to ask if he knew of furnished accommodation for her and William.

The rector hurried his meal and then pleaded work to be done in his study, left the three to their own devices.

He and Jane had been married for eighteen years, and none of them had been particularly happy ones. Jane had proven over the years to be a shrew, nagging him at every turn. With no intention of doing any work at all, he sat in his favourite chair next to the fire, which was unlit with the weather getting warmer. He pulled on his pipe, relishing the peace and quiet.

Jane was upstairs creating a fuss, for none were paying attention to her, but with the study door closed, her crying was thankfully muted. Rectors were supposed to marry, to show the way to their flock, that the union of man and woman was a gift from God. He didn't consider his marriage a gift from God. He looked at it more as a penance for Lord knows what.

How much longer can I put up with Jane, Mary, and Anne? What is stopping me from telling them I have had enough? That either they all stop behaving so badly or I shall leave them? I could tell the bishop I am ill and need to escape to the fresh air – though where I will find fresher air than here, I don't know. He thought of all he had that was unknown to Jane. There just might be a way.

His thoughts continued long into the evening. The house at last settled for the night, and still the rector sat in his study deep in thought.

The following morning Jane had deigned to join the family for breakfast, but was still in a vile temper. Patience gone, he asked her when she thought her main grieving would be over. She burst into tears once more, rushing from the room with a wail. Mary and Anne, despite their bickering, ate heartily; eating was never a problem for them, no matter what their mood.

'I have thought about accommodation for you and William, Elizabeth. Come to my study after we have eaten and we can discuss it.' He didn't want his daughters to hear his suggestion, though they were too busy eating; neither Mary nor Anne showed any interest in finding out their father's plan.

Elizabeth sat straighter. Hurrying her food, she left the board without asking permission and rushed to the study to await the rector. She didn't have to wait for long.

'I have given much thought to your enquiry for lodging, and believe I have the answer. A member of my congregation has died, a wealthy widow. She lived in town, alone except for two servants. She had a son, a good-for-nothing sort who has gone to the Americas to seek his fortune. I doubt if he will find it there any more than he did here, though that's neither here nor there.'

'The town solicitor is the executor, and he will of course need to communicate with the son to tell of his mother's death.

All this will, of necessity, take time. At the time of leaving, the boy stated he would never return, and his mother put the house

233

into the solicitor's hands, specifically to be sold with the contents upon her death. The funds were to be remitted to him in America.'

'I can think of no reason why the solicitor would not obey her instructions, and it would be to everyone's advantage to have the house occupied. It would also mean that the servants have no need to find other employment. It wouldn't be easy for either of them, for they are no longer young. But that's not your worry. What do you say? Shall I approach him on your behalf?'

Elizabeth didn't hesitate. 'Yes please, uncle, it sounds as if it would suit us well. We would still be in town but have our own lodging, which we both seek.' She stopped, aware she sounded churlish to this gentle man. 'I don't, however, want you to think I haven't been happy here, for I have.'

'Nonsense, Elizabeth. You've been no happier here than I am. It will do you good to get out of this wretched house and find your own way. It shan't be easy, mind, but I've a notion you and William will do well. I hear that Peter Brigginshaw has offered William employment. I hope he accepts, for young Peter is a good businessman. He does good work, and his reputation is known far and wide, his furniture much in demand. William could do far worse than be involved with him.'

'I know William will accept; especially now he doesn't have to return to London. With the chance at lodging of our own, it will make his decision even easier.'

'And what of you? What plans do you have for yourself?'

'I haven't given it thought; there's nothing I am good enough at to make a living. As you know, Timothy's letter said Father had been wealthier than even we had thought, so we have no worries in that regard.'

Suddenly remembering the rector's poor living, she went to him, her arm round his shoulders.

'Timothy, William and I have indeed been fortunate in spite of the deaths in our family. Would you accept help from us to ease your way, Uncle?'

He smiled sadly. 'That I wouldn't, child, though I shan't forget such a kind and thoughtful gesture, but don't you fret about me. I have plans of my own. I shall speak to William directly on this matter, and suggest a price he should offer. As I said, it is a good house, and you will both be comfortable there.'

With that, Elizabeth had to be content. All she could do now was wait and hope that the rector could convince her brother of the merits of purchasing the widow's house.

After speaking to William, and true to his word, he knocked on the door of the solicitor's office that same morning. Laying the offered price before the executor of the will, he could almost see the man's mind turning over. The solicitor promised to have an answer for William the following morning.

Walking back to the rectory, he thought how everything seemed to be working out well: A ready-made home for his niece and nephew, continued employment for the servants.

Chapter 51 ❧
Honiton

The deportation of Philip was imminent. Lady FitzGerald had been to see him, allowed to enter the cell in which he was kept. Accompanied by Thomas, it was a heart-breaking visit.

Philip begged her to speak on his behalf to the magistrate, plead for mercy and have his sentence commuted. It was embarrassing for all of them, Philip on his knees clutching his godmother's skirts with grubby hands. Sobbing, he vowed to change, promised anything so long as he wasn't deported.

The visitors didn't stay long. Lady FitzGerald said her goodbye to a pathetic figure of a man who grovelled in the straw laid on the floor. Thomas didn't speak; he had nothing more to add to his comments at the time of Philip's sentencing. Neither looked back when the heavy oak door was locked after them. Left alone once more, Philip lay in the straw, all hope now gone. He was to be taken to London the next day.

He had no idea how things could get any worse. Prisoners for transportation were kept in hulks on the River Thames. The gaols in London were overflowing, and the hulks had been pressed into service as temporary gaols. Living in horrific conditions, Philip was frightened and confused. The chains round his ankles bit deep, making sleep difficult and the constant pain unbearable.

He thought he would be sent to the Americas, which he had heard was the land of opportunity. He held on to the glimmer of hope he could make a go of it there.

One night, as he lay in the dark, the odour of fear from the dozens of men kept with him was almost touchable. He listened with distaste to the coughing and snoring, the whispered conversations and the skittering of the rats. Restless in the close quarters with his body pressed close to men either side of him, he overheard several others talking. What he heard terrified him. It wasn't to the Americas they were to be sent. It was to Australia. Things had indeed had become worse.

⁂

Earlier, Jeffrey Browning heard of the Watch's journey to Exeter from talk about town. Avoiding the innkeeper was taking its toll, and Master Beaker eventually caught up with him as he returned to his room one afternoon.

'How much longer do you intend to take the room?'

Jeffrey, caught off guard, stuttered. 'Just a couple of days, then I'll be on my way.' He tried to sound confident, assertive; instead, his voice had a wheedling tone that wasn't lost on the innkeeper.

'You are aware your tally is now quite large, and I shall need payment today,' replied Master Beaker. He had people skip out before without paying their way, and wouldn't be caught again. If the man was leaving in a couple of days, best to get payment now.

'Ah, right. I was awaiting funds sent by coach, but they haven't arrived.' The innkeeper was aware nothing had arrived, for he'd been the one to greet the coach, the driver telling him there were no deliveries.

'I fully expect they will arrive tomorrow, and I will pay you immediately when I receive them.' He thought while he was talking of how much he had in his possession, but it only amounted to a few shillings, hardly enough to satisfy the innkeeper. But, he reasoned, it would be best to lull the man into a false sense of security. He also made the mistake of doubting they would be accepted. He was ever a fool.

'I can give you three shillings now, on account, if you wish,' he said, fumbling half-heartedly in his pocket for the precious coin.

'That will do well,' replied the innkeeper in his turn, holding out his hand.

Left with no choice, Jeffrey handed over his few coin, leaving him with fourpence.

'Your tally comes to six shillings, what with the room, food, and drink. I'll take the three shillings now, with three more to come tomorrow.' He emphasized the 'tomorrow.'

Jeffrey smiled, a sweat breaking out on his brow and upper lip. Where am I going to find three shillings? It's good I had already determined to go tonight. Damn the man.

He ate a good meal that evening smiling benignly at the innkeeper when he came into the eating room. Who knew when his next meal would be, and he faced a long journey back to Exeter.

By eleven o'clock the last of the customers had left the inn, and he lay on his bed listening to Master Beaker locking the doors and windows, sending the maids to their beds after a long day.

He waited another hour, and then quietly opened the bedroom window that gave on to the small roof of the house that adjoined the inn. Carefully he lowered his ready-packed bag on to the windowsill, and then leaned further out only just reaching the roof below. Taking care not to make any noise at all, he followed the bag, carrying his shoes so they didn't sound on the roof and alert those sleeping below.

The roof was about seven feet above the ground, and with no other way down, he dropped the bag and jumped after it. He landed awkwardly, knocking his breath away. He lay in the dirt, ears straining for any sound that would mean the innkeeper was alerted to his escape. Hearing only silence, he put on his shoes, picked up his bag, and quietly slipped away from the inn and out of Honiton to wait for the morning.

⁂

There was only one road to Exeter, so the Watch had no option but to use it. Certain in the knowledge he had escaped, Jeffrey set off to find a suitable place to wait, from which to attack the Watch and take possession of the plate come morning.

Reasoning that the Watch would set out after first light, Jeffrey hunted around for a fallen branch that could be used as a weapon, then curled up, trying to keep warm. With funds now critically low, life was unbearably hard, but he had no other choice, he had to take possession of the plate.

The Watch, the plate held in panniers on a pony led by a rein, set out reluctantly for Exeter. While the magistrate had said it must be returned to its rightful owner now that sentence for Philip was pronounced, he didn't want to be the one to take it. Exeter was a long hard ride, and he begrudged the time away from his family. All too often he had to go here and there, away from hearth and home for days at a time.

As spring was now well and truly arrived, it should have been a pleasant time riding along and enjoying the beautiful Devon countryside, but he was tired and dispirited. This was merely a journey to be endured, not for pleasure, over as quickly as possible.

Whistling to keep himself company, the Watch wasn't on his guard. His horse whinnied, the pack animal trotted behind carrying the plate pulled on its leading rein.

Jeffrey, hiding in dense brush at the side of the road, waited until the group had passed him then leapt out, caught hold of the Watch's leg and tipped him out of the saddle. The horse, startled, took off down the road. The packhorse, the rein held by the Watch, was oblivious to the attack, and put its head down to graze on the newly grown grass.

The Watch, unsure what had happened, had landed on his belly. As he prepared to turn over and get to his feet, Jeffrey hit him on the head with the branch, laying him out cold.

The runaway horse was now a small figure in the distance; all that was left was the packhorse and the precious plate. Quickly returning for his bag, Jeffrey ran back to the scene of his crime, grabbed the rein that lay on the road, and pulled the reluctant animal into a trot.

With too much plate for him to ride, he had no choice but to run alongside. He huffed and puffed, dragging the reluctant animal behind him, and within a short while he was absolutely worn out. Cursing loudly, he awkwardly climbed onto its back, jostling for space with the baggage. Without saddle or stirrups, it soon proved not only extremely uncomfortable but also unmanageable. He had never been a good horseman, and the animal quickly sensed his inexperience.

Reluctantly, he dismounted and went back to walking. To keep himself going, he thought of how grateful Nan would be to him, what he would say to her when he arrived. He envisioned her happy face as she unwrapped the bundle and knew she couldn't refuse him lodging.

Chapter 52 ≈●
Honiton

With the solicitor dealing with the widow's house, the rector set his mind to his own worries. He wrote a letter to his bishop begging an audience, 'As I have something of great import to tell you.' The bishop replied in due course, giving a date and time.

He told Jane the bishop had summoned him for some unknown reason, and he would be leaving on the coach the following day. Jane showed no interest, only glad he would be out from under her feet.

He had given much thought to what he would tell the bishop, and had settled on telling him that he had lost his faith. How could he be expected to give comfort to others, he reasoned, when he had lost his faith?

Shown into the bishop's study, the rector told him that he wished to resign from his assignment in Honiton. Taken aback, the bishop sat with mouth agape. The rector had previously given no indication of dissatisfaction with his life. When he asked what had brought this on, he kept to his pre-arranged words. Seeing he was to get no further, and not interested enough to delve deeper, the bishop said he should return home, and a letter would be sent shortly with his decision.

Returning to the rectory the next day, hardly noticed by Jane, he went immediately to his study to contemplate his next steps.

In fact it was over a week later when the bishop's letter arrived. He would accept that the rector would be leaving the hurch. He would also, he stated, expect the rector to remain at his church until a replacement could arrive. The rector, however, had no such intention.

A year previously, he had heard of an elderly man who had moved around, earning his living making charcoal deep in the woods. The news was he had been seen last to the east of Honiton. Needing to escape, he had set out to find the man. The walk was long, and he had stopped frequently to bathe his face in the stream he was following, which would lead him to the man's last known location.

In reality he didn't really care now whether he found him or not. He saw the remains of a stone-built structure were close by, and hot and tired; he walked towards the ivy and lichen-covered walls that remained standing. Sitting down, his back against the warm stone, he took his ease.

His hand brushed back the grass and weeds, and he had taken up a handful of dirt, more dust than anything due to the lack of rain. When he had looked down, it was to see a piece of hessian, rotted and filthy, poking through. He tugged at it, with more appearing. He knelt and dug with his hands, breaking nails.

The top of a sack tied with twine was now visible, and he pushed aside more dirt, giving him access to what was inside. The sun at its apex caught the metal and caused a glare from which he had to shield his eyes. Objects that looked like goblets and plate, a large candlestick all gold in colour were revealed.

Frantically he continued to dig until the sack could be wrenched from the hole in which it had been buried. For buried it had must have been.

Once it was clear of the ground he put it on his lap and rested, his filthy hands resting on the sack, fearful it would disappear. The beads of sweat ran freely down his face, causing his eyes to blur. He sat back, gasped for breath and threw off his coat. He wondered if this were the only treasure to be found. He poked a sturdy twig into the ground next to the newly dug hole, but it didn't go far, for it seemed something hard lay below. Frantically with his heart racing, he continued to dig. He soon became dirty and dishevelled. Now tired, for he was no longer a young man, he had to pause frequently.

Soon there was revealed a rusty metal box, handles at either side. With a struggle, he had tried to pull it out, but it was heavy. There was no lock, nothing to prevent the lid being raised.

Inside, it was filled to the top with gold sovereigns. No wonder it had been heavy. The rector sat back, hardly believing his eyes. Here, at last, he thought, is the answer to my prayers. Far too many coin to count, and too heavy to bring to the rectory, he shoved and pushed the dirt back, then covered it up with weeds and leaves. He did the same with the sack of plate until he was satisfied no one would ever know they were there. All the time he looked around, scared someone would see him and come after him to steal his new property. Now he had his salvation, no one and nothing would stand in his way.

All thought of finding the man had now gone. His back to the wall again, his thoughts raced. Who had left it there; it must have lain buried for many years, for the sack to become rotten. He was well aware that his future lay on which way he turned next. Obviously, its owner had been wealthy. Had they forgotten where they buried it? Or had they died without passing on the information? Perhaps it was stolen and the thief apprehended before he could return?

All his training told him he should share it with the parish. How many times had he spoken in church against theft? Too many to count, he thought. But here was his new life, ready-made. Could he, should he, turn his back on a lifetime of teaching? He reasoned that if he didn't take it, some other fellow would find it. Why should they have the benefit and not he? Hadn't he worked long and hard for little reward? Hadn't he wasted his life with Jane? Didn't he deserve his ease now, as the years grew short?

He sat until clouds threatened rain. Casting a look at the hidden treasure to assure himself no one would discover it before his return, he set off for home. When Jane saw him, she shouted about the state of his clothes, asking how he expected her to clean his hose that were filthy. She demanded to know where he had been, screeching at him until he thought his head would burst. That decided it. He would keep the knowledge to himself until such time as he could put the treasure to its best use; escape.

Relieved beyond measure, he sat at his desk, took fresh parchment, sharpened the quill and dipped it in the inkpot. He proceeded to write a detailed plan of his escape from Jane and the girls. He would tell her of his leaving, for it would raise considerable talk in town. He would tell her they wouldn't lack for a place to live and sufficient funds to live in comfort. He doubted any of them would even miss him.

As he wrote out his plan, he added time lines, the last being the anticipated day of his leaving. He would have to retrieve the coin in bits and pieces so as not to draw attention, and then hide it in the study. No one was allowed to enter without invitation. He looked down at the threadbare rug that covered the floor. Flinging it aside, he used a small knife he kept in his pocket to pry up one of the boards, peering into the space below.

There was a good two feet of space between the floor and the dirt, the house raised up in case of damp. The coin and plate could easily be hidden here. He was now more confident than ever that God had intended for him to find the treasure, for He never did anything without reason. He meant him to escape this purgatory and had shown him the way and given him the means.

It took but a few days to finalize his plans and to move all the findings to his study. The metal box had to be abandoned, the bottom starting to rust away, the contents moved piece by piece. The attic of the rectory contained many discarded objects, and the rector found a trunk there that would well do. Waiting for Jane and the girls to be away from home, he pulled and pushed it down the stairs and into the study, ready for the day of departure.

Telling Jane had proven easy, and as anticipated, she showed no anguish at the news. Once he had assured her that he would purchase a house for the women, and they would have sufficient coin to live in comfort, he was left with the uncomfortable feeling she was relieved. With the parish now expecting a new rector, they would have to leave their present accommodation.

A suitable house was quickly found, much newer than the rectory, and paid for from the hidden gold coin. Jane never enquired where her husband had found the money for it, only grateful he had. The new house lacked the draughts they had been plagued with these past years. There were many windows to let in the light; it was situated halfway down High Street behind the shops. Jane, when she saw it, was ecstatic.

He assured her coin would arrive every six months, that they would be able to afford two servants, one to cook and one to clean. The girls would be able to order all the dresses they wished without worrying. As far as Jane was concerned, it would be a perfect arrangement.

Her only concern was what the townsfolk would say when they found out the rector was leaving them. He had anticipated this, and told her to tell everyone that he had been given another living some hundred miles away – the likelihood of anyone visiting him so far away was small – and that she and the girls had decided they loved Honiton too much to leave.

All were satisfied with the arrangement. The rectory was emptied of their personal belongings; the two new servants were hired. Coin sufficient to last the six months was left with Jane.

At the last service he held in Honiton he told the congregation of his move, telling the same story that Jane would then confirm. All shook his hand as they left, thanking him for his care over the years. The church now empty, he removed his surplice and knelt before the altar to beg understanding for what he was about to do, and without looking back, he left St. Michael's church for the last time.

A bag with his few clothes was packed and waiting. The large trunk containing the treasure so carefully hidden from the household was strapped up securely. He had paid three men with a cart to wheel his belongings, and with a final look around the now empty rectory, he walked outside.

Closing the door behind him, and without looking back, he made his way down the hill to Cross Keys Inn to await the coach. He didn't care where it was going, so long as it was far, far away from Honiton.

He didn't even care about the inheritance left to him by the wealthy widow. The solicitor had told him it was in the amount of three guineas. He had no need of such a paltry amount and told the solicitor to give it to the new rector. 'Tell him to use it for the poor,' he said. From start to finish it had taken a very short while to bring his plan to fruition.

಼಼಼

William, on being told Elizabeth had to leave the rectory, had made arrangements with the solicitor to move into the empty house immediately. Happier than she had been for a long time, she worked with the servants to clean throughout. Husband and wife, they were only too eager to help, for with the rental it meant they didn't have to find other employment.

Rose, the kitchen girl so badly treated by Jane, had decided to move with Elizabeth when presented with the opportunity. A new dress was purchased for her, and she had her own room, not a pallet under the table in the kitchen. She too, had never been happier. The small, newly formed household soon settled into a comfortable routine, respect received and given by all.

William had accepted the offer of employment from Peter Brigginshaw, left the house in the early morning, returned for dinner at noon, then back to the shop for the rest of the day. The new buildings were nearing completion, and some of the supplies were now moved into the various places allotted them.

Life was pleasant, the summer galloping into its transition to autumn. Elizabeth and William sat before the fire in the parlour one evening, and were startled by a knock on the door. Rose answered it. Poking her head round the parlour door she said, 'The solicitor is here to see you, sir.'

'Show him in, Rose,' replied William, and both stood to greet their guest.

Giving a small bow of greeting, the solicitor came straight to the point. William and Elizabeth's offer of thirty guineas was accepted, all that remained was payment and transfer of the deed. The only article the owner had requested, should the house ever be sold, he said, was a small miniature of his parents, commissioned by himself, which he had kept by his bed upstairs. It was one of a pair, the other he had taken with him. Elizabeth left the men to talk, and collected the small piece from upstairs and gave it to the solicitor to send onward to the Americas.

When Peter heard that Elizabeth was to remain in Honiton he was thrilled, only too willing to give William leave from his duties to travel to London two days later. A visit to Timothy was necessary to explain they had purchased a new home and to obtain the necessary funds. The coach travelled the same road Jeffrey Browning had travelled on foot.

Chapter 53 ❧
Exeter

Jeffrey tied the horse to the fence outside Nan's house. He knocked on the front door and recognised by the servant, was allowed entry. Shown into the parlour, he was told Nan would join him shortly. The maid rushed to the garden where Nan was picking herbs, and on hearing Jeffrey was inside, she threw the herbs onto the path and followed the maid to the parlour. Closing the door on inquisitive ears, brother and sister stood facing each other.

'Nan, I have the plate. I returned it. I told you I would.'

Nan looked at the sewing bag that had been used to carry the loot. Without a word, she opened it and began taking out each piece. Much to her amazement all were accounted for, and still without speaking, she began re-filling the dresser shelves.

Jeffrey didn't know whether to say more or stay silent. He decided to hold his tongue, sure now that Nan would ask him to return. He was hot and sweating, and he smelt, even to himself, like a pigsty. As the last plate and jug were positioned in pride of place, there was urgent knock at the door; Nan left the maid to answer once more.

The parlour door burst open, the Watch standing there. Red of face, sweating like Jeffrey, he said, 'Got you. You'll pay for this, attacking a keeper of the law. I can't believe you were stupid enough to leave the horse tied outside, you might just as well have put a notice on the door announcing your presence.'

Jeffrey stood, rooted to the spot, his face a mask of pure horror. Clamping his huge hand on Jeffrey's collar, the Watch made as if to drag him to the door. Nan stood transfixed, not comprehending what was happening.

Jeffrey, already feeling ill from the long arduous walk, began to shake. His eyes turned up in his head and he fell to the floor with a resounding thud, the Watch letting go of his collar as he went down. He lay on the floor, limbs thrashing about, his face a deep purple colour. Only the whites of his eyes showed, and the other two stood looking down at him wondering whether this was real or pretence. When the froth started to flow from his mouth, Nan hollered for the maid who was in the hall listening through the door to all that occurred. 'Fetch the physician,' she demanded. The maid scuttled off, leaving Nan and the Watch to remain with Jeffrey.

It was only a matter of time before Jeffrey's bowels loosened and the stench filled the room. Opening a window, Nan covered her face with her wrap and fled for the door, the Watch short steps behind, closing it firmly behind him.

They spent the time waiting for the physician in the kitchen drinking ale. When he arrived an hour later, only then did Nan open the parlour door. All were assaulted by the lingering smell. Reluctantly the physician entered, took one look at the now still Jeffrey, felt for a blood pulse and not finding one, told Nan, who was standing in the doorway with the Watch, that Jeffrey was dead. It was statement obvious to both of them. Only saying that he would send the cart for the body, he then held out his hand for his fee, which wasn't forthcoming due to his tardiness.

Neither Nan nor the Watch could believe what had occurred. They left Jeffrey where he had died, both retreating into the kitchen for restorative ale. Nan had to sit down, but didn't offer the Watch a seat.

He recovered his thoughts first. Perhaps it has worked out for the best. The plate had been returned to its rightful owner as the magistrate had instructed, and I'm not about to let others know that I was set upon or they might think I'm easy prey. Deciding it was best to keep the attack to himself, with his duty done, he finished the ale and bid Nan goodbye, making a hasty departure.

It took nearly three hours for the men with the cart to arrive, loading Jeffrey inside without appearing to care about either his soiled clothes or the stench that emanated from them. Asking Nan for instruction, she replied that she would arrange for burial in the churchyard, and to take Jeffrey to the church, where a woollen shroud would be made available. With no intention of keeping watch over her brother's body, and definitely no intention of washing and preparing it for burial, she watched the departing cart with no feeling of guilt whatsoever. Leaving the maid to clean up the mess, she went back to the garden to continue picking herbs.

She had the plate back, she was rid of Jeffrey and his irritating nature once and for all, and her life could continue with its main aim, that of amassing even more money. Life, she said to herself, and unable to keep the smile from her face, has a way of working itself out.

Chapter 54 ❧
London

William arrived in a London, to his mind, much changed from the one he had left. Walking to the family house from the coach stop, he wondered if it was his imagination that the streets seemed less congested, the usual raucous sounds muted. The typhus had passed, thanks to God, but the atmosphere, he felt, was almost palpable with anticipation of its next visit.

While he had been in Honiton he had felt carefree and confident of his future there. Now, as he walked the streets, he felt a gloom settle on him. What if Timothy had changed his mind and needed help at the warehouse? What if he wanted to sell the house? He told himself not to anticipate trouble before it came, but even so, he approached the front door with a sick feeling in his stomach.

He hadn't had opportunity to write to Timothy to tell him of his impending arrival, and knew he would be at the warehouse until time for supper. Using his door key, he let himself in and set down his small bag on the bottom stair.

The air inside smelt fresh, the stone floor beneath his feet recently swept. The door to his father's office stood open, and William entered slowly. Nothing had changed. If anything, it was tidier, the shutters folded back to let in the morning light.

Papers were stacked in a neat pile, his father's quill and inkpot in their place. William felt a sense of overwhelming silence. The last time he had been here his father had been sitting in the chair, while Mother and Simon had been upstairs. Now all were gone. The house didn't feel empty, just quiet. Timothy still lived here.

He left the office, turning right down the corridor to the kitchen. This, too, he found orderly and clean. Looking out of the window to the small plot of land behind the house, he gave himself time to adjust to the loss of his life as it had been. He took a seat at the table, remembering how he, Elizabeth, Timothy, and Simon had all sat together when younger, before Simon turned so cruel.

He felt no sadness for Simon's death. If he had survived the typhus, it would just have been a matter of time before his cruelty had been found out, and the inevitable punishment given. William was glad his parents had at least been spared that. With no idea of the time, he continued to sit at the table consumed by memories. It was only when he heard the front door open that he roused himself, moving to the kitchen door to greet Timothy.

A stranger stood before him, a frightened look on his face, which matched the look on William's face.

'Who are you?' asked the stranger.

'More importantly, who are you?' retorted William, bunching his fists in readiness to defend himself.

'James Morbeck and I live here. By what right are you here?' The two men were matched equally in height, though James was leaner. He drew himself up as if to be more intimidating.

William laughed with relief and held out his hand in greeting. 'I'm William, Timothy's brother. Glad to meet you, James.'

James visibly relaxed, blowing his breath out with a loud noise. He took William's hand in return. 'William, you gave me such a fright. I wasn't expecting anyone to be here, for I know Timothy won't be back until evening. I noticed a bag on the stair and couldn't think where it had come from. When did you arrive?'

'You gave me a fright, James. Timothy had written that you were lodging with him and that you attended school. I wasn't expecting anyone until evening. But come in, I expect you could do with a drink, I know I could.'

'That I could. I came back early to study, it's peaceful here, and I've an essay to write for tomorrow.'

'Well, I shan't disturb you,' assured William. 'Where do you normally study?'

'Here, in the kitchen. When it's cold I light the fire, but there is no need of it today.'

While he spoke, James took down two tankards from a shelf, filling them with ale from a barrel in the corner. William accepted his, then said, 'I'll leave you to your essay. Which room are you using upstairs?'

'I believe it was Simon's.' He spoke hesitatingly. 'I do hope you have no objection?'

'No, best to have the house used and Timothy is grateful for the company.' He left the kitchen, returning to the stairs. With the ale in one hand, and picking up his bag with the other, he climbed the stairs to his bedroom.

He knew that he was dreading walking past his parents' bedroom, knowing they were not there, and would never be there again. He put his bag on the floor, the tankard of ale on a small table to the right of his parent's door. Steeling himself, he grasped the latch, pushing the door back.

Here also the air smelt fresh, no ghosts to greet him on this sunny day. The linen on the bed had been washed and folded neatly, placed on the wooden struts. The mattress and bolster pillow was missing, which William presumed had been destroyed when the house had been cleansed. He opened the linen press, but it was all but empty. All his mother's clothes were gone; the only pieces it contained were her personal linens and the fur wrap, kept for Elizabeth.

William felt his eyes prickle and knew that tears were close. He backed up to the bed, climbing onto it; he sat on the wooden boards. With none to hear, he gave way at last to his grief.

⁂

Timothy arrived home to the sound of talk from the kitchen. Wearily he laid his coat on the bottom stair, he smoothed his hair with his hands. Obviously, someone other than James was here and he didn't feel in the mood for casual conversation. He pulled back his shoulders and he opened the kitchen door.

'Timothy!' William stood at the sight of his brother, noting the tired face. 'You look weary, come sit down. Can I get you an ale?'

Timothy looked in disbelief at his brother and came forward to hug him. 'Goodness me, is it really you, William? This is a good day. I heard voices as I came in and felt disheartened at having to appear pleased to see whoever was here, but this is indeed a good day! When did you arrive? How is Elizabeth? Did the typhus reach Honiton? Are all there safe?'

William held up his hands. 'Wait, wait, let me get your ale, then we will talk.' He nodded in James' direction. 'James and I have been getting to know one another, and I can see why you enjoy each other's company.' He placed the ale before Timothy, who took a great gulp and smacked his lips in satisfaction.

James looked at the two brothers, at how alike in looks they were, demeanour, too. He closed his study books, covering the pot of ink. 'We'll need more dinner tonight. I'll leave you to talk and go to the pie shop.'

He doubted whether either heard him, both busy talking nineteen to the dozen. James slipped out the back door, feeling a little jealous of the brothers who were so obviously fond of each other. He thought of his own brother, and the void that seemed to have opened up between them at his last visit home. Shaking his head to clear the thought, for there was nothing to be done about it while he was in London, he made his way to the pie shop to get dinner.

After they had eaten, the plates washed and stacked, William and Timothy moved to the parlour. Not only did they have family business to discuss, but also James was eager to return to his studying, preferably done in peace and quiet.

'Tell me, how fares Elizabeth?' asked Timothy.

'She is well, even better now she has moved out of the rectory.'

'Moved out, but where has she gone?' asked Timothy with concern.

William conveyed the news and repercussions of the rector's departure. 'We have provisionally bought a house in the town, and the solicitor has given permission for us to live there until the sale is complete, given the circumstances. Living with Aunt Jane, Mary, and Anne was proving completely impossible. Mother had sent her there in the hope our aunt would be able to tame her, but from the little I saw, she was incapable of taming her own girls, and you know Elizabeth's nature.'

Timothy smiled, nodding. 'Oh dear, it must have been a real battle of wills. Are Mary and Anne still as irritating?'

'Even more so, I fear. If they ever find someone foolish enough to marry them, I would feel nothing but pity for the poor men.'

'As bad as that, eh. But enough of them, tell me how you found Honiton? Is it a pleasant town?'

'Extremely so, though the hill it's situated on means a goodly climb from the bottom to the top. The house Elizabeth and I are purchasing is halfway up the hill. It sits on acreage, and is a good size. A fellow who has gone to the Americas presently owns it, and that is one of the reasons for my visit. As I said earlier, the solicitor has agreed to the sale, and I shall require funds. I shall need to draw from Elizabeth and my portion of Father's estate.'

'Of course, any assistance I can give, I will,' replied Timothy. 'The business is doing well, and I have been thinking I will have to hire more men sooner than I anticipated. There are some new Italian wines that look promising, and I already have several customers eager for them. Father left us a good business, money is certainly not a concern either now, or in the future. Do you want me to accompany you to the bank tomorrow?'

The sudden change of topic surprised William. 'Ah, no thank you. You have enough to do.'

Timothy nodded. 'How long do you plan to stay in London?'

'Just a day or so. I need to get the funds back to the solicitor in Honiton. I hope I'm not attacked as I was last time I made the journey.'

'Attacked! Were you hurt?' Timothy leaned forward, looking at William for signs of injury.

'Knocked on the head. Worse than that was the loss of my new horse, Endeavour. The bastard took my clothes, too.' They both laughed. While their mother was alive, they would no more have been able to use that word in the house than fly to the moon. They both fell silent at the memory of times that used to be.

⋆⋆⋆⋆

The next morning, with James already gone to school, Timothy readied for work. 'You'll be back tonight?' he asked William.

'I will. If I can get the funds today, I hope to catch tomorrow's coach. Failing that I will have to wait for two days when a coach leaves again. But I foresee no problem.'

'Nor I, but I must leave for the warehouse or the men will think I am ill.' He shrugged on his jacket, picked up his hat, and opened the door. 'James will pick up dinner again tonight, that's part of our arrangement.' He paused, the door half open. 'What do you think of him?'

'James? He seems a nice enough fellow. As you said in your letter, this house would be empty with just you here. I think it's an arrangement that has worked out well for both of you. But get you away, and I must get ready to leave also.'

As he anticipated, there was no problem in getting the necessary funds, given as a note for the Devon house purchase. The only concern was carrying such a paper. William's head ached with even the thought of another attack, though in reality this was almost non-existent since he would be travelling by coach. If on one of the night's stopovers he had to share a chamber with a stranger, he would make sure it was kept on his person.

That night was spent as the first, James studying in the kitchen and William and Timothy reminiscing in the parlour. William spoke of Peter Brigginshaw, and the offer of work given to him and accepted. Both drank too much, went to bed too late, and woke the next morning with heavy heads and grumpy demeanours.

William set off early to take passage on the Honiton coach, Timothy walking part way with him. At the corner of the street where they would part, they hugged each other. 'Keep in touch, Timothy. If you need me to come home for any reason, send word.'

'I will. Give my love to our sister; I hope you will both be happy in your new home. Perhaps one day I can hire a manager for the warehouse and be able to visit you.'

'I look forward to that day,' replied William fondly.

Timothy watched William make his way to the coach stop with a heavy heart. Standing amid the crowd of hawkers, peddlers, and those out looking at what was on offer on the various stalls, he felt alone.

William arrived back in Honiton in a violent thunderstorm. His bag, luckily, was inside under the seat. The thick leather curtains were down and fastened closed, but all the passengers could hear the rain beating on the roof and sides of the coach. With each loud clap of thunder the horses screamed, frantic to escape their traces. The driver had to work hard to control them, the last quarter of an hour a nightmare not only for him but everyone.

The last to leave the coach, William ducked straight away into the door of Cross Keys Inn, to be met by Master Beaker.

'You'll not go far in this weather,' he told William. 'Might as well have an ale while you wait it out.' They both looked out of the doorway, the downpour showing no sign of abating. William readily agreed, following his host down the flagstone hallway into the main room, already filling with customers with the same thought. With no other choice but to remain until the storm had passed, he heaved a great sigh of relief. He had arrived safely back in Honiton. With the inn so close to the solicitor's office, he thought he might as well take the note to him on the way to his and Elizabeth's house – a house that would soon be theirs. The sooner he handed over such an important piece of paper, the better.

Chapter 55 ❧
Honiton

During the few days of William's absence, Elizabeth had kept herself busy. Re-organizing the furniture to better suit their way of living, she, Rose, and the two servants turned out each room for a good cleaning. Flinging the windows wide, the walls and floors were scrubbed, furniture polished and rearranged.

The servants who had worked for the previous owner were elderly, and it wasn't surprising the house hadn't been kept as it should have been, especially since their previous mistress had died. With the thought they would be released from their employment when a new owner bought the house, they had, frankly, ceased to do any work, unwilling to put any more effort into a lost cause.

But now Elizabeth and William had moved in, and their services were needed. With the knowledge that the two would purchase the house and that they would be retained, they creakily moved from taking it easy to hustle and bustle.

A washerwoman was brought in to freshen curtains and linens, and rugs were taken outside and beaten within an inch of their lives. Where there were no rugs, the old rushes were taken out into the garden and set alight and new ones strewn on the wooden floors. Cupboards were emptied; shelves were washed, along with anything they contained. When William returned, it was to a house considerably cleaner than the one he had left.

He and Elizabeth sat talking after supper. The air was still chilly after the storm, and a fire was lit to ward off the damp. 'I stopped at the solicitor's office on my way here and gave him the note. All should now be in order, and he told me it would be but a matter of a day or two before we receive the deed.'

'Good,' replied Elizabeth. 'I can't tell you how nice it's been to have this time to clean the house, though I don't know how good the servants will prove. I'm beginning to understand how Mother must have felt, trying to keep things in order. Rose is a godsend, small she may be but she works hard and keeps telling me how grateful she is to be away from Aunt Jane and the girls. Oh! I saw them the other day.'

'What did they say? Have they been here?'

'Aunt Jane spoke; she asked how we were settling in. I didn't tell her we were buying the house, she'll find that out soon enough, I've no doubt. Mary and Anne were with her and said not a word. Mary didn't even look at me, not that I was sorry about that. I wonder how they are doing without their father there.'

'I wonder,' replied William. 'It must have been a difficult decision for him to leave as he did.'

'Yes, but I can't blame him. I was only there a short while, which was bad enough. I can't imagine how awful his life must have been. Aunt Jane is telling everyone he has taken a living a distance from here and will be coming back, but she's not fooling anyone. Tell me, how is Timothy? Is he coping all right? What did you think of James Morbeck?'

'He's doing well, already thinking of expanding the selection of wines he carries, and he has more customers than Father had. He'll be taking on more men soon to help with the increased business.'

He picked up the ale pot from the table beside him, staring down into the liquid. 'It was strange going back to the house without Mother and Father there. I even felt the loss of Simon, strange to say. I admit when Timothy wrote to say that he had someone living there I felt unsettled, but now I can understand. It's a large house, and it would be empty without James. He seems a nice lad, intent on his studies. I told him I would visit his parents on my return and let them know how he fares. He gave me a letter for them, so I'll take it tomorrow on my way back from Peter's. Have you seen him since I have been gone?'

'Peter? No.' Elizabeth chuckled. 'I've been far too busy sorting out everything here. We will need to buy some linen for the beds; the ones in the press are shabby and threadbare. I could turn them sides to middle, but we can afford new, and I don't see why we should deny ourselves that comfort.'

'No, we can well afford new. I visited the bank to get the note. I never realised Father was such a wealthy man. I knew he wasn't poor, but I never imagined he was that well off. Is there anything else we need?' He looked around.

'Not that I can think of.' Elizabeth sat staring into the fire, at the logs crackling and spitting. 'William, where do you think our uncle got the money from to buy the house for Aunt Jane? Before I left there, Anne told me that from now on, money would be no object to them, that Aunt Jane would receive funds every six months that would keep them well fed and even better dressed. He had never seemed a rich man, so where did the money come from?'

'I don't know. Could he have sold something?'

'Like what? All in the rectory belonged to and stayed with it. Aunt Jane was grateful for the guinea Father paid her each month for my care. It doesn't make sense to me. They even had to buy all new furniture for the house, and have taken on two servants.'

'We'll probably never know,' replied William. 'Just be grateful you didn't have to move with them.'

'I am, more than you know, for I couldn't have stood another moment under the same roof. But I still have to wonder about that money.'

※※※

The next day, William returned to the joiners to be greeted by Peter. 'Welcome, William, it's good to have you back. How was London, and the journey?'

'Everything was well. My brother is doing well, and seems as happy as he can be under the circumstances. The journey was good, at least this time I wasn't attacked.' Peter laughed.

'Well, that's something at least. But come along and see what I have been up to. There's lots of work for you to do, the orders for furniture are flowing in. I need you to look over the figures and see if I can support another apprentice.'

'Another? I'll look straight away. Do you already have a lad in mind?'

'I do, but I'll wait until I hear from you.'

Peter returned to the workshop, where William could hear him talking to the old man who swept and tidied after them.

Chapter 56 ❧
Leaving Honiton

Reverend Cardwell had left Honiton without a backward glance. In his mind, his wife and daughters didn't exist, indeed had never existed. He rode the coach for two days, and when he considered he was far enough away, got off at the next stop, watching as his bags and large heavy box were brought down from the roof.

All his fellow passengers disappeared into the inn for refreshment, and their journey would continue. He stood looking around him. He didn't know the name of the place. What he did know was that it was totally unlike Honiton and, therefore, must be right for him. It wasn't surrounded by hills, he couldn't see any sheep and more importantly, his wife and daughters weren't there.

At the last stop, with all new passengers joining him, he had removed his religious collar and purchased a new stock, jacket, and breeches from a shop in the town in which they had spent the previous night. He hadn't enquired of the name of that place either.

He had left his old clothes tied in a bundle under a chair. No one need ever know he was recently a cleric. Names weren't important to him. Peace and quiet was. And money. His new life had begun.

He had spent the days, as he bumped and rolled his way on the coach, thinking of a new past for himself. If anyone asked, he was a recent childless widower looking for a fresh start.

He had even decided to change his name, lest someone track him down. From now on, he decided, he would be known as Robert Hannford. A good English name, strong sounding, reliable.

Until he decided where to live permanently, he would need accommodation. Three lads nearby were chasing each other with sticks, and he called them over. 'Carry my bags into the inn there and I'll give you a penny each,' he said. Pushing and shoving, they quickly picked up a bag each, taking them into the inn. Two of the tallest and strongest returned for the large box, groaning with the effort of moving it. The innkeeper met him at the door.

'I'll require lodging for a few days,' he said. 'I'll take your best chamber. Have my bags taken straight there.'

'Certainly, sir,' said the innkeeper. Not many stayed over at the inn, and paying custom was gratefully received. Robert handed each boy a penny, and they ran off, pushing and shoving each other again, shrieking with laughter. The innkeeper had two male servants carry his belongings up, a third servant required to help shift the box up the narrow, curving staircase. A great deal of loud cursing accompanied their labours.

'It's three pence a night,' the innkeeper told Robert. 'In advance.'

Robert reached into his pocket, bringing out two shillings and handing them over. 'I'm uncertain how long I shall remain with you; this should do for a while. I'm looking for a property to buy. Do you know of anywhere?'

'Depends on what kind of property. There are plenty of empty cottages around. There's not much employment here, so people go to the towns and cities, hopeful for an easier life. I don't know whether they find it.' He sighed. 'What are you leaning towards?'

Robert had given this much thought on his journey. 'Somewhere with land, and it must be away from noise. And not a small house, either, something substantial.'

The innkeeper stood scratching under one arm, giving thought. 'Well, there's the manor, but it is a bit out of the way.'

'Is it for sale?' asked Robert.

'Aye, I reckon it is. The man who owned it died and he had no kin or heirs that I'm aware of. The best person to ask would be the solicitor, he'd be certain to know.'

263

'I will. Now, if you would show me to my room I'll get washed and settled. Perhaps you would be good enough to have some food and hot water sent up?'

The innkeeper nodded, leading the way up the same narrow, curving stairs.

Robert lay on the wide bed. It had to be after midnight, for he'd heard the church bell strike ten, and that had been awhile ago. It was as black as ink outside, the silence deafening. Tomorrow I'll visit the solicitor, and find out about this manor the innkeeper mentioned. If not that one, there's bound to be another, and I'm in no hurry. He turned over, pulling the coarse linen sheet up over his shoulders. How wonderfully quiet it is he thought, before drifting off to sleep.

Chapter 57 ❧
Honiton

Try as she may, Elizabeth couldn't get the thought of her uncle out of her mind. He had to have gotten the money from somewhere. He hadn't been left it, for she would have heard that news, and it would have spread like wildfire in the town. It seemed all her waking hours were taken up with the puzzle. She spoke of it again to William that evening.

'Elizabeth, you're surely not still thinking of that. Let it be. What do you care where he got the money? They had so little, and perhaps he had been saving it all these years, unknown to Aunt Jane. Why do you care so?' he spoke somewhat impatiently.

'That's just it. I do care. I liked him; he was always kind to me even though we weren't real family, just through marriage. He knew I was unhappy and tried to temper it. I have the awful feeling that he's in trouble.'

'What trouble could he possibly be in? He's away from Aunt Jane and the girls; he's away from Honiton. It's obviously what he wanted, so do stop fretting, Elizabeth.'

She turned away, unsatisfied. Where are you, uncle? Are you all right?

Elizabeth had turned seventeen the week before. There was no celebration, for the anniversary brought memories of her parents, so the day was spent quietly at home. Not even the old servants were told, and Rose was also kept from the knowledge. She had asked William not to mark the day, and he grudgingly agreed.

Appearing at breakfast, he had bent to kiss his sister's cheek. 'Are you sure you want no mention of this day?' he asked. 'It is a special birthday, you know.'

'Yes, thank you, William. I just want to be alone today.'

'Very well, but can I mention it to Peter?'

'Peter? Why tell him? Why would he care?'

'Because he cares for you, that's why.'

Elizabeth shrugged, turning to look out of the window. 'If you wish,' she replied, keeping her head turned away as she felt her face grow warm at the thought of Peter.

True to her word, she spent the day mending her petticoat and writing a letter to Timothy to tell him details of the new house. The solicitor was coming that evening with the house deed, the sale final. Two important events in a day.

When William returned that evening, he brought Peter in his wake. Elizabeth, hearing voices, put down the book she was reading.

'Good evening, Elizabeth, I hear this is a special day for you,' Peter greeted her.

'Well, if you mean the house will be ours, then yes, it is,' she replied, smiling at him.

'You know that's not what I mean. I understand the servants are unaware, so I shall keep my voice low. A Happy Birthday Wish to you.'

She laughed. 'Thank you, Peter. It's certainly a day I shall remember.'

William poured wine for them from the bottle on the side table. Handing each a glass, he proposed a toast. 'To Elizabeth and the new house,' he said.

Elizabeth and Peter raised their glasses and took a sip of the sweet wine. She sat down again, arranging her skirts round her feet. As she was about to speak, there was a knock on the door, and she glanced quickly at William, eyebrows raised.

'That will be the solicitor,' he told her. 'I will just be a moment.' He left Elizabeth and Peter alone.

'You must be thrilled to have a house of your own,' remarked Peter.

'I am. Luckily I had a good teacher in Mother, so I am coping well. It's pleasant to have the two of us here. I only wish Timothy could visit.'

'Perhaps he will one day. William tells me he will be hiring more men, and hopefully he will be able to leave the warehouse for a few days and journey here.'

'I do hope so.' She picked up the letter she had written to their brother, which was on the table beside her chair. 'I have to give this to the coach when it next comes. I told Timothy all about the house and gardens, but it would be much better if he could see it all for himself.'

They heard the front door close and footsteps coming down the hallway towards them. William opened the door, a huge smile on his face. In his hand was a parchment, rolled up and tied with a red ribbon. 'We have it, Elizabeth. The house is ours!'

Elizabeth leapt from the chair, running into William's arms, and he twirled her round and round, both of them laughing. Peter watched them, or rather watched Elizabeth, her face flushed with joy.

'We have to name it,' she pronounced, clapping her hands with pleasure.

'Name what?' William and Peter asked together.

'The house. We must have a name for it. Everyone has a named house.'

'The house in London didn't have a name,' remarked William, bemused.

'Well, this one shall. I have to think of a suitable name.' She rushed from the room in search of Rose, anxious to share the wonderful news that this was now their house, none to take it away from them.

༺☙❧༻

The next morning, Elizabeth walked up the hill towards the church. She felt the need to give proper thanks for their good fortune, and to say a prayer for their parents. High Street was already busy, and she stopped to speak to several people on the way. All gave their congratulations on the purchase of the new house, and she was left to wonder, once again, how such news was spread so quickly.

Continuing up the hill, she noticed a commotion ahead. People and carts had to weave around a mound in the middle of the street. Some shouted in anger, while others looked on in pity. There was the same old woman she had seen before. She was digging in the street. Still dressed in rags, she was grovelling in the dirt using fingers black with ingrained dirt. While she dug, she looked around her, cursing at those who came too close, heedless of the sharp hooves of the horses passing by. Elizabeth stood for a few moments, watching not only the woman, but those around her. The woman started screaming, making all jump, some laughing at the poor soul.

Eventually reaching the church, the new rector still not arrived, she slipped through the heavy, oaken door. It was empty, the sound of her footsteps echoing on the stone floor. The air struck chill after the warmth of the day, and without a wrap, she wouldn't stay long. But Elizabeth was unsettled by the old woman, and finding prayer evasive, returned to the sunshine.

The woman had gone, carts and people moving freely once more. Back at the house, she asked Rose if she knew of the woman.

'Oh, you mean Mad Meg. I don't know what her real name is, but that's what we call her. Been at it for years she has, digging in the oddest of places. Once, my ma used to say, you could get sense out of her, but not now. Now she just shouts and curses at anyone who comes near her.'

'But why does she dig?'

'Who knows? Perhaps she lost something and is trying to find it. All I know is she is mad and should be locked up. Mad Meg.' Rose laughed. 'Best to steer clear of her if you know what's good for you.' She turned back to her task of peeling apples for a pie, the sad plight of Mad Meg an old story and of no interest to her.

Summer was slowly turning to autumn, and with the house now spic and span, Elizabeth found time on her hands. There were two things left that needed thought. The first was naming the house, the second, and most important, the mystery of her uncle and his newly found wealth. She didn't begrudge him his good fortune, for if anyone deserved it, it was he. But she couldn't let it go.

The naming of the house was something else. The house itself was imposing, standing well back from the lane on which it fronted. With no neighbours close by, the gardens were completely private. Composed of two stories, the black painted timbering showed a solid, trusting home. The plaster between was painted a mellow pink. The front door, reached by two well-worn stone steps, was to be found more to the left side of the front of the house than the middle, as was usual. This gave on to an imposing hallway, a large stone framed fireplace on the left. The rooms were spacious, almost all oak panelled with linen fold panelling, wide oak planks for the floors.

Obviously, whoever had commissioned the house to be built was a man of taste and stature. This information should be found on the deed, and Elizabeth promised herself to ask William to see if it was. The more she thought of it, she wondered why it had even been built in the town at all. Normally a house of such standing would have been built outside the town. Though perhaps it had been, and the town had gradually encroached on it. Whatever the reason, such a house needed a name worthy of it.

That evening, Elizabeth broached her suggestion to William. 'But it's not a manor, Elizabeth. It's a house; it has no need of a name.'

'I know that, but it is such a beautiful house. And who is to say it's not a manor? We can name it whatever we wish. It's our house.'

'Do what you want, so long as it makes you happy.' He smiled indulgently at his sister. 'So, it will be 'The Manor'?'

'Don't be silly, William. Of course it won't. There has to be another name. I have one in mind; I'll let you know when I'm ready.' With that, he had to be content. He knew Elizabeth. If she wasn't ready to tell, she wouldn't. He would have to wait.

Elizabeth now knew the name of the house. She spoke it aloud a few times when she was alone. It felt right. More importantly, it sounded right. She hoped people wouldn't think she and William were getting above themselves, new to Honiton as they were. When William came home, she told him of her choice.

'What? You can't be serious, Elizabeth.'

'I am. That's the name I have chosen. You told me I could. You said whatever made me happy, and this makes me happy.'

William shook his head, resigned. 'Very well, if that's what you want.'

She kissed him, dancing around the room. 'You'll see, everyone will love the name.'

Chapter 58 ❧
Honiton

Peter Brigginshaw moved to his new buildings. All completed, he moved all the wood over with just a few more things to be seen to. Mistress Chapman had moved into the new house and was filled with joy at the kitchen. She and Master Chapman were to have their rooms on the ground floor at the back of the house, no more having to trudge up and down the stairs. Peter, sympathetic to their age, had also employed a young girl who would assist her in the care of the house. The girl would be responsible for the heavy work, and for cleaning upstairs. A cook would come three times a week to prepare food, or more often should it be needed.

Henry Chapman was very frail, finding walking both difficult and painful. Only comfortable when he sat before the fire, his legs resting on a stool, customers would visit him there. With the move to the new house, Peter made sure Henry would find everything as he liked it, almost as if he had never moved.

The apprentices, including the newly hired boy, were housed above the workshop. As Peter had promised, each had a room of his own. None had such luxury before, each believing themselves the most fortunate of boys.

Only one thing was missing, a wife.

Once all the wood, equipment, and personal belongings had been moved into the new buildings. Peter, seeing no point in waiting, approached William. The life he anticipated for himself looked prosperous and fulfilling, and he wanted to share it with someone. His chosen one was Elizabeth Sharpe. Confident she felt the same about himself despite his infirmities, he wanted to tell one other before he approached Elizabeth. At the end of a long and tiring day, he sat in his new office, quill in hand, composing a letter to his sister, Susannah.

The two women had met when Susannah had been on a visit to Watermead. That was the same time there had been the awful events surrounding her Ladyship's godson, Philip Goldworthy.

Blotting the ink, Peter looked over his letter one last time. Crossing out one word, substituting it with another he thought more descriptive, he folded it, placing a seal on the join.

It would be given to the next coach going to Salisbury, for it was to their estate in Wiltshire for an extended stay that Susannah and Thomas had travelled when they left Watermead. If they weren't there, it would be sent on. With plans in place and his mind easy, he walked round the house and buildings, making sure all was secure, all flame extinguished for the night. Expensive and rare woods were stored in two of the outbuildings, their potential loss a huge blow to Peter both personally and his business. It was for this reason that he had had the new premises built away from the town and any danger of fire. All the new buildings were of stone, roofs of tile. He had told Susannah once that there would be enough room for her should she require it, but she had been raised up now, in no need of Peter's benevolence.

Crawling into bed, he lay imagining how his life was about to change.

Chapter 59 ૐ
Spitchwick House

The subject of Elizabeth's thoughts, the self-proclaimed Robert Hannford, stood outside a different house. The late owner's solicitor, Master Bigby, accompanied him. 'It's a fine building,' said the solicitor, casting his critical eye over the prospective buyer. Privately (for he thought of himself as being an expert judge of men), he doubted if this man could afford the price of 150 guineas being asked. Still, a sale was a sale, and appearances could be deceiving.

It was to be sold with all the contents, lock stock and barrel, but Master Bigby nevertheless felt the price excessive. A fine house it may be, with 300 acres of prime wood attached, but he knew repairs were needed, and quickly. The last time he had entered, a bat had flown uncomfortably close, causing him to screech in fear. Upstairs, the roof in one of the bedrooms was leaking, the bed beneath wet and mouldy. Grime and dirt lay thick on every surface, and in the solicitor's opinion, it would take an army of tradesmen and cleaning women to bring order where now there was chaos. He was obliged to tell the prospective buyer of the failings, but he had no intention of dwelling on them and losing the sale.

Robert Hannford had already made up his mind, however. It would take more than bats and a leaking roof to put him off. For before him was the house of his dreams, with no Jane, no Mary, and no Anne. Lying awake night after night as he had beside Jane, listening to her stentorian snores, he had dreamed of such a house; two-storied with many windows, with views through them that lasted forever.

He listened to Master Bigby recite the house's failings, and cared not a whit. When the solicitor gave his estimate for repairs, Robert gave a shrug. It was meaningless to him. He wanted the house.

Master Bigby unlocked the front doors with a large iron key, which made a loud grating noise as it turned. Before them was the most exquisite block floor made of different coloured woods. Though a thick layer of dust lay on top, Robert could imagine instantly how it would look once swept and mopped. His eyes moved round, seeing tall double doors to left and right, both now closed, on either side of the entranceway. He couldn't wait to see what was behind them. Striding away from the solicitor, he flung open the doors to the left. A large wood-panelled parlour was revealed, with chairs and tables covered by white cloths. A large fireplace faced the two floor-to-ceiling windows, the mantle above it high enough to be beyond Robert's reach. Fine woollen rugs lay on the wooden floor, and he knew that once they were taken outside and given a good beating, their beautiful colours would shine through.

Back into the hall he went, followed closely by the solicitor. He opened the doors to the right to find a library within. Three walls held floor-to-ceiling bookshelves, fully stocked. Hardly able to contain his joy, he walked to the nearest and looked at the titles and authors.

He didn't care how much the house cost. He had to have it. He wasn't interested in seeing the rest, but forced himself to follow the solicitor through the downstairs rooms, then up the curving staircase. Four bedrooms, each spacious and well appointed were revealed. The largest, with wonderful views over the surrounding hills, would be his. The large four-poster bed looked comfortable, and he sat on it, testing the mattress. The bed hangings would have to be replaced, but no hurry for that. The bedroom with the leaky ceiling was the priority; no doubt the bed as well as the linen would have to be replaced there.

Back downstairs, Master Bigby led the way out of yet another parlour's doors onto a flagstone terrace that ran the length of the house. Facing south, it would catch all the afternoon sun. A perfect place in the summer to read, enjoy ale, and a pipe. In the cooler weather there was the library. With no wife or daughters to complain of tobacco smoke or how long he spent in reading, Robert Hannford could have wept with anticipation at the joy to come.

'You'll want to think about it, I suppose?' asked the solicitor, locking the doors behind them.

'No need. I'll take it. One hundred and fifty guineas, you said?'

'Yes, but, well, forgive me, sir, but can you afford it?'

Robert laughed. 'No need to concern yourself on that score, Master Bigby. Though I will only pay one hundred and twenty guineas. As you told me, the roof needs fixing, and I will have to get someone to deal with the bats, no doubt the attics are full of them.' He looked the solicitor firmly in the eye.

The solicitor quavered. 'But the price is one hundred and fifty, sir.'

Robert shrugged. 'Oh well, I have several other houses to inspect, all no doubt eager for a willing buyer. I'll do that this afternoon. You can get back to me on the price. One hundred and twenty is my only offer. Take it or leave it.'

'I'll take it,' said Master Bigby, somewhat unhappily.

Robert held out his hand to seal the deal, the solicitor took it. He would have been happier with the full price, but since this newcomer was the only one who had shown even the slightest interest in the house over the past year, one hundred and twenty was better than nothing. The money would go directly into his own coffers; he would make sure of it.

'As soon as payment is received, I will hand over the deed. Do you intend to live here alone?'

'I do, though I'll require some servants, no doubt you can help me with that.'

'Indeed I could. When, um, do you anticipate having the funds, if I might ask?'

'Tomorrow soon enough for you?'

'Tomorrow?' squeaked the solicitor. 'So soon?'

'No point in waiting, sir. I want to move here in three days' time. I'll bring the funds to your office tomorrow, you can give

275

me the deed and the names of anyone you think would be honest and reliable servants. I'll have the house cleaned and move in as quickly as possible. The repairs can be done under my supervision once I am there.'

Master Bigby stood looking at the declared buyer in amazement. It's as if the one hundred and fifty, no twenty, pounds, was nothing to him, he thought.

Robert Hannford returned to the inn, happy in the knowledge that his time in the noisy establishment was almost at an end. Entering his room, he closed and locked the door, and checked the locks on the large chest in which he kept his wealth. All secure. He lay back on the bed, his arms behind his head, staring at the ceiling. Tomorrow, wonderful tomorrow, Spitchwick House would be his and his alone.

⁂

With autumn approaching, morning frost was heavy, taking its time leaving even in the weak sunshine. Robert had been at Spitchwick for two weeks, each one more enjoyable than the one before, which he hardly thought possible. The servants he had hired, all grateful for the work, proved diligent and honest. The house, sparkling with cleanliness, was an absolute joy to its grateful master.

Each morning, come rain or shine, Robert inspected the stables, home to two gentle and obedient horses, and one that proved not so gentle and obedient. The man hired to care for them was knowledgeable and subservient. Sometimes Robert would ride out onto his land, grateful beyond measure for all he had been given.

Afternoons were usually spent in reading or exploring the house itself. At the time of his initial visit, only a cursory glance had been taken in each room. Now he enjoyed taking his time finding out all of its secrets.

He couldn't work out why there was a smaller sitting area in the library upstairs. Situated next to his bedroom, the bookshelves here were on two walls, and ran from halfway up, with cupboards and drawers beneath. There was sufficient room for two large wingback chairs with a table between. He moved one chair and the table nearer the window to take advantage of the meagre light. With only one window, the room was gloomy, and it wasn't centred on the outside wall. A small fireplace was set in the corner. The room didn't make sense, and because of that, Robert found himself drawn here more and more often.

It was here one day that he heard whispering, which appeared to come from behind him. Getting up, he looked out of the window that overlooked the gravel driveway to the front door. There was no one there. Returning to his seat, he picked up his book, finding his place once more. But there it was again, the whispering, though he couldn't make out the words. His book now on his lap, he looked around, but the door was closed, and he was completely alone.

As the rector in Honiton, he had regularly been called upon to exorcise ghosts, real or imagined. Usually dreamed up by the elderly, fevered or just plain mad, he would use the cross that hung about his neck when he entered their room, spouting Latin that meant less than nothing to the afflicted. Upon leaving he would assure them that the ghosts had gone, and they would not be bothered again. Usually it worked.

He tried it now. Hesitant to totally give up his former life, he still wore the cross beneath his clothes and brought it out now, burnishing it with his sleeve. Though certain there were none to see, he still looked around, embarrassed to be caught in such a questionable practice. Holding the cross in front of him at chest height, he repeated the still remembered Latin phrases. At the finish, he stood silently. No sound, the whispering had stopped. Convincing himself he had imagined the noises, he returned to his chair, tucking the cross into his undergarment and laughing at himself.

Then he felt the hair stand up on the back of his head, his body grow suddenly cold, starting to tingle. For next to his chair, not a foot from him, he heard the whispering again, louder this time. He fled.

⁂

The whispering in the small library had unnerved him. Despite his attempt at exorcism it continued, hearing it whenever he entered. He constantly asked the servants if they too could hear it, taking them, sometimes forcefully, to stand in the room and listen. Each in turn looked at him as if he had gone mad, for none could hear whispering, each leaving, shaking their heads, laughing behind their hands. Honest servants they may be, and grateful for their employment, but it didn't prevent them spreading the tale of his imaginings around the town. The master of Spitchwick House soon became a laughing stock.

Robert lay in his bed, knowing the ghosts, for what else could they be, were on the other side of the adjoining wall, afraid they would visit him in his room. Every night he buried his head beneath his pillow trying to block out the noises, and he fell asleep in the early hours while holding tightly to the cross.

From a happy, guileless man, he had now become obsessed with the small library. Frightened of it on the one hand, he couldn't prevent himself from entering it on the other, peering repeatedly in all the corners, behind the books, opening the cupboards and drawers. Once exhausted, he would collapse in a chair, knowing full well the whispering would begin again. Convinced the servants were trying to drive him mad, he dismissed them all except for the stable man.

He convinced himself that the ghosts were forcing him out because they had a secret hidden in the room they didn't want discovered. Whispering couldn't hurt him, he reasoned. They, whoever 'they' were, would soon find out he was the master.

He spent the days pulling the room apart, repeatedly checking the books and cupboards. He had been searching for three days when he found it.

Between two of the bookshelves there was a small carving high up, out of normal reach. Dragging a chair over, he stepped up to inspect the intricate design above him: A coat of arms, a bumblebee in high relief. He ran his trembling fingers over it, feeling the fine carving, the intricate detail.

His legs felt suddenly cold, and looking down, saw a yawning space opening up. In fright, Robert fell off the chair and landed with a thud on the floor, giving his head a nasty crack.

Sitting up he rubbed his head and looked into a black space where once had stood a bookshelf and set of drawers. Drawing slowly to his knees, he pushed the chair out of the way.

The shelves had moved inwards, no sound heard of its movement. He pulled a huge tome off the adjoining shelf, placing it on the floor. Should the door close, the book would prevent it closing completely.

Taking a candle and holder off the table, he lit the wick and stepped carefully over the threshold, stopping to reassure himself again the book would prevent his entombment. With all the servants gone, there could be no hope of rescue.

Holding the candle high, he looked around. His mouth dropped and he almost let go of the candle, for before him was a treasure trove. The plate and coin he had found in the woods in Honiton looked decidedly paltry next to this.

He stood in a narrow room, and he now realised why the window in the adjoining room was off centre. This room contained its partner, though now roughly boarded up. The space had been taken from the small library as a vault. It too had shelves, but these were floor to ceiling, no drawers or cupboards. A thick layer of dust lay over everything. As he moved the candle, dead rats and mice could be seen, there so long their bodies now desiccated

But it was the shelves that he stared at, for they contained untold treasure. Rolled up parchment, paintings, cups and plate, rough gold nuggets piled in a metal dish, open boxes of gold coin, some spilling onto the wooden floor. On a shelf by the window was a small chest no more than two feet long, black with age, thick leather straps that proved brittle when he tried to unfasten them.

The candle now at his feet, he struggled to open the straps. Sweating with the effort, and with no servants to hear, he cursed loudly. When eventually his efforts were rewarded and the lid lifted, it contained nothing but one piece of parchment.

He touched it. It didn't feel brittle. A large seal was affixed to the bottom. Carefully he took it from the chest, but unable to see clearly, he carried it to the doorway, again stopping to ensure the book he had left would prevent the door closing. Carrying the parchment across the library, he stood before the window. The seal proved heavy. With one hand he pulled the small table to the window, carefully laying down the parchment and its attachment.

He peered at the large round disc, but couldn't make out the writing stamped around the edge. Pushing it to one side, he carefully unrolled the parchment, the bottom slowly appeared. Robert rubbed his eyes, uncertain of what he had read. He looked again.

It was dated 15 June 1215 written in Latin, old Latin at that. It can't be, he thought. It can't be the Magna Carta. But if it were, how did it get to this place, to Spitchwick House?

It was signed near London. Everyone knew that, and more importantly, what it stood for: Justice for all.

It looked old enough. Why shouldn't it be? And if it proved to be so, how much was it worth? Leaving the parchment on the table, he went back into what he now thought of as the secret vault. Standing in the middle of the room he tried to gauge the worth of its contents. Whatever it was, it was priceless. Add to that the parchment in the library.

Unable to think any more and feeling totally fuddled, he left the room, replacing the large tome on the shelf and pulling closed the door behind him. When he looked back, there was only one thing to show the entrance had ever been. There was no crack between the shelves to give it away, but there was dust on the floor from his shoes. Taking out his handkerchief, he dropped to the floor, wiping away any trace of his activity.

Robert took the parchment and heavy seal, attached by a length of ribbon, back to his bedroom. He stopped halfway along the corridor. He realised he hadn't heard the whispering all the time he had been in the secret vault. The ghosts, or whatever they were, had vanished. Hopefully, they would never return. Perhaps my exorcism worked after all, he thought, chuckling to himself for the first time in a while.

The next afternoon, he dragged the chest containing his own treasure, now somewhat depleted along the corridor and into the small library. Using the chair again to reach the door lock, he pushed and pulled the chest into the vault, lifting it with difficulty onto an empty shelf. He replaced the parchment in the chest in which he had found it, closing the lid.

Wiping his dusty hands on his handkerchief, he looked around. He decided to look one more time in the chest containing what he was convinced was the original Magna Carta, he lay his handkerchief down beside it. The candlelight confirmed again his hope. Though the writing on the seal remained a mystery, he had no doubt what he had in his possession.

He closed the door behind him, stepping once more into the small library. Reassured now that he wasn't going mad and hearing voices, he was convinced the whispering had been leading him to the secret vault all the while.

Excited beyond measure, he walked to the stables to visit his horse, breathe some fresh air and decide on his future plans. The man would be there, but no matter, no need to talk to him, a servant. The day was proving to be a fine one. He could smell rain in the air. However, he thought, that wouldn't be for a while.

The man was indeed there, busily grooming Robert's favourite horse. Leaving him to his work, Robert went into the stable to saddle another horse, but as he was leading it outside the horse was limping slightly. He told the stableman to check it, leaving the animal tied up waiting for attention.

He turned to go back into the stable to get the remaining horse, but the stableman advised against taking it, as it had been acting strange, advising him to wait for the one he was grooming. Robert assured the man he could handle the beast, and shooing away the offer to saddle the horse for him, did so himself.

Without another word, he set off. The air was mild considering the time of year, with the hint of rain, the fallen leaves clattering under the horse's hooves. Pleased beyond measure with the way his life was going, he set the horse to a canter. It kept shaking its head as if angry to be taken from its warm stable and plentiful food, but Robert hit it a couple of times with his whip.

'Now you'll see who the master is,' he said aloud.

With more than enough money to last him to the end of his life, whenever that was to be, he hadn't a care in the world. He couldn't contain the laughter that bubbled to the surface, and he raised himself in the saddle, shouting with utter joy. Why, he thought, I could even stop sending money to Jane and the girls. They have no idea where I am, and what could they do about it anyway? With the habit of a lifetime, Robert gave thanks to God for his life, his fortune, and his overwhelming happiness.

⁂

It was the stableman who sounded the alarm. When his master hadn't returned by seven o'clock, the night fully dark, he rode a horse into town heading straight for the inn to raise a search party.

Once there he met up with fellows he hadn't seen for a while and sat down for one tankard of ale to fortify himself, both from the journey and for the search ahead. One tankard turned into three, and before he was aware, he had fallen into slumber where he sat, only to be pushed out the door by the tired and irritable innkeeper at close to midnight.

Curled up against a wall, he shivered his way through the night just steps away from the horse he had ridden into town. When he awoke, it was to a thudding head, freezing body in wet clothes from the mizzle, and dawning realization. Quickly asking for help from those he met in the street, he led the search party back to Spitchwick House, he riding a hungry, thirsty and angry horse, four others walking behind.

The stableman had seen Robert take the path to the north, and they now took the same route. It didn't take them long to find him. With no sign of the horse Robert had been riding, they quickly approached the recumbent figure. It was apparent he had been thrown, his head striking a large rock to the side of the muddy track. Blood and brains spilled out into the wet earth and leaf mould, life absent for many a long hour, for he was stone cold. The stableman took a moment to silently berate himself for going into town the night before instead of taking this path in his search, but quickly managed to turn that around to blaming his master for taking a horse with which he was unfamiliar and had indeed been warned against.

Between them they managed to haul the heavy body up onto a horse, which was extremely skittish when it smelled the blood. But the stableman calmed it down, and they all made their way back to the house. Two of them carried him up to what they presumed was his bedchamber, dumping him unceremoniously on the bed. They all then raided the kitchen, finding little food since the cook had been dismissed, and the wine cellar, which proved exceedingly well stocked. He then headed into town to tell the solicitor, there being no one else to tell or who would be interested in the knowing.

Chapter 60 ᚨ
Honiton

Peter stood waiting anxiously for William to appear the next morning. Now his mind was set, there was no reason to wait any longer. William hadn't even removed his hat before Peter sent an apprentice to ask him to come to his office.

'Sit down, sit down, William.' He indicated the beautiful chair made by him that stood at the side of the desk. Peter took his seat behind the desk.

'I'll come straight to the point. As you know, I have become extremely fond of Elizabeth over the past while.' He looked quickly at William, to see if he could guess what was coming. By the look on his face, a faint smile playing round his lips, he could.

'As you well know, I have a vibrant and well-run business here; the only thing I lack is a wife.' He leaned forward, his arms on the desk, the eagerness on his face belied by the sweat beading on his forehead.

'Do you think Elizabeth would have me for a husband? Even with my deformity? Be honest with me now.'

The silence was pronounced. Peter sat back, anxiety beginning to replace eagerness. 'Say something, William.'

William burst out laughing. 'Of course she will have you! I'm sure she's been waiting for just this moment. When do you intend to ask her?'

Peter whooped with joy, standing up and leaning across the desk to shake William's hand. 'You had me worried there for a while. Are you certain? She doesn't mind? You're sure of it?'

'Yes, I'm sure of it. You should have more confidence in yourself, Peter.'

'That's what Susannah keeps telling me. I will come round after supper, if that's all right with you? But you won't say anything ahead of time, will you? I want my visit to be a surprise.'

'I won't say a word about the reason for your visit. I will, however, let her know you will be calling. You know what women are like, they like to have the house neat and tidy when anyone visits.'

Peter laughed. 'No, I don't know, but I'm looking forward to learning. I'd best get on; there's lots to do today. Two more orders came in yesterday; business is growing faster than I can keep up, William.'

'I'm delighted to hear it, for I should not like my sister to be marrying someone without a future.' William left Peter's office to start on his own work. So, he thought, I'm to have a brother-in-law, and I couldn't wish for anyone better.

⁂

Elizabeth sat in the window seat, neglected sewing lying on her lap. She looked out over the dying garden. The supper dishes had been cleared away, and the evening stretched ahead of her. William had told her Peter would be joining them later, and now she found herself unable to settle to anything. Sewing didn't interest her, and each book she had picked up couldn't hold her attention for more than a page. All the rooms were neat and tidy, nothing more to be done there. It was with relief she heard the knock on the door, looking forward to seeing Peter. Unconsciously her hands went to her hair, smoothing it once more into place as she walked into the hallway.

She had told Rose she would answer the door, and she greeted Peter warmly. Of William there was no sign, and she presumed he had walked to the adjoining house to speak to the neighbour. For now the house was quiet, even the usual kitchen sounds were muted.

She led Peter into the parlour, where they sat next to each other on the settle. After the usual enquires of health, Peter decided to summon his courage. He opened his mouth to speak, but instead of the carefully rehearsed speech which, now, had seemingly flown completely from his mind, came the words, 'Will you be my wife?'

Elizabeth stared at him blankly. 'What did you say?'

'I asked you to be my wife,' he repeated, his face reddening with embarrassment, unable to look her in the eye.

'Of course I will. I wondered when you would get around to asking me.' She was smiling, her eyes crinkling with sheer delight.

'You will?'

'I will, and gladly.'

Peter took up her hand, which felt warm and soft to the touch. 'I asked William for permission this morning. I did it all properly. Susannah told me I should, that I should ask William's permission before I asked you.'

'Yes, you did it all properly.' Elizabeth laughed, Peter joining in. They both jumped when the parlour door was suddenly flung open, with William and Rose coming in, followed by the two servants, all laughing and smiling.

'Congratulations to both of you,' said William. He addressed Peter directly. 'I told Rose and the others not to disturb you, as you had an important question to ask of Elizabeth.' He came forward to kiss Elizabeth's cheek and to shake Peter's hand. 'When is the happy day to be?'

'Slow down, William, we haven't even thought of that. Besides,' said Elizabeth, 'We have to write to Timothy, for I will want him here for the wedding.'

'Of course he must be here. I only hope he has someone at the warehouse who can look after the business in his absence, for he'll be away for a good few days.'

'I hadn't thought of that,' replied Elizabeth, a frown appearing. 'Well, if he can't come here, we have no choice but to go to London to be married, for I shan't be wed without him.'

'Let's not anticipate problems, Elizabeth,' interjected Peter. 'Going to London would cause problems for me here, so let's wait until you hear from him.'

'There stands a man with common sense,' laughed William. 'Write to him tonight, hopefully he will have it in two days' time. In the meantime, while you are waiting for his reply, plan your wedding!'

Elizabeth and Peter looked at each other, their eyes locked onto the others as though no one else existed.

Rose and the servants left, chattering amongst themselves with all the excitement that was to come.

'It's a pity Reverend Cardwell isn't here to perform the ceremony,' said Peter. 'The new rector is a solemn fellow.'

'Yes, it is a pity. He was nice to me, and I miss him. I still can't help wondering how he suddenly became so wealthy,' she mused. 'That reminds me, have you noticed that old woman, William, the one I see who sits digging in the dirt with her bare hands?'

'Yes, I've seen her a few times. I think she's mad, isn't she?' He turned to Peter for confirmation.

'Well, I don't know about mad. Apparently her family was wealthy at one stage in their lives. They lived the other side of the church many years ago. Apparently, for some reason they lost all their wealth. Rumour has it the old man had lost his mind, and was convinced someone, specifically the servants, were trying to steal his coins and plate. His wife and children realised their wealth was disappearing, presuming it to be the servants stealing. It was only later, in a brief moment of sanity towards the end of his life, that the old man told them he had taken it into the woods and buried it. They tried to get him to say where it was, but the moment had passed and he slipped into his madness again, dying shortly after.'

'No one knows where? Has it never been found?' asked Elizabeth.

'No, no trace of it. Apparently he used to run around without any clothes on, much to his wife's horror, and in the end had to be confined in the house. As I said, he died not long after, never having revealed the place he had buried the family fortune. If truth were told, by then he probably couldn't remember where he took it. The old woman you have seen is the last of his children. She is trying to find it, has been for years. Some say she is as mad as her father, and who's to argue with that. But whether mad or not, it's a sad story.'

'It is indeed,' said Elizabeth, her mind racing. They stood in silence, pity in their hearts for the poor woman desperately trying to recover her family's fortune.

The happiness of their own events, however, couldn't keep the mood sombre for long. Soon all were laughing and smiling once more. Peter left for home after a celebratory toast, promising to return tomorrow to discuss wedding plans.

William lay awake, wondering how he would feel with Elizabeth gone. They hadn't had the house long, and it didn't feel like home yet. I only hope Timothy is able to travel here for the wedding, for it's certain Peter can't afford the time to go to London. Work is coming in faster than he can keep up. It's Elizabeth who will have to give way on that. But hopefully all will be well.

He chuckled at the thought. It would be interesting to see, for she had rarely given way before. He settled his head more comfortably on the pillow. The window, with the curtains drawn back, looked out at an inky black sky, only a few stars visible through scratchy clouds.

What of me? Will I marry one day? Will I be content working for Peter for the rest of my life? I have funds of my own; I can do anything I want. But what do I want? Father started out with nothing and built up the wine business, but that's Timothy's responsibility now. If Father could do it, why can't I?

Peter bought the joinery from Master Chapman, a business ready-made. What business could I start? Perhaps I should think of my talents first. I'm a good manager of men. I am excellent at getting people to buy things. What are people lacking here that is readily available to those in the big cities and towns?

The wine is imported, what is there I could import, even from far away? It's usually women who make the purchases, what would they buy if it were available? We are fast approaching 1800, what will the future need that I can provide? With all these thoughts swirling round in his head, William drifted to sleep.

Elizabeth also lay awake, certain she had found the answer to her uncle's sudden wealth. He had to have come across the buried plate and coin and taken it for his own. Long into the night, tossing and turning, she wondered where he was and what he was doing. Her mind turned to the poor old woman who dug in the streets. There is no hope now of finding her inheritance.

288

She felt unsettled that the new rector would be marrying her to Peter. She wanted her uncle to perform the ceremony. With no idea where he had gone, only that it was far away according to town gossip, there was only one way to find out. She had to visit Aunt Jane.

🙢🙠🙢🙠

The next morning after breakfast, she told Rose she would be gone for a while. Wrapping herself warmly against the cold wind, Elizabeth set off up the hill to the house newly purchased for Jane and the girls. This was the first time she had seen them since they had all moved from the rectory. She had never received an invitation to visit, indeed didn't expect one, and she was looking forward to seeing how this house differed from the rectory, though not to seeing its miserable occupants.

Set back from the street, the small front garden looked neat and well kept. She stood admiring the large stone-built structure, thinking how much more space must be inside compared to the rectory. Unbidden came the memory of the time she arrived in Honiton with her mother. The screeching from inside the rectory at that time had been something to behold, with this time being no different.

Although Elizabeth was unable to make out which one of the girls was making the racket, for one screech is almost identical to another screech, Aunt Jane's lower-toned answering screech was easy to recognize. Nothing changes, she thought with a sigh.

She approached the door, hardly able to contain her laughter and giving a thought to taking flight, but she hadn't come all this way to turn back now. As before, it took three hefty raps with the knocker before the door was answered. Anne stood there, snot running from her nose, her eyes red with weeping. She took one look at Elizabeth and turning her head, yelled into the empty space behind her, 'It's Lizzie, Mama. Should I let her in?'

'Don't be stupid, Anne, of course you should let her in. What does she want?' came the yelled reply. Elizabeth couldn't see Aunt Jane, but could hear Mary snivelling from somewhere within.

'I don't know. What do you want?' The last was addressed to Elizabeth who walked through the door, not bothering to answer such a rude question.

'Aunt Jane?' she called, for it appeared her aunt's voice had come from somewhere in the back of the house.

'Coming, coming.' Jane appeared from a doorway set at the end of the hall, which Elizabeth presumed to be the kitchen. Jane was wiping her hands on a towel, the usual bad-tempered scowl on her face.

'What is it, Elizabeth? As you can see I am very busy.'

'Yes, I see that. I shan't keep you, Aunt; I wondered if you knew where Uncle had gone? I'm getting married, you see, and would like him to perform the ceremony.'

'Married?' screeched Anne. 'Married to who?' She pulled at Elizabeth's arm, forcing her to spin round and face her.

Aunt Jane pulled her back again to face herself. 'Married? Who's the boy?'

'Peter Brigginshaw.'

'The joiner? Why are you marrying him?'

Elizabeth had no intention of answering. Taking a breath, she asked again. 'Do you know where Uncle is? As I said, I would like him to perform the ceremony. I will need to contact him quickly.'

'No, he sends us money every six months, that's all I care about,' replied her aunt. 'When are you getting married? Are we to be invited?'

Absolutely not, thought Elizabeth. 'Peter and I haven't had a chance to discuss those details yet, Aunt, the decision only reached last night.'

'But what's to become of William? Will he be staying at the house on his own?' Jane asked. Her eyes narrowed, settling on Anne. 'He'll be in need of a wife now without you to care for him.'

Elizabeth knew exactly what was in Aunt Jane's mind. Better put a stop to that right here and now.

'No, he won't. He has no intention of getting married, he has servants to help him.' she looked pointedly at Anne. 'And definitely not to anyone in Honiton.'

Reddening under the rebuke, 'Well, that is for him to say, not you,' replied Jane.

Elizabeth once again brought the conversation back to the reason for her visit.

'So you've no idea how I can contact him?'

'No.'

'Well, in that case, I'll bid you all a good day.'

Mary still hadn't appeared, though the sound of crying was plainly heard from upstairs.

Anne opened the front door, waiting for Elizabeth to pass through, with the usual sneer on her already unattractive face. 'We will get an invite to the wedding, won't we, Elizabeth?' tried Aunt Jane one last time.

'As I said, our plans haven't been laid down yet. Good day.' Ignoring Anne, Elizabeth left the house, barely making it to the bottom step outside before the door was slammed behind her. The screeching began again, with Elizabeth certain she was the cause of this episode.

Unable to contact her uncle, there now was no choice but to accept the new reverend would marry her and Peter.

Chapter 61 ❧
Honiton

Elizabeth and Peter decided on a small wedding, with only close friends present. Peter's sister, Susannah, had been given word of the marriage and would be attending, though her husband, Thomas, was out in the country and wouldn't be able to accompany her. Susannah would stay with Lady FitzGerald for the length of her visit. Elizabeth decided not to tell Aunt Jane of the day. No doubt word would spread on the wind as it usually did, but as to an invite, none would be given. Let Aunt Jane be upset; Elizabeth owed her nothing and definitely nothing to her two brats.

On the way back to the house Elizabeth dropped off the letter for Timothy at Cross Keys Inn. Master Beaker would give it to the next London-bound coach when it came through. It would be at least a week before an answer was received, and in the meantime she would plan for the wedding, plans that definitely wouldn't include Aunt Jane, Anne, or Mary. Family they may well be, but none could be trusted to behave in an acceptable way, and she was terrified they would cause a fuss and spoil a wonderful day.

In the letter to Timothy, Elizabeth had told him she and Peter planned to wed on Sunday, 1 October, which should give Timothy enough time to join them. As she would be moving from her present house to Peter's on that day, there was little work in that regard to be done. Peter's house was brand new, all the modern conveniences including an indoor pump for water in the kitchen.

Rose would remain to help William, along with the two elderly servants. Elizabeth knew she would need to take on at least one more servant at Peter's house. Mistress Chapman had her hands full dealing with her husband, now completely bedridden, his mind wandering more and more often.

※※※

On 29 September, the day dawned dry and clear. Elizabeth looked out of her bedroom window over to the hills beyond, wondering if today would be the day they heard from Timothy. With no word received, she wondered if her letter had reached him. Perhaps he was upset she was marrying while still young, though she would be eighteen on her next birthday, and lots of girls were married far younger than she. Even if a letter arrived today, there was no time for him to arrive for the wedding, and she had to accept that, while pleased she would be given away by William, Timothy would not be there to share in her joy.

She dressed slowly, a headache threatening, a churning stomach already with her. She returned to lie on the bed, the sounds of the house awakening unheard beneath her now throbbing temples. When she awoke, the sun had moved a considerable distance in the sky, and unsure of the time, Elizabeth made her way carefully downstairs.

'You slept well,' said Rose, greeting her in the hallway, her arms full of freshly washed linens.

'I did. What time is it?'

'Nearly noon, you're just in time for lunch. Master William will be back soon.' They both heard steps approaching the door. Not expecting the doorknocker to sound, for William would have a key, they both jumped at the sudden noise.

'I'll answer it,' said Rose. 'You go and sit down, you look ever so pale.' Gratefully Elizabeth made her way to the parlour, closing the door behind her and taking a seat by the comforting fire.

'So, no greeting for your poor brother?' asked a familiar and much missed voice.

'Timothy! You're here!' Elizabeth, headache forgotten, she ran to him, clasping him in her arms, all thoughts of queasiness gone. 'I didn't think you would be here in time, why didn't you write and tell me you would be coming?'

'And spoil the surprise? Did you really think I would miss my only sister's wedding?'

Both heard the front door open, Timothy turning raised eyebrows to Elizabeth.

'Is this William?' he asked.

She nodded, grinning. Timothy held his finger to his mouth to indicate they be quiet. Elizabeth suddenly thought Rose would tell William a strange man was here, but she heard no voices through the door while they both stood holding their breath, waiting for the door to open.

'Timothy! What a wonderful surprise,' said William, greeting his brother warmly.

'Now Elizabeth can enjoy her wedding day, she has been fretting you wouldn't be with us.'

'So I gather. I wouldn't miss such a joyful occasion. Besides, I want to meet my new brother-in-law.'

'You will like him,' promised Elizabeth. 'You know he has an infirmity? I told you in the letter I wrote.'

'I know of it, but if you love him, then I will too.'

He turned to William. 'You're working for him now?'

'I am. He has a busy shop, orders coming in from far and wide. He's taken on another apprentice to help with the heavy lifting and carrying. A young lad, but Peter is particular who he hires, and this one is promising so far.'

'Timothy, you must be hungry and tired after your journey,' said Elizabeth. 'I will get Rose to prepare some food for you, and then I'll show you to your chamber. I hope you will be comfortable there.' She paused, her hand on the door latch. 'I am so glad you are here. You boys are the only family I have.' She left the room, so happy she was close to tears.

William took a seat, indicating a chair for Timothy. When both were settled, William asked, 'What of the warehouse, who is taking care of it in your absence?'

'I hired a reliable man several weeks ago. He came with experience of both wine and managing the men. He had a good position up north, but his previous employer died of the typhus, like so many others.'

They looked at each other, remembering their dear parents and not-so-lamented brother, Simon. 'The man's widow didn't want to keep the business, and with no buyer, it was dismantled. He came south looking for work.' William started to interrupt, but Timothy held up his hand.

'Don't worry, I wrote to the woman to ask of his reputation, and checked with others too. All remarks on him were positive. He's not a young man, but he's as strong as an ox. You should see him move the barrels; he makes it look like they weigh nothing. The men already respect him, and all get on well together, even though he is new. If it weren't for him, I wouldn't be here now.'

'I'm glad you are,' replied William. 'Elizabeth was getting anxious you wouldn't arrive in time. You'll like Peter; he's a good, honest lad. He's young to have such a business, but he runs it well, and as I said, he can hardly keep up with the orders. I anticipate much success for him.'

'I did bring one thing for Elizabeth from home,' said Timothy. 'I thought she could use it, I just hope I did the right thing.' He looked worried, unsure how his sister would react to the gift. When he told William what it was, William replied he couldn't have thought of anything better.

There was a knock on the door, and William called out, 'Come in.' Rose entered, carrying a tray laden with food, along with a tankard of ale. She left it on the table at Timothy's elbow, gave a small curtsey and scurried from the room, stopping at the door to glance at this new arrival from beneath lowered lashes.

❧❦❧

The wedding breakfast was to be held at William and Elizabeth's house. The two elderly servants would have done their best, but Elizabeth sensed early on that preparing the amount of food that would be required would be beyond them, even with Rose to help. She had asked two women in town to help for the day. The payment she offered them was more than generous, and they had both willingly given of their time. Preparing the food Elizabeth requested in their own homes, it would be brought to the house during the ceremony, which was to be held at ten o'clock in the morning, ready for the returning guests.

As was usual, Elizabeth and Peter would be married at the church doors of St. Michael's, and then come back down the hill to the house. The newly married couple would ride in a carriage loaned by Lady FitzGerald, while the guests would walk back. Lady FitzGerald had been extremely kind to both Susannah and Peter in their younger years, and she would naturally be one of the guests.

It wasn't to be a large wedding. Peter's family was small, consisting only of his sister, Susannah, and Master and Mistress Chapman. Master Chapman was too ill to attend, and would be left in the care of the servants, but Mistress Chapman would be there to see them wed.

Elizabeth's family consisted of William and Timothy. No invitation had been given to Aunt Jane and the girls, Elizabeth hoping they wouldn't just turn up at the church and then expect to come back for the wedding breakfast. Deciding there was nothing she could do about it if they did; she tried to put it from her mind. She would, she had decided, leave the dealing of that to William and Timothy.

Elizabeth was to wear her best dress, freshly washed and pressed. The morning of the wedding, Rose was to help dress her hair, weaving a yellow ribbon that matched the dress through the curls. There were few flowers left in the garden, the frost having seen most of them off, so she decided to carry a small Bible she brought from London.

ಜಿಜಿ

The morning arrived. Elizabeth woke early, lying in bed and anticipating the day. She could hear noises from below, recognizing them as Rose, who had awoke early and was moving from room to room opening the wooden shutters, even though it was still dark outside.

Peter was also awake. He lay with thoughts of work going through his mind. Reminding himself to have this and that done, he wondered how he was going to fit in everything he had to do.

Aunt Jane was up, looking at her dresses and deciding what to wear, which hat was appropriate. Invitation or not, she intended they all would be at the church. And the breakfast that was to follow.

Anne and Mary still slept, both worn out from yet another of their temper tantrums the night before. Jane stopped what she was doing. 'The girls really are getting out of hand. I wish their father was here to control them,' she mused. 'But I have to admit, life is a lot easier without him. So long as he keeps sending the money, we will be well.'

Elizabeth had spoken to William and Timothy the day before, warning them the vile women may appear at the wedding breakfast. William asked of her wishes, should they be given entrance? Elizabeth thought for a moment, carefully considering her answer.

'No, I think not. There was only one time Aunt Jane was kind, and that when Nathaniel died. I have to say she made my life there a misery, and I'm grateful I didn't have to be there any longer. Anne and Mary, well, what can I say about them, you know my thoughts in that regard, William.'

William nodded, turning to Timothy. 'You haven't seen them since that time they came to London, and you remember what we thought of them then.' Timothy nodded. 'They are far worse now, spoiled brats as far as I can see, truly their mother's daughters. I think Elizabeth is right, they shouldn't be allowed entrance. We can't stop them coming to the church door, but we can bar their entrance here.' He turned to Elizabeth. 'Don't worry, they shan't be allowed to spoil your day.'

'Thank you, William. I feel badly, for she was Mother's sister, but I can't abide them, and that's that.'

Elizabeth, followed by a beaming Rose, came downstairs on her wedding day to a waiting William and Timothy, the two elderly servants peeking round the kitchen door. Dressed and coiffed, she was ready. Over her arm she carried a woollen wrap against the morning chill.

'I have something for you, Elizabeth,' Timothy told her. 'I told you I would keep it, and I think Mother would wish you to wear it today.' From the chair behind him, hidden from view, he took up Sarah's fur wrap, holding it out to his sister.

Elizabeth gasped. 'How wonderful! I hadn't given it a thought, but it's perfect. Yes, I'm sure Mother would want me to have it today.' She turned around, allowing Timothy to lay it over her shoulders, feeling the softness and warmth. It should, perhaps, have smelt musty, but instead, when Elizabeth pressed it to her nose, she caught a faint, precious trace of her mother's odour. She hugged the wrap to her.

'Thank you, Timothy.'

Lady FitzGerald's carriage waited outside the door attended by a footman, and several of the neighbours had gathered beside it, waiting for Elizabeth to appear. When the front door opened and Elizabeth stepped onto the path, it was to see neighbours smiling at her, two of the men digging each other in the ribs, silly grins on their faces.

Helped up the coach step by William, she settled her dress around her, the carriage rocking slightly as William and Timothy joined her. Peter was waiting at the church door, dressed in his best clothes while more of the town folk gathered around. The new rector, visibly nervous, stuttered over the all-too-familiar words, but once the rings were exchanged, for Peter had decided to wear one also, and they were pronounced man and wife, he relaxed, leading everyone in a rousing cheer.

The wedding breakfast was a huge success, the two hired women bringing their contributions over in plenty of time. The house was full of well-wishers, and Elizabeth and Peter were overwhelmed with gratitude.

All day Elizabeth hadn't given a thought to Aunt Jane and the girls, she had too much else to celebrate. She wasn't even aware of the scuffle outside the door when they turned up. William, chancing to glance out of the window, saw the three making their way down the lane towards the house, and hurried to the front door to fend them off.

He spoke bluntly. 'You're not welcome, Aunt. Elizabeth has asked me to bar entrance, for she doesn't want the day spoiled.'

'What's this? Barred from my own niece's house! I've never heard of such a thing. Didn't I give her shelter when her mother asked me? Wasn't her mother my own, much missed sister? What would she say that we are barred entrance?' Jane's face was bright red, her breath coming in great gasps. 'Let us in, I say.' She pressed William back, trying to get at least a foot in the doorway.

But William held his ground. 'Don't cause a fuss, Aunt Jane. That is Elizabeth's wish, and I will use force if necessary.'

Jane looked at his face, which showed steely determination.

'Why can't we go inside?' asked Anne in a whiny tone. 'Why?

'Yes, we want entrance,' Mary backed up her sister. 'It's the least we are owed after all we did for Lizzie.'

'No, you were paid for Elizabeth's stay,' stated William.

Jane looked over his shoulder, seeing behind him another young man, the family resemblance clear. 'This must be Timothy,' she simpered. 'Can we not even greet him?'

'I will visit you one day,' said Timothy. 'But not today.' He stood ready to reinforce William should it become necessary.

'Well! Wait until the reverend hears about this,' shouted Jane. Furious, she grabbed Anne's hand, twisting it painfully, causing the girl to squeal in pain. 'Come along, we know when we're not wanted.'

They turned, marching down the short path to the lane, all three shouting at each other. William closed the door, leaning against it in relief. He hadn't been sure how, or what force he would have used had it come necessary; he was only relieved he hadn't had to follow through on his words, for he wasn't of a violent nature.

When the time came for the young couple to leave, Elizabeth, now a married woman, took a moment to return to her room for the last time. She only took a few things with her that day, intending to return in the morning with a cart for the rest of her belongings.

She looked at the small, neatly made bed, the jug of flowers beside it left by Rose the day before. She would miss this room, indeed would miss the whole house. But now she was mistress of another. Rose would take care of William, and who knew, she thought, perhaps he too will marry soon and bring his own bride here. I never told William the name I chose for the house, but it's no longer mine, and not for me to name. But it's such a perfect name. I would have named it 'Fables,' for that's what my life has been. Mother told me a fable was a story that teaches a lesson, and I know now that no matter how terrible things are, there is always lessons, hope, and love.

She walked downstairs where Peter was waiting. Holding out his hand, which she took gladly, and he raised to kiss, they went out the front door and were helped up into the carriage by the footman. Surrounded by a cheering crowd of friends, neighbours, William, Timothy, and Mistress Elizabeth Brigginshaw smiled.